PULASKI'S
CANAL

ROBERT F. LACKEY

Heron Oaks, Murrells Inlet, SC

Copyright © 2014 Robert F. Lackey
All rights reserved.
Republished under Heron Oaks imprint 2016
ISBN:0692625267
ISBN-13:9780692625262

OTHER PULASKI BOOKS BY ROBERT F. LACKEY

Blood on the Chesapeake (#2)	*ISBN: 0692688676*
Ravens Risk (#3)	*ISBN: 0692831320*
Kingdoms in the Marsh (#4)	*ISBN: 0692625267*
Brazen Deceit (#5) –	*ISBN 0692063145*
Serpent's Compromise (#6)	*ISBN 0692057730*

DEDICATION

To my wife Sandi,
who was my greatest supporter to finish the manuscript
and bring this story to print.
She was my inspiration for Sonja,
and the reason why the character has so much life and charm,
as does she.

-   Robert F. Lackey

ACKNOWLEDGEMENTS

No book can make its way to print without the hard work of many people.

I wish to acknowledge the valuable assistance of stalwart beta readers and thank them for their contributions.
Notably
Judee Cooper of Edgewood, Maryland,
Kathy Cullum of Havre de Grace, Maryland,
and
Caroline Zeitler

who aided significantly in finalizing this manuscript.

Also, among the wonderful people of Havre de Grace, Maryland, who patiently answered my near-unending questions for material, photographs and personal knowledge,
I extend my gratitude especially to
Robert Magee
and
Joseph Kochenderfer,
of the Susquehanna Museum at the Lockhouse,
Havre de Grace, Maryland.

- Robert F. Lackey

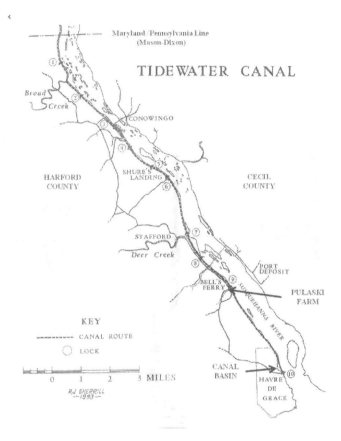

Tidewater Canal Drawing by Richard James Sherrill, used by permission. Map and Canal Era article by Mr. Sherrill were previously printed in Harford Historical Bulletin Number 58, Fall 1993, published by The Historical Society of Harford County. Map labels were rearranged to enhance reader references for this novel, and compress the map layout to fit this page.

1

"He's Alive!"

Aaron burst into the shanty, angry light from a bloody setting sun knifed into the darkness of the front room. He shoved a crumpled paper into his mother's chapped hands. The widow pulled herself awake from the nightmares that tormented her, even a rare nap in her battered rocking chair. She stared into his face with empty eyes. Her fingers drifted up to push away unruly hair, spiraling strands of rose painted brass caught in the fading sunlight.

"Wha-what?"

"He's alive, Ma! He's alive! They were all wrong! He's alive and he's coming home!"

She forced her eyes to look down at the telegram in her hand, clawing back from exhausted sleep, barely finding the sense to understand the words neatly penciled on the lined telegraph office paper.

April 17th, 1841. It was sent today. It was from him.

He is alive! she thought.

Her words barely an audible rasp, "Oh my God. What will I do?"

Her face leached to white. The paper slipped away unnoticed from her trembling hand, and drifted down like an autumn leaf onto the worn plank floor in front of her. Thundering blackness stormed through her brain and she slumped from the rocker, collapsing onto the telegram from a dead man.

"Ma! Ma!"

Seagulls screeched overhead under a warm blue sky feather-brushed with occasional clouds and crossed by long coal smudges from steam tugs churning down the Susquehanna into the Chesapeake Bay. The hard cobalt of the river gave way to the translucent green of the upper bay, its lazy surface crowded. Work boats dodged each other, slipping in and out of the little harbor under light wind and full sails, with loads of fish, oysters and lumber. Ben Pulaski looked along the Havre de Grace waterfront, shaking his head.

"It was never supposed to be this damned long! Nine months - That's what I told Sonja before I sailed away, Anthony- maybe a year. Now I've been gone over two years- almost three!"

He twisted his back to ease the pull of tightened skin around the long angry scar, still too fresh and irritated under his wool shirt.

"I have a daughter, Anthony. She must be almost two by now, and I've never seen her. And the money the company sent them, has it been enough? Are they all well? How has Sonja endured? What have Aaron and Isaac had to do in their father's long absence. There is so much I need to know."

Ben slapped his fist on the ship's railing. "Twenty months. Seventeen days. Fourteen hours. Time lost in China. Time spent in Hell!"

"Calm yourself Ben. You endured all that time in China. You can last a few more minutes. All will be well soon enough."

Anthony Renowitz stood next to Ben near the bow of the little schooner that had brought them up from Baltimore. They filled their eyes with the dozens of ships stuffed against the wharves, and the waves of chattering people moving between the ship gangplanks and the warehouses. As the little packet ship bumped gently against the dock, still nudging forward and eager to be on its way, Ben tossed his sea bag over his shoulder and offered his hand to his shipmate.

"Come see me when you can Anthony, unless you're

shipping out again."

"No. I'll not go to sea again, Benjamin. I am just happy to be going home, and I never want to see China again. We saw too much of it; saw too much of too many things. When I make it to Philadelphia, I will be home to stay."

Ben's hand slipped from Anthony's grip and up onto his shoulder. "Can we ever be human again, Anthony? Do we have enough soul left to be called that?"

"We do what we can, Ben. A man does what needs to be done."

A deck hand snapped at Ben. "You gonna jump off or stay on board?"

Ben nodded to the sailor and turned back to Anthony. "I only wish Simon had come with us and was going north to Philadelphia with you. It would be better for him there."

"He has his papers."

"Southern Maryland is not a place for a black man to be wandering loose. He should have come up the Bay with us."

"He will fare well, Ben. Simon always does."

Ben shrugged his shoulders and stepped across the growing gap onto the dock, the schooner already pushing off and resetting its sails toward Chesapeake City and the Delaware Canal. He traded a final short wave with Anthony, then turned away.

Home at last.

Ben scanned the docks for a familiar face and saw nothing but strangers; dozens and dozens of them. Havre de Grace had exploded with new people and businesses. New shops elbowed space next to old ones, their fresh yellow rough cut boards butting up against old gray ones, all competing for trade with the incoming ships, forming a wall around the docks that imprisoned the faint breeze off the bay. The air was stale and tangible with the aromas of new wood and fresh tar, roasted coffee and fried fish and sweaty wool. Crowds of clerks, warehousemen, seamen and farmers and slaves flowed among the buildings and brushed against each other, only barely touching like schools of fish pushed by the waves. From within the crowd a hand reached out to tap his shoulder.

"You Pulaski?'

Ben spun to face the voice. "Who's asking?" The face was broad and familiar, but taller than he remembered it. "Isaac??"

"Welcome home Pa."

Ben grabbed his son in a bear hug, feeling the growth of his chest and the firmness of his shoulders, but Isaac stepped back picking up Ben's seabag.

"Follow me. I'll take you to the... the house."

Ben scanned the faces around him again. "Where's Aaron? Is he with you?"

"He went on to tell Ma you had come. We almost didn't recognize you. " His eyes drifted away from his father's as he turned to walk. "Come this way."

Ben let loose a broad smile, patting his growing younger son on the shoulder, but Isaac outpaced Ben's reach. "I think I can find my own..." Ben reached for Isaac again. "How is your mother and your sister. I ache to see them at last." Ben caught up and threw his arm around Isaac's shoulders and turned them both toward Water Street.

Isaac looked away. "N-No, Pa. Not that way. Follow me this way. We... uh...live in a different place now.." He looked over his turning shoulder. "You look so different." He pulled away from his father stepping quickly along the new gravel slope up toward Market Street.

"Isaac?? We live in a different place??"

But Isaac had already covered several yards ahead of his father at a pace Ben had to struggle to match, barely catching glimpses of his son's back as he rounded street corners and went along Adams Street. They came to Doc Harper's house then Isaac darted along a side walkway to its back yard.

4

Ben allowed himself a small smile. *They must have a celebration for me.*

He followed Isaac around the yellow belles and onto a footpath in the thick dark grass of the side yard. He looked up to see only a glimpse of Isaac turning yet another corner. He was uneasy walking through Wallace Harper's own yard without even stopping to say hello or ask permission, but the eagerness to keep up with his son brushed away the petty social concern.

Behind the big house, at the end of a neatly trimmed emerald lawn edged with hundreds of daffodils, where the property touched the back service lane, was a little plank cottage barely holding its single narrow green door and front window. The old rough cut vertical boards had been freshly whitewashed. The door held a small bunch of baby's breath tied with a pink ribbon in its center.

Isaac stepped up onto the uncovered porch. He stopped with his hand on the iron door latch and looked back at his father again. "You look so different. I guess everything changes."

Ben smiled and cocked his head. "Seamen look like this son. It will all be back to normal soon, I promise."

"I don't think so, Pa."

Isaac took in a deep breath and blew it out. He pushed open the door and stepped into the dim front room. Ben hesitated and then followed Isaac through the door. He recalled visiting the little building when Dr. Harper started his practice back in '28, before he built the main house. The waiting chairs were gone from the front. An iron stove was against the back wall on the left, a small stack of kindling wood laid neatly beside it, a rocking chair snugged close and a small table beside that. On the opposite wall there was a narrow counter below two meager cabinets. On his right a small overly worn table and two ladder-back chairs were under the single front window. Light from the window lay across the table top and reached to the back wall on that side and touched the bottom of a simple door.

Isaac took a stand in the back corner near the stove.

"This is where we live now, Pa."

"Son, what is this? I don't understand. Why didn't we go to Pearl Lane?"

Isaac nodded toward a plank door on the other side of the iron stove. "Aaron and I mostly sleep on the barges, and Ma sleeps in that back room now."

"What is this, Son? Why do you want me to believe you live here? Really now, where is everyone? Where could a baby be in this little shack?"

Ben stepped to the door and pushed it open. Rusted iron strap hinges squeaked in muffled complaint. The unpainted room held a single narrow bed, nightstand, and battered chair beneath a small cracked window high in the back wall. Dusty sunlight painted a yellow rectangle across the faded bed quilt losing its edging in a sagging loop just above the floor. A few worn dresses hung in the corner from a wooden bar decorated with a short lavender ribbon tied in a bow at one end. The threadbare dress in front was patched in several places and only a faded reminder of the deep blue it had been the day Sonja saw him off at the docks. The bright white collar and lace edged cuffs were now sickly and frayed. A chipped oil lamp sat on the nightstand, its stained base nestled within a snow white crocheted doily. A bible lay next to the lamp. The once supple leather cover was water stained and stiff, and the edges of the linen pages rippled in confusion, unable to close flat. He remembered Sunday afternoons when she sat by the fireplace and read aloud from that bible to him and the boys.

Ben shook his head and folded his arms in front of his chest. *This cannot be!* He spoke to the walls of the little room, his voice booming within the shanty.

"I want some answers, Isaac. I am seeing no humor in all this. If this is some kind of joke, it has failed and you need to end it right now."

Isaac answered quietly from the front room.

"Please, Pa. Don't be angry. You need to talk with Ma. She needs to tell you things."

Ben stepped back into the front room waiting for his son to say more. Isaac only pulled out a chair and sat at the narrow table, placing his hands together in front of him and looking down at them, unable to meet his father's gaze. Ben walked up to the table and placed muscular palms on its surface, leaning toward his son. His breathing was shallow against the band tightening around his chest. He stared down at the top of his son's head.

"Oh, Ben."

The words floated into the room from miles away. The sound of her voice caressed his heart and soothed the emotions raging in his head. He stood away from the table straightening his shoulders and turned toward the door.

"Sonja...", he whispered. She stood in the doorway silhouetted by the sunshine behind her, the harsh details of her face and her gray pinafore dress lost in the shadows. The years and the miles vanished between them as he swept her up in his arms. His heart filled. Again and again he whispered her name and tried to kiss her, but she snatched his hands down and stepped back. Tears filled her eyes. She slapped his face with all of her strength.

"Where the Hell were you?!! We heard NOTHING from you! They said you were DEAD! And then your telegram came. Nothing for almost three years, and then you decide to send a telegram to me?!! You decide to come home again?!!. You were gone so long. You were dead! And I killed our baby. I couldn't hold on to her and I let her die. And you weren't here to help us!" She opened her arms and swept them around the meager room. "Well, by God, Welcome Home!"

Ben stood in shocked stillness, his hands still in mid-air where Sonja had stood, trying to understand what was happening. He looked into Sonja's eyes gone ice cold and her face alabaster stone. Isaac looked out the window through misted eyes to study the blooms on the flowers edging the back yard, not wanting to be there.

Ben let his arms settle by his sides. "I don't understand."

Isaac rose from the table and went to the door past his parents. He hesitated briefly by his mother and patted her back, and then left the little house to them. Tears flooded Sonja's eyes and slowly slipped down her cheeks and onto her dress, but she held her chin up to him, her back straight, she would not approach Ben. Sonja pointed her finger at his face.

"You were dead to us. And I couldn't hold on to our baby, so I let her die. And you weren't here to help us. You were dead and we have become accustomed to that! I am a widow and the boys are fatherless. You were DEAD!!""

"Why did you think I was dead?" Ben moved his mouth several more times, but no words or sounds disturbed the heavy silence settling around them. He absently reached for her last letter he still carried in his pocket, but then let his hand fall by his side.

Sonja slowly raised her clinched fist toward him. "I have lost everything! My baby was dead...and then you were dead!" Fire in her eyes burned through the tears welling up around them. She stiffened her back and spat out the words. "I told you in my letters and was sure you would never come home again! I even thought for a while that if you were really dead before you knew, maybe it was a blessing – maybe the letters never came. I have told you a thousand times in my nightmares, and now I have to tell you again! God Damn you!"

Sonja slowly pounded her fist into the center of her chest. "You should have been here. You didn't have to leave! The depression ended. Things got better a couple months after you left, and they were building the canal again, and men were working again, and coming home every night. But not you! You had to sail to China! -

Pulaski's Canal

Another BIG adventure in your life! You and Anthony, and that Simon! You should have been here. With US! But you were gone and our baby died, and you never even saw her. Now you'll have to live with that too!"

She folded her arms in front of her, glaring into his eyes. In dumb silence, Ben placed his hands gently on her shoulders, but she jerked herself free of him and pushed him away, clawing at his arms, slapping his face in a frenzy while her face bled tears.

Ben gripped her hands in front of him, confused by the rage in her face, the hatred in her eyes. "You lost the baby? How? What? When?"

Sonja wrapped herself in her arms, heaving sobs racked her body. "I let our baby drown! I had her in my arms when I fell, but I didn't hold on! I should have held on tighter. I should have died to save her! The precious little angel! Oh God! I let our baby die! And you should have been here, you bastard!"

"No... No Sonja. This can't be so. Surely not, Sonja! Surely not...Tell me what happened? Where is the baby? Where is my daughter?"

Sonja stepped back from Ben, gripping her skirts tightly in her hands. Ben stared at her, the pounding in his brain beating down around his eyes, blurring everything but her face. The pain in her face cut his heart as she searched deeply into his eyes.

"She's gone?" he rasped.

Sonja fixed him with cold eyes. She took in a deep breath and balled her chapped hands into fists again. The strain of the moment, the wear of the years drew deep lines in her face and she looked old and frail. She held her fists between them, her skin pale and her knuckles red.

"I wish I had died instead of her! God knew I didn't deserve her! I didn't hold on to her and the river took her! I should have died then too!!" Her shoulders jerked with her sobs. Ben tried to wrap his arms around her, but she twisted her shoulders away from his hands.

9

"Where the Hell were you? Why didn't you come home? Damn you! You should have been here!!"

"But no. Sonja... I... I... - You need to know..."

She beat her fists against his chest and slapped his face again in a frenzy of flying hands. Ben grabbed her wrists and pulled her to him, holding her and caressing her shoulders as she raged at him. He stood there, not knowing what else to do, stroking her shoulders, stroking her head, letting her cry and letting the tears run down his own face.   Sonja jerked herself away from him again, folding her hands against her breast, fighting away the tears and letting the anger refill her. Ben heard a footstep in the doorway.

Isaac stepped beside his mother and placed his hand on her back. "It wasn't her fault, Pa." He leaned forward and kissed her sobbing shoulders and then straightened his back to look at his father. "We had a real bad winter the year you left. There had been a lot of cold rain, then tons of snow, and the river froze. Even the little creek by the house was full and overflowing all that fall and winter. Aaron and I built a little footbridge across it so Ma wouldn't get her feet wet going into town. Later, the river ice got so thick they talked about running rail tracks over it since the steamer was iced in. We had a small flood from under the ice in early December."

Ben turned his head to look out the window at the darkening trees as Isaac continued.

"Right after Alisha was born, about the middle of December..."

"Alisha was born December 19th.", Sonja spoke, brushing stray hair from her face and wiping her eyes with her apron.

Isaac nodded to his mother. "People were talking about an ice dam forming up the river. Mr. Boyd said someone needed to do something about it. The Canal Company brought down an engineer to look at it; the engineer and Mr. Boyd got into a big argument over it. The engineer said all the water was running under the ice out into the Bay, but Mr. Boyd said they should blow up the ice dam so it wouldn't hurt the canal. They yelled at each other for a long time out there, but I guess it didn't do any good, because the company left it alone."

Isaac held out his hands toward Ben. "They should'a done something Pa, but nobody ever did. Then, in early January the water started coming over top all the ice. Some of the Irish had a work camp down near Bell's Landing, and came by saying they were heading for town. More ice and water started rushing down over the top of the ice that was already there and then it all sort of broke up, I guess"

Sonja spoke in a toneless voice without turning her head. "I should have gone then. Isaac said we ought to, but I told him Will said we would be all right. I didn't know where else to go. I should have just taken the baby and the boys and gone to the hotel until it was over. I shouldn't have stayed."

Isaac looked down and continued. "Aaron was working up at the lockhouse that night. There was a terrible cracking sound out in the yard, like someone shooting. We lit a lamp and saw the yard full of water and ice, and I said we better go then. People were outside running through the yard and over our little bridge with whatever they could carry. We got dressed as fast as we could, and Ma wrapped Alisha in her quilt."

Sonja rubbed her hands over her arms. "I had to go get that damned tin box. The money. It was all we had and I made us wait too long while I went in the bedroom to get it out of the dresser." She laughed. "I lost it too, anyway."

"No Mom, it wasn't your fault. None of it." Isaac turned back to his father. "By the time we got to the little bridge, the whole yard was flooded with ice flow, blocks bigger than bales of hay, and you couldn't even tell where the creek had been except for the bridge. The water was almost knee deep and pieces of ice were grinding against the side of the house and the bridge. There were some men on the other side of the bridge yelling for us to hurry. Ma and I were almost over the middle of the bridge when it cracked and twisted in the middle. It went over before we could get to the other side."

"I should have built that bridge much stronger, Isaac." Aaron had entered the room while Isaac was telling Ben the story. "It was all my fault. Not Ma's," he added looking at Ben, but Ben did not see him.

Isaac slapped the top of the table. "Bull shit, Aaron! It wasn't anybody's fault. It wasn't Ma's fault and it wasn't your fault! It was the river. The ice flood! It was that goddamned river!"

Ben turned to Isaac. "What happened when the bridge gave way?"

"I yelled for Ma to jump, but there didn't seem to be anywhere to jump. Everything was spinning around and then we were in the water. We weren't more than six feet from the bank, but the ice flow pushed so hard we couldn't stand up. We rolled in the water and I got hit in the head with a big piece of ice, and then started trying to swim to get my head above water. I was never so cold. I couldn't even breathe the first time I came up. I could see men running along the bank, and I yelled for Ma. One of the men yelled that she was behind me and so I turned around as fast as I could. She was already under, but I saw her hand holding Alisha out of the water and then we were all pushed down again. I kicked and reached and grabbed for anything I could find under the water and finally got a hold of Ma's arm. Aaron was on the bank by then and threw us a rope, and some other men helped him pull us in."

Isaac looked at Aaron unable to say anymore.

Aaron continued. "We got Ma out of the water and someone had a blanket. She was all blue and only barely breathing. Mr. Boyd tried to take her to Doc Harper, but she started kicking and screaming for Alisha. I heard the splash when Isaac went back in. I called for him, but he was already under in the current. We ran along the bank to try to find him, and then about twenty feet down he came up with the quilt..."

"I touched her foot, Pa," Isaac said. "I know I did. I

almost had her that time!" Isaac searched his father's face for his reaction, but Ben was still staring out of the darkened window, not looking with his eyes but seeing the tragedy in his mind.

Aaron spoke again. "Somehow we got him back on the bank and tried to pull him back up the slope to where Ma was, but he just pushed away. He took the rope I had and tried to tie it around himself, but his fingers were so numb he couldn't even make a knot. I knew he was gonna go back in so I tied it for him and then me and John Mitchell held on to the other end. Isaac went back in and went under for the longest time. I was afraid he was drowning so I started pulling him back, but when he came back up he yelled `No!' and started going back in again."

Isaac grabbed the air in front of his face. "I almost had her!"

Aaron shook his head and looked back at his father. "He could hardly move. His skin was all blue and his lips were almost black. He couldn't swim a stroke, he was just reaching out in slow motion not knowing what he was doing anymore, but he wasn't gonna quit until he was dead too. I told John we had to pull him in, so we did. Then we took him and Ma to Doc Harper's."

Aaron looked at Isaac. "You couldn't have done any more."

Isaac's lip trembled as he spoke to his Father. "I tried, Pa. God, I almost had her! Then she was gone." Tears filled his eyes again and he turned his face away.

Sonja raised her head and shoulders and looked into Ben's face. "I don't remember much until the next day. LuAnn Harper had put me to bed in her own room. Wallace came in after LuAnn told him I was awake. He told me that Isaac was safe, but he had hurt his foot and there was no feeling in one of his toes."

Isaac looked out the doorway while his mother continued.

"Wallace said the toe was frost bit and he would

probably lose it. Later that week it turned black, and LuAnn and Aaron held him, while Wallace took it off."

Ben said nothing.

Sonja took in a deep ragged breath. "I have to finish it. I have to tell it all." She looked at nothing on the rough plank wall, her expression a death mask, her voice toneless. "Ben, we lost everything. We lost our daughter. We lost our house. We lost everything in the house. We lost the money that you had left. Everything that was in the house, and it's all gone."

She turned a hate-filled face to Ben. "All that you wanted to save from the bank was swept away by the river. Everything that you promised before you left, that-you-promised, you promised - was a hollow damned lie! What was left of the yard was just a gouged field in the spring. The Canal Company offered me a good price for the land, but they couldn't pay for a house that wasn't there."

She curled her hands into chapped fists and held them together in front of her chest. "I sold the land so we could buy food and clothes, and try to pay some of our debts, but there wasn't enough. A year had gone by since you left us. I took a job cleaning house for the Binterfield's over on Union Avenue. We didn't have a place to live then, but the Binterfields said I could stay there through the winter. Aaron and Isaac stayed some at the Boyd's and then found work helping to repair the canal basin for room and board on barges."

Sonja opened her arms to the small room. "In the spring, Wallace had this place cleaned out and said we were welcome to stay in it until you got back. When we heard you were dead, he just said stay as long as we needed."

"Who told you I was dead?"

"A letter came from the company that owned your ship. It said the ship went down with all souls."

"I don't understand. The captain said the company would send you money."

"They only sent notice of your death."

Sonja stared at the wall, empty with nothing else to say, waiting for Ben to speak.

"Why didn't you go stay with your father?"

Sonja offered no answer.

Ben reached out his hand to Sonja, but she pushed away, not looking at him. "I am so sorry, Sonja. I am sorry I was not here to help, to be here for you and my daughter when you needed me most. I could not get back…"

Sonja turned her back to him and walked to the little stove and began stabbing at the bed of coals with the poker. Ben then turned to Isaac, placing his hand gently against his face and then around his neck and pulled his head down and kissed him on the forehead, motioning for Aaron to come to him as well. He wrapped his arms around their necks and pulled them to him. Aaron pulled away and stepped to the other side of his mother and held her hand.

Ben spoke to his sons. "You did the best you could do. Sometimes that's all a man can do. I don't think I could have done any better or maybe even as well. A man does what needs be done. I am proud for what you tried to do, and how you did it. I am home now."

Darkness settled upon the heavy silence within the shanty as the last of the outside light faded. Sonja lit an oil lamp on the table, then stepped into her room speaking over her shoulder as she lit her lamp. "Stay or go as it pleases you. It's what you have always done." Then she closed the door behind her. With few words barely spoken, Aaron and Isaac left to sleep on board one of the canal barges.

Ben watched his sons leave, unable to find words to assure them, struggling to fully grasp what had become of them. He stood moments looking at the closed door between him and Sonja. He rubbed the scar beneath his shirt, searching for words to say to open that door; to begin the story of where he was and how his thoughts of coming home gave him strength when others lay down and died in China. All that was unsaid was useless and unimportant against the empty cavity growing in his chest, but he needed to speak.

"Sonja. I have things to tell you. You need to know what happened."

She spoke from behind the closed door, her voice muffled by the wood. "I know enough things; things a mother should never have to know!"

"But, it matters."

"...will it bring my baby back? Does it really matter?"

"No, but it matters to us."

"There is no us."

He stared at the door, finding no words worth uttering. The light beneath her door fluttered out as she put out her lamp. He stood there in silence. He placed a hand on the door. "I am here and I will stay. I will not leave you again."

Silence filled the little room and pressed against him. He took a chair out onto the roofless little porch at the front of the cottage. A full moon rose, painting the world in silver light. He pulled out a worn leather folder and withdrew the tattered letter protected inside. Looking at it again, trying to regain the moments when he had a new baby and a family and a home held within its brittle pages, and looked up at the stars through misted unseeing eyes, trying to find places in his mind to put all he had heard, and then returned the letter to its folder.

Later, as the moon began to set he was still no closer to his answers, Ben gently withdrew Sonja's letter. The letter had kept him alive in his heart when nothing else could have. Read to him countless times by his friends Anthony and Simon, he had memorized every word. Holding the letter up, not even looking at the words he could not read, he chanted in a desperate whisper to himself.

"I am doing well and the baby is kicking - come home to us soon – Mrs. Johnson says it will be a girl - we will name her Alisha - come home in time to see your child born – come home to see your child christened – you should be proud of your sons – I love you always – come home to us..."

He carefully refolded the old letter and returned it to its folder. Hearing a sound of movement within the shanty, he stepped back inside to find a faded pillow and quilt laid out on the table, but her door had already closed. He spread the quilt on the floor in front of the old stove and slowly lay down on the threadbare pad, easing his hands behind his head and staring up at the ceiling. He waited for the emotional cyclone of the day to finally end and sleep to take him, and he waited. He watched the moon beam crawl across the floor and onto the far wall. As the moonbeam faded to darkness, sleep at last came for him, bringing new nightmares.

Blood covered his opened hands, dripping onto the body of the man he had killed in China. Jason Seeger lay at his feet with Ben's knife still plunged into his chest, the abdomen slit open to his crotch. Blood gurgled and the man's intestines writhed like snakes within the horrific wound. In the middle of the writhing lay a dead baby, and all was covered in flowing blood. The wound closed over the baby. Seeger's eyes opened, looking up at Ben, and the dead man laughed.

2

At dawn, Sonja emerged from her room. Ben awoke as she stepped near him to place a kettle on the stove and feed a few pieces of split wood on top of the smoldering coals, and then tapped them with the poker to encourage the flame at their edges. She looked down at him.

"Still here? No new adventure come to mind during the night? Well, you might as well go sleep in my bed and be out of my way. I have to get ready for work."

Ben said nothing, but moved to the rocker on the other side of the room. In silence, Sonja built a modest fire in the old iron stove, filling the room with the smell of burning oak, and brought the pot of coffee to boil, and then readied herself for work at the Binterfield's. Ben watched her move, his mouth opening slightly at moments, but found nothing worth saying. The iron stove ticked and pinged, expanding from the heat of the fire, giving the only other sound in the warming room except for their breathing until the coffee boiled.

"Why didn't you go stay with your father in York Furnace?"

She set a cup of coffee for him on the table, not sitting with him but taking her cup to stand near the other window, staring out at the flowers in the Harper's back yard, sipping her coffee and rubbing the sides of her cup with her finger tips. "I did."

Ben studied the hairline crack running down the side of the dark stoneware cup holding his coffee, waiting to hear more. She spoke to the window, the faint daylight painting the curve of her throat and the delicate shape of her lips and nose like an ivory silhouette. "It did not work out. We were not welcome."

"That's hard to believe of him."

Her back stiffened and she glared directly into his eyes. "Believe it." She set her half full cup on the other end of the table and went back into the small bedroom returning with a full white apron over her faded gingham dress, tying the apron behind her as she walked toward the door.

"You don't have to do that anymore, Sonja."

She opened the door without turning back and spoke over her shoulder as she opened the door.

"I'll finish out the week and give them notice – if you stay. If not, it's all I have."

"I am staying."

She stopped in the doorway, looking outside. "Why?"

"We will have a new home. I have money for that now."

She did not look at him when she spoke, nor did she wait for an answer.

"Do you have enough money to buy back your daughter?"

Sonja stepped through the open doorway and left the cottage, speaking over her shoulder as she left.

"You can stay if you want; or not. I have grown proficient at being a goddamned widow."

He stood and watched her go, and stared for a moment into the yard through the open doorway, the sky lightening to blue, but shadows still covering the trees. He then went to the corner of the room where his seabag leaned, and withdrew a small sack. Holding it by its cord tied closed in a long series of square knots, he tossed it over his shoulder, reached down and closed the air vents to the little stove, stepped out into the early morning air, and pulled the door shut behind him.

Ben needed to speak with Wallace Harper, but it

was still too early. He walked down to the wharf to look again at the new buildings and lengthened dock serving the once sleepy town at the top of the bay. He stopped at the old bakery and bought a hot roll, but the baker's helper was new and did not know Ben. There were many faces he did not know, most were new to him. Catching his reflection in a store window he realized that with his rough sailor's appearance, some who might have known Ben Pulaski would probably not know him now.

Just as well.

As he struggled again with the terrible news, he freed his legs to take him aimlessly along street and walkway. He let his feet find their own pace and direction while he fell into thought, and soon found himself at the end of Water Street, and then at the corner of Pearl Lane. Rather than a gently curving lane ambling around the edge of the trees, it was now only a short driveway into a muddy lot. After a few steps he stopped and looked ahead, cognizant of where he was.

Behind the lockhouse where a cornfield had been was now a holding pen for a dozen mules. Harnesses hung along the split rail fence, ready to hitch the mules to new barges, eager for the tow up the canal and then back home. He remembered the lane had been much longer when his home was near its end, and it had curved slightly back to the west. Now, Pearl Lane ended before it even began, no longer even posting a sign calling it by its old name. Where houses had once lined the narrow end of the curving lane, stood two large warehouses. None of the ground out there looked familiar to him. The original houses, trees, and roll of the ground had all been scraped away by the ice flood two winters ago, and then rutted by legions of mule-drawn cargo wagons.

He walked along the drive as far as it would take him, and then walked the packed earth around the warehouses. Very little grass grew around the warehouses. Very few landmarks remained to help him place where his house once stood. It was all barren and unrecognizable to him. He stood between the warehouses listening to the mumbled voices of the men inside and the sound of iron wheeled dollies and shipping crates being shifted over wooden floors within. A small tree limb had been cut and left in the dirt. Absent-mindedly he picked it up using it as a thick walking stick, and stepped away from the warehouses walking up the gentle rise from the basin toward the post road. He walked higher up the slope away from the packed barren earth, letting the heavy dew on thick unkempt grass wash his boots to a watery shine and sprinkle them with grass seeds and little burrs.

He stopped before a stout oak tree. It stood away from the other trees, which allowed its branches to reach their full spread. He had always thought it was one of the handsomest oaks in Havre de Grace, even more so than some of the well kept young trees along Union Avenue. A milk cow munched among the wet grass to his left and tugged on her tie line within the perimeter of its circular reach. He could see another well-worn circle where she had been staked before, and beyond that the small barn farther along the slope where she was kept at night. The modest Johnson house and little barn had not changed. His own barn had been almost a mirror image of that one, both had been built by the same man who had then sold him the calf that became their own milk cow, Nadja.

Ben turned around in front of the majestic oak and looked back down the slope toward the warehouses. Looking to his right at the Johnson barn and keeping the oak over his left shoulder he knew where he was. Dropping the small bag he carried at the base of the tree, he paced back down to the first warehouse, and walked along its side.

No. This isn't right.

He returned to the oak and then studied the lay of the land to his left.

There! There are the braces for the Baltimore railroad, where the train loads onto the steamship for its ride across the river.

He turned himself slightly north and walked down

the slope with his eyes half closed, remembering this same walk from a hundred times before. He walked down the slope counting his steps, to the left corner of the second warehouse and stopped abruptly.

No! Not yet! Just a few more steps and I would be there!

He stepped back and glared at the warehouse. That corner of the warehouse sat on his property; sat where his house had been. Suddenly he wished with all his heart that he could see the spot again. He felt that it would be better if he could just see the spot where his house had been and his family had lived. He hated the warehouse for being there, as if somehow the warehouse held some cruel responsibility for his losses. And now he could not even look over his home site to even mourn it. He raised the heavy stick and swung it with all his might against the corner of the wooden building. The shock of the impact ran up his arm to his shoulder. It was as if the building was fighting back, and only added to the fire of Ben's growing hatred. He swung again smashing wood into wood. The sound of the impact echoed over the packed earth between the two buildings. Grabbing the stick with both hands, he firmed his grip and steadied his stand. Ben smashed it into the building again.

And again.

And again.

The pounding reverberated within the cavernous warehouse. Ben pounded again and again, cursing the building and the world around him in a barrage of profanity. He ignored the rebounding punch up his shoulders and slid into an internal rage of pounding noises and the rush of blood in his ears. The roar of the noise and the pounding and the cursing and the hatred and the pain of his loss merged into a momentary madness where his only existence centered on smashing the corner into splinters. He let the madness take him. The pounding of his own heartbeat thundered through his brain. His vision focused down to the spot where the stick smashed into the corner of the building. The violent collision became his only world.

Men within the warehouse stopped to listen to the mechanical pounding that loosened small cascades of dust jumping from the rafters and floating down through narrow sun beams onto their shoulders after each blow. Inside the warehouse the supervisor followed the noise out through the side door near Ben.

"Hey! What th'Hell is going on here? Hey you! What the HELL are you doing?".

The supervisor stepped toward Ben reaching his hand toward the stick. Ben's shoulders rounded forward with his ragged gasps. His shirt was soaked with sweat and pasted to his back. Unsteady on his feet, Ben put the tip of the stick to the man's chest, pushing him back. He screamed through clenched teeth, the veins in his neck standing out below a contorted crimson face.

"Stay away!"

More men came out of the side door to see what was happening. Ben attacked the corner again. The pounding increased. Several of the nailed boards had cracked and splintered. The bark on the heavy stick was ground away to pulp. The supervisor looked from Ben to his men, deciding what to do about him. The pounding became faster. Sweat poured down Ben's face burning his eyes and mixing with the tears that would not stop. Pulp shavings and splinters flew from the corner.

The supervisor's anger rose and he motioned for his men to come. In the midst of the pounding and cursing, the stick finally shattered, and the space between the buildings fell silent. Ben held the stub of the stick in his hand staring at the corner. Nearly exhausted, folded over sagging knees, and gasping for air, he dropped the piece in his hand and stooped to retrieve the larger piece on the ground before him. He fell to his knees picking up the remaining piece of wood and began to slap it weakly against the building, barely making a sound with the gentleness of the movement.

Before the supervisor could give another order, Robert Hannah stepped forward and placed his hand on the supervisor's forearm and pulled it slowly down.

"I'll take care of this. That's Ben Pulaski. His was one of the houses torn from here by the ice flood."

The supervisor leaned over to examine the damage to the building and then looked back at Ben.

"Well it ain't here now. That's company property he's hittin'."

Robert walked over and knelt down beside Ben.

"Ben. Ben, what are you doing here?"

"My house is in here"

"No it's not Ben. There's nothing under here but dirt. And there's nothing inside that was yours."

Ben looked up at the man, almost pleading.

"My house, Rob. My house! It was here!"

Robert slipped his hand under Ben's elbow pulling him to his feet.

"No Ben. Not anymore. I'm sorry, but there's nothing here for you."

He led Ben back up the grassy slope to the great oak and helped him lean against the tree.

"Oh God, Rob. I should'a been here."

Robert stood back up and brushed the grass from his trousers, looking down at the tortured man and then looking away, out toward the bay, so the agony would not touch him.

"It's done, Ben. And it can't be undone. A lot of folks lost people and things they couldn't live without, and now they have to. I'm sorry for your loss, but everybody did all they could, and it just happened, and it's done. You got to let it go somehow. You start whacking on that warehouse again and the super's gonna call the law."

Robert stood over Ben in silence for a moment resting his hands on his hips.

"I wish to God there was something else to say Ben that would make things different for you."

Then he walked back down the slope leaving the

man to work through his misery. The men in the warehouse returned to their tasks and the supervisor to his clipboard after assigning one of his men to find planks for new cap boards over the damaged corner.

Ben leaned back against the tree and looked up at the sky through its branches and let the slight breeze from the river cool his eyes. He rubbed his hands slowly in the still wet grass in the shadow of the tree and wiped his face with the dew, letting a ragged breath escape from his chest. A voice far in the back of his mind, Sonja's voice, called Alisha to come in for supper.

He pulled his knife from its sheath on his belt and looked at the reflections in its mirrored steel surface. He saw pieces of the sky between the new leaves and branches of the oak above him, and then his own eyes in the reflection.

Did I pay for Seeger's life with the life of my daughter?

He watched the sun play along the razor edge of the blade and he rocked the handle back and forth letting the sunlight pulse into his brain. He then held the blade still and looked once more into his own eyes.

I cannot let you out again.

Then he turned the blade and gripped the handle firmly and held it up over him, and studied the handle for a moment. With a grunt he pulled the knife down with all his strength and drove the blade through the tender grass roots and deep into the soft soil beside him. Withdrawing the blade and plunging it down again, he began to dig a small hole in the dirt at the base of the tree.

When the hole was deep enough, he reached into his small canvas bag and withdrew a tightly rolled parcel. He returned it to the canvas bag and rolled the bag into a tight bundle. He laid the bundle reverently in the hole and studied it for a few moments, his eyes not focused and his mind reaching into his memory to retrieve the image of her he had formed since the day of the letter. He then reached into his trouser pocket and withdrew the leather folder holding the old letter from Sonja and slowly whispered its words again. Then he laid it carefully on top of the bundle, tapping it lightly into place, stroking it with his finger tips. He sighed and shook his head no.

No. I will not give that up.

He returned the folder to his pocket and gently covered the hole with loose dirt and capped it with grassy turf brushed clean with his hand, and then patted it all firmly in place. He wiped the dirt from his knife on his trouser leg, returned it to his sheath and then stood up examining the ground where he had dug. He was satisfied there were no signs left that might tempt some youngster to dig it back up. The little spot at the foot of this oak was much better than some unknown place under the building down the slope- or out in the Bay with the crabs. He stood and looked up at the broad oak. This would be Alisha's tree.

Ben turned his back to the tree and slowly walked down a slope where no one lived anymore, crossed the remnant of a nameless lane that went nowhere, and trudged back into town where he was now a stranger, returning from the dead where no one mourned him.

3

Sonja watched from Lydia Binterfield's bedroom as two men walked up the slope to the giant oak tree. Sun sparkled off the canal basin beyond. The Binterfield mansion sat on Union avenue with upstairs views of the Bay and the canal basin. She would look out over the place she once lived each day as she re-made the bed and put away Lydia's sleeping clothes. It seemed to ease the pain. Today she looked out, cradling Lydia's pillow gently in her arms, watching the grassy slope. People rarely walked there anymore, except for Mr. Johnson when he tethered his cow. It was only as Ben walked down the slope heading back into town that she recognized him at that distance.

"Herbert tells me your man is back from the grave."

Sonja spun around and began smoothing out the surface of the pillow and placed it quickly on the bed, answering as she pulled the coverlet over the pillow.

"Yes Ma'am."

Lydia pushed a perfectly curled raven black ringlet back away from her eyes and walked to her chiffonier, threw open the mirrored doors and began picking through the dozens of dresses hanging within it.

"Well, when you're through daydreaming out my window, take some of my dresses downstairs for ironing."

She pulled out three gowns and tossed them onto the bed near Sonja, and then sat at her ornately carved dressing table, spreading her powder blue day gown out from the bench as she sat.

"Cook tells me Herbert has managed to miss the damned chamber pot again. It's all I can do to get her to serve the man his breakfast in his room where he wants it. Sissy'll tell me things like that but do you think she'll lift a finger to take care of it? Hell no. I can't get her to do anything in there now. Anyway, you'll need to mop in there. Just don't touch his damned tintypes of the canal. Sissy knocked one off the table last Sunday and I thought he was going to leave a scar on the girl - ruined a perfectly useful work dress."

Lydia took up a tuft cotton pad to smooth the powder on her long neck and oval face, examining her near-perfect cheeks one at a time in the tall ornate mirror. She slipped her hands up under her coiffured hair and carefully lifted the wig from her head and set it on one of several ceramic mannequin heads lining the back of her dressing table. Each head held another style wig of the same beautiful black shining hair that had once graced the heads of oriental girls. Sonja picked up the dresses and left the room as Lydia began brushing the rust colored nap that covered her head.

Sonja took the dresses down to the laundry room in the basement and handed them to Sissy's mother Junie.

"Junie, Lydia asks that these be ironed..."

"That woman don't ask nothin', Sonja."

"Shshsh! She's going to hear you one of these days..."

"That prissy man ever beat my baby again and they're gonna hear a whole lot."

Sonja ignored the comment.

"I need to take a pail and mop up to the man's room."

"He miss the pot again?"

"Mmm-mm"

"Better you than me, chile. Don't you touch those..."

"I know, I know. Don't touch the tintypes."

Sonja walked to the two narrow doors in the back of

the laundry room and gently touched the little bunch of dried flowers tied with a pink bow pinned to one.

"I been havin Sissy sleep in there since you left, but I can have her move back in with me if you planning on comin back."

"No. Ben's back now."

"He gonna stay?"

"I don't really know yet. Maybe."

"He changed much?"

"Everything has changed Junie. Mostly me. I got used to him being dead and I guess I need to find some way of wanting him to be alive again. I'm not sure I can do that – not sure if I want to do that."

"Well chile, you can't be wantin to stay here. Don't you be lying to me or to yourself saying that."

Sonja blew out a sigh and folded her arms together in front of her.

"No I don't want that either."

"Well unless you got other choices, you best be pickin between those two."

"I feel like it's between working for a Banshee... or being one."

Junie cackled.

"Be one, chile, be one! That ain't no choice. It's always better than working for one. And that's the damned truth."

Sonja stepped beyond the narrow doors into the darkness of a rough brick recess and took up the mop pail.

The chamber pot in Herbert Binterfield's bedroom was full to overflowing with everything that came out of the man. Sonja strained with the big ceramic pot down the back servant's stairs, but could not avoid spilling dollops along the way to the outhouse. She had to mop her way back to the master bedroom, changing the pail water several times.

In the master bedroom she returned the pot to its cabinet below the chamber seat, closed the cabinet, and stood in the middle of the room, letting the shame wash over her again. He had been sitting at the table near the fireplace holding his new pictures of the canal when she brought in his breakfast. He was kind to her, letting her talk of herself. She had finally accepted Ben's death as Herbert had encouraged her to do many times since he first brought her the news.

People have to adjust to their losses, he had said. *You need to start a new life, Sonja. Leave the old one behind or it will hurt you forever. You are a widow, Sonja, but you still have a life to live.*

Tears flowed down her face and he wrapped his arms around her. It was the only human contact she had felt since Ben sailed away; since Herbert had told her the ship's company listed the ship lost at sea. He kissed her on the forehead like her father used to and patted her shoulder and gently rubbed her back.

Even now it was a confusing memory. She sobbed into his vest and he stroked her back, kissing her cheeks. She was desperate for the feel of human kindness, and then he began to loosen her blouse. She was overwhelmed by grief and need and she did not stop him. The blouse had drifted open and he untied her cotton shift, caressing her breast and pulling her against his lips.

It was then that Sissy opened the door to clean the room. Herbert stepped back, pushing Sonja away.

Really, Sonja! You must control yourself! He turned back to his desk, dismissing them both with a flip of his hand.

Both of you, get out of here now! And pray I don't discuss this with Mrs. Binterfield. Go!

Sonja's embarrassment and shame only doubled through the expression on Sissy's face. Sonja pulled her blouse together and dashed down the servant's stairs to the basement. That night she stepped into the bitter cold soap water of the laundry tub and scrubbed her body red, but the lye soap would not cleanse what had been soiled.

She would never have gone back to the Binterfield's if she had had any other place to work. She pretended it never happened. Would not let herself think of it again. Ben's return had opened her memory. She had cursed Ben for returning, but even in her anger knew he would stay. She stood in the middle of his room again now and the shame of that day Binterfield touched her poured over her like slime and her stomach turned. She stood there sobbing, beating her chest slowly with her clenched fist, letting the mop handle fall to the carpet.

"Oh God."

Looking back at the glass covered tintypes on the table, she bit on her lip to help move her mind to other thoughts, but only stood there as blood trickled down from the corner of her mouth. She stooped down to retrieve the mop, grabbing the handle near the mop head and walked over to the table, staring down at the framed pictures.

"God Damn you!"

She pushed the mop handle back over her shoulder and then swung down and across, emitting an animal growl as the wooden shaft arced through the air and smashed into the pictures, shattering the frames and sending a spray of the glass shards over the room. She threw open the cabinet to his chamber pot, and drove the mop handle into it like a whale harpoon, shattering the pot. Ceramic pieces gushed out of the cabinet onto an oriental rug in front of it. Then she pulled down the bedcovers and shoved the mop onto his bed and walked out of the room.

Lydia threw open her bedroom door at the far end of the hall, wearing only her sheerest slip and her long neck craning above narrow exposed shoulders.

"What was that?"

Sonja reached the top of the servant's stairway and did not look back. She spoke into the echo of the narrow unfinished staircase, her words punctuated by the clomp of her footsteps on rough hewn boards.

"Sounded like something broke to me. By the way Lydia, I quit!"

Ben ascended the steps to the large front porch on Adams Street. The walk from the grassy slope and a brief stop at a public water pump had been just enough to settle him down. He still had much to do and his first call was to be with Wallace Harper, MD. Ben lifted the brass knocker in the center of the right hand double door and let it fall against the highly polished strike plate. A moment later after the second knock, the door handle turned and the heavy lacquered wooden door swung silently inward. Morning sunshine flooded the entrance, casting a yellow glow on the oak flooring and the round teak face of the Harper's maid, Eudora. The cheerfulness of the sunlight was unmatched by the stern countenance on Eudora's face. The voice was devoid of friendly tone and the eyes attempted to sweep Ben from the porch in spite of the polite formality.

"May Ah he'p you, suh?"

"Good morning, Eudora. I would like to speak with Dr. Harper, if I may."

The woman looked closer at the stranger, but still no recognition crossed her face. "An who may ah say is cawlin'?"

"Eudora, I'm Ben Pulaski. You've only known me for ten years!"

Eudora leaned slightly forward to re-examine this visitor, and then beamed a smile.

"Lo' mistah Ben, you spossa be dead, and now you comes lookin like a pirate. Ah' didn't know you from Adam."

Still looking closely at Ben to reassure herself that she was not mistaken after all, she ushered him into the front waiting room and guided him across highly polished oak flooring to a cherrywood parson's bench against a side wall.

"Ah'll tell the Doctah you wishes to see him."

Her dress and apron billowed as she pirouetted her broad frame and headed for the private door to Wallace Harper's office.

Watching her leave the room, Ben was reminded of a frigate coming about on the starboard tack. He glanced about the room as he waited, noting the daisy yellow color of fresh paint on all the walls and the snow white of the trim and mantle. The neatness and cleanliness of the room made him self-conscious of the loose grass and tar stains still on his canvas trousers. He brushed away some grass and picked with his thumbnail at one stain still holding a small fleck of tar, in a meager effort to improve his appearance. He had finally dislodged the little tar ball when Eudora sailed back into the room.

"Doctah Harper says for you to come in to see him now, Mistah Ben."

Ben smiled at Eudora. Holding the little piece of tar in his open palm he walked across the room and tossed it into the fireplace. Eudora stepped back to allow Ben entrance to the private office.

Wallace Harper was making a final note in one of many record books piled on a wide cluttered mahogany desk. He turned and rose with a quick agility almost surprising for his bulk and height, his massive hand engulfing Ben's in a firm handshake. Wallace had always looked more like a lumberjack than a doctor to Ben. The gentleness of his voice and eyes were often seconded by his physical presence to those who did not know him. Wallace motioned Ben to a padded chair next to the ornate desk and returned to his own chair. New leather rubbed noisily against its own folds and the wood frame creaked under his weight as he settled back into it.

"Welcome home, Ben. I'm sure Sonja and the boys are very glad to have you back."

Wallace's eyes twinkled under dark bushy eyebrows, his smile spreading over his entire face, lines furrowing up his forehead to his balding pate.

"There was a time when we weren't so sure you were going to come back to us, you know."

Ben looked around the office as he sat in the offered chair.

"It took a lot longer than any of us ever thought it would, Wallace. If I had just known what would happen,- both here and there - I never would have left."

Wallace looked down at his desktop, not seeing any of the many papers laying in front of him, slowly nodding his head.

"What did happen over there, Ben? I read in the Harford News about the return of your ship"

Ben looked up. "You read about my ship?"

"Yes, read about it last week. These are modern times, Ben. We have telegraph here in Havre de Grace. Why I understand they were still unloading part of the cargo off the *Philadelphia Star*, even as the story was sent to Baltimore. Our Gazette had it early the next day."

"Well Wallace, if you already read about it..."

"No, Ben, what I don't understand is why the Chinese king would impound an American merchant ship, let alone its crew! Why on earth would they do that?"

Ben sighed and relaxed the tension in his back. "Well, as far as that is concerned, it was because at first they thought we were British."

"Now that war is out between the Brits and the Chinese, I can understand why the Chinese might impound a British ship, not that I care a fig for the Brits. There is certainly no love lost for them here in Havre de Grace, since the bastards nearly burned it all to the ground back in '13. Old man O'Neill still talks at Mrs. Sear's tavern about firing the cannon at them as they came ashore. Still, it does appear awfully aggressive for such a backwards country to confront an empire like Britain. Seems damned foolish of them."

"The local prince was trying to protect his people from the opium the British were shipping in from India. By the time he was convinced we weren't British, he was too embarrassed to tell his uncle, the emperor, what he had done. So, he just kept us prisoner."

"I didn't know that!"

"I didn't either. Not then. The General guarding us spoke English and told our captain. Said the prince wouldn't be in power much longer. He would visit the ship saying it would all be cleared up in a couple weeks. Then he stopped visiting, and the food stopped coming. Later, the captain had us up anchor and we tried to sail back down the river, but we were stopped by gunboats. Then they fired on us..."

Ben looked down and shook his head.

"They had us moor up at a wharf so they could keep a closer eye on us, but soon all the guards left. We had to get off the ship to find food...it all became so insane...twenty months in Hell...six in ten came home."

"Ben...it must have been..."

"I never heard from Sonja about the baby until last night."

Wallace jerked his head up to stare at Ben's face, his expression displaying the unspoken questions.

"Only some of her letters caught up to me, Wallace. I had one from her just before we left from Charleston going down to the horn, and another written shortly after the first that I got when we finally returned, but the other ones never found me, nor mine to her. After about six months the captain had us sign some papers to be sent to a US Navy Ship in local waters, so the company could send some money to wives and mothers of the crew, but it never found Sonja. There ain't no post road from the Orient, and we suffered all the more for that."

Wallace nodded again, searching for the words to say.

"I'll never leave them again, Wallace."

Silence settled between the two friends. A moment

passed and Ben spoke again.

"I want to thank you for taking care of my family, Wallace. I can never repay you for the friendship and kindness... but I can pay you for your services. I was well paid for my voyage. My family was in great need and I know there are debts to square Wallace, and yours is the first account I wish to settle."

Ben withdrew a thick wad of bills from his trouser pocket.

Wallace sighed and reached for another record book in the hutch next to his desk.

"There's no rush about this, Ben."

"I appreciate that, Wallace, but it's the only thing I can do now-now that it is all over. I can't undo any of it, but I can at least repay the money debts. The debts of kindness will always be there."

Wallace smiled again at his friend and then turned the record book so Ben could see it. Ben squirmed in his seat before the page and looked pleadingly at Wallace. There were still many men who could neither read nor write, and Wallace remembered that Ben was one of them. He searched his mind for a polite word or two to help Ben keep his pride and still understand the entries.

A glimmer of understanding swept mercifully across Ben's face, to Wallace's great relief, as Ben found the total at the last entry. Ben could not read, but he could recognize his own name and he knew his numbers. He did not understand the other words written in long hand that looked like a length of knotted fishing line with unruly loops, but he trusted Wallace, and he knew that the numbers in the margin represented his fee. He could not read most words, but he could read people, and he knew that Wallace would have reduced his fee to his friend well below what it should have been. He added twenty dollars to the sum and hoped it would be fair, and pulled out the necessary bills. Wallace slipped the bills into his cash box in the desk without counting, almost embarrassed at handling money in front of Ben, and Ben hoped Wallace would be satisfied when he counted it later.

The cash box was quickly returned to the desk and the drawer locked with the key Wallace had attached to his watch chain. He then leaned back in his chair, lacing his fingers together in front of his broad abdomen, resting his elbows on the arms of his chair. The twinkle returned to his eyes and a small smile returned to his lips. His face now in its most natural state, framed by the thick side hair and full sideburns. The smile struggled to remain small as Wallace spoke.

"Now that I am in your employ, Ben, I would offer some unrequested advice."

Ben waited in silence, his head cocked slightly to the side, one eyebrow raised in question.

"Ben, you look like shit. You should really do something about that."

Ben smiled broadly and nodded his head slowly in agreement.

"So, Ben. What are your plans now?"

"There are still other debts I need to set aright. When I left we were buying our house and land at the end of town, as you know, but even though Sonja had to sell the land, I still owe Binterfield for the house. I'm not sure how we're going to settle that, but I suspect it will not be to my advantage."

Wallace frowned.

"Whatever arrangement you have with Herbert Binterfield, it will always be to his advantage, I can tell you that."

"We appreciate being able to stay in your old office out there, Wallace, but we can't impose on you any longer than we have. You have done a great deal for my family as it is."

Wallace raised his hand, but Ben shook his head before he could speak.

"No, we have to find our own place. There are always two or three places that could be bought or rented cheap, until we can do better."

Wallace shook his head.

"Not any more, Ben. With the completion of the canal, real estate speculation has become rampant here in town. Almost every square inch of land and anything with a roof on it has been bought up by men like Binterfield. Even some of our town commissioners are up to their eyeballs in real estate. It'll make them rich if anything can. Rent for a small house is five times what it was when you shipped off! A laboring man can't hardly afford it."

Ben stared down at the floor digesting the unwelcome information.

"Well, I need to see Binterfield next, and then William Boyd. Will and I planned to partner over a canal barge. He had it started when I left."

Ben rose from the chair. The two men shook hands, then Harper watched the resurrected man step out into the sunlight and straighten his shoulders for his next task. The doctor sighed and shook his head, then returned to his ledger.

On Oyster Street, Ben found the new building of The Tidewater Bank and Trust Company. The humble frame building of '32 was now encased in fine red brick and given a white painted lap-sided second story. Once inside the bank, the view was only little changed from his last visit. The meager writing counter for depositors was still nestled under one of the front windows, and the two cashier cages opposite. A friendly but unknown face smiled at him from the first teller position.

"May I help you, sir?"

"Morning. I would like to see Herbert Binterfield."

"Just a moment, please. I will see if Mr. Binterfield is available."

Ben smiled to himself as he could see Binterfield not more than twenty feet away in the back office area sitting at his desk.

"Who may I say is calling, Sir?"

"Ben Pulaski."

The teller withdrew from his stall and approached Binterfield's desk. The teller leaned slightly toward Binterfield's desk from a respectful distance, addressing his employer. Binterfield stiffened in his chair, gave a quick glance in Ben's direction, and exchanged a few hasty words with his teller. The teller backed away from the large carved oak desk and stepped slowly to Ben, tapping his fingers together in front of his slight frame like some squirrel trying to remember where he buried his acorn. The teller cleared his throat twice before he could speak again.

"Mr. Binterfield is terribly busy. Perhaps you could come back some other time?"

Ben's patience at dealing through an intermediary across a distance of twenty feet evaporated immediately.

"Bullshit!"

Looking directly at the banker and raising his voice so that it would be impossible not to be heard across the room, Ben spoke.

"Binterfield, you and I have some business to settle, and I want to settle it today."

The teller looked from Ben to Binterfield for a response. Binterfield looked quickly at Ben and then at the private door to his left; looked at Ben again, took in a deep breath and then nodded to the teller. The man returned to the front, quickly opened a small door beside his window and motioned for Ben to enter.

Ben approached Binterfield's desk and extended his hand to the man. Binterfield flinched slightly, but quickly accepted the offered hand. His hand was damp and yielded noticeably in Ben's firm handshake. Binterfield displayed a broad smile of perfectly even white teeth under a finely combed chestnut mustache in the middle of an unblemished face that would have rivaled a Greek statue. His nearly feminine pale blue eyes were without wrinkle, or frown, or arched eyebrow, or other indication of emotion that Ben was accustomed to reading in men. The smile stopped precisely with the lips and did not disturb the rest of the face.

"Welcome home, Ben. Please, have a seat. I had not heard of your return. W-when did you get in?"

Ben sat in the offered chair to the left of a desk far too large for the small room.

"I came in from Baltimore yesterday afternoon."

Binterfield looked repeatedly about the room as if searching for something, rolling his pen rapidly within his fingertips. He edged his chair slightly farther away from his desk, and Ben, leaning back against the springs of the chair.

"So, Ben, what business do you wish to settle today?"

"Well, first I wish to speak to you about my wife..."

Binterfield swallowed and blinked his eyes several times, clearing his throat.

"Yes?"

"Sonja tells me you and your wife hired her on as housekeeper after the flood took the house,- and the baby."

"Yes? Yes, yes we did, that is Lydia wanted her help. Yes. We did. Lydia and I." Binterfield swallowed again.

"That was a hard winter for my family. I hate that they couldn't stay together, but I am glad at least she had a warm place to stay until she could get her feet on the ground."

"Well,.. We, that is Lydia, was very pleased with her help in the house."

"Well Herbert, I thank you for that. And now I need to settle with you about the house."

The banker sighed.

"Yes, of course. The house. We do have some unfinished business with that, don't we?"

Turning to the teller with a flourish, Binterfield requested him to bring the necessary ledger and found the necessary entries.

"Yes, here it is. Your balance at the time of the flood was two hundred seventy five dollars and twenty-seven cents. And then there is the building interest since then, and of course there is the problem of the land your wife illegally sold."

Ben started at the mention of the word illegal.

"What do you mean by that?"

Binterfield tapped the ledger page with the end of his pen and continued.

"Yes. You see she sold the land to the Tidewater and Susquehanna Canal Company for a modest sum in cash. Money was still owed to the bank for the property, and it was not really hers to sell. I spoke to her at length about this when she came to live with us. Although the tragedy of the flood destroyed the house, the land was all that remained of the original note. This bank still held that note, as it does to this day. In ordinary circumstances I should have foreclosed on the note and regained possession of the land. The Canal Company acted brashly and your wife acted without the benefit of proper financial or legal counsel. She sold that parcel of land for a pittance of what it was actually worth. This bank lost significant profit due to that illegal sale, which I must therefore transfer to your debt."

Ben could sense the shark circling its prey.

"So what is the debt, now?"

The banker looked from Ben's face to the ledger sheet in front of him.

"Well, Ben, the debt,-that is, your debt, is now four hundred eighty four dollars and fifty five cents."

The shark had struck. The breath caught in Ben's chest. He gripped the edge of the desk with his right hand and placed his left hand on the wad of paper notes in his trouser pocket. He stared into Binterfield's face without expression as he inventoried the damage this kind of debt would do to his pay. Months of dangerous shipboard work, exposure to disease and dysentery, risks taken in storms and in foreign ports, to earn this money. And in a few seconds, sitting in a small bank in Havre de Grace, it began to evaporate as if it was never there, never earned.

Binterfield slid his chair slightly farther away from the desk, slightly farther away from Ben. He eyed the private door to his left.

"You won't mind me having that debt reviewed by a lawyer, would you?" Ben asked through thinned lips.

"No. No, of course not. As a matter of fact, I can recommend a good lawyer for you to see this very afternoon."

"No thanks. I know of one who can assist me with this."

He hoped the shark would choke in the meantime.

"We may not be able to settle this today after all."

Binterfield had his teller provide Ben with the necessary copies of the original and additional debt amounts and dates. Ben stood and nodded to Binterfield, and then left the bank.

Once out in the sunshine again, he took a deep breath of fresh air, shook his head and cursed to himself.

"God damn the man for a thief!"

Ben curled his hand around the handle to his knife, barely withdrawing the blade more than an inch. The sound of pulsating thunder reverberated within his head, the blood pulsed painfully behind his eyes, and the glare of the day became shrouded in blackness running in toward the center of his vision. His grip on the handle tightened and the blade withdrew further. He clinched his teeth and closed his eyes.

No!

A man and woman walking together along the wooden walkway stepped around him, looking in curiosity at the man with closed eyes.

I will not let you out!

Ben took in a ragged breath and then blew it out.

Again. He opened his eyes and relaxed the grip on his knife, sliding it fully into its sheath. He placed his hand in his pocket. He blew out another breath.

I will go see George Milton, then I will see the others.

He blew out another breath.

I will not let you out.

The sun was down over the western side of town before he tramped wearily back to the little cottage behind the Harper house. The grocer and dry goods stores had been visited and accounts settled. The time with George Milton had been almost painful, but George wanted more time to review the sale of Ben's land at the court house in Bel Air and asked Ben to return to his office the next evening.

The only consolation of the visit was learning of an available small farm in Lapidum along the first section of the canal, too far away from the town to suffer much from inflated prices.

The frustration of being legally cheated blazed in Ben's mind, but the fire waned as he entered the small house and found Sonja cooking their supper. He would not stress Sonja with his financial worries tonight. They were far from poor, and his desperate need for home and family called to him.

Aaron and Isaac arrived at the door soon after Ben. Sonja had only brief words and meager smiles for him when they at last sat down to dinner together. The quiet of the little main room pressed down upon all four of them. Sonja cleared the table with little conversation and was soon gone to her room behind closed door. Ben sat with his boys and began to talk of his voyage to China. He wanted them to know what had happened and where he had been. Only moments into the story, Aaron stood.

"We have to get Number 32 ready for in the morning." He sent a sharp look to Isaac and left the room without another word.

Isaac watched him leave and then turned to his

father.

"Pa, Aaron and me spent all day getting Number 32 ready to go north to Wrightsville and it's going to leave at daybreak. I didn't know so much could be put down in one little cabin. And we need to sleep on board her tonight so we can have the mules hitched up before dawn."

Ben was left alone at the table, his hands held up in front of him in silent question, for which the room offered no answer. He looked at the closed door shielding Sonja from his presence, and took one of the chairs out onto the little porch. The early evening chatter of night bugs and still busy birds had settled into the quiet deeper night chorus of bullfrogs and owls as Ben smoked his pipe on the tiny porch and sipped at a small glass of rum. He delayed another night on the floor a while longer, trying without success to understand the form of Sonja's grief and the manner in which she was adjusting to her husband's resurrection. He reached into his pocket for the letter that had been part of his nightly ceremony for long lonely months, and then softly recited some of its lines in a whispered rosary chant.

The setting moon, a second bowl of tobacco, and a third tumbler of rum finally escorted Ben to his pallet on the floor, and a fitful dream where he struggled down through ice cold water to reach a tiny white lace gown. The water became blood and he floated to the surface of a red ocean holding on to the corpse of John Seeger, first mate of the *Philadelphia Star*.

Pulaski's Canal

Ben arose before dawn and left the cottage while Sonja still slept. He walked down to the docks where everything was draped in fat morning dew and watched the sun rise slow and ruby gold over the Perry Point tree line across the Susquehanna flats. Schools of shad rippled the surface of the flats, fleeing the larger fish arriving for the feast. The air was from the south and the smell of the bay was the same as the ocean. He helped a tottering seaman return to his ship from a night of too much celebration, and then shared shipboard coffee with the captain of the schooner preparing to leave for Annapolis. As the wharf came full to life and the merchants began opening their shops, Ben thanked the captain and walked to the lockhouse to meet with William Boyd.

The Susquehanna and Tidewater Canal joined Pennsylvania's thirty-mile Susquehanna Canal to Maryland's fifteen-mile Tidewater Canal. The Joint effort connected coal-rich Wrightsville to Havre de Grace, the gate way to the Chesapeake Bay. From Havre de Grace at Maryland's lock number 10, barges were towed by steam tug to Philadelphia or Baltimore. The lockhouse was both the superintendent's office as well as the lock office and the locktender's residence. William had done well for himself and had become the canal's first superintendent. It would have been Will's prerogative to live in the residence, but he kept a small room in the Harford House Hotel and allowed the locktender and his wife to stay in the lockhouse.

Will stood leaning against the corner column

to the front porch of the lockhouse, his usual morning coffee steaming in the tin cup almost dangling from his looped finger, and his hat pushed back high on his forehead. He idly looked at the time on his pocket watch, then slipped it back into its pocket, and let the brass chain dangle across his unbuttoned vest to the fob in the other pocket. His slender frame stood upright and he keened his head to watch a familiar form walk down from Water Street. Ben waved as he approached the porch. A smile spread across Boyd's narrow face.

"Heard you weren't dead anymore, Ben. It's good to see you again."

"It's been a long time coming home, Will. There were times I didn't think it would happen."

The two men shared handshakes and talked as they stepped down across the front lawn toward the small cove below the lock, the dew shining their shoes and wetting the edges of their trousers as they walked.

"What happened over there, Ben?"

Ben only shook his head and looked out at the Susquehanna Flats. Then he turned back to his friend and smiled. "Maybe someday soon over a long drink."

Will nodded his head and kept walking, sweeping his arm over the grounds ahead of them.

"Like most else, the ice hit the barge pretty hard. I had it moved back up closer to the edge here and staked down so it wouldn't get pulled on down the Bay at high tides, but little else had been done for it. T'be honest, I couldn't see putting any more money into the thing to rebuild it since I no longer had a partner to operate it. That was to be your part. My work is here, I can't leave to run a barge up and down the canal."

Neither spoke as their short walk ended at a low grassy slope that thinned into mud as it slipped into the water's edge. Trapped in the exposed mud of low tide, the unfinished barge lay at an angle showing her bare forward struts and uncovered interior filled with stale water and algae. Ben's heart sank. The unfinished boat was a mere derelict partially buried in the gray mud. The higher side had suffered months of use as a seagull perch and was showered in layers of white crusted bird droppings.

"The wood's not as bad as you might expect, Ben. I had a man dig down a ways last fall and poke into the bottom wood as far down as he could get. Adam Tuttle? He said it was still good wood. Said the mud was keeping it covered like salve on a wound. Said he could probably fix it. I just couldn't find the interest to try to pull it out."

"If the bottom and the framing is still good, Will, it might still be worth the effort to me."

William patted Ben on the back and smiled.

"With you back, we're partners again, Ben. See what you can do."

The two shook hands again, turning away from the boat skeleton and walked back toward the Lockhouse.

Hanging his near empty tin cup loose from his hand, Boyd pointed it at Ben.

"Ben, I was real sorry about your... your loss. But you'd have been mighty proud of your sons, the way they took care of Sonja, and what they tried to do. And when the company bought your land, I saw to it Sonja got all the money she could. I guess it just wasn't enough."

Ben looked out beyond the lock where the mouth of the Susquehanna River climbed out of its trough and slipped wide across the flats and then down into the Chesapeake, and nodded. He let his eyes wander along the shore of Perry Point on the far side of the flats and then followed the downward flight of a seagull swooping in to collect a small fish swimming too close to the surface. He let out a small sigh to push away the silence that had filled the space between them, and then turned back to Boyd.

"I'm probably going to take the old Walker place upriver at Lapidum. Thought I'd just walk along that new towpath out there, if the Canal Superintendent wouldn't mind. Shouldn't be more than 4, maybe 5 miles from here"

"The Canal Superintendent can do better than that Ben. Dan Bartlett is taking Number 26 past there this morning. Why don't you just ride with him?"

An hour later, Ben sat at the rear of the canal barge watching reflections of the sky and tree lines on the canal surface slip by the barge as the mules traced their way along the towpath far ahead. Dan Bartlett talked about the opening ceremony of the canal, a year late because of the ice gorge and the damage to the canal; and now the almost constant canal traffic between Columbia up in Pennsylvania and Havre de Grace, occasionally nudging the tiller to keep the barge in its place. The barge trailed after the sagging tow rope behind the mules like a huge black bass slowly tracking a minnow, never gaining nor falling behind. Dan pointed his thumb at the mule tender up on the towpath.

"That'd be Thomas. He's old t'be tendin mules, full grown, 'bout twenty, I'd guess. His owner had no room for him in Bel Air and didn't want to sell him down for cotton work in Mississippi if he could help it, so he offered him to the Company at half rent if they give him a place to sleep. The county gave him a numbered copper tag to wear on his neck so nobody'd snatch him up as a runaway when we cross *The Line* into Pennsylvania. "

Dan fixed a firm eye on Ben.

" 'Course the Company has t'vouch that he's comin back. There's a lot of serious armed men from deeper South that hang around *The Line* watching for runaways."

Ben watched the black man walk with the mules.

"Why doesn't he run away when you go into Pennsylvania?"

Dan shrugged his shoulders.

"Used to worry about that. All the trouble I'd be in if he didn't come back with me. I mean, it'd be like losing part of a consigned cargo, and I sure couldn't afford that.

But we kinda got used to each other. I give him a few cents, and he goes off to a tavern for his kind in Wrightsville, while we wait our turn to cross the bridge to Columbia for coal. He has a couple drinks with'em, but then always comes back."

"He earns half pay, but you still have to give him money for drinks?"

"Ben, his rent goes to his owner. He never sees hardly any of that. Now and then a note comes from his owner by post, telling the Company to give him a quarter or maybe a half dollar, and deduct it from the next rent, but that ain't often. Thought you were from around here?"

Ben frowned and stared at Thomas in the distance.

"I am. Just never thought much about the blacks. Which was free. Which was slave. What people had to do with them to stay inside the law. Never went up into Pennsylvania, either."

Dan nodded, looking Ben steadily into his eyes. He spoke slowly.

"It's a complicated thing, that's for sure. Seems to stir up a lot of hate, either for or against."

Dan kept his gaze into Ben's eyes for a long moment.

"You got an opinion?"

Ben shook his head no. Dan leaned over the other side of the barge's stern and spit tobacco into the canal, and fixed his eyes on Thomas.

The Harford County shore was over a hundred yards away to the west across the open manmade lake, called the basin, that ran a half mile north enclosed by the towpath. The river width stretched eastward a quarter-mile wide beyond towpath to touch its eastern confines in Cecil County.

Dan pointed with his thumb toward the towpath.

"Looks like just a thin ribbon of dirt out there, don't it? Water on both sides of it. But it was packed hard on hundreds of tons of rock, gripped between cypress log walls pounded deep through the mud into the ground. They hauled rock and pounded cypress everyday for over a year to make that."

It was both a pathway and a wall, caught between the weight of the manmade lake water draining down from Wrightsville, Pennsylvania, forty five miles to the north, and the surging force of the untamed Susquehanna River on the other side. The river was engorged with the spring run off and roiled with undulating humps and frequent splashes against the outside of the towpath like a wild animal trapped just below the surface and begrudging the area of the basin stolen from it.

Gradually the wooded countryside of the west bank edged back toward them as the mule team continued its steady pull, drawing the long rope leading out from the bow of the front barge, taking them closer to the mouth of the actual canal. Palmer's Island rose out of the middle of the river blocking the view of Perryville back down to the east. Great Blue Herons squawked complaints at being disturbed during morning wades in the shallows and majestically flew away over the river.

The recent rain water still gushed and splashed downriver with large eddy currents shouldering their way around the big rocks standing at the edge of Palmer's Island, while the mirror of the canal basin reflected the forest on a surface almost perfectly still. Ben looked at the wide charging river nearby and almost felt hatred for the thing that had taken his daughter. The reflections of trees and sky on the canal surface were marred only by the small rolling wake pushed out from the rounded bow of Number 26, as it glided almost silently against the modest current. The barge still smelled of fresh cut wood and new tar. The off-shift mule team munched lazily on hay under a canvas topped manger at the bow. Thin smoke drifted slowly toward the west from the small stovepipe in the top of the little center cabin as the last embers of the morning cook fire in the stove died away.

Pulaski's Canal

Beyond the towpath, on the other side of the river, Ben could see small sailboats from Port Deposit and Perryville coming out to the middle of the river north of Palmer's Island, anchored against the rushing current. The boatmen had fishing poles angled out in all directions to catch the spring run of huge rockfish, making the rowboats look like spindly legged spiders on the rippling surface. Ben pointed out toward the boats.

"I can remember taking home twenty pound rockfish that made great white fish steaks for dinner during happier days. Some of those men make a good living selling rockfish to the markets and taverns. Fish and crabs in the spring and summer, oysters in the fall and winter until the ice comes, and then ducks and geese. And the hills along the river offer a good chance for a deer or two almost every week when the weather gets too cold on the Bay. A man just has to go out and get it."

"Not so much anymore, Ben. Got so many people down in Havre de Grace now, you'd be lucky to get two or three deer a week."

Ben leaned on the stern rail of the barge and watched seagulls hover around the fishing boats looking for their own dinner, absently rubbing the scar at his back. He straightened up from the rail and lifted his new straw hat to rub his head. The barber had trimmed his beard and hair, cutting off his seaman's pigtail. It had seemed a normal thing to have while he was at sea, but the queue was more an oddity among the good folks of Havre de Grace.

The mules continued along the towpath leaving behind the ribbon across the water and mounted grass covered firm ground, as the barge channeled northbound into the mouth of the canal proper. The openness of the canal basin was replaced by a dense old forest on the left, where huge oak, maple, and poplar trees rose high among crowded saplings, firs, and leafy underbrush competing with each other for sunlight under dark green canopies. Thomas hailed a southbound mule team pulling another barge downstream. The barge sat low in the water with only two feet of hull showing between the waterline and the white painted gunnel strip.

Ben was interested to see how these two barges sharing the same narrow canal and with mules sharing the same towpath, would negotiate the problem of the towrope. Ahead, the oncoming mule team was ridden by a small boy of only six or seven years. The boy and Thomas traded easy waves. The southbound barge swung slightly to the left of center as Ben watched it, while Number 26, empty of cargo and high in the water, drifted toward the right skimming the shallows. As the two mule teams met on the towpath, the little boy slowed his team, allowing his cable to sink low in the canal. Thomas slowed his pace to gather slack in his line and tossed his towrope over the little boy. The descending barge continued its slow glide toward the position of the little boy as Number 26 easily slipped over his submerged line. The little boy played with a grass twig and gave Number 26 a lazy wave as it passed. Ben and Dan returned his wave and smiled at his good-natured gap-toothed grin. Then, on the left the two barges began to pass each other. The loaded barge was three feet lower in the water. Ben read the name painted on the bow of the oncoming barge: *Piglet*, and smiled to himself at the name, Number 26 passed easily over the lowered towrope without the slightest hesitation, the two tiller men nodding to one another as they passed.

"Mornin', Dan" The man on *Piglet* spoke.

"Mornin' Fred."

Dan pointed his chin toward the other barge.

"There's a woman on board there."

Ben looked carefully along the deck of the barge but could see no one but the other tiller man.

"Where? I didn't see her."

Dan smiled at Ben and pointed his thumb toward the *Piglet's* center cabin.

"Curtains in the cabin. Always see that when a woman stays on board with her man. First thing she does is put up curtains in the cabin windows."

Ben smiled again and absorbed this new information. As soon as Number 26 had passed the little boy, unseen nudges by his bare feet started the mules, but they already knew what to do. They trotted down the path until they had taken up the slack of the towrope and could feel the weight of the barges begin to come against their collars, and then slowed to an easy pace, pulling the barges smoothly on their own way.

Ben watched the operation with keen interest.

"Is that the way it's always done?"

"Yep. The De-scending barge is always deeper in the water and the A-scending barge is almost always empty going up to Wrightsville. Only makes sense for the boat riding higher in the water to move to the shallows and pass over th'other fellah's line."

"Why are some barges numbered and some have names?"

Dan eased Number 26 back into the center of the canal and spat tobacco juice over the side.

"The ones with numbers belong to the Company. I'm hired as boat Cap'n and draw monthly pay from the canal company. Same pay full or empty. But now, barges with names belong to the man at the tiller. Empty runs cost him big, but he gets all the profit when she's full. Trouble is though, there ain't no profit until the cargo is sold. Usually in Philadelphia or Baltimore, but sometimes right there in Havre de Grace. Boats with numbers get first rights to steamer tows through the Chesapeake & Delaware Canal or down the Bay. Sometimes private owned barges wait a couple weeks until they can get towed, 'cause the company has a contract with the steamers and their barges go first."

"Seems to me, that a barge could get down to Baltimore under it's own sail and not have to wait like that. It wouldn't be as fast as a steamboat, but it would be a hell of a lot better than waiting in the Basin for two weeks."

"Barge ain't got a keel, Ben. She'd crab sideways like an old river ark, goin' this way and that. Don't think these tubs would take to sail worth a damn. These things are only good for what they do: gettin' pulled along by mules or tugs." He ended his statement with another spit of tobacco juice over the side.

Ben nodded to Dan's remarks, but watched one of the fishing boats out in the river current raise a sail and slip almost effortlessly past them for another fishing spot farther upstream. The thought of owning a barge held prisoner in the canal basin for weeks at a time placed a dim light on the very business he wished to begin. He began to run his eyes along the deck of Number 26 with keener attention to detail, comparing it to the little skiff out in the river. Ben's thoughts were interrupted when Thomas began to blow through a conch shell, sounding like a hoarse trumpet. He looked at Dan who answered his unspoken question.

"Lock number 9 is just up ahead 'bout half a mile. We blow on the conch to let the lock keeper know we're comin. That way he can move the swing bridge, and make sure the gates are open in the right direction. According to my wife's Pa, up here around Lock 9 used to be called Bell's Ferry. A couple small farms and the ferry across to Cecil County was here long before the canal was built. That was back long before Doc Archer had his covered bridge built down at Rock Run Mill. But this place up here has been 'Lapidum' to me long as I can remember, though some of the ol'folks that don't live up here still call it Bell's Ferry. More houses now, since the canal, nearly seven altogether I think, and a dry goods store."

Ben nodded at Dan's description.

"Sonja and I once rode the mares up this way. Crossed over and had dinner at the Union Hotel. It was a fine time, but between the bridge fare going both ways and the dinner at the Hotel, it cost me over half a dollar. A working man just can't live like that for long."

The arrow straight towpath softened into a long

gentle westward curve that finally brought the buildings of Lapidum into view and where the towpath began to rise higher above the canal surface. To the left a small cabin and the roof of another building beyond it sat back from the canal within an overgrowth of tall weeds and saplings, barely visible between a matched pair of massive low branch oaks facing the canal, and only touched by the morning sun in their higher branches. Dan pointed to the property with his thumb.

"That'd be the Walker place there."

Farther along the canal beyond the cabin and another short stretch of hardwood forest, Ben could see the mule barn and stable on the right side of the towpath where the land expanded. About four acres were enclosed between the canal and the river there. Beyond that on the left he could see the two-story building of the dry goods store. It stood at the corner created by a dirt road descending the hillside into Lapidum and turning north to run parallel with the canal past the lock in the distance. A roof of moss-edged gray split oak shingles gave cover to a vertical plank upper story holding two modest glass pane windows looking out over the road. A single large river rock chimney rose through the center peak where it sent blue-gray smoke up into the morning smoke cloud hanging over the little village.

The air smelled of burning oak and hickory that mixed with the aromas of roasted venison and fish stew. The first floor was a windowless wall of brown brick and cut stone offering only a single doorway at the front. Stacked wooden barrels and a row of new iron farm tools were set against the front wall under a generous front porch, and an apron clad man sat in the lone chair next to the doorway watching the approaching barge.

Small gray stone and weathered plank cottages marched in close order up the steep hillside along the road beyond the store. Fir trees decorated a peak of speckled granite boulders rising another fifty feet behind and above the buildings to mark the beginning of a forested ridge that continued south parallel with the canal. Some of the meager homes were separated by slender lines of dark green tufted grass and others butted against one another sharing common dark rock foundations of higher and higher steps, all of them with their backs against the side of the peak and the doorway to the highest house well above the roof of the store.

Beyond the store and farther along the canal stood a single story brick house, the younger brother of the Lockhouse in Havre de Grace. Lock Number 9 was directly across the road in front of the house and Ben assumed it was home to the lock tender.

The swing bridge was turned parallel with the granite walls of the lock and the lower gates were open. The lockkeeper stood on the wall edge above the closer gate and barely waved a finger pointing the way toward the lock as Number 26 eased into the little granite canyon. Ben admired the lock wall of massive granite blocks, cut so well by the Irish quarrymen that mortar had not been necessary. Rising onto his toes Ben looked beyond the upper gate and could barely see the next level of the canal a full ten feet higher than the water floating the barge under his feet.

Thomas snubbed the tow rope around a broad post set next to the far end of the lock, bringing the bow against the upper gate and pulling number 26 into the center of the lock with barely six inches of clearance on either side between the granite walls and barge. The lock keeper leaned into a chest-thick lever beam at the top of the gate and slowly closed the lower gate behind them. The mules on the towpath took the opportunity to munch on nearby grass and flick their tails at bothersome black flies, ignoring the mechanics of raising the barge.

With the southern gate sealed, the lock tender walked to the north end of the lock and began to push angled rods along the tops of the upper gate that opened iron sections at the bottoms of the gates and allowed torrents of water to fall into the lock chamber from the higher canal. Number 26 floated gracefully on the rapidly rising water within the lock as Dan used his pole to keep the barge from drifting against the lock wall and scraping its sides against the granite.

Thomas took up the slack in the towline as the barge rose, drawing the tow rope through shallow spiral grooves around the snubbing post. Ben watched the surface of the lower canal back away as the barge continued its rise to the next level. When the water flow had stopped, the lock keeper took up a clipboard and pencil and made a record of the time of day and the barge number. The water surface calmed within the lock and the barge thumped gently against the upper edge of the lock wall.

"This is where you get off, Ben. John will point you in the direction of old man Walker's place."

"Thanks for the ride, Dan."

Ben shook hands with Dan and stepped off the barge onto the granite ledge facing the lock keepers house. The lock keeper leaned into the lever beam and slowly opened the upper gate. The mule team had already started their trek northward along the towpath, taking up the slack on the towrope. Daniel Bartlett poled Number 26 out of the lock and into the next section of the canal as the towrope tightened to pull the barge again. Dan gave a crooked finger wave to John and Ben, and then steered the barge toward the center of the canal.

Ben turned to the lock keeper to introduce himself,

"Hello, My name's Ben Pulaski. George Milton in Havre de Grace said the Walker place was near here?"

The lock keeper accepted his hand.

"John Bartlett. The Walker place is only about a hundred yards back down the canal."

He pointed a crooked finger toward a small trail entering the woods where the road rounded the store to ascend the hill.

"Ya' passed it coming in."

Ben looked at John and then back at Number 26 as it drifted along the canal, and then again at the lock tender.

"Bartlett? You any kin to Dan?"

"Yeah. He's my older brother. You lookin' to buy the Walker place?"

"Rent, more likely, at least for now. What kind of shape is it in?"

"Can't say anything about the inside. Old man Walker never invited me in. Kept to himself, mostly. Was just his Pa's place, and the Bell's next to it, back when the ferry was here and they called this spot Bell's Landing. Long before my time, though. Walker didn't seem t'care for much visiting, and damn sure didn't like the canal being dug on this side of the river. Anyway, his place looked all right from the outside, 'cept for the weeds and brush now. A lot of rock around the place for terracing. The field out back needs some work, I don't think it's been planted for six or seven years now. Barn looks to be in fair condition."

John raised an eyebrow at Ben.

"Don't think I make it a habit of looking into other folks business, but there is a good fishing spot couple hundred yards below his place so I always go through his land to get there. Did it when he was there too, and he never even acted like he noticed. Never had much to say."

"Thanks. I guess I'll go up there and have a good look around before I make up my mind."

"I won't be going up there any more, though."

"I won't mind, John. Come ahead."

"Not that, Ben. Not so many fish up there since they enclosed the canal basin. Bass and trout from the inflow creeks, but the big rock fish can't get in there."

Ben turned and headed in the direction of the path to the Walker place. John Bartlett called after him.

"You're welcome to come up at lunch. The wife cooks a good meal for fifteen cents. Nothing fancy but it's real filling. Serves it on the front porch at noon."

Pulaski's Canal

Weeds and small brush grew close to the trail narrowing it almost to a game path. Ben crossed an old arched wooden bridge over a small creek gurgling its way down to the canal. The bridge was wide enough to take a wagon, but would probably need to be shored up some, Ben thought. The path continued slightly uphill and then left the brush to wind its way through a small stand of trees that allowed not too many briars and saplings to grow under their shade among the years of leaves. Beyond the trees, the ground cleared of heavy growth and Ben stepped back under open sky, although the sunshine was now gone. Looking up he could see waves of gray clouds rushing across the sky from the south.

Ben remembered his father's voice. *If you don't like the weather on the Chesapeake, just wait ten minutes - it'll change.*

The wind began to rustle the leaves and higher branches began to sway. A large silver maple stood at the southern edge of the clearing with its leaves turned to the sky.

Looks like I'm going to get a chance to see if the roof leaks.

The clearing was grassed down to the edge of the canal to his left, but had been neglected for more than a few years for the weeds, brush, and saplings to grow up. Ben could see a pair of rabbits hopping about in the tall grass, unaware of his presence. A few half submerged broad stumps from once towering oaks marked the edge of the short front field, cut down to make way for the canal. Two oaks of wider girth matched the stumps in a row farther up to the middle of the front yard. These were the matched pair he had seen from the barge, and would give plenty of shade in the summer. To his right the grassy slope led up to the front of the house. The center of the house was obviously the original log cabin. Mortar had been added to the mud that once filled the seams between the logs. He could see that an effort had been made to adze the sides of the logs flat when they were stacked and pegged in place.

There was a door in the center of the cabin and a window on either side of it. Vertical plank rooms had been added to either side of the cabin, set slightly back from the front, and the peak of the original roof extended over the two rooms. A low front porch ran the full width of the house. The foundation was river rock and mortar. More rock and mortar made up a knee-high wall running across the yard in front of the house half way between the standing oaks and the porch. Ben passed through the opening in the rock wall and up to the front porch, watching a young squirrel scamper along the peak of the roof to leap onto a nearby tree branch. Once in the safety of his tree, the squirrel turned to bark bravely at Ben's arrival. The front door leaned at a slight angle, suspended from the remaining upper iron hinge; the lower long since rusted away, replaced twice by leather straps still nailed in place one over another and now worn in two. The door had seen long and rough use, and had to be lifted to open inward.

The cabin had wide wood floorboards pegged into place at their ends. The river rock fireplace was located in the center of the cabin with gray slate flooring in front, a thick slate slab jutted out above the fire box as a mantle, and the chimney rose to the exposed underside of the roof peak between thick rafters. Walls ran to the left and right of the fireplace separating the cabin into front and back rooms. The firebox itself was open both front and back, and he could see the floor of the back room through the opening above the grating. He admired the planning that would allow one fireplace to heat both rooms, but wondered whether the draft of the chimney was sufficient to draw smoke from two rooms. He looked at the walls near the fireplace and the beams above.

No blackening to suggest a smoky house. That is a good sign.

The wall to the left of the fireplace held a doorway to the rear room. Doorways had also been cut through the log walls on each side of the front room for entry into the added plank rooms. Vertical board doors with good iron hinges and latches were hung in each doorway. Ben liked the way the house was laid out.

Dust stirred under his feet as he walked across the room toward the rear door.

Just needs some cleaning. Everything but that front door looks to be in good condition. A few cobwebs here and there still tended by their landlords.

There were no water stains on the floor to indicate roof leaks, at least not in the front room. Ben looked up and examined the underside of the roofing planks. There were split oak shakes on the outer roof, so they must be nailed to the planks above.

The old man's father built a good cabin in his day.

Looking closer at a seam between two planks above, he could see small spreading stains of pitch.

Very good. It should be a dry house in the heaviest rains.

The sky challenged his quiet thoughts with a rolling thunder coming up from the south. The room darkened slightly as more clouds gathered overhead, blocking the last of the sunshine on the house. He turned to look at the graying day through the collected dirt on one of the two front windows to the room.

The old man had a beautiful view of the river from here. Small wonder he disliked the canal being build practically in his front yard. Sonja will like this view.

Ben imagined tying his barge up at the front of their own yard.

The rear room was the same size as the front, with room to cook and for the four of them to sit at table for supper. There was a rear door from the kitchen out into the back yard.

The bedroom on the right has plenty of room for a large bed and maybe a wardrobe for Sonja.

The single rear window gave view to the terraced wall of the small field behind where the barn was sited. He could also see the outhouse to the right of the window, and on the same level as the house.

Not too far a walk, even in the cold or during the night.

Sonja hated such trips in the night, and had always awakened him to escort her with a lantern on those rare trips while at their place near town. The room on the left was the same size and would provide the boys even more room than they had on Pearl Lane – whenever they came home.

Yes, this place would do very nicely.

In back of the house, the barn was in less sound condition, but not ready to fall, just in need of repairs. Sky shown through a few places over the four stalls, and the singlewide door would have to be replaced. The corn crib had not seen use in many years, but the hay loft looked dry and had room for plenty of feed for the winter for one or two working animals. He had hoped to once again have a horse and a milk cow, but would need to make room to keep four mules for his barge. He re-examined the stalls and crib and decided he could rework the walls to create enough room for the mules and a cow.

Still unsure if that would be sufficient, he walked out of the barn to look at the small cornfield next to it, and then the old outhouse. The little field looked large enough to provide fresh corn for his family and some feed for the work animals, but not enough to feed four mules through a hard winter. He found a small hog pen on the left of the barn, and a good sized chicken coop on the right. Both needed new enclosures, but the low roofed areas were still sound. The hillside behind the farm kept the field from going very far in that direction, but it was wide enough. Hay would have to be bought or traded from another farm. The field was satisfactory, but the outhouse was not. It would have to be re-sited and rebuilt.

Another thing to pay for, and I've not finished the barge details with Will, or settled accounts with that shark Binterfield!

Pulaski's Canal

He kicked a dirt clod hard across the little field, watching the little dust cloud drift away from where the clod landed.

Damn the thief!

Fat raindrops began to pelt down upon his hat and shoulders as Ben walked back toward the house among the little spurts of dust kicked up by the drops. The raindrops turned into cascade before he could reach the porch, he hunched forward against the pouring rain and stuck his hands into his pockets as he trotted back. The sky had opened its sluice gates to rid itself of a heavy load, and celebrated the release with a concert of lightning and thunder. From the porch Ben could see lightning strikes on the river surface and the rock cliff face across the Susquehanna. Somewhere on the opposite shore the fishermen had dragged their wooden boats up the banks after a hard pull against wind and current to escape the lightning.

The late spring heat of the morning was brushed away and a slight chill trickled down Ben's back as the fresh rainwater seeped down his shirt. He shook water from his hat and stamped his feet on the porch to shed some of the water, and reentered the front room of the house. He could hear the water gush from the roof overhead feeding small streams developing in the ground on either side of the house, eager to make the journey downhill to the canal. The rain beat on the roof in a rolling drum tattoo looking for ways to get in, but no rivulet of water could be seen from inside. Ben could only find a small drip of water in the rear room window, but the others performed their duty well. He noticed more of the telltale signs of pitch at their edges.

Old man Walker had been determined to keep his house dry.

He stepped into the rain to find the trail back to the lockhouse. Hands in his pockets, he fingered his coins and decided he would sit down to Mrs. Bartlett's front porch lunch.

Ben set the bell dancing above the door as he entered the Tidewater Bank and Trust Company, wading through swirling dust mites sparkling in the early morning sunbeam shining from the window. Beyond the teller stalls, their faces and chests brightly lit in the sunbeam but waist deep in shadow, Ben saw Binterfield and a man unknown to him leaning over a ledger book on Binterfield's desk, deep in discussion over its contents. The man pointed repeatedly to a spot on the page, his hand dipping from the sunlight into the shadow, while Binterfield repeatedly shook his head to the unheard question. Ben stepped through the swing gate and strode to Binterfield's desk with the teller quick stepping behind him.

"Good morning, Mister Pulaski."

Binterfield opened his hand toward the other man at the desk.

"Do you know Mr. Briscoe, here? He handles the real estate concerns of the bank."

Ben and Briscoe nodded without further introduction. Binterfield exchanged a quick glance with Briscoe.

"It was very efficient of your lawyer to notify Mr. Briscoe to attend our meeting today. Kindly have a seat and let us discuss your delinquent account."

Ben stiffened at Binterfield's remark but remembered the advice of the lawyer to be both friendly and wary of Herbert Binterfield.

"Thank you, Mister Binterfield. If I may place some

of my papers on the edge of your desk.

Ben set down a bundle of papers, most were not even related to his business with Binterfield, but Ben wanted to make Binterfield believe he had more facts than he actually did.

Ben leafed through the bundle to the solitary document that had been found by the lawyer, which he had suggested might be of value if Ben only allowed a portion of the official looking document to be seen.

Raising his eyes from straining to see the obscured details of the partially displayed papers, Binterfield looked at Ben and nodded.

Ben mumbled to himself as he rescanned the lines of wording on the document he could not read and let out a small "Ahhh, yes. This was my question." And tapped the paper gently with a calloused fingertip at a spot he selected at random.

Binterfield spoke before Ben could say anything, "The property suffered the loss of the dwelling during the ice flood of '39, leaving only the bare land and it in almost unusable condition. And, the original mortgage, the original debt, is still outstanding, for which Mr. Pulaski is responsible.

Ben tapped the document again, "Yes, but according to this..."

Binterfield went on, "The flood was an unfortunate act of God, but the money for the property was advanced by this bank. The debt arose from the purchase of the land and house, and regardless of the loss of the house, the amount owed still legally exists. We advanced that money and require repayment, with interest, as defined in our mortgage contract. And... there is more..."

"And what is that?"

"There is the recent destruction of property and the hand of your wife while she was in my employ... in the amount of...Five Dollars and sixteen cents."

Ben raised a finger, "And of course I pay my debts and those of my wife. My confusion rests in the actual amount owed, against the actual amount paid to Mrs. Pulaski."

Binterfield and Briscoe exchanged frowned glances as Briscoe tightened his hold on the ledger on his lap.

Ben continued. "In discussion of the parcel of land with an official of the Susquehanna and Tidewater Canal Company, I am informed that the Company paid the sum of..."

Ben referred back to his document.

"...the sum of six hundred twenty five dollars. Is that not correct, Mr. Briscoe?"

Briscoe swallowed and looked at Binterfield and then answered.

"Yes, that is correct."

"Excuse the inquiry, Mr. Briscoe, but what is the customary commission paid for acquiring land for the Tidewater Canal Company?"

Briscoe responded quietly, "Ten Percent."

Binterfield leaned forward from behind his desk and fixed his eyes on Ben.

"What has that to do with this discussion?"

"Just a moment, Mr. Binterfield. Mr. Briscoe, or should I address these questions directly to you Mr. Binterfield?"

Binterfield shook his head and leaned back in his chair.

"No, I am certain that Mr. Briscoe knows much more about the real estate acquisition than I. I am more of a silent partner in that office. The bank merely handles the financing before the sales are made final."

"And shares in the profit, does it not, Mr. Binterfield?"

"Yes. Yes, of course the bank shares in the profit... as a stockholder."

"Thank you. So, Mr. Briscoe, since it is fair business that your company earns a ten percent commission, then the property in question was purchased by you for five hundred sixty-eight dollars. Is that correct, sir?"

Briscoe slowly opened the ledger book so tightly held to his chest and answered softly, "...and eighteen cents," and looked back at Binterfield who would not meet his gaze.

Ben sorted through more papers on the corner of the desk.

"I am informed that Mrs. Pulaski received only seventy-five dollars when she signed over the deed?"

Briscoe cleared his throat.

"Oh, no. That is not so. The poor woman was distraught with the loss of her home and child."

Briscoe looked into Ben's eyes and quickly looked back at Binterfield.

"We paid her the entire amount. Why we did everything we could to assist her in her time of need."

Ben grunted in dissatisfaction with the boldface lies flying about the room and shifted noisily in his seat.

"I am amazed that she cannot recall such a large sum of money being placed in her hands. Was it in cash, sir?"

"No, we rarely provide cash. She was given a bank draft for that amount. See here. Here is the payment entry in the office ledger."

Briscoe opened the book for Ben to examine and pointed to the entry. The smudge around the entry suggested it as the likely topic of much animated discussion ongoing as Ben had entered the bank.

"Still, a lot of money to burden a woman with. And she only remembers seventy five dollars."

Binterfield stiffened in his chair.

"What people receive and what they say they receive can be argued forever. That is why ledger entries are made; to keep people honest. Who's to say what she did with the money. She also said she had over two hundred dollars in cash lost in the flood. We can't help what people lose, or what they say they lose."

Ben shifted in his chair again, its legs dragging audibly on the wooden floor.

Briscoe glanced at Ben and leaned slightly away.

"That's right. We gave her a generous sum, and she lost it, or spent it, or buried it. I don't know. What I do know is that we gave her a check and she signed over the property."

Ben repeated the sum for effect.

"For five hundred sixty eight dollars...and eighteen cents?"

"Yes."

Briscoe pointed again to the columns dissecting the recorded line in the ledger.

"Here's the entry for the check, the date, the amount, and who it was paid to. Why, Mr. Binterfield there even offered her a place to work and live, and I even suggested she bank her money."

Binterfield swung his head toward Briscoe, not showing the expression to Ben. Briscoe leaned back as if slapped, closing his mouth and the ledger like sprung traps.

Ben grunted in satisfaction, considering Briscoe's revealed information as settled among them, and then followed with another question.

"Mr. Binterfield, does my wife have an account with this bank?"

Binterfield offered up both hands.

"I can't possibly remember everyone who holds an account with us. I mean, it's possible, but I cannot answer from memory."

"May I see the ledger entries for Mrs. Pulaski's account?"

Binterfield stammered slightly.

"Well, I suppose. I don't know what good it would do. I mean, if she only remembers seventy-five dollars, and that is all she deposited, it would prove nothing. And, accounts of customers are quite confidential, perhaps if you were to return tomorrow with proper papers..."

"I am her husband! No business or law can keep a husband from knowing the activities of his wife. I am responsible for her and I will see what is legally mine! Have your teller show me the ledger book of her account. Now!"

The teller had been listening to the conversation from his stall at the front counter and moved slightly from his perch on the high stool, but did not turn around, waiting for his employer's response.

"Very well. Brown, bring the ledgers for Mrs. Pulaski's account."

Brown went to the bookcase on the sidewall of the inner office, pulled a single large ledger book from its shelf not far from Binterfield's desk and handed it to Binterfield saying, "Here are the M-N-O-P's, sir."

Binterfield accepted the ledger from Brown, who hesitated near the desk.

"Well, get back to work."

Brown spun on his heels and returned to his perch while Binterfield leisurely flipped through the pages.

Ben frowned. *That's not the book I need. He's too smug about this.*

Binterfield opened the book and spread it on the desk so Ben could see it and punched a well-manicured finger at one of the first entries.

"There it is, gentlemen. January the 22d, Eighteen hundred thirty nine. Opening balance was five hundred sixty eight dollars...and eighteen cents. Deposited by bank draft from the Havre de Grace and Lapidum Real Estate Development Corporation."

Tapping the book harder he added "and two days later, a withdrawal leaving her with a balance of seventy five dollars. And that, gentlemen, is the seventy-five dollars she remembers. I can't say what she did with the money, but I can say what she did not do with it. She did not pay off the debt owed the bank for the Pulaski property!"

Ben gripped the sides of his chair.

The lying Bastard! He has doctored these books already.

Blackness crept into the edge of Ben's vision. The page was perfectly clean without smudge or pencil mark. All entries were exactly the same shade of ink. It was obviously a fabrication.

"And I suppose there are the customary withdrawal slips for that action?"

Binterfield leaned back in his chair smoothing his vest and picking imagined lint here and there.

"I suppose so, but you know that sometimes such little papers do get misplaced. That's why we have ledgers as the final record."

He leaned forward over the open ledger book again saying, "This is all that's really necessary, you know. It is all entered and initialed properly by my tellers."

Ben watched the backs of the tellers stiffen and twist at their windows. They knew full well what was happening here, but were pretending to be oblivious to the crime. Slowly Brown turned on his stool and faced the group seated around Binterfield's desk. He stepped down from his stool, looking at Ben, and took in a deep breath. Wringing his hands in front of himself, the teller quietly approached the desk, hesitating at the respectful distance Ben had observed before. Brown spoke to Binterfield, his voice squeaking under the strain.

"W-Would you be needing the day ledger, sir."

"No! Brown, I have this well in hand. You stick to your duties and earn your keep, such as it is."

Binterfield glared at Brown as he spoke, but Brown did not back away.

Ben was quick to see an important moment.

"Is that a written record of each activity throughout

each business day?"

Binterfield cleared his throat and continued to glare at his employee, but Brown summoned the strength to answer Ben's question.

"That is correct, sir. The daybook activities are transferred to individual account ledgers at the end of each week. "

Binterfield raised his voice slightly.

"I am sure it won't be necessary to dig through all those stored ledgers to find a single entry that is shown perfectly well here. Brown, I'll call you if I need you."

Binterfield stared hard at Brown, willing the man to go back to his perch on his stool where he belonged, but Brown remained where he stood.

"I-I thought it would be helpful to have everything available for your review, Mr. Binterfield, so the day books for that week were pulled and cleaned for handling."

Brown was visibly trembling. Binterfield's face was nearly crimson.

"That won't be necessary Brown, and that will be all."

Ben held up a hand.

"You are probably quite right, Mr. Binterfield. I have intruded so much into your busy day already..."

Binterfield's face faded to normal and he exhaled slightly offering up a smile.

Ben continued, "However, since your man has already gone to the trouble of pulling the things and cleaning them off for our review, it's only right we review them. After all, we want to put this whole thing to rest and then do what's right here, don't we?"

Binterfield and Briscoe nodded in unison, both glaring pure hatred toward Brown.

As the clerk brought the tidied ledgers toward the desk, Ben overreached Binterfield taking the ledgers directly into his possession and holding Brown's hands in his grasp.

"I assume these are simply by date?"

Brown nodded and stepped back, but not back to his teller stall. He would not look at Binterfield, but he remained nearby. Ben reviewed the slight little man with new respect and he breathed a light sigh of relief since he could read dates. He also knew he could recognize Sonja's name, and by God he knew his numbers. He sat up straight in his chair, and confidently flipped through the pages, watching the date advance.

Just like on a ship. The day log and the weekly log, of positions and times. All numbers – and I know my numbers well.

Briscoe kept his own ledger book held close to his chest, thrumming its cover with his fingertips, his wide eyes tracking the progress of the day ledger. Running his finger down the date column Ben paused at the first entry for January 22. He continued his perusal onto the next page and halted half way down the sheet.

"How odd. How interesting," he muttered absently to himself. "Mr. Binterfield, this ledger shows an opening deposit by Mrs. Pulaski for..."

He intentionally looked up at Binterfield with a confused simpleton expression, to extend the pause.

"Seventy Five Dollars? I am sure you know much more about banking and accounting procedure than I, but shouldn't the day ledger and the account ledger match?"

Binterfield could only nod in agreement, pressing light lips tightly together. With a slight flourish, Ben withdrew a cancelled check and a single deposit slip that had been placed between the pages; displaying the signatures of both the teller and Sonja Pulaski. Ben knew when he had been dealt a winning hand. He also suspected what this hand would probably cost the dealer. Ben continued in his most innocent tone. "And what day was the withdrawal? Oh yes, two days later, you said. If my poor math is up to the task, that would be the 24th, wouldn't it?" and he scanned the next few pages, counting to himself. Binterfield said nothing, his glance shifting from Brown to Ben with equal malice. Ben announced to all present, "There were thirty two entries on the 24th. There are many names here in this ledger, but alas, no entry for a Pulaski. Why do you suppose that is, Mr. Binterfield?"

"A mistake," Binterfield croaked, and eyed Brown. "Someone obviously made an error in the ledger entries. I am sure there have been some... inadvertent errors; errors that have put us all at unfortunate and unnecessary odds. The question is, which ledger is in error?"

Ben tried to enjoy the moment. He stretched out his arms, holding the ledger out in one hand as he had seen traveling preachers hold the Bible at prophetic moments, and searched the faces of his little audience. Ben arched his eyebrows and gave a gentle outward smile, even as he suppressed the stronger urge to the thundering beginning at the back of his head.

"Is this ledger right, and the woman never received the balance, or is your account ledger correct and her account is simply under funded by some five hundred dollars?"

Ben cleared his throat.

"Five hundred sixty eight dollars and eighteen cents."

Briscoe held his book before him. "My books are correct. Binterfield and I reviewed them together. We both signed them. We both signed the checks."

Binterfield rolled his reddening eyes at Briscoe and stood from his chair.

"We obviously have some, er, corrections to make, Mr. Pulaski. If you will allow me a day or two to investigate these terrible mistakes, I assure you that I will get to the bottom of it and produce an accurate accounting once and for all!"

"That's very kind of you, Mr. Binterfield, but I do

not wish to bother you unnecessarily. You have lost valuable time from your bank business by my intrusion already."

Reaching down and absently touching against the partially exposed legal documents, he added "I'm sure that we can find some good folks to help us search all this out, if we are unable to settle the matter now."

Binterfield paled and looked from face to face among the small group. He eyed the private door momentarily, but then returned his attention to Ben and smiled his toothy smile.

"I am sure that the day book is in error. As Mr. Briscoe has so nobly informed you, I helped him settle his ledger and the account ledger. No, the errors must be in the withdrawal in the account book and the daybook entry for the deposit. Obviously a clerk must have entered someone else's deposit rather than the full check amount we had authorized."

Ben smiled genuinely from Brown to Binterfield.

"So what you're saying is that our account actually has five hundred sixty eight dollars more than the account ledger shows?"

"And eighteen cents." remarked Brown.

Ben turned back to Binterfield.

"What amount does the account ledger say she has?"

Binterfield looked down at the account ledger and spoke demurely without looking at Ben.

"Forty seven dollars and thirty cents."

Ben quickly calculated the sum of the two numbers and then asked Binterfield.

"And how much is the remainder of my original note?"

Binterfield exhaled slowly over the book not looking up.

"Four hundred eighty four dollars and uhm, oh hell just call it four hundred eighty dollars."

Ben slapped his hands together.

"All right! Let's settle the damned note."

Binterfield fixed Ben with a cold stare and tapped his desktop with his middle finger for a lingering silent moment.

"There is still the matter of your wife's destruction of private property. There is that additional amount of five dollars and sixteen cents."

Binterfield slowly pulled out a pen to correct the amount to be paid to Ben by that amount. As he wrote he spoke, not looking up.

"Your wife broke a set of glass covered tintypes. Pictures of the canal. I am an investor in the canal, you know. She also broke an imported chamber pot."

He raised his head looking unblinking into Ben's eyes.

"Her job was to clean my bedroom, and to empty and clean my chamber pot. That was her job. But, you knew that didn't you, Mr. Pulaski. You knew that it was your wife's job to clean out my chamber pot, didn't you sir?"

Ben's lips were compressed into a thin line.

"No."

"Yes, it was. I believe that's when she broke it. While she was cleaning it. Pity. I really enjoyed using it, and I will certainly miss her being there each day... to clean it."

The sun was shining on the slice of bay visible between the tavern and market across the street when Ben left the bank and stood out on the plank sidewalk. Ben slammed his fist into his palm.

That bastard cheated Sonja all that time. All that time Sonja sweated as a maid at his own house, cleaning his goddamned chamber pot, and he had her money! She lived in a shack and he had her money!!

Ben rubbed his palm over the handle of his knife and partially withdrew it from its sheath, tightening his grip on it. He stood there, fingering the handle, looking out at the bay between the buildings but seeing nothing. The sounds around him were muffled by the beating of his own heart pounding in his skull, and the light around the edge of his vision slipped beneath a surging red tide dragging blackness behind it. His skin drew tauht around his arms and shoulders and down his spine, tugging at the ugly scar under his shirt; an ungodly mark from an ungodly place. Ben closed his eyes, remembering the feel of a fighting knife jammed against human bone; the feel of hot blood gushing over his hands. The pounding in his head grew louder and louder and then went silent, his vision blurred and his view of the street was like looking through a frosted window at the end of a dark hallway, passersby only silhouettes against the ice. In the distance a deck whistle blew long and mournful, and he listened to the sound of his own breathing, waiting for it to slow, wishing it to slow. He whispered to himself his private catechism. The lines of her letter came back to him. *Come home to me*, her last letter had said. *Come home to me.* He forced the air from his lungs, and listened to his breathing begin to slow. The sound of people on the sidewalk returned to his ears and the light filled his eyes, and he could see a slice of the bay visible between the tavern and market across the street. He breathed deeply again and slid the knife back into its sheath, and then crossed the road heading for the canal.

We are not finished, Binterfield!

Binterfield stood at the front window with his hands in his pockets staring intently at Ben's back, chewing the edge of his lower lip, not noticing the trickle of blood tracing down his chin. Without turning he spoke,

"Brown, you're fired!"

As Brown scurried from his cubicle and out the door, Binterfield walked back to his desk. Briscoe still stood dumbly by the desk clutching his ledger. Binterfield snatched the ledger from his grip.

"Get out, you fool!"

Pulaski's Canal

Holding it with both hands, Binterfield beat the ledger on the top of his desk several times, scattering other papers and spilling his ink well across the surface and onto the floor, then flung the ledger against the back wall, splitting its leather spine.

"God Damn it!"

As the remaining teller at the front of the bank busied himself intently with minor duties within his cubicle, Binterfield opened his desk drawer and began wiping spilled ink off papers and envelopes kept there. Underneath an envelope from the Pennsylvania Shipping Company now stained with black ink, he picked out an old letter, as yet unstained and never mailed. He held it to his nose. Inhaling deeply of the fading scent of Sonja Pulaski, savoring the feminine aroma, he turned it over and read the address.

Benjamin Pulaski

Pennsylvania Shipping Company

Aboard The Philadelphia Star

He smiled to himself and returned the letter to the drawer with the others, and slammed it shut. Blood dripped off his chin onto his starched white shirt.

We are not finished, Pulaski.

6

The treetops across the mouth of the river from the lockhouse were barely visible in a gray dawn, and the moon's reflection still rippled on the surface of the water. The river flowed serenely out of its course and onto the wide sandy shelf of the Susquehanna Flats, where under the surface the river found its channel beyond Concord Point and continued its trek down the bay. The air was thick with flower pollen and the smell of the spring shad run.

Will Boyd was already at work at the Lockhouse when John Mitchell, the new lock tender walked into the supervisor's office and poured a cup of coffee.

"I saw a dead dog in the shallows of the basin."

Will looked up.

"You get it out?"

John shook his head slightly in the steam rising above the tin cup.

"Not much there to get. The crabs were all over it."

Will shivered within his shirt.

"Hope he was dead when they got to him."

John frowned and twisted his mouth.

"Hadn't thought about which came first. Sure as hell hope it wasn't the crabs."

He set his cup down on the window sill and walked back out onto the porch. He stood there a moment with his hands in his pockets, looking at the canal basin, then shook his head and walked over to the mule barn.

Pulaski's Canal

Will was still at his desk writing in his ledger when Ben scraped the mud from his boots and stepped up onto the wide porch facing the canal basin and the river. Ben paused to look out over the basin, making a quick count of nearly thirty barges waiting to be towed, and all of them low in the water full of cargo. A mule team was far up the towpath pulling another barge back toward Wrightsville, floating high in the water. Ben's gaze drifted over toward the new warehouses where he once had a small farm, then abruptly stopped his loitering and went in to the office.

Will Boyd sat at the narrow desk set below the front window of the office. His dark brown vest unbuttoned to allow cooler air into his white shirt and held partially in place by his watch chain. The side window to Ben's left held a higher desk where barge captains would list the content and weight of the cargo, usually coal. An iron stove stood in the far right corner with a well-used tin coffee pot still simmering on the top.

Will looked up from his ledger work and smiled.

"Well Ben, how did it go up at Lapidum? You get caught in that rain squall yesterday?"

Ben glanced at the ledger on his desk.

The damned things are everywhere.

"Yeah, some. You have the time to discuss our venture?"

"I've been looking forward to it, though it will not be all good news. That pile of beams and planks will do nothing for us unless we can turn it into a profitable barge. Let's step outside and go look at the wreck again and see what can be done for her."

Will stood reaching for his wide brimmed hat in a single practiced motion, then stepped with Ben back onto the porch and across the yard to just beyond the lock.

"I hope we can resurrect this thing, Ben. The cost is already in it, and I don't know if I can afford to start over with another one. The company pays over a thousand dollars for them now, made by a builder up in Pennsylvania."

Ben walked around the unfinished skeleton and looked closely at the bottom planks.

"I was thinking that maybe we could finish her up so we could sail the cargo to Baltimore."

Will frowned at the mud-trapped barge.

"I don't see how in the world we'll be able to do that. You can't put a mast in a barge and then try to pull it up the canal. There isn't enough room overhead. And the canal isn't more than three feet deep in some places, maybe five when the spring creeks fill'er to the brim of the towpath. No, I just can't see it in my mind."

Ben smiled and reached for penciled drawings stuffed in one of his pockets.

"I don't want to make it into a sail boat, I just want to make it a barge that can be sailed."

Will took the drawing and laid it against the closest rib beam to steady the picture.

"Looks damned ugly. Looks kinda' like a beached Orca... with its head cut off. What are these fins here?" He pointed to the midships of the sketch.

Ben held his arms out from his sides, bent at the elbows with the forearm and hands pointing down and his palms facing inward.

"Those are outboards. They go on the outside and take the place of a deeper keel. The Dutch have used'em for hundreds of years."

"How far down will they stick? She'll still have to stay above the mud in the canal and the flats."

Will raised his hand in the direction of the Susquehanna Flats, just beyond the mouth of the river where a thousand years of river silt kept the bay bottom there barely three feet below the surface even at high tides.

"Doesn't matter. Well, it does matter. They do have to stick down as far as a keel, but they'll come off while she's in the canal."

Will raised his eyebrows and smiled momentarily, but returned to his frown.

"What about the mast and sails. How is all that going to get out of the way? This thing needs to be opened from stem to stern so we can load and unload cargo."

Ben quickly nodded again.

"The mast is stepped down into an open brace, like an ink pen stuck in its holder. Same with the 'sprit. Then we rig it like a schooner. We leave the mast, sprit, boom, gaff, and sails ashore when we go up canal and then step'em in after we come back down. Then, we sail the cargo to Baltimore, or Annapolis, or even Philadelphia."

Ben smiled again with excitement over the plan and then remembered his arms were still held out and dropped them sheepishly to his sides, looking around to see if anyone was watching.

Will continued to frown at the drawing.

"Well, Ben, it sounds good, and I'm sure you could sail it, that is if we could actually make this thing sail. Stepping the mast coming and going may sound easy enough, but you'll need a lot of mast to hold enough sail to move even a sailing barge full of coal. You can't just reach out and pluck the thing up and stick it in your pocket. That mast will have to weigh hundreds of pounds."

"Just need leverage, Will. I've helped manhandle top masts down from the upper rigging with a storm coming on. 'Course I won't have that kind of manpower, but I can have enough leverage so I won't need it. I'd put twenty-foot spars in pocket holes on either side, and braced below like the main mast, then use block and tackle to lift it up. I'd also put an iron bar through the base of the mast so it stuck out on either side and then slide it down in slots. That would keep the base of the mast where I wanted it until we laid her down. Just lift her up, lean her back, and lay her down."

Ben bobbed his head up and down emphasizing each point of the operation he had in mind.

Will looked out at the current of the Susquehanna flowing into the upper reaches of the Chesapeake, thinking about Ben's plan. A log canoe eased away from the wind near Perry Point, leaning out as the wind took her on a new course.

"It would be a great savings not to have to pay the steam tugs to move the barge. Going into Baltimore or Annapolis under sail meant that the cargo could be sold to anyone with the money. Company barges deliver their cargo wherever the contract tugs take them. The company controls that. This is a good plan."

He watched the sail boat glide across toward Havre de Grace harbor and noticed the small boat trailing in its wake by a towline.

"Ben? Reckon a sailing barge could pull another one?"

"If there was enough wind from the right direction."

Will nodded to himself and looked back at Ben.

"Then let's do this thing."

He frowned, then hesitated before speaking further.

"Ben, I have to tell you that I have already put up all the money for this venture that I dare. There doesn't seem to be enough to show for the money already involved, with the damage to the frame and all the lumber washed down stream and lost."

Ben unconsciously patted the money belt wrapped around his waist under his shirt. His future was in that snug band.

"I know, Will. I am prepared to carry the costs to finish her. Looks like half of it is already here. Only right that I take care of the other half."

Will let out a breath and let the frown slip from his face.

"There's a boatwright over in Concord Cove. I hear he's honest and does good work. And I hear two more things about him that ought to sit well with you."

"What's that?"

"He once crewed for your father, and he don't like Herbert Binterfield."

Ben laughed and slapped Will on the back.

"I like him already."

Adam Tuttle was ankle deep in wood shavings, planing the surface of a keel beam that seemed intent on staying crooked. He arched his eyebrows sending a wrinkle high up into his pale spotted crown. White bushy hair sprouted out from the sides of his head and chin, framing a reddish oval face. Another bush of white hair expanded out from under his nose covering his upper lip from view. A pouty lower lip showed under the moustache and he clenched the stem of an unlit corncob pipe between large crooked teeth. He had planed the outer surface of the beam several times to carve away a little rise that kept the beam from being perfectly flat. He laid down the plane and pulled his square from his leather apron and ran it along the top of the beam. Mumbling small grunts of satisfaction as he slid it along, when he came to the area that he had given additional attention, the square rose almost imperceptibly showing the surface still not level and causing Adam to stand upright and throw the square across his shop.

"Well, damn you to hell!"

He stomped back over the packed earth floor to his workbench to pick up the plane again, then tossed it back.

"No. I ain't cuttin' wood when I'm pissed. Just make a little problem a big one."

He walked across his shop and retrieved his square and returned it to its rightful pocket in his apron. Adam stepped outside into the cooling breeze and generous shade provided by his favorite red maple growing beside the small building he called both business and home. He stepped over to a small cooking fire still heating too old coffee, placed the end of a small twig into the fire and then used it to relight his pipe. He returned to the outside corner of his building and sat down on a short shiny topped barrel that had served as a stool for many years. Adam leaned back against the building, closed his eyes and blew smoke into his maple.

"Adam Tuttle?" the voice in the sunlight asked.

Adam opened one eye and squinted into the direction of the voice.

"Yeah. That's what my mother always told me, anyway."

Ben stepped out of the sun and under the big maple offering his hand.

"My name's Ben Pulaski."

Adam extended his hand in Ben's direction without moving any of the rest of his body or even turning his head to look at him.

"What can I do for ya'?"

Ben looked at the man and his shed and the dozens of boats in various stages of repair and disrepair scattered around the cove.

This man obviously does nothing but work on boats, and he doesn't know what I want?

Ben thought a brief moment and then smiled to himself.

"I need a new corset."

Adam turned to look at Ben and then gave a small chuckle.

"You sure are a smartass. Wha'd you say your name was?"

"Pulaski. Ben Pulaski."

"Knew a Pulaski once. Had a fair sized schooner out of Baltimore a few years back. I crewed for him a while. Had a little..."

Adam leaned forward and looked keenly at Ben.

"You Lenz Pulaski's boy?"

Ben grinned at the old man from his childhood.

"Hello Mr. Tuttle."

Adam took Ben's hand again.

"You are Lenz' boy! And you're STILL a smartass. Always was. You sneaked off from school every chance you got to go on your daddy's boat. Use'ta drive us crazy keepin' you from fallin' overboard or getting your noggin beaned with somethin'. How is your daddy?"

"He's been gone some years now."

"Sorry for that."

Adam puffed a small cloud of smoke from his pipe and sent it up into the maple after the others.

"He was a regular rounder, and a damned fine Cap'n."

Ben paused in the silence for just a moment.

"Mr. Tuttle, I need you to build an unusual boat."

Two hours later Ben had left his drawings with Adam Tuttle to study and had visited the leather shop near the shanty town at the south end of Union Avenue. He settled with the tanner for the new boots Sonja had arranged for the boys, and had been paying him on time. Again Ben was impressed with the intricate plans Sonja had created to provide for her children even while she had next to nothing of her own. The kindness and generosity she had shown to others before the flood had also come back to her when she needed it; not from everyone, but from enough. He walked back down Union Avenue as far as Bourbon Street and then crossed over to Washington Street passing a small office. The sky had darkened again blocking out most of the remaining sky light from the late afternoon sun and a clerk had lighted a lamp so he could make final entries in a large ledger.

Another damned ledger book.

He crossed Washington Street near Granite Lane, hardly noticing the man standing in the shadows at the entrance to the lane. The new office building at the corner of Washington Street and Granite Lane extended out into the wooden sidewalk almost a foot farther than its neighbor. Obviously the builder wanted to crowd on as much floor space as he could get from his narrow parcel. The slight extension of the building created a sharp border between the lamp light of the sidewalk and the shadow of the lane, making it more an alley. Ben looked beyond the lane and farther down Washington Street to the sign above the First National Bank. He was sure it would still be open. The graying sky only made it feel later than it really was. He focused his walk toward the bank's location as he stepped off the sidewalk in front of the narrow office building.

Ben did not see the dark brown muscular arm reach out after him from the darkness. In the swiftness of a fish hawk swooping to grab his prey from the water, Ben's form left the sidewalk almost silently. The massive arm wrapped around his neck and upper chest, and suddenly he was trapped within the grip of a big man, snatched into the deeper darkness of the alley. Ben could feel the man's warm breath against the nap of his neck. He could smell old whiskey, the mustiness of wool clothing left damp far too long, and the pungent odor of stale sweat. Something hard pressed against his right side and a rasping voice spoke calmly into his ear.

"Give me your money."

Ben struggled against the grip of an iron bear hug. The voice rasped again into Ben's ear.

"Give me your money or I'll blow your kidneys into the street!"

Ben managed to turn slightly within the massive arm, seeing a partial profile of his attacker in the edge of his vision.

"It's 'gimmie yo' money!' not 'GIVE me YOUR money'"

Struggling to maintain his grip, the assailant answered in confusion, "What?"

Ben repeated.

"You gotta say "Gimmie and yo, else, it just don't sound right."

The big man took his fingertip from Ben's ribs and ducked farther back into the shadows as he released his quarry. Ben turned and offered his hand to the would-be robber.

"Hello Simon."

Simon Bond smiled broadly.

"Hello Ben, how are you?"

Ben slapped his friend on the shoulder.

"I'm alright, Simon. It's good to see you."

Ben looked around to see if anyone else nearby was watching them.

"You know, Simon, a man with a gun could have taken your joke with me very seriously, and shot you before you could have explained. That was a dangerous thing to do in Maryland."

"I know. It was a spontaneous idea."

Ben smiled and shook his head.

"When did you get into Havre de Grace?"

"Just this afternoon. How'd you know it was me?"

Ben placed his hand on his hips.

"Simon, you're the only black man I know in this world that speaks like a professor, and you can't hardly speak like a desperate man. It doesn't sound natural. But, I'll tell ya' what else, for a second there, before you spoke, my heart was in my throat, I was so scared."

Simon smiled again.

"Ben, you're too honest. Never tell a man he scared you. Besides, you have no idea how desperate I have been."

Ben tilted his head slightly.

"Well, I can tell a friend. Listen, where are you staying? Do you have people up here? You never said anything about that."

"Well, I don't know where I'm sleeping, yet."

Ben slipped his hands in his pockets looking around the lane and cleared his throat.

"Simon, I, uh, wish I could invite you to stay at my home, but, uh, I don't have it anymore."

Simon looked into Ben's eyes, but said nothing.

"Can you wait here a few minutes? I've got to get over to that bank as I promised Sonja. They will close soon and I don't want your robbery joke to come true. Give me a few minutes to go there and I'll meet you back here."

Simon shook his head slightly, looking around at the lane and the narrow office buildings.

"I suppose I had better not hang around here any longer. Let's meet at the little wharf south of town. There are a few shanties and free blacks that way, and it is getting dark."

Simon was still wearing the wide striped pullover and nankeen trousers they had all worn on the *Philadelphia Star*. It was obvious that Simon had not lived well since their departure from Baltimore. The trouser knees were badly soil stained and his shirt had a rip along one side. Ben felt a twinge of regret as he realized that Simon's appearance was likely more acceptable in public as he was, than if he was wearing a fine English suit. He also realized the soundness of meeting Simon near the shanties rather than near the center of town at sundown.

Ben went on to the Bank and opened his account. He was comfortable with the numbers they showed him, but when presented written material he apologized for arriving without his reading glasses and asked the clerk to assist him by reading the few sentences aloud. Although it was to Ben's humiliation that he could not read, it was certainly not unusual for the clerk to assist others who could not. The clerk demonstrated no awareness or suspicion of Ben's inability to read. He was either very kind or very accommodating, but in either case, Ben's experience with the bank was a satisfying one and as he stepped out of the bank and onto the wooden sidewalk the clerk quietly locked the door and drew the shade behind him. Nearby a clock chime struck six times. He left Washington Street and crossed the wide dirt Union Avenue and then down toward Chesapeake Lane to the warehouses south of town.

It was only a short walk, and brought him back near Concord Cove for the second time that day. Beyond the last warehouse, sitting on land only inches above a small marsh and draped in thick humid air waiting for a breeze off the bay, were a collection of one room shanties of free and leased blacks. The common space between the shanties was wrapped in dusk, pushed away at the center by a brightly burning fire, and several men were gathered about it standing or sitting on barrels or stumps. Aromas of roasted meat, burning tobacco, alcohol and mildewed cloth mingled with the musky vapors rising off rich fertile mud exposed at low tide. Congenial voices and deep laughter drifted into the evening air from the fire and swarms of mosquitoes hummed among the trees standing in the shadows at the edge of the light.

Shading his eyes from the brightness of the fire, Ben looked among the group, but could not distinguish any form that could be his waiting friend. A voice among the group gathered at the fire pulled his attention and he recognized the baritone voice and the too-well pronounced words of Simon Bond in the midst of a tall sea tale. Ben walked through the weeds toward the clearing surrounding the fire. He spoke as he approached.

"Evening."

One or two men quickly stood to peer through the gathering darkness trying to recognize the face that went with the voice coming from the lane. As Ben's face became visible in the reaching firelight, silence drew over the group. They stood almost as one and stepped back slightly to the opposite side of the fire. A few men stepped back farther into the dimness of the firelight closer to the marshy bank. Those that had remained nearest the fire smiled broadly at Ben and bobbed their heads in mute greetings, waiting for the white man to state his purpose – or complaint. They stared at each other across the tip of the wood fire for a few lingering seconds until Simon stepped forward to shake Ben's hand. Glances were traded among the other men as Simon turned and introduced his friend.

"We sailed together on the *Philadelphia Star*. Ben's a good friend."

He added with significant emphasis on the last word. Simon pulled another wood stump closer to the firelight for Ben and handed him a carved wooden cup of cool beer. Most of the other men relaxed and retook their seats, though some remained in the twilight and quietly took to their shanties. The largest man in the group stepped over toward Ben and extended his hand, stating only his name in the way of greeting.

"Jedediah."

Ben shook Jedediah's hand, and the hands of two others who offered and gave their first names. He finished his beer among murmurings regarding the weather, the bay, and the fishing, but the camaraderie Ben had observed from the lane had clearly been replaced by a formality too stiff to be endured long. These men were obviously not comfortable with his presence among them. Ben thanked them for the beer and apologized for the intrusion, then he and Simon moved away from the fire and the shanties farther down Chesapeake Lane in the rising moonlight. They walked in silence as the firelight faded behind them.

"We lost our house while I was away, Simon. Lost the baby too."

Simon stopped walking, hesitated before he spoke again.

"I'm terribly sorry to hear of that Ben."

Ben said nothing. His expression hidden from the moonlight by the brim of his hat.

A crow squawked overhead, disturbed in its nightly perch by another bird settling too close on its branch.

After several seconds Ben cleared his throat.

"How did it go for you in St. Mary's County? Is Lettie coming up?"

"There was trouble, Ben. Lettie had been sold…"

"Oh No. Not down to Mississippi?"

"No. To another place there in the county. I almost bought her, but there was trouble. They took my money. I hurt a man."

Simon turned his face toward Ben and lowered his voice.

"A white man."

Ben looked up at the moon.

"Is he dead?"

"Yes."

Ben turned toward Simon. Their moon shadows merged into one.

"Did he deserve it?"

Simon paused, taking a deep breath and letting each word fall heavily into the night air.

"Yes, by God, he did."

Ben's hat brim rocked forward in the silver light, his face still in shadow and he sighed before he spoke.

"How can I help?"

"I'm not ready to go north, just yet, but I don't know exactly what am going to do, except that I know I'm not going without Lettie."

"Does the law know you're up here?"

"No."

Ben thought for a long quiet moment.

"Then help me start my business on the canal, until you decide."

"Doing What?"

"Right now, I don't have the damnedest clue."

Both men chuckled in the moonlight.

A candle flame arose within the nearby cabin and shown from a small window not far from where the two men stood. Noticing the light, their conversation halted as a door opened and the candle bathed the darkness in front of the cabin with its brave little glow. A voice grumbled.

"You gonna talk out there all night?"

Ben smiled in the darkness, but before he could respond the voice spoke again.

"Who is that? What'er ya doin' down here?"

Ben recognized the voice and then realized where they had walked. He had spent half the day listening to that voice

"Evenin' Mr. Tuttle."

Adam Tuttle twisted his head to see the figures in the meager candlelight.

"Pulaski? What th'hell're you doin' back here? Who's that with ya'?"

Ben and Simon stepped farther into the candlelight so they could be seen. Ben answered the last question first.

"This is Simon Bond. He and I sailed together in the Pacific. He's going to work my barge with me on the canal."

"Is that right?"

The old man's face swiveled toward Simon.

"What'er you gonna do 'til I git it finished?"

Simon shrugged his shoulders.

"Haven't decided yet. Haven't decided I'll stay either."

Tuttle grunted and turned toward the inside of his shop, then stopped and turned back toward Simon and Ben, pointing the candleholder toward Simon.

"You know anything about woodworking?"

"I helped a carpenter for a while when I was younger."

Tuttle grunted again.

"Well, that worthless helper of mine has run off for crabbin' with his uncle. Does it to me every spring and summer. If ya' care ta help me turn that pile of trash Pulaski has into a sailing boat I'd pay ya fer it. Same as my helper woulda got, if ya do it worth a damn."

Simon opened his mouth to answer, but Tuttle was already shutting the door again. From inside the shop they heard Tuttle's voice yell out.

"Come back in the mornin' an' talk about it. Now git th'hell outta there and let a man get ta sleep!"

The lone candle was extinguished leaving Ben and Simon standing in the darker night as they began to pace back toward the shanties. Simon spoke in the darkness.

"Well, I really don't have any other plans right now, Ben. I'm going FROM more than I'm going TO anything. Helping that ol'geezer would give me a place to be and a chance to make some money while I'm deciding what to do next."

"You know where the canal lockhouse is? Have you found that yet?"

"No, but one of the blacks back there is leased to work at the mule barn for the canal company. He and his woman are letting me stay at their place tonight. He can get me there."

"Meet me there in the morning."

The two men shook hands and went in separate directions.

It was late when Ben entered the little cottage behind Dr. Harper's house. He was aware how similar it was to the shanties near the marsh. A lamp burned low on the table near the window. The door to Sonja's room was closed, but yellow lamp light shown under it.

"Good evening, Sonja."

There was no sound from the little back room, and he dropped a small bag onto the floor.

"I met with Binterfield today. He told me you quit his house."

"Yes."

"George Milton, the lawyer, helped sort things out with Binterfield's bank. The matter of the mortgage is settled. What I found out was..."

Ben stepped toward the door, but there was only silence on the other side of it.

He took in a deep breath and slowly let it out.

I can control myself. I will control myself. I will give her time.

He turned away from the door. On the table under a clean frayed-edge cloth he found a plate holding two fried shad and a biscuit. A new crock of cider and an empty mug sat near the plate. After he ate he opened the bag and withdrew two iron hooks and a new canvas hammock. Stepping next to Sonja's door, he spoke to the planks.

"There'll be a little noise out here."

She did not respond. He withdrew a mallet from the bag and began pounding one of the iron hooks into a corner beam, and drove another in to the beam near the window. While he was hammering, the light in Sonja's room went out. He hung the hammock from the hooks and tossed the old quilt into the center, then blew out the lamp on the table, slipped into the hammock, and spoke to the darkness.

"Good night."

He watched the moon a long while through the window, until it began its fall and sleep finally came to the man and to the woman; each dragged down to their own nightmares.

At sunrise the next morning Will Boyd made his ritual walk by the trapped barge frame and then past the nearly cleaned dog skeleton lying in the shallows of the basin. Ripples on the water rolled up by the morning breeze latticed views of the skeleton below the surface between mesmerizing reflections of the blue sky above. He stared at the patterns popping between darkness and brightness for lost moments, then climbed the porch to the lockhouse for his morning work. Will heard hollow wood thumping on the river and turned toward the sound. Coming around the point below the outlet lock, like a duck followed by her brood of ducklings, Adam Tuttle slowly rowed his workboat, towing a long line of empty barrels bobbing over gentle bay ripples. Will smiled to himself, relieved that the work to rebuild the barge had finally begun. He had invested all the money he dared in the project, more than he actually had and was still in debt to Binterfield for it. He silently cursed himself for not having the nerve to tell his wife.

He unbuttoned his vest, letting his brass watch chain drape from its pockets and stuffed his hands into his trousers, leaning against a corner post on the porch watching Tuttle array his barrels around the barge. The muddy bank was lost from view at this distance, but he could see each barrel bobbing on the cove surface and then pulled from view as Tuttle attached it to the unfinished frame. There was too little of the barge to float on its own accord, but too much bottom and frame for Tuttle to haul it overland to his shop. Will could still see Tuttle's tattered sea cap, perched upon bushy white hair, flit in and out of view below the bank or behind shrubs as the old man moved around the barge. Tuttle's voice drifted across the grassy yard to the lockhouse in pieces and parts brought by the early morning bay breeze. Single word profanities and commands given to errant barrels mixed with the skreels of cormorants and squawks of the herons debating ownership of the shad minnows among the cove shallows.

Will's sense of relief grew as he watched Tuttle's progress, and he straightened to enter his office. The barge would earn good money for him as well as Ben. It would earn more than enough for him to meet his debt payments to the Tidewater Bank and Trust Company. He entered the office in a very good mood, and was greeted by a hearty 'good mornin' from John, and the aroma of fresh brewing coffee. This was going to be a fine morning.

Ben and Simon rounded the corner from Water Street and made their way down among the brush and rocks to the gray mud shoreline where Adam Tuttle was already busy attaching lines to the barge frame.

Adam grumbled over his shoulder as the two men came up to him.

"Thought you two might come by to help. Though I had hoped it would be not so near noon before ya got here."

Ben only smiled at the old man while Simon shook his head and looked at the opposite shore across the mouth of the Susquehanna, where the sun had not yet poked itself above the low lying trees.

"Can't be six o'clock, yet." Simon murmured to Ben

at his side.

Ben nodded to Simon and then addressed Tuttle

"What can we do to help?"

Tuttle stood and waved an arm toward his brood of barrels.

"Got sixteen of them forty gallon barrels there. Plugged and sealed. Each one has a ringbolt in its side, and a line fixed to it. I need th'other end tied onta' the ribs, as low to the bottom as possible. Use a sheepshank knot and loop th'free end underneath. That'll let us snug'em up one at a time, pullin' th'barrel down toward the bottom so the barrels can start pullin' this frame up. Do that at every other rib 'til we got eight on the free side."

He stopped to look for a sign of comprehension among his small audience, and then raised his hands to demonstrate the action of barge and barrels.

"That'll give the frame enough buoyancy t'float on that side. Then we heave from the other side 'til it's in the shallows, and then do the same thing again. Reckon you two SAILORS can manage t'help do that?"

Ben and Simon chuckled as they bent to their assignments. The barrels were attached, tied and snugged to even Tuttle's satisfaction. Sluggishly the outer side of the barge frame rose from the muddy bottom of the shallow water. Tuttle begrudgingly released a grunt of satisfaction and the lines to the barrels were given additional tugs to bring them closer to the line of the bottom frame and planking.

Heaving the landward side of the barge into shallow water took a great deal of effort from them. Heavy fence poles had to be borrowed from the mule barn and additional help sought from Will and John before the water soaked frame was finally wrenched from the muddy grip of the bank. The unused barrels were then tied high on the freed ribs to keep the frame from settling back down in the mud of the shallows. Dark gray mud covered the men to their waists as they tied and retied float lines, edging the barrels lower down the ribs while slowly bringing the landward side to an even keel.

Sonja visited the men in the early afternoon with a large basket of fried chicken and biscuits. Even as she approached, the smell of freshly cooked chicken drifted over the men mired waist deep in stale water and mud, creating a chorus of growling stomachs that even Tuttle could no longer ignore. Waves of muddy water and showers of gray mud were kicked into the air and over the bank as the men charged the basket. Sonja squealed in mock horror, quickly setting down the basket and retreating in her clean dress to the protection of the Lockhouse. Picked over biscuit crumbs and muddy plaid napkins were the only remaining contents of Sonja's basket when Ben set it at the corner of the porch. He looked into the office to thank her, but she had already gone, leaving behind a reminder with Alice Boyd for Ben not to forget the basket.

The sun had risen to its zenith and then begun its slow set over the hillside behind town, before the frame finally floated within the nest of barrels and rocked slowly at the mouth of its prison cove. A line was tied to its bow strut and secured to a gunnel pin near the stern of Tuttle's workboat.

Will worked at scraping the mud from his trousers and boots before he could return to his office. John returned the fence poles to the mule barn and used loose hay to wipe away some of his collected grime. Still soggy from a last valiant dip in the cove to rinse away at least some of the mud, Ben and Simon sat within Tuttle's boat each pulling at an oar to push the workboat and its tow over the flats and down the bay to Concord Point.

Adam Tuttle worked the tiller, steering the boat and keeping a close practiced eye on the floating skeleton drawn along behind them. He watched the wicks blink to life in the nearby lighthouse as one of the O'Neill family lit the sixteen whale oil lamps to show late returning watermen their way home. He gave almost no thought to the mud. Today it is mud. Tomorrow it would be dry clumps. The day after that it would only be a little more

Pulaski's Canal

dust in his shop. He had other more important things to consider. A small flight of ducks flew overhead in the fading daylight, landing in the tidal marsh in front of the shanties just beyond the lighthouse. Tuttle pushed the tiller over to bring the little caravan on a course into Concord Cove, and listened to a hymn rising gently from the group gathered around the fire in the middle of the shanties, and hummed the tune with them.

8

"Ugly, ain't it?"

Tuttle spat into the water, adding rings on the surface slapping onto the muddy bank near his feet. The sun had just risen, but already the air was sultry and the surrounding trees filled with the sounds of cicadas. The spring river rush had finally faded and lazy water drifted over the Susquehanna Flats. The sky was bright blue and full of seagulls chasing after great schools of perch with no place for them to hide over the sandy bottom. There were little islands of froth in the middle of the Flats where the terrified fish thrashed to escape the seagulls diving in large splashes to catch them. Mallards and Coots paddled along the shallows near the boat muttering to themselves, agitated by the raucous seagulls celebrating their breakfast in a chorus of screeches.

Ben stood silently next to the old boatwright with his hands in his pockets looking at Tuttle's finished work float a few feet from shore. Tuttle pointed at the boat with his thumb.

"The mast is yet to be stepped, but even so, she'll still be ugly when it's up."

Ben slowly shook his head.

"I knew the design was a bit odd when I asked you to do it. On its own a scow is a boxy thing without the comely line of a true sailboat. I knew that..."

He rubbed his hand on the back of his neck, and sighed.

"And I certainly knew that a barge, which at best has the lines of a cheap coffin, was not going to be an artful thing... but good God a'mighty, Mr. Tuttle, I think calling it ugly is charitable to the seventh time."

"It's your design Ben..."

"I know. I know."

Both ends were straight across from side to side, and both beveled down toward each other at the waterline, one more so than the other. Determining stern from bow, the end with the tiller was the primary indicator of the stern, and the bow was identified solely as the only other choice to be made for the other end. The sides were high, especially high without most of its rigging and cargo weight. It set within the water not quite two feet, and stood above the water line another five feet.

Simon stood beside Ben, opposite Tuttle, in tactful silence. A small smile struggled to stay under his facial expression. Simon leaned forward catching Tuttle looking in his direction and rolled his eyes toward Ben. Tuttle spat into the water again.

"Don't you look at me like you had nuthin' to do with it, Simon. You helped build the goddammed thing."

Tuttle turned his gaze to include Ben.

"I told you from the beginning that the thing was gonna be ugly!"

Ben kept staring at the boat.

"Yeah, I know."

Silence continued another minute before Ben spoke again.

"Well, I sure as hell can't name that thing after my wife. Sonja thinks poorly enough of me these days, without me adding an insult like giving this thing her name."

"I said it'd be ugly, Ben..."

Tuttle put his hand on Ben shoulder.

"But I also said I'd do a good job, and I did. While you been working the canal with Dan Bartlett on Number 9, me and Simon have been coaxing as much boatiness out of this box as can come. Its sturdy built, dry as a cracker, and it WILL sail. So, let's get the mast rigged, drop her side boards and take her sailin'!"

The three men pulled the hulk against the small pier below Tuttle's workshop and tied it in place. With the help of a few free hands from the nearby marsh village, the mast was stepped and rigged into place with mainstays and tackles attached at the peak. The boat would be sloop-rigged: a single mast, fore jib sail, but a gaffed main sail. The gaff, a short boom riding the top of the sail and suspended from the mast, would hold out the sail to catch the faint breezes notorious on the upper bay. The jib sail was raised along a line from the bow sprit to the tip of the mast. Two dozen large rocks were set in the bilge for ballast, and four large oars brought aboard as sweeps for when the wind died. Soon the boat was ready to make its first tentative moves under sail.

Sonja walked down the slope of Market Street and passed between the shops to watch the new boat move ungainly across the shallows of the flats, standing on the dock near where she watched Ben leave three years earlier. She looked down at the faded dress she now wore. The one she had worn then.

It will soon be more patches than dress.

She picked absently at the frayed cuff with hands no longer red and chapped.

The boat lost a line from the mast and dropped the foresail into the bay beside it and the breeze blew it in a circle. The men reattached the line and raised the jib, and while their attention was on the forward sail, the breeze stiffened into a gust and pushed the main sail far over. She brought her hand up to her mouth in concern as the wind pushed the main sail farther over tipping the boat up onto its side, dumping the crew and settling into the water.

"Oh, No!"

She watched Ben then Simon and then Mr. Tuttle stand up in the waist deep water, pull the sails down, and began working to right the boat. She exhaled a small chuckle and allowed herself a rare smile.

Once upright, bucketfuls of water began to shoot over the sides and back into the bay as the men bailed out the boat. They were going to be out there for the rest of the day doing that. Sonja let out a long sigh and a hand gently landed on her shoulder, its fingers working along the fabric of her dress, the tips kneading softly into her skin. She turned abruptly into Herbert Binterfield's smiling face.

"Watching your man in his new toy, my darling?"

She slapped his hand away from her shoulder.

"No!" and left the dock.

Binterfield stood there, his smile still frozen on his face, his eyes iced and focused on the odd boat temporarily stranded in the shallows of the Flats.

On a sunny mid-June day Ben borrowed a wagon and mule team from Will Boyd and brought it up the service lane to the little cottage behind Doc Harper's house. The oak trees along the lane were filled with Blue Jays yelling to one another in the shade, and several local dogs were ambling around the wagon sampling the aromas. Curious children with little else to do stood watching Ben and the boys load the wagon. Wallace and LuAnn stood together near the great magnolia tree in the center of their back lawn as Aaron and Isaac loaded the last few items onto the wagon. Most of the furniture in the cottage either belonged to the Harpers or had been loaned to Sonja, so the size of the wagon was more than ample. The Boston-made rocking chair was Sonja's, a gift during happier times, and had benefited from Ben's attention and new stain. The boys wrapped it in an old quilt to protect it from scratches, and gently set it in the half filled wagon. The cottage had been scrubbed inside and newly whitewashed outside, white patches and drops still decorated spots on the boys trousers. LuAnn gave Aaron and Isaac each a warm embrace, pulling them down one at a time to her short height so she could kiss them on their foreheads. Sonja promised to visit as often as she could, trading sisterly kisses with LuAnn, and was then engulfed in the huge bear hug of Wallace Harper. Sonja gripped a hand from each of them in hers as tears slipped down across her cheeks.

"I would not be alive today if it were not for you two wonderful people. For what you did for my boys and for me, I will always hold you dear in my heart, and there is nothing, nothing, that I would ever refuse you. If you ever need me for anything, you send for me."

LuAnn only smiled and kissed Sonja again on the cheek, wiping the tears from Sonja's face with her fingertips as her own eyes filled. Sonja reached up and brushed away LuAnn's tears, and for a moment the women gently held each other's face, smiling and sharing thoughts beyond words.

Ben offered his hand to Wallace.

"If you ever need me, just let me know."

Wallace smiled and touched the side of his nose with his finger.

"I may just do that someday, Benjamin."

"I'll always be in your debt, Wallace."

Wallace placed his thick hand on Ben's shoulder and his other arm around Sonja, and walked them to their wagon. LuAnn stayed in her spot by the magnolia, and brought a lace cloth to her eyes.

Ben helped Sonja onto her seat, checked that the boys each had a good place to sit in the back, and then taking the reins in his hands climbed into his own seat.

Wallace tapped a heavy finger on Ben's knee.

"Don't get up there in Lapidum and forget you have friends here in Havre de Grace."

"It's only five miles from here, Wallace."

"Then remember that, Ben."

Sonja looped her arm around Ben's and leaned into him as he drove the mule team down toward the canal basin. Ben turned to her and smiled, but she quickly withdrew her arm and sat straightened in her seat. Will

104

Pulaski's Canal

Boyd was standing on the front porch to the lockhouse as they passed it to cross the swing bridge and swung his hat off in a wide deep royal bow to Sonja.

"Madam, the towpath is yours!"

Sonja smiled broadly at his demonstration and returned a small wave in his direction. The mules and wagon clomped and creaked over the wooden swing bridge and crossed onto the end of the towpath with a slight jolt as the wheels dropped off the edge of the bridge onto the ground.

The trip up the towpath to Lapidum was almost too quick. Isaac blew the conch shell horn as they rounded the last gentle curve before coming to Lapidum, so John Bartlett could swing out the bridge. The new Pulaski place, framed and shaded by the giant oaks in the morning sunlight, slipped past them on the other side of the canal. Soon, the little tavern and the dry goods store were reflected off the canal surface between the towpath and Lapidum, the blue sky and clouds above the hamlet was duplicated as a blue and white band along the canal shore nearest the wagon. Then it was time to guide the mule team through the sharp left turn off the towpath and cross the second swing bridge over the lock and past the front of the lockhouse. Another left onto the hardpacked dirt of Stafford Road took them past the stores again and headed back down to the farm.

Margaret Bartlett was already coming out of the front door of the lockhouse carrying a large pot still giving off steam through the green plaid cloth cover, and yelled back at John as she went.

"Get that other stuff."

She and John stepped out a quickened pace following the Pulaski wagon.

A yellow dog came off the porch to the drygoods store at the corner and trotted along beside the mules sniffing at their hooves and then dropped behind the wagon. Isaac quickly checked to ensure everything was tied and then let down the back board whistling to the dog. The dog made a single leap onto the wagon and dove into Isaac's lap to be petted.

The store owner set up in his chair and pointed a finger at the wagon.

"Don't you steal my dog, Isaac Pulaski!" but followed the warning with a smile.

"I'll send him home, Mr. Nilson."

Lars Nilson smiled again and shook his head speaking mostly to himself.

"Dog already spends more time with that boy than he does here. Maybe I need to get a cat; a good mouser."

Aaron twisted in his seat until he could see up the hill along the road that came down to the store. His squinting eyes flitted from window to door of the plank homes perched on the hillside until he spotted a little patch of white apron surrounded by a pale blue dress. Red curls unfolded beneath a crisp white cap, and big eyes the color of her dress looked out at Aaron. Holding a dish and drying cloth in her hands in front of her apron, she raised her fingertips above the drying cloth and waved to him. He waved broadly back at her giving her an open mouthed grin. An older, heavier woman with gray hair but matching eyes appeared next to the girl and pulled her back from view. Sonja and Isaac had seen the exchange and were looking intently at Aaron for some bit of information, but were only given a curt single word question instead.

"What?"

Isaac pulled a handful of shed dog hairs from his lap and tossed them at his brother.

"Oh, nothing, Aaron."

Aaron stared in determined silence at his mother and his brother, so Sonja turned back to face the road ahead. The wagon crossed a little wooden bridge holding several new planks and entered the freshly cut wagon trail to the farm. None of this was new to Sonja. She had spent a great deal of time putting finishing touches in the house, and even spent a few nights already. Now she was coming to another home. Ben pulled the wagon around to the right along the low stone wall and brought the wagon next to the porch. After locking the wheels of the wagon Ben and Sonja crossed the porch toward the door and paused to look out between the massive oaks at the canal and the river beyond. The barge sat on this side of the canal, staked down where the lower end of the yard sloped down to the still water. Out in the river men fished from row boats in the current, circled above by chattering seagulls.

"You'll want to eat this stew while it's still hot!"

Margaret clomped onto the porch in sturdy work shoes under her skirts and pulled them all inside with the tilt of her head and her bright smile as she walked ahead of them into the kitchen. The Pulaskis followed her into their own house and in turn was followed by John, hauling a large basket of biscuits and jam by one hand and a large cool earthenware jug of sassafras tea cradled in his other arm.

Supper and visitors came and went and their meager possessions were deposited in the places they now belonged. The boys were off exploring more of the woods over the hill. Ben and Sonja had pulled chairs onto the front porch and watched Simon come up the slope. Ben raised his hand in a short wave.

"We were starting to think you'd changed your mind, Simon."

"No, I'm happy to come up here. Get's to be too noisy sometimes down in the cove. I'm ready to take that first trip on the *Ugly Boat*."

Sonja said nothing to Simon, but looked at Ben.

"Are you really going to call that poor thing the *Ugly Boat*?"

Ben nodded over his pipe.

"Already did it. Name's painted on her and all. I think it fits."

"At least it sounds better in Polish. *Brzydka Lódź* is much better than just *Ugly Boat*."

Simon grinned as he sat against one of porch

columns.

"That Polish name sounds more like 'Breezy Loads' to me."

Ben sent a small cloud of blue-gray smoke into the porch rafters.

"Yes, Sonja, it's the Polish name painted on her bow and stern – not that most folks will be able to tell which is which."

Simon stood and stretched.

"Well, I already ate in town with some friends, and probably had more beer than I should have, so if you will excuse me I will 'retire to my abode'."

As Simon rounded the side of the house toward his room at the corner of the barn, a great blue heron glided down from the evening sky, sailed across the open front yard between the oaks and landed silently in the canal shallows near the barge. Ben pointed at the large bird with his pipe stem.

"He's become a regular visitor here, Sonja. I don't think I could have finished getting it ready without him."

When she did not answer he turned to look where she had been sitting, but she was gone. Ben lingered on the porch watching the heron until darkness hid the bird and then stepped sleepily through the front room into their bedroom. The lamp was out, but he could see well enough in the moonlight. Sonja was on the center of the bed wrapped into her quilt cocoon facing away from the doorway. On the floor next to the bed was a cloth pallet, blanket and pillow.

Damn! Will this ever get any better?

He picked up the pallet from the floor and threw it into the corner, and then sat on the side of the bed to remove his shoes. Determined not to sleep on the floor in his own house he stretched out on the bed against Sonja and covered himself with the other blanket. Sonja stiffened and slid away from him to the far edge of the bed, but said nothing. Ben lay there looking up at the ceiling unsatisfied with his small victory.

Pulaski's Canal

In the dark the heron stopped in mid step as the human came back out on the porch and lit his pipe. Ben lit an oil lamp on the porch and pulled out a pencil and paper from his pocket. Placing a short split wood plank across his lap, he bent over the paper with his pencil, copying yet again the much repeated list of letters printed by Simon at the top of the page that neatly spelled his name.

Ben grunted in dissatisfaction with the forms of the letters and wrote them again and again, following each with a muttered curse.

The cabin door hinge gave a mute squeak and Aaron stepped out onto the porch.

Ben quickly folded the paper and slid it under the plank in his lap.

"What are you doing up, Son?"

Aaron dropped into the chair on the other side of the lamp.

"Somebody outside my window keeps saying 'shit-hell-damn-shit-hell-damn'."

"Sorry, Son. I didn't realize I was speaking out loud."

"Why did you do it?"

"I was just, uh, making some records for our business. It's, uh, adult things that need to be written down..."

"No. I mean why did you have to stay gone so long. Didn't you know Ma would worry. And you didn't ever send a letter. And everyone said you were dead, even the shipping company. Why did you do it?"

Ben sighed and looked down at the barge sitting on the surface of the canal with the moon reflected next to it.

"There's more story than I can tell in one sitting, Son, and your mother doesn't want to hear any of it."

"I want to hear it! I need to hear it! Tell me at least some of it!"

Ben looked at his face through the lamp light, and then looked down at his own hands laid flat on the plank in his lap.

"China was at war with itself. We didn't know that when we left in '39. The British are on one side helping them to kill the other. The other side captured our ship in one of their harbors. They thought we were British. Their prince kept us prisoners for two years. We went months when we couldn't leave the ship, and nothing could be brought on board. No one ordered the guards to feed us, so no food came and we ate everything we had on board. Some of the crew starved to death. Some killed themselves. Some started killing each other."

Ben looked out toward the canal, but not seeing it.

"One morning the guards were just gone. We thought we were free, but the ship still could not leave. We were nothing. We had nothing in a place where most people had very little. We did things to live. Whatever needed doing."

"Like Ma," Aaron said.

Ben paused and swallowed hard.

"I've been waiting to tell what happened, but now that it's coming out, I can't say anymore. I have done things that I am ashamed to describe, just so I could come home."

The lamp oil had been used and the flame faded out. In the darkness, tears fell onto the plank between Ben's hands, and he sobbed.

Aaron stood in silence and put his hand on his father's shoulder, then walked quietly back into the cabin.

Out in the shallows, the heron put his head down watching the water for his next meal, and speared a small shad that filled the bird's stomach after its slide down his long neck. Full and satisfied he stepped among the small branches of a thin bush growing at the water's edge and closed his eyes for a nap.

He was startled by loud thumping noises and voices

a few hours later, and flew off complaining of his treatment to anyone listening.

The heron squawked overhead in the dawning light. Ben and Simon loaded their few possessions needed for the first trip to Wrightsville and poled the barge sideways across the canal to the towpath where the harnessed mule team stood patiently with Isaac. The sound of poles thumping against the oak hull or wooden heels on fresh planking echoed within the thin warm mist rising off the canal. Summer had come heavy to Lapidum. Ben's voice drifted over the water.

"You boys stay close to your mother while I'm gone."

Isaac nodded sleepily at his father's command, then he headed back to the swing bridge so he could cross back over to the other side and return to his bed for another hour's sleep. Ben called after him.

"Don't forget to move the swing bridge back."

They were ready to pass through the lock and make their way north. Simon led the mules up the towpath pulling the barge into the lock. Ben shifted the tiller full to the right to bring the rudder flush against the stern of the barge as it slipped into the lock and Simon wrapped the bow rope tighter around the lock post. John Bartlett pushed the lock gates closed from above, and walked to the mid-lock gates to open the slews. A slender unshaven man in wrinkled clothes stood in the growing light at the edge of the lock wall wearing a battered gentleman's hat pushed back high on his forehead. He stood by idly watching the lock fill with water from the upstream canal and sipping coffee from a dented tin cup. As the boat floated above the level of the lock sides the man nodded to Ben and looked closely at the bow of the boat, frowning. John brought the clipboard to Ben for his signature on the daily register, and Ben proudly printed his name with the pencil John handed him. Satisfied with the display of his renewed skill of printing his own name, he nodded to himself and returned the clipboard to John.

The man in the bowler stepped toward the stern of the boat, and spoke over the rim of his coffee cup.

"Mornin'"

Ben nodded and began walking toward the bow of the boat. The man in the bowler pointed toward the boat with his cup.

"Strange name ye' got there for yer, uh, uh, boat, Mister."

Ben looked at the man without smiling.

"It's Polish."

The man nodded again squinting at Ben over the rim of the cup as he took another sip through the steam.

"What's it mean?"

Ben turned to the man and spread his arms slightly to include the whole of his barge.

"It means *Ugly Boat*."

The man coughed slightly and quickly turned his head away, but then returned his glance, working unsuccessfully to suppress an escaping grin, and then allowed a full smile that wrinkled the skin around the corners of his eyes.

"Tis a righteous name you've given her, sir, if I may say so."

Ben's resolve to endure another insult to his boat evaporated into his own grin matching that of the idler. The man leaned over toward Ben extending his right hand.

"Th'name's Micheal Patrick O'Grady."

Ben took his hand in a firm handshake, feeling the

easy strength in the Irishman's hand.

"That's a mouthful of a name, Micheal Patrick O'Grady. Which name do people call ya' by?"

O'Grady spoke within the well of the cup as he sipped again.

"Well, me mother always called me Micheal Patrick an' me father called me Micheal – when he wasn't callin' me 'that little bastard' and trying to beat me. And me brothers an' sisters called me Mickey."

Ben smiled.

"So what do your friends call ya'?"

O'Grady shook his head, pouring out the last of the coffee and grounds into the canal.

"Don't have no friends. But the bastards I worked with buildin' this damned canal called me Stumpy."

He patted his right leg.

"No toes on this hoof. Lost'em when I was ten. Frostbite. Plays hell with me dancin'." And offered up another broad smile.

"Well, people call me Ben. I guess you could too. What would you have me call ya'?"

"Micheal'll do. I hear ya rented the Walker place."

John Bartlett began to swing open the mid lock gates. Simon whistled and clicked to get the mules walking down the towpath, taking up the slack in the towrope. The boat snugged slightly as the rope took hold and began to pull it slowly down the lock toward the upper canal.

"I'd like to talk with you more, Micheal Patrick O'Grady, but as you can see the *Ugly Boat* has to get back to work."

Ben waved his hand at Simon and pulled the tiller back to centerline, guiding the boat away from the path side of the canal.

O'Grady began pacing the barge, walking alongside toward the end of the lock.

"I hear ye' need a second barge.."

The pace of the barge quickened and the man walked faster.

"... and I have one ta' give ye!"

Ben looked over at John, who offered back a sheepish smile knowing that Ben had just recently told him that very thing. Ben looked at the Irishman and then at the progress of the barge.

"Jump aboard and ride with me, or we can talk on my way back from Wrightsville."

Even as Ben finished the last of his statement, the Irishman was in the air and landing ungainly on the deck of the barge almost tripping off the far side into the canal. Righting himself with arms flailing backwards.

"I think I'll ride with ye', if it's all the same to you."

John yelled out from the edge of the lock.

"Hey! My cup!"

O'Grady glanced down at the tin cup still in his hand and gave it a quick overhand toss, sailing it hard into John's grasp. John called after them.

"And ya still owe two cents for the coffee!"

O'Grady bellowed over Ben's shoulder.

"On the way back, John. On the way back!"

Looking again at Ben, O'Grady flashed another broad smile.

"An' call me Mickey."

Ben looked closely at his haggard unshaven passenger.

"Tell me more about your barge- Mickey."

"I can do even better that that, Ben. It's nestled into the brush and rocks not more than a mile up the canal from here."

"Why didn't you just bring it on down to the lock?"

"Well, it ain't exactly IN the canal, Sir. And it needs a spot of work done to it."

Ben frowned slightly.

"John said you might be worth listening to. I know John, so I can give you that. But I think I need to hear some serious details."

Mickey looked into Ben's face, down at the smooth canal surface, and then out beyond the towpath to the river water slapping the large rocks standing against the current. The sun had not yet reached down to the river but the sky overhead was already turning bright blue, and the choppy waves around the boulders were a mix of black and bright blue triangles. The river current pushed a man-sized tree branch thumping it hard against one of the rocks. The branch spun wildly in the eddy current to the side and then flew past the rock riding the undulating surface of the water.

"There's a power in that river the folks down stream don't usually think about. Down stream it gets wide and flows in the deep channels around both sides of Palmer's Island with hardly a ripple on top. But, there's a Bitch in that water. She's as sinister as the devil himself and ready to snatch up a life quicker than a bat taking a moth."

Mickey focused his attention on the swirling water around the rock jutting up through the current, while he retrieved thoughts and memories to complete his explanation to Ben Pulaski.

Just tell him how ya got here, ya idiot! Ben's a good man, John told ya. He'll understand, because he already knows the hardest part of it.

Outside the canal, swirls of debris and foam pirouetted out from the sides of the rock and raced after the tree branch. Water slapped the upstream front of the rock sending a constant spray over the granite dome. The sound of the water trying to force the rock downstream only added to the constant low roar of the river that most people forgot to hear after a while. Ben adjusted the tiller slightly to keep the barge in the center of the canal, watching Simon's easy pace next to the mule a hundred feet ahead on the towpath, and the towrope still bent down toward the smooth surface even though the mule was pulling against the gentle southbound current of the canal, and waited for the Irishman to go on.

Mickey took in a deep breath and faced Ben.

"I helped build this canal. I've worked in stone since I was in my teens. Thought I'd be over here helping to build big buildings in New York, or maybe Philadelphia, but they had no use for me. Too many Mick's already at it. The Canal Company wanted stone men to build the locks, so I came here and they hired me. I came here with my Emily. Her wishin it was somewhere else, somewhere cleaner, somewhere with little wooden houses instead of tents, but she never said a word against it."

He kept his attention on the water spray over the rock.

"She knew it was all the work I'd find, knew the Irish were not welcome in this place. Too many of us. Starvin', looking for work, and tryin' to keep some hold on to our pride, even when we were diggin' table scraps out of the tavern trash heaps in town."

Mickey turned his attention back within the low rails of the barge. Ben rummaged through his pockets pulling out his pipe and retrieving his tobacco pouch. Both men settled onto the locker near the tiller. Ben watched Mickey in silence, waiting for his story to continue.

"winter of '39 the river was froze and Emily's belly was swollen with our coming baby. Our little village in those days was on a rocky shelf beside the river a couple miles up; we called it Pebble Beach. We had finally been paid for the month and the children and the women folk were all warm and snug in our shanties, so we gave ourselves a little time with the drink. Me and some of the boys hoofed it down to Havre de Grace that Sunday to visit a tavern that welcomed the Irish. We were only into our third pints when we heard explosions outside.

"We came coatless out of the tavern, beer steins still

in our hands, breath in frosty clouds in front of our faces asking what it was. Then the ice blocks bigger than humble houses began to rip up from the frozen river and push up onto the banks. Men ran up from the canal basin yellin' about an ice gorge. Wasn't sure what that was, but ice boulders along the river was danger for sure. We scrambled for our coats and were running down toward the canal basin as the water began rushing out of the river and through communities near the edge. The explosions continued as the sheets of ice holding the river sent cracks racing across to the other side and up the river even past Port Deposit. Miles of pent up river water burst from the ice and flooded Port Deposit.

"We scrambled along the towpath, but there were many places where the ice had already gouged the earth away. We waded through iced water in the canal to reach Stafford Road on the other side and ran on to Pebble Beach..."

Mickey pointed ahead.

"It's up here. If you'll pull up here, I can show you where the barge is."

Ben whistled several times before he received Simon's attention and signaled that he wanted to stop at this place. Curiosity filling his face, Simon walked back to the barge after tethering the two mules to trees and placing a feed bag over each of them. Ben answered his unspoken question.

"This gentleman says he has a barge up here that we can have."

"Have?"

Mickey raised a finger.

"Have. In exchange for steady work."

Ben brought the barge against the berm of the towpath, then he and Simon staked bow and stern lines to keep the *Ugly Boat* in place. They followed Mickey into the thick stand of saplings growing on the thin strand between the towpath and the river. They passed through and stood in a small clearing that fed a well worn path down into the river.

Mickey stood for a moment staring at the water slapping against the path where it slipped under the water. He picked up a small rock and heaved it overhand at the flowing river.

"This was Pebble Beach."

He paused, then continued his story.

"It pretty much looked like this when we all got back here then. We crossed the canal again and on to the towpath. Men ran along the towpath screaming and yelling and cursing the water they could see pushing into the trees. Some spun in circles looking carefully at all the landmarks, hoping they had made a mistake, that this was not the right trail, that this was not the trail that led down to Pebble Beach."

He swallowed and took in a breath.

"It was all gone. Everyone. Everything. There was the beginning of the trail and everything above on Stafford Road that was supposed to be there, but below that there was only the damned river. Men stared into the rushing water just inches below the edge of the towpath. There was only the water. There was no one, no item, no remnant of anything. There was nothing. There was nothing on the edges, nothing in the bushes or tops of small trees still standing at the edge of the water. There was nothing."

Mickey stared in silence down into the swirling water.

"The Bitch took it all. Then she gave me that."

He pointed to a barge trapped between the outer towpath and a large oak standing in the shallows several yards up the river.

"When I didn't sleep in the Havre de Grace jail, I'd come up and sleep in that or in John Bartlett's barn, 'til I decided I was still alive."

He cleared his throat and gave another smile that did not go all the way up to his eyes.

"So there she is, Ben. The cabin and stern as fresh as the day she was built. John says he asked William Boyd if the Canal Company was still looking for the barge, but Will said the insurance company paid for it long ago. Said we could have it for scrap, he had one about like it near the canal basin. I think she'll swim yet, if the box ain't too rotten and someone could fix it."

Ben stepped carefully down along the tilted deck and pried open one of the forward cargo covers. He set it against the upper edge of the cargo hatch and slipped down into the hold. He managed to move his boots along the interior hull and find most of it in tact by the feel of it. Ben looked up at the faces of Simon and Mickey looking down at him, his voice echoed within the barge.

"Mickey, say your price for this is to have a job crewing it if we get it fixed?"

"Yeah. But, don't pay me much. Too much still goes for whiskey. Couple dollars right now would probably kill me with all the whiskey that would buy. All I want's a place to sleep, food to eat, and occasional drunk money. Someday I'll be asking you for the rest."

He looked over the towpath to the river beyond.

"If the Bitch don't come for me,.. or I for her."

Ben put his hands on his hips looking around the half submerged cargo hold.

"I know someone who might be able to put this thing on top of the water again."

Simon looked down at Ben and said one word, a name.

"Tuttle."

Ben grinned up and raised his hands for them to help him back up. Once on deck again, steadying his feet on the tilting deck, and shivering slightly from his early morning soak, he released Simon's hand with a nod of thanks, but kept his grip on Mickey's. He looked into Mickey's eyes, still gripping the man's hand.

"Deal."

"Deal," Mickey answered.

The remaining miles and locks to Wrightsville went smoothly without incident except for the frequent ribald comment about the barge's appearance or its name. The canal basin at Wrightsville, however, was a jumble of confused barges, inaudible orders, frequent bumps with other barges and screaming captains. First they entered the line to the Wrightsville wharf and waited four hours to find out that since they had no cargo to off-load they were in the wrong line. Simon had already taken both mule teams to the main barn for their wait in the stalls. The *Ugly Boat* waited again while Ben and Simon retrieved the mules from the holding barn and tugged them still munching on mouthfuls of hay back to the towing harness, to pull the barge along the mile-long covered bridge across the Susquehanna to Columbia on the opposite shore.

"You shoulda' already been told!" the man at the barn had said, and still charged them full price for the mule stall and feed.

The coal mountains were staggering high and coalers looking everywhere for barges to take more coal. Ben allowed too much coal to drop into the barge holds; no more than the other barges, but the *Ugly Boat* did not have as much buoyancy with the loss of the original bow and part of the stern. The shape of the scow brought the bottom up at an angle allowing it to face the waves, but robbing it of tonnage for its cargo. The barge squatted on the silt bottom of the Wrightsville inlet lock blocking all barge traffic to and from Columbia, suffering the curses of several other barge crews. Some of the other crews reluctantly helped them shovel out excess coal to lighten the load in the *Ugly Boat* and finally let her float again through the jeers and shaking heads of more experienced canallers.

It was with great relief that the crew of the *Ugly Boat* slipped back down the canal and away from Wrightsville to find their way home toward Lapidum and Havre de Grace. Two miles below Wrightsville they were joking over the wild confusion they had encountered and their happiness to be on the quiet canal, when the *Ugly Boat* ran aground again. They spent the next two hours tossing more shovels full of coal onto the far bank, and were passed by a laughing barge crew that had already helped them once shovel coal out of *Ugly Boat* at the inlet lock.

One of the other crewmen yelled across the narrow gap between the barges.

"You boys done thrown away all yer profit!"

The crew of the *Ugly Boat* all agreed that the laughter on the passing barge was much longer than necessary and barely tolerable to the red faced shovelers. They also agreed to mark the maximum level of coal the *Ugly Boat* could accept and still float in the canal.

In the fading light of a long day the crew of the Ugly Boat pounded stakes into the canal bank and tied up for the night still above the Pennsylvania-Maryland state line. Sonja had sent an iron pot full of white bean stew aboard the barge before it left Lapidum that morning, and the men attacked the stew as soon as the little iron stove in the barge cabin could heat it and the coffee. After cleaning up, Mickey took his coffee and walked across the plank to the towpath and stood watching the river current sweeping by the canal. Ben joined him, looking into the river.

"It took my daughter the night it took your family. I never got to see her."

Mickey kept his eyes on the river, feeling it more than seeing it.

"I heard."

"How did you do it?"

"Do what?"

"Decide that you were still alive, even after you lost them."

"The Bitch wouldn't take me, even with me sleeping in that barge just inches from her. I even dared her to come get me. Some nights I would stand on the tilted deck in the moonlight, drinking and daring her to come."

"So you decided if she didn't take you, you would live?"

"No. The Bitch only takes you when you want to live."

Mickey swallowed hard and clenched his hand tightly around his coffee cup.

"There was a lot of grief along this river. It took awhile before I could see it in some of the others. Somehow knowing others were able to keep going, it made me think maybe I wasn't all dead inside after all. A few times I saw a retched woman stand on the shore and scream at the river, almost like we were both waiting for the Bitch to come. One night I saw her finally throw herself into it, and before I even realized I had done it, I was in the current with her dragging us both to shore. She just about scratched my eyes out trying to go back in there, and we both almost drowned, but I would not let her go. Then she scrambled up the bank kicking away from me and was gone."

He turned toward Ben.

"Maybe she went back in farther up the path, I never knew. But after that woman was gone, lying there in the mud with my legs in the water where the Bitch could come get me, I knew I wasn't ready to die yet. So I had to accept that I was alive."

Ben put a hand on his shoulder and then went back to the barge.

They stopped at Lapidum late the next morning to swing the mast and leeboards onto the deck. After passing into the canal basin at Havre de Grace and signing out for their canal fee with Will Boyd as he had his first morning cup of coffee, the crew poled the barge through the outlet lock into the mouth of the river, raised the mast, and at last set sail down the bay for Annapolis and a coal merchant Will knew. The gentle breeze pushed the barge along, taking advantage of the scow design and the bustle-extended leeboards. Less than a mile below Havre de Grace the *Ugly Boat* ran aground again on a sand spit too near Spesutie Island. After shoveling more coal out of the holds, Ben made a note on his map of the upper bay to give the point a wider clearance, grumbling loudly to himself.

"I hope t'hell we have some coal left when we get to Annapolis!"

"Just another reason t'have a second barge!"

Mickey smiled brightly to a stern faced Ben, handing him a steaming cup of coffee and returning down to the cabin.

Ben shook his head and sighed heavily into his coffee.

"At least the damned stove works."

Moments later Mickey stumbled up from the cabin coughing in a whirl of black smoke billowing from the stairway and out through the cabin windows.

"Stove pipe bracket gave way," Mickey coughed. "Fire's out, but looks like your bedding got singed pretty bad Ben."

Simon turned to look back toward Turkey Point, his smile hidden from Ben and his shoulders shaking. Ben kept his attention riveted forward in tight-lipped silence.

Early the following day, after sleeping in the little cabin overnight, Ben steered the *Ugly Boat* into the mouth of the Severn River. With almost a mile of water between the two shores, it was still a stressful challenge to guide the little boat among the hundreds of large three and four masted ships and then dodge the churning water in the wake of several coal fired steamers charging through the water. Ben steered the boat close enough to the Annapolis City Dock for them all to catch a glimpse of the Maryland State Capitol building high up on the hill, before tacking back to the west for his run up the river to Weems creek. Will Boyd had helped him identify a couple Annapolis merchants always hungry for more coal.

"Hardly enough coal there to make it worth my while to shovel it out, Mr. Pulaski."

"Me and my crew will do that. Just lower the catch

buckets and we'll keep filling them til we're done."

The clerk looked down at Aaron and Isaac.

"These your boys?"

"Yes sir, and their father is proud of them."

The clerk smiled at the boys and nodded at Mickey, then pointed a pencil at Simon.

"You'll keep an eye on that one, right?"

Ben looked at Simon then back up to the clerk.

"Sure. Simon is here to help me."

"That ain't my point, Mr. Pulaski," he pointed his pencil back toward the capitol. "City Dock over there does a brisk business in newly arriving slaves, fresh from Africa. You let your man get too close to a herd over there and he'll get snatched up before you know it." Then he turned back toward his warehouse and called for a loading bucket crew.

Four black men with skin the color of the coal they worked, pushed out a hand cart having a large lift bucket at the end of a pivot pole that they centered over the *Ugly Boat*, then lowered it down. While Ben and his crew shoveled coal into the man-sized bucket again and again over the next three hours, the black men operating the contraption worked at a near frenzied pace until every lump was taken back into the warehouse. The clerk came back out with a clip board for Ben to sign, handed Ben six dollars, then walked back to the office speaking over his shoulder.

"Believe you need more draft in that thing or something else."

Ben, Mickey, Simon, and the boys sat around the cabin roof catching their breath, drinking water and trying to wipe off black sweat. From inside the warehouse some of the black men stood watching Simon share water with the two white men on the odd little boat.

"They're new, aren't they," Mickey said to Simon.

Simon nodded. "No English yet. Probably still

thinking about how to get home. They never will."

There was no complaint when Ben asked them to get the boat ready to sail back to Havre de Grace.

It was late in the evening of the fourth day when the *Ugly Boat* was poled across the canal to the edge of the Pulaski place. Ben spoke to the men in a grunt as he pushed the poles with them.

"This trip has cost me more money than the price of the coal we managed to get in Annapolis, and that much only because the dealer is a friend of Will Boyd."

The gangplank was shifted over the side to kiss down on the dew-covered grass and Simon led the mules off the barge and headed for the barn. Ben and Mickey staked the barge to the shore and trudged up the slope between the great oaks toward the house. Yellow light filled the doorway to the cabin as Sonja came out onto the porch.

"You were supposed to be back in two days, not four!"

Ben pulled off his hat and scratched his head.

"It took longer than we planned. We had to..."

"It always does with you, doesn't it. Who's that?"

Ben turned toward Mickey and pointed to him with his hat as Mickey stepped fully into the lamp light. Ben smiled at Mickey as he spoke.

"This gentleman has joined our crew and has brought us..."

The door slammed and Sonja was gone inside.

Ben stood in silence a moment, then sighed heavily.

"She has endured much, and can barely hold on at times."

"Some scars take a long time to heal, Benjamin, especially the ones you can't see."

"Well, let's get you settled in our little bunkroom in the barn. I can introduce you to Mrs. Pulaski tomorrow."

The introduction did not happen the next day, nor

the next. It was days before Sonja spoke again, and even then it was only one word answers to necessary questions.

Sonja cooked and cleaned and watched over the boys as they became friends with the other children of Lapidum. During the long silence that continued between her and Ben they did not rediscover the rhythm of a marriage, only the cool politeness of shared space in a boarding house of strangers.

One evening in the heavy quiet that hung in the cabin Ben said, "Someday we will find our way back to what we were, to who we were. We will.", but there was no answer.

10

The following five trips with the *Ugly Boat* continued to earn less money than Ben paid for the coal, but each trip came closer to breaking even, while the summer slipped in cooler days. Ben continued to serve on other barges to keep at least some coins coming home and protect the withering remains of his seaman's pay. At last the second barge was repaired and ready to join the *Ugly Boat.* It had taken so long that the three men agreed to name it the *Turtle,* after Sonja refused to offer a name when asked. Ben never had an opportunity to introduce Mickey to Sonja, she would not allow the moment to come, but she seemed at last to accept his presence.

Mickey settled on the edge of the Pulaski porch, resting after his last chore of the day, watching the barges at the end of the gentle front slope down to the canal, waiting for Ben. The first oak leaves drifted down from great branches framing the view of the canal. Sonja stepped out of the cabin, looking down the slope and then noticed Mickey sitting on the porch. She started, rubbing her palms together and turned to go back inside. Mickey saw her and stood up, removing his hat.

"There's the smell of autumn in the air, Ma'am. Are you well this day?"

She stopped in the doorway, but did not turn back to face him.

"Yes. I am well."

She took in a deep breath and placed her hand against the door frame.

"I don't believe I ever thanked you."

Mickey smiled at her back.

"As I recall you slapped me and questioned my lineage. Both likely worthwhile endeavors."

Sonja turned to him, her hands gripped tightly together, her eyes wide.

"Does he know?"

"No Ma'am, least not from me. T'be honest, I wasn't really sure it was you until just a couple days ago. It was dark and all...I was half asleep myself."

"Thank you for that..."

She rubbed one hand over the other.

"...though I am still not convinced you did me a favor by keeping me from the river that night."

"We both lost kin to the Bitch, Ma'am. But don't be givin' yourself to her. She'll have you when she wants you, there's no doubt about that. "

Sonja nodded and opened her mouth to say more, when Simon returned from the barn. Sonja smiled at Simon.

"Would you gentlemen like some coffee?"

They both nodded with smiles, and Simon turned to Mickey.

"Not often we get called 'gentlemen'."

Mickey looked at the doorway to the cabin.

"The Irish are called many things these days my friend, but rarely that."

The last of the sunlight had faded and the moon rose while the men discussed chores assigned and completed. Mickey's barge had been resurrected by Adam Tuttle and finally floated primly in the cooling canal water at the edge of the Pulaski property. Ben was at last satisfied the *Turtle* was ready for the morning. He ambled up the slope to the house between the giant oaks, taking in the view of the cabin under a bright harvest moon. Wisps of thinning silver smoke rose from the chimney, feather brushed by the cool air. The fortress-appearance of the old stacked log walls were softened by new gingham curtains hanging in the windows, backlit by the warm yellow glow of oil lamps in the front rooms.

Simon and Mickey were relaxing on the front porch with their coffee, watching moonlit autumn leaves drift down from the old oaks, when Ben walked up.

"Autumn is nearly upon us. I think we are ready for tomorrow, and have done enough this day." He barely waved a tired hand to them and received silent friendly smiles and nods as he went inside. Sonja had finished supper, but had left him a bowl of venison stew and some bread sitting next to the coffee pot on top of the iron stove. The stove fire was out, but enough heat remained in the coals to keep the food warm. The coffee pot was still more than warm to the touch and Ben pulled his old cup from the shelf under the window, filling it with the dark liquid. He could hear Sonja stirring in the bedroom. He stood near the door, sipping his coffee while he decided what he would say to her, could say to her. The silence between them grew oppressive as evenings fell.

He could not find joy to draw upon to give her a carefree face if he entered the room. His money from the *Star* was almost gone, and the shallow draft of the *Ugly Boat* had gained only meager profits. The *Turtle* had to make the difference. It had to.

This WILL work!

He stopped his pacing and stood before the door to their bedroom, fingering his cup. He heard her footsteps come closer to the door. She would know he was out here, standing like some boy-child not knowing what to do next.

We cannot mourn forever!

That thought only increased his anger over the situation and his anger with himself for his self-pity. He turned and walked back toward the front of the cabin and out onto the front porch. Blessedly, Simon and Mickey had left the porch to arrange their beds in the barn's tack room turned bunkhouse. They would surely be back in a few moments. It was too early to go to bed and there were still matters to discuss for tomorrow, but for now he had the porch to himself. He sat there in the dark sipping his bitter coffee and looking out toward the river for the heron.

Sonja brushed her hair while he stood outside her door. He was late. She could tell by the way he hesitated in his steps in the kitchen that he was deep in thought. His feet always gave him away when he was worried. She knew it when they were each standing near the door that either could easily and quickly pull open. There were too many heavy emotions leaning against that door, like a bar across it, too heavy to lift. Sometimes they both let it get too heavy, and in their moments of doubt they lost the confidence to move it aside. She had set her shoulders, knowing that her sadness would need to find another host for just a few minutes, while she would go out and ask him to share his troubles; their troubles. She hesitated for a moment, fighting the heaviness that fell upon her sometimes and kept her from doing things that she knew must be done. The heaviness pressed in and held her to her spot. She listened to him sip his coffee from that old cup. She listened to his few additional footsteps on the wood floor, moving only inches at a time as he wrestled with his decision.

She braced her shoulders, took in a deep breath, and forced her arm to reach out against the force of the shadow holding her back. She willed her leg to step and her foot to take the ground and carry her to the door. She forced her hand to rise toward the latch, so she could open the door hanging between them. She took her step and reached out taking the latch in her hand and then heard him shift his boots. She heard him turn on his heel and step away from the door. Maybe she could catch him, but no, there was the sound of the front door, and his boots on the front porch. She stood there listening to the sound of her own heart keeping pace with the pendulum clock and his boot steps on the porch boards. She let her hand drop down by her side. The moment was gone.

She was asleep when at last Ben entered the room to lay claim to his side of the bed and lay waiting again for his own sleep to join him.

The morning slipped in almost unnoticed within a torrential downpour that began during the night. Lightning and thunder woke Ben at three o'clock after only two hours sleep, but he rose and began preparations for the trip to Wrightsville. The wind shoved coal-colored clouds across an angry night sky. At dawn the gray of the horizon merged with that of the sky and rolled up together toward the barge in the downpour as visibility shrank to only a few yards. The two barges would tow as one, with more than enough hands to work, even within the rain storm. Mickey and Simon began their work, and then both Aaron and Isaac joined the crew to help. Both boys had already more experience on canal barges than any of the men. Hordes of fat rain drops hurled themselves down onto every surface, exploding like watery shrapnel, slapping faces huddled under soggy hat brims, and racing down in cold rivulets, rushing into any crevice where warm dry skin attempted to hide. Simon lead the mules to pull the barges like a slow funeral procession under the heavy rain pelting down on them.

The rainstorm continued all day allowing little northward progress until it was enfolded by the night without the slightest promise of a reprieve. It continued to dump inch after inch of heavy water on the valleys around the Susquehanna River. Rock Run, Deer Creek, and other tributaries that fed the canal and the river swelled out of their banks. The waste weirs, so carefully built all along the canal to free excess water into the river, could not release enough of the millions of gallons racing down the hillsides from over a thousand square miles in Pennsylvania.

Pulaski's Canal

The morning sun was hid behind gunpowder gray clouds still engorged with more rain to come. The current within the canal pushed stubbornly against the barges as the mules strained to pull them toward Wrightsville. Three-mule teams were increased to four, the rain mixed with the mule sweat, and still the body steam rose from their backs as they leaned into their water-soaked harnesses. Mules slipped, the rider was forced to stumble along the muddy paths leading them, and all legs were covered in mud to the knee. The blunt bows of the near empty barges bucked against the current, yanking the tow rope right and left trying to avoid making way directly into the current.

Canal walls usually five or six feet above the canal surface were now less than a foot higher than the water. All along the canal, barges were being pulled to the side and tethered to deeply driven pegs to wait out the rain. The storm blew the entire day, never allowing more than meager portions of light to leach through blackened clouds. Thunder and lightning added to the fear and unsteadiness of the mule teams. Tenders had to stay close to the mules to keep them from sprinting blindly into the canal or river, trying to escape the explosions of lightning and thunder. Rainwater seeped into the packed earthen pathway turning it into a quagmire and sinkholes all along the canal. Tons of precious towpath soil slid into the canal or the river. Ben's barges moved only begrudgingly along the canal, still well below the Mason-Dixon Line, and more than thirty miles from Wrightsville.

Trying to pull themselves within the confines of their leaking ponchos, heads bowed against the rain and wind covered with meager flopping hats, Simon and Isaac pulled the lead tethers of reluctant mules, urging them farther along the towpath. The surface of the canal water eddied and bounced in miniature demonstration of the raging river only a few feet away at the other side of the towpath. Water spouts shot ten feet into the air as the river current smashed into boulders and launched from their angled surfaces. Fallen trees and logs raced by in the turbulent froth, crashing into rocks and adding the occasional crack of massive trunks to the roar of the river. Curtains of rain shouldered through the downpour as the wind slapped at anything so foolish to stand against it. After each white hot flash of lightning, they were blinded for eternal seconds until the dim light and grateful breaks in the rain allowed momentary view of the soggy world around the barges. Oak, poplar, and beech leaves hung pitifully from their limbs, afraid to look up into the storm.

Two more hours drew them closer to darkness and only another mile had been put behind the barges when Ben rang the old deck bell mounted by Adam Tuttle. Isaac, Simon, and Aaron looked in his direction. Finally resigned to the storm, Ben pointed to the towpath side of the canal. They would make no more progress today. The risk of a twisted ankle or broken leg was too high for man or mule. The blunt bow of the *Turtle* bucked against the towrope as Ben turned the tiller handle to the left and allowed the barge to be pushed to the side. Simon pulled the towrope down to the pathway, but did not yet release the strain on the mule tree. Pulling a three-foot peg and heavy wooden mallet from the pack on the canal side mule, Simon twisted the peg on the rope forcing the line to spiral around the neck of the peg, and then forced the peg into the mud. Holding the peg while his poncho slapped his side and face, Simon began to pound the peg deeper into the mud until it sank into firm ground. Simon repeated the process with two more pegs before he would release the strain on the mule team. He tied the team to a nearby tree and went to help Isaac triple peg the towrope for the *Ugly Boat*. Cold raindrops stung the skin on his face and forearms as O'Grady jumped from the *Turtle* to bring the stern rope with him to the towpath. Six pegs anchored two feet into the towpath at last held each barge against the side of the canal, and still they jumped and rocked like a sloop on a lively bay.

The wind and the thunder and the roar of the river made talking outside almost impossible except for the shortest one or two word shouts from man or boy. Slowly the specters stumbled into the barge cabin. In the meager twilight the storm marched grimly into darkness. The roar of the nearby river and the constant downpour seemed to reach deafening levels as the last of the pitiful light retreated behind the tree line on the hillside above the canal. Inside the small cabin of the *Ugly Boat*, rocking within the yellow glow of a single lantern, the walls and floor jerked and the barge was pushed again and again against its tether lines on the bank. O'Grady had finally managed to light a fire in the small wood stove. The stove bucked gently within its gravel bed footing and tugged against the long iron bracing bolt reaching behind from the wall beam. Soon a pot of steaming coffee was shared among the sodden crew as they gathered around the growing heat of the stove. They were too wet and too tired to speak much. Water drops danced and hissed into steam on top of the little stove as they fell from drenched coat, shirt and hat of anyone reaching for the coffee pot. Each man and boy had a small puddle of water beneath him and around his boots where he sat or stood. Aaron shivered slightly within layers of wet wool allowing his body to regain its heat lost during the day.

The rolling blows of rain beat down on the cabin like a host of angry drummers risen up from the Susquehanna. Again and again the hull was snatched up to a jerking halt at the end of its tethers, sending the contents of the few shelves jumping to the floor. The Susquehanna roared louder on the other side of the towpath, raging against the fragile wall of mud separating it from its shallow pretender. After another tremendous slam against the bow tether, Aaron looked around the cabin meeting the eyes of the others.

"I'm closest to the door. I'll go check the lines."

At the top of the narrow steps, he pulled his coat tight against his neck and bent forward into the driving rain, stepping out quickly and closing the short door and roof hatch behind him. One line of the bowlines to the towpath was loose, but the other two were well anchored by the long pegs driven deep into the ground.

Aaron looked forward toward the *Turtle*, trying to peer through the curtain of rain. In the next flash of light he could make out the rear tether lines holding well. A rush of rain-filled wind slammed against the bow of the *Ugly Boat* suddenly jerking it away from the towpath and sending Aaron sliding along the outer walkway, driving his knee into one of the iron deck shackles. Pain shot though his leg and he grabbed for his knee as the wind snatched his hat from his head and poured water down his collar. Cursing against the pain and chilling water, he rolled onto his back trying to find a position that would ease his knee and allow him to catch his breath.

The deck jerked upward again and he sloshed along the tilting deck with the running rainwater until he could grab hold of the low outward rail. He was able to keep himself still long enough to assess his throbbing knee without further injury. He braced his other foot against the hatch in front of him, pinning himself against the rail and slowly tried to extend his injured leg. He had slammed the iron shackle hard, but the slow tolerable progress in straightening his leg assured him it was not broken. His head was drenched in the cold rain, but the pain had given him a quick sweat, which was now fading into chills as rivulets of cold water found its way down his collar soaking his shirt inside his rain slicker.

"Damn!"

He did not have another hat. Maybe Father would have something in the cabin from a previous trip. Aaron had been tossed down the deck walkway like a bowling ball to the stern, and would have to make his way back to the protection of the cabin. He propped himself up onto the hatch cover and massaged his leg before he could put weight on it, and then pivoted around to face forward, looking for another hand hold. Again the deck bucked in the swirling water, leaving him in the air for a fraction of a second before his rear slammed back into the hatch cover, twisting his injured knee to the side.

"Damn!!"

Looking forward he could see that the cabin roof was now within a stretching reach. He leaned forward stretching his hand and arm as far as he could without yet leaving the temporary support of the hatch cover, wanting to secure his hold before another jerk of the barge deck would send him sprawling again. He spit out the rain pouring down his face and pushing into his mouth by the wind. He found the roof trim with his fingertips and grabbed with all the strength his fingers could muster. Turning to face the cabin corner, he brought his good leg around and pushed himself up so he could hold with both hands. The cabin roof was not quite waist high, but gave him enough support to straighten his legs. Tears mingled with the cold rain in his eyes as he put weight on his knee. That thing would be sore for weeks. Maybe Father would put him at the tiller for a couple days until the pain eased. He knew Isaac would tease him if Father did that, but the knee hurt like hell! He took a step with his good leg and then braced himself against the roof edge to ease his injured knee into place.

Aaron looked forward trying to see the current surging in the canal, trying to foresee if the deck would suddenly pull out from under him or shove his poor knee into the air. Another flash of light illuminated the low cliff up the canal on the hillside. Aaron peered again into the blackness that befell eyes after a lightning flash.

"What cliff?" he said aloud to himself. "The canal doesn't turn there. This is a straight shot."

Another flash and Aaron saw that the low cliff stretching to the hillside actually extended all the way from the river itself, was the river itself.

"Oh, shit!!"

Aaron ignored the pain in his knee and banged on the cabin roof yelling to the top of his lungs. In the cabin Ben raised his head from his coffee cup at the sound of the banging on the roof, asking to no one

"What'd he say??"

Even as he asked the question the answer came

from the barge herself.

Aaron yelled out.

"Flood!!"

The bow of the *Turtle* stood almost skyward as the wall of water hit and lifted it like a dried leaf. Deeply driven pegs flew into the air at the end of flailing tether lines as the stern of the *Turtle* and the bow of the *Ugly Boat* rose together in a death's kiss. The *Ugly Boat* stood on its stern and then rolled toward its side as the *Turtle* folded along side trying to pass it, hinged by the tie lines and riding the rushing flood crest over the towpath into the river.

Mickey grabbed at the corner of the table as the world within the cabin tumbled around him. Wide-eyed, he bared his teeth in a demented grin.

"The Bitch is come!!"

Aaron was thrown out beyond the barge into a numbing tumbling black airless world. The flash flood charged down the Susquehanna at forty miles an hour, sweeping over the canal like an angry hand, and pulling it all to her deadly bosom. It all became a churning rolling watery avalanche, twisting and flipping everything in its path unable to withstand it. A human body was among the smaller debris washed out of the canal and into the raging Susquehanna. The roar of the water was muted in its depths.

Aaron was powerless against its strength and spun beyond his ability to think. Again and again objects reached out of the blackness to do him harm. His lungs were ready to burst. His body was wracked by continuous jabs, slaps, and punches in the blackness. His body slammed against something large. Instinctively his hand shot out to hold it, but it was too large to grasp. He was pushing hard against it as colored dots floated closer and closer to the center of what should have been his sight. The large thing shot ahead dragging him onward and twirling in the maelstrom. As it rolled, he found himself almost entirely out of the water, but even as his mind instructed him to gasp for air, he choked his mouth closed again only barely in time as the huge oak tree rolled again taking him under to the bottom of the Susquehanna.

The world of the barge cabin upended and rolled, sending men, supplies and burning coals tumbling within its belly. Isaac and Simon fell into each other as the barge flipped into its back. Ben and Mickey were tossed onto the ceiling of the cabin and peppered with burning coals and hissing loose stove parts. They all clawed toward the sides of the boat as it continued its roll. The side became the bottom and the bottom became a blunt ram to the occupants as the barge slammed into trees and rocks in its path. Loose coals hissed their way into human skin and the river water mixed within the spinning cabin. Glass jars of green beans smashed into the bulkhead adding a shower of shards to the air. Whale oil from the tin lantern in its wall mount poured from around the wick and mixed with the rolling bilge. Red-hot coals not yet found by the sloshing water were kissed by the whale oil and fire spread along the bubbling surface of the fast rising water. Again the barge flew into another object and shuddered. The boat quivered on its side, but held its position for a moment. Water surged maddeningly along its roof and submerged side. Sprays of water erupted around the caulking of the cabin windows facing the current. Mickey and Ben were covered by the whale oil and their sodden jackets erupted in flames.

Mickey stood back up and kicked at the burning surge, flames leaping up his jacket.

"Come git me, ya' Bitch! Take me! Take me if ya' can!"

Simon and Isaac began splashing water on the flames and tugging off the jackets.

Ben spun around the center of the cabin looking for the stairs and their way out. In the frenetic motions of the barge he couldn't remember if the stairs should be up or down. There was no time for other thoughts as the boat was snatched from its purchase and spun around sickeningly on its side sending everyone down into the water again. The barge rolled again onto its back, the cabin roof smashing into rock or stump, opening a gash in the roof and crushing the windows. The water charged in with a fury, knocking the bodies away like toys and foaming the whale oil fire. The barge continued its roll, stopping the rush of water within as the cabin pointed up for a brief moment, and then dove back down into the current half filling the cabin with water.

Mickey was thrown hard against a support beam, hitting his head. He slumped into the water, his head slipping under, when Isaac grabbed his shirt collar and pulled his face back up into the air. Ben and Simon were on their knees trying to splash the flaming water away from themselves and backing toward Isaac and Mickey.

The boat shuddered to another impact and spun again on her side like a feather in the wind. The men were thrown down toward the broken windows, and then pushed aft, and then pushed hard against the bottom as the boat was swung by its bow. The barge was then propelled on its side cabin-first in its new direction. Breathing and pushing the fire away was all they could do. The cabin roof exploded inward from another impact, pummeling the interior with splinters and more glass shards, and the barge shuddered to another momentary halt while the motion drove them all toward the jagged claws where the roof corner had been. Isaac sailed against the bulwark still holding Mickey by his shirt collar. A pain shot across his chest and stole his breath.

Simon reached out for any handhold only to grasp the lower half of the stove still bolted to the floor and yelled out in pain as his palm burned against the still hot iron. The water in the cabin was dashed against them in a single wave finally putting out the fire and plunging the cabin into darkness. Ben was thrown toward the roof and groaned out as a long wooden splinter forced its way into his thigh. The flood water roared against the bottom of the hull as the trembling barge lay on its side, locked by its forward-pointing roof, sharing a maze of splinters with whatever it had smashed against. The barge continued to jerk and buck on its side, pounded against its confinement by the furious river, still desperate to get at them.

Farther down the river, a large tree trunk plucked from the riverbank by the flash flood bobbed to the tumultuous surface and rolled its trapped passenger over into the air just as Aaron felt he could no longer hold his breath, could no longer hold his life. His hands and feet were numb. He did not know if he still held the trunk or if it held him in a death grip. He did not know if he could survive another trip to the bottom of the river. The tree bolted as it hit something else in the river. He could see a light run by in the distance through a break in the night rain.

It must be a house on the shore.

He wondered for a moment if it was even his own house. The light moved past so quickly, it told Aaron how very fast he was hurtling within the river surge, and it terrified him. The tree slewed around in the darkness and the light ran away. It felt as if the tree was then speeding down the rocking torrent side first. The air was cold on his back, but at least the rain seemed to be thinning. Aaron began to squeeze his hands, trying to make them work, to feel where he was, how he was being held to the trunk. His fingertips told him they were against bark. They hurt like hell and he smiled grimly; at least he still had them.

He flexed his right leg and his knee gave him new pain, worse than before. He flexed his ankles forcing his feet to move and tell him they were still his. His feet told him he had lost his boots. His right ankle was wedged deep within the narrow fork of two branches and would not come free.

Fighting the shivering that racked his body and the pain in his left knee, he inched his hands along the massive trunk toward his right foot. When both of his knees were bent as far as he dared on his precarious perch, he gripped the trunk as much as he could with his arms and began to push away with his left foot and pulling up with his right. Lightning shot up his left leg from his injured knee. He clenched his teeth and groaned against the pain. A moment later he stopped and went through his limb-by-limb assessment, trying to gauge his progress.

Nothing.

He began his push again. As if sensing Aaron's meager attempts to free himself from it, the huge tree slowly rolled forward as one of its branches deep within the floodwater snagged against a rock. Aaron's right foot slowly sank back into the chilled water, forcing him to strengthen his grip on the trunk to keep above the surface. He pushed with his left leg again, growling against the pain and the fear of being trapped under water again, trying desperately to free his foot, but without success. Again he strained.

Nothing. Damn!

The exposed tree roots scraped against a large rock outcropping and spun its top facing down river, the spin causing it to roll Aaron further into the water. He struggled to keep his grip on the trunk and continued to pull up on his right leg and push down on his left. His hand and forearm went into the river and the angry brown water ran up his arm coming for him. He gulped air as the water surged around his chest and shoulder, to his neck, to his chin, his lips, and then the trunk pulled his head under the water. Only his left foot and hand were above the water and the rolling stopped.

Keep rolling! Keep rolling!! Oh God, Keep rolling!!

Unencumbered by the frantic struggle of the pitiful human boy trapped in its branches, the tree ignored the frothing water around the hand and foot at the edge of its exposed side. Slowly the trunk rotated further, taking Aaron farther and farther from blessed air and deeper under the muddy water. He couldn't hold on any longer. He couldn't hold his breath as long as the last time. The pain in his chest was almost unbearable. He had to make it stop. He couldn't hold the air in any longer. The numbness was coming to release him from his agony. His heart pounded in his chest and drove needles into the backs of his eyes.

Roll damn you, Roll! Roll!

He punched and kicked with his free foot trying to loosen its grip.

He slapped at the bark; his free hand totally under the water now, but the tree was huge and nothing Aaron could do would make it move. Only the river made it move, and it sailed farther south, caught in the current of the billions of gallons of water charging down toward the Chesapeake Bay.

At last his chest felt as if it would explode and he could no longer hold it in. He began to release some of the air into the dark water to release the pressure in his chest, even though he knew there was no new air to replace it. Blessed fresh spring air only inches away that he would never taste again.

He let go of the trunk and floated beside the behemoth oak, his arms and free leg drifting outward in the current, held to the body of the tree by his trapped ankle in a grotesque ballet. The air bubbles no longer escaped from his open mouth. Light could not find his open eyes in the muddy water.

Like a great whale swimming home, the tree glided among the rushing currents of the Susquehanna River into the Susquehanna Flats on its way to channel into the Chesapeake Bay.

Panicked fear slipped into nightmare, then dream, as the air-starved brain began releasing jumbled memories to twirl haphazardly among fading thoughts of a life drifting away. He stretched out his hand in the liquid blackness, reaching out to the little sister he had lost in icy water.

Don't worry, Alisha. I've got you. I'm here now. Ma will be glad I'm with you.

11

The tumultuous flood surge tossed and slammed the barges like mere twigs farther down the river course in the darkness and the downpour, until at last the *Ugly Boat* and the *Turtle* came to a precarious perch among boulders lining the western shore of the Susquehanna River. Miraculously still held together by the thick hemp line fastened between the barges, a single massive oak tree among the boulders snagged the line and held the barges against the charging current. The barges ground against each other, cabin roof to cabin roof, like warriors tied together in deadly combat. The worst of the flood crest passed on allowing the hulks to settle uneasily among the rocks, laying the *Turtle* on its side in the continuing Susquehanna turbulence, with the *Ugly Boat* lying against it and wedged between the rocks and the scarred riverside of the towpath. River waters still charged and splashed among the rocks and against the *Ugly Boat*, slapping and rocking the hull. The stairs to the cabin hatch now ran down into waist deep water to the submerged exit.

Gasping and coughing, the four trapped men tried again to stand on the inner side of the hull and look for a way out. The rain poured down in cascades through the missing window panes now above them and through the smashed corner of the cabin roof. The sky was only slightly lighter than the blackness of the disoriented interior, but offered faint light to move toward the window. Using the cabin roof beams as step holds, Simon and Isaac helped each other climbed up through the small window and onto the outer wall of the cabin that now provided them an unsteady and narrow deck barely large enough for their feet. Mickey had not regained full consciousness and they had had to pull him through the window while Ben pushed him up from below. The clouds were thinning and the rain began to diminish as Isaac and Simon slid across the upturned side of the hull and dropped down into ankle-deep water slapping the rocks at the base of the towpath.

Ben helped the disoriented Irishman move across the hull to reaching hands, and then turned back toward the *Turtle*.

"Aaron!" he yelled. "Aaron, are you all right son?"

No response came to his question but the increasing wind and steady roar of the river. Isaac took up the call from the towpath. Ben stepped across the crumpled roofing onto the side wall of the *Turtle*'s cabin. He knelt down to find the window panes there missing as well. Looking through the window frame he could see darker forms among the shadows within the rotated cabin. With the *Turtle* held by its stern rope, the cabin door and roof hatch were on the upper side of the barge. Ben pushed the roof hatch back, pulled the short door up, and stepped carefully down into the blackness. Frantically he pulled and pushed his way among the shapes that were stove, bedding, or ruined supplies.

Don't you take another child from me!

He began looking for anything that might help them. After rummaging through the jumbled cabin for several moments, he pulled up a small unopened wooden box and pried it open with his sheath knife. Still packed snuggly in dry shipping straw, Ben pulled out two new lanterns. He found the dented but capped lamp-oil can and then returned to the opening.

"He's not in here! Have any of you seen or heard anything?"

Isaac had already begun tracing the towpath northward back where the flood had struck. Simon and a much-recovered, but slow moving Mickey, began moving south looking for Aaron as well, but none could find any sign or sound in the night that might lead them to Aaron. Ben climbed up through the jagged opening and stepped back onto the upper wall of the *Ugly Boat*'s cabin. Gripping the wire lantern loops by his sides, he looked up in the darkness.

"Don't you take another child from me!" he screamed to the breaking clouds.

Simon was still exploring the canal side of the towpath and yelled back to Ben.

"The current's still real strong in the canal, he could be down this way!"

Ben jumped off the side of the *Ugly Boat* and scaled the side of the towpath. He looked toward Simon then north, back up the canal, remembering that Aaron was on deck when the flood rushed against them.

"He could still be back there, up canal!"

Isaac fished a flint from the cabin of the *Ugly Boat* and managed to light both lanterns.

"We need to search both ways, Pa."

Ben passed one of the lanterns to Simon. Torn between wanting to search both north and south, and not allowing himself to think of Aaron being tossed into the river, Ben decided on a northward search.

"You look south and I'll look north. Go about a mile, then come back. I'll do the same. Isaac, you stay here with Mickey."

"I ain't stayin' here, Ben! I'm goin' with Simon. I ain't sitting on my ass while you boys go look for Aaron!"

"You need to stay here, Mickey. You took a bad hit to your head."

Mickey pointed in the lamp light at Ben's upper leg.

"You best tend your own wounds, Ben. That ain't water running down your pants."

"Pa! You're bleeding!"

Isaac approached Ben to assist, but Ben made to push him back.

"Pa, what are you going to do for Aaron if you bleed to death?"

Isaac wrung out and folded a water-soaked bandana and then pressed it against the gash in Ben's leg. Mickey passed his neckerchief to Isaac, who then tied it over the folded patch. Ben patted his son on the shoulder.

"Good a field dressing as any. Thanks, son."

Yelling between them as they moved farther away in opposite directions they agreed to be back at the barges within two hours. If either pair was not back, the other would then move in that direction to join them.

Dawn was in the skyline when Ben and Isaac returned breathless and hoarse to the barges and had stepped out only a hundred yards when they saw Mickey and Simon in the gray light. Ben's face was lined with smut and grief, having found no sign of his other son even after retracing each foot between the resting point of the barges and the location where the crest of the flash flood had hit them. Without waiting for the sky to lighten into dawn, Ben and Isaac moved southward. They let the lantern go out, having enough sky light to see by, but continued to investigate any dark form spotted near or in the canal.

Several more times Ben or Isaac waded through the bone chilling current to investigate a log or limb lying on the far side. Once they both charged through the water when they noticed a dark form moving on the landward side, but it took most of their remaining energy to dodge the antlers of a near-berserk and seriously injured white tailed buck. They could only leave it to its struggle and climb again up the muddy slope onto the towpath. There were only a few places on the landward side where they could walk for more than a few yards without having to divert deep into the woods or slip back down into the canal itself, so they were forced to keep their vigil from the towpath.

At least staying on the towpath allowed us to check the river shore as well.

Dawn finally came with Ben almost knee deep in

swirling river water, having found yet another log trapped in the rocks and covered by a mantle of leaf debris. He heard voices up on the towpath and called out

"Aaron?? Is that Aaron up there??"

Simon's voice penetrated the sound of rushing water near Ben's ears.

"No, Ben, we couldn't find him!"

"Maybe you should have looked farther south!"

Ben yelled into the trees and bushes, and did not hear the heavy sigh or see the look of exasperation on Simon's face.

When Ben stepped from the underbrush and briars onto the towpath and before he could ask any further questions, Simon spoke.

"The towpath is gone, Ben, about three, maybe four hundred yards down. There's a section where the canal water is just pouring into the river. There's about twenty yards of towpath that's just gone."

"Well, did you look down at the river shore? Maybe he's just down from there. Did you look? Did you?"

Mickey stepped close to Ben.

"Aye, we looked, Ben. We looked hard for about another half mile. He ain't there, Ben. If we was taken that far, then it took him out into the river."

Ben looked from one man to the other figuring what action he could take next to find his son, but nothing would come into his thoughts except the picture of Aaron's face lying pale in a coffin. He turned away from them.

"Damn! Dammit to Hell and back!!"

Isaac placed his hand on his father's shoulder and looked down, shaking his head.

-------~✦◉◉✦~-------

Long before the barges came to rest against the tree, the flood crest had charged down the canal and into the river. The racing river hardly noticed the addition of a paltry flash flood charging out of the swollen creeks and down the canal. It required no assistance to continue rolling house-sized boulders and ripping 100-year-old trees from the shore and propelling them southward toward the bay. One old oak tree slipped by Lapidum in the darkness as it floated quickly along in the swollen current. The rain began to wane at the southern edge of the storm clouds, near the mouth of the river where it slipped into the Chesapeake Bay. The river gave forth its anger and its debris every spring and every autumn, when the rain fell heavy in Pennsylvania. Several trees floated out of the river onto the Susquehanna flats.

Aaron?

Is that you, Ma?

Aaron opened his eyes in the black water of the Susquehanna. In the distance he could see a light coming toward him. He could feel nothing now, except the awful headache pounding in his forehead.

Ma?

The light was in front of him now.

Alisha?

If he could only let the last of the air out of his chest and stop the pain he would be all right, but there was no more air to release. He wanted to go closer to the light but the pain kept him away. Suddenly there was a new pain in his arm, sharp, searing; almost as much as the pain in his lungs. The light came closer. He looked with eyes wide open and saw Alisha floating in the water next to him. She was smiling and reaching for him. The pain in his chest came again, and the pain in his arm grew worse, and Alisha drifted away.

No! Alisha don't go!

Alisha's face swam into view again. Her face was almost nose-to-nose with his. She was saying something, but Aaron could not understand her, and began drifting off to sleep. They could talk in the morning. He was so tired now. He just wanted to sleep.

The pain shot into his arm again

Not now, little sister.

She spoke again frowning at him, shaking him.

I don't understand, little sister.

I've got you! I've got you!

What?

"I've got you!"

Adam Tuttle yelled again.

"My God, man!"

He yelled to the other in the boat,

"Ya' didn't have to stick him with that goddamned gaff!"

"I wasn't tryin' to stick'im, ya ol' fool."

"Well, get a rope around his chest so I can see what's keeping him t'this damned tree?"

The rope squeezed the water in his lungs and Aaron coughed out water and gasped the air in ragged breaths as the blackness in his head and the water in his lungs surged back into the river. Adam leaned beyond the gunnel of his boat holding the lantern over Aaron. Adam patted his head gently.

"Don't worry, Boy, I've got ya."

Aaron smiled as they freed his foot, hauled him onto the boat and then covered him in the most wonderful fish-smelling, raggedy wool blanket he had ever known. Aaron drifted into unconsciousness smelling the musty blanket and mumbling to his sister.

When Aaron returned to the world of light through a fog of watery darkness and confusion, he found himself tucked snuggly under fresh ironed sheets in one of the Harper's guest bedrooms. The room was well lit and as his eyes focused, he surveyed the room around him. Doctor Harper was asleep in the wing-backed stuffed chair against the wall beyond the foot of his bed. Mrs. Harper was sitting in the old wooden rocker near the lamp at his bedside reading a book, and looked up as Aaron shifted his position and emitted a murmuring grimace to the twinges of pain in his shoulder and his knee and his ankle.

Mrs. Harper smiled brightly reaching over to gently push the hair from his forehead.

"Good morning."

Doctor Harper awoke and stood in a single almost effortless movement. His large form grew to his full height and he stepped quickly to Aaron's side. He felt the boy's forehead and then pulled back the bedcovers to examine the shoulder bandage. Sliding a huge hand across his face, the doctor lifted one of Aaron's eyelids and peered close.

"You've got a small poke in your shoulder that needed just one stitch to close, and your left ankle was twisted a good bit, but it isn't even broken. It also looks like your knee is wrenched pretty good by the amount of swelling."

Aaron began to sit up, still working to separate his last clear moments.

"Pa! The barges! There's a flash flood!"

Before he could say more the room began to spin and the pain in his shoulder sent a stab of pain across his chest.

"Settle down, youngster. You damn near drowned and you're bruised up quite a bit. You need to rest. I've sent someone to tell your mother where you are and that you are going to be all right, but you need to lie still so things don't get worse. I'll let you know as soon as we hear anything about Ben and the others."

Mrs. Harper retrieved a green glass bottle sitting near the lamp and poured a few drops into a spoon. She gently lifted Aaron's head and allowed the medicine to dribble across his lips. Aaron instinctively swallowed the warm liquid and felt the burn of its alcohol content as it slipped down his throat. The cloud quickly returned and the lights faded.

Ben led the small party farther south looking for the body of his oldest son among the rocks at the river's edge. The hours and the miles of rocky shoreline and briar thickets yielded only begrudgedly to the four men. All thoughts that Aaron might yet be found within the shallow canal were abandoned. Where the towpath had washed away they crossed to the land side and worked their way beyond the rent and then re-crossed to the path. The men stumbled on in the fading darkness long after the oil in the lantern had given out, moving farther south along the towpath back toward Lapidum. Twice Ben and Simon had waded almost waist deep into the rushing water, leaning out to feel a trapped log of tree top and yelling for Aaron, as Isaac and Mickey held on to them from whatever anchor they could grab on the bank.

"Pulaski! Ben Pulaski!"

The trotting rider called from the towpath

"Here!" Ben yelled back, "We're over here!" and slogged out of the water and up the bank in the direction of the voice. Ben dashed toward the rider, water droplets cast off his sodden pants and spraying from his boot tops as he ran.

John Bartlett reined the horse to a halt.

"Sonja sent me to look for you. She was afraid you were all drowned."

"We lost Aaron! Did you see any sign of him?"

"No sign, Ben, but plenty of words."

Ben's heart gave a tremendous thump in his chest.

"I think he's all right, Ben. One of the sheriff's deputies rode down the towpath to tell Sonja that Aaron was at Dr. Harper's. Seems like Adam Tuttle and another fellah were tagging logs and such washing down the river and they found Aaron tangled up in one."

Ben dropped to his knees and pulled Isaac close to him in a tight bear hug.

"Thank God!"

Mickey limped up to the rider.

"I'm mighty glad the old fart was there when Aaron needed help, but what the hell was he doin' out there in a storm, for God's sake?"

"Tagging trees. Adams goes out to the flats when it storms upriver. Tags free floating trees with little wooden signs that says they belong to him. When the winds die down he hauls them into his cove. Gets almost all his wood for free. Been doin' it for years"

Ben laughed and slapped John's leg.

" Ol' Tuttle charged me for lumber when he rebuilt the *Ugly Boat*. And he got it for free! Well, hell, I'll never be able to pay him enough for pulling Aaron out."

John smiled and pulled the reins to the side to turn his horse around.

"You boys well enough to walk the rest of the way back? Or do you need to go back and get the barges?"

Simon placed his hands on his hips and shook his head.

"Those boats are going to need a lot of work before we can bring them back down – once we get them out of the trees and rocks!"

"Your barges are in the trees??!"

Ben pulled on John's stirrup.

"We can finish the walk back to Lapidum, John. And our steps will be a lot happier. I'd appreciate it if you would trot back to the farm and let Sonja know that all her men are coming home."

At full sunrise the four trudged up the gentle slope between the giant oaks and clomped onto the porch boards. The house was empty, but a small note was written on the edge of butcher paper and wedged into the doorframe. Ben tried to read it in mumbles to himself, but then relinquished the note to Isaac to read aloud.

"Gone to Dr. H to get Aaron."

Ben stood on the porch smiling and looking out over the river toward Port Deposit.

"You know, it took us a day and a half to pull those barges as far as we did. We lost three good mules, and both boats are beat to shit. And then it just took us through the night to walk back down here. Next time it storms like that, we're staying home."

There were no objections to the idea in the following silence.

When Sonja returned from Havre de Grace late that morning, Sarah, the mule pulling the wagon and Aaron resting among a pallet of quilts in the back, her front porch was full of mud-spattered, thorn-scratched, bandaged canallers, all in deep heavy sleep. She and Aaron stepped quietly over sprawled arms and legs and into the house, where she put Aaron to bed and started a large pot of coffee. While she waited for the coffee to boil, she stood in the middle of the front room, arms folded across her chest, looking out of the open door at Ben's booted feet lying on the porch boards.

I've already lost a daughter waiting on you. I'll be damned if I will stand by and let you kill my sons.

12

Even as the sky returned to a peaceful blue, flood waters roiled three more days before the current slackened enough to permit attempts at freeing the trapped barges. Ben, Simon and Mickey made their way back to the barges. Aaron and Isaac were no longer allowed near the barges and were being home schooled by Sonja. Ben could not argue the point with her, could not disagree with her fear.

They are safer with her than with me.

The water level slowly settled, allowing the hulls enough freeboard to float if they could be separated without losing them to the remaining current. Ben and Simon ran long heavy ropes from trees on shore to secure the two barges, and then tied lighter lines around their own waists. Several solid chops with a newly sharpened axe severed the faithful tether that had kept the hulls together during the flood and saved the barges. Once freed, the *Ugly Boat* was pushed off the rocks by the residual flood waters racing down from Pennsylvania and quickly snapped at the end of its new line, bobbing and bucking in the current like an animal trying to escape its tether. The open jagged maw that had once been the cabin roof would need a great deal of carpentry work. The *Turtle* remained on its side, wedged between the boulder under the tree that stopped them and another large rock several feet farther from shore. The river pushed against it bottom, locking its position with brute force.

Still wrapped in white linen bandages, Mickey shook his head, grinning in admiration at the sturdiness

155

of the barge. "Damned thing just likes to swim, Ben! Wants to stay where it is!"

"Well, it's not going to stay where it is," Ben yelled above the roar of rushing water. He slogged waist-deep through the muddy current above the barge, pushing off the hull against the oncoming water and working his way along the exposed bottom, looking for a way to dislodge the boat. He turned back toward Simon who was gauging the damage to the *Turtle*'s rudder. "I think the water's pushing hard enough against the bottom and the bow to keep it wedged at an angle between these two rocks."

Simon looked along the line of the upturned deck at the other side and nodded in agreement. "Looks like it'll need that block and tackle we brought. If we can pull the bow back toward the shore, the water ought to just push the thing out. Better not let anybody be downstream when it slips loose though, this water's still pretty mean!"

Even as Simon spoke, Ben's boot slipped on the muddy rocks and he was forced deep into the brown surf surging under the hull. Ben's safety line was tied securely upstream, but he had to allow himself enough slack to assess the length of the barge. As soon as his body fell completely into the water, the current shooting under the side of the hull snatched him along and yanked him to the limit of his line. Suddenly Ben found himself in furiously churning darkness under the far side of the barge, and the rushing river trying to push him down stream; his safety line holding his position under the hull and keeping him from getting his head above the water. He struggled to grab at the side of the barge, kicking with his feet to fight the current, but could find no hand hold. Several seconds went by as Ben twirled in the rushing water under the barge like a helpless rag doll, before Simon and Mickey realized Ben had not surfaced on the other side. Ben struggled to untie the safety line and float free with the current, but could not get the knot untied.

Simon saw the safety line go taut and could not see Ben surfacing anywhere. "Ben's trapped!"

Pulaski's Canal

Simon could not reach Ben from the far side of the barge. He turned back to tell Mickey to cut Ben's line, but even as he opened his mouth to yell, Mickey already severed the line with the ax. Mickey quickly spun around to wrap the line's newly freed end around his own waist. He allowed himself to slide down the scarred muddy face of the bank, giving what he hoped was enough loose line so Ben could surface on the other side. Mickey managed to tie a loop around himself as he slid into the current without his own safety line.

Ben's chest felt like it was going to explode as he tumbled in the water; felt the tension release of his line and he bobbed gasping to the surface just beyond the hull. He tried to stand, but the river swept him off his feet again and shot him farther down river toward the next jumbled collections of boulders at break-neck speed. The water ahead of him foamed and surged up the sides of the onrushing rocks almost as if they were rising up to meet him, to slap him down. He was thrown faster at the boulders.

This is really going to hurt!

As Mickey slid into the current he yelled to Simon. "Grab me Simon! Grab me as I come by!"

Simon gave a quick tug to check his own safety line, prayed it was knotted correctly at the other end, and then threw himself at the rope between Mickey on one side and Ben beyond the barge on the other. Mickey was already being drawn down into the tumbling water at the edge of the hull. Simon grabbed the line holding Mickey and Ben, kicking hard with his legs to push it and himself out away from the barge. Ben's safety line popped out from under the end of the hull and sent him closer to the rocks. Angry muddy froth pulled Simon deeper into the water behind Mickey, and they were both swept beyond the *Turtle*.

Ben shot on toward the pile of rocks, pushed hard by the current and freed to fly by the additional slack in his line. Simon grabbed Mickey's waist just as he reached the length of his own safety line. The rope stiffened and reverberated, individual hemp strands twisting and grinding and popping within the weave under full strain. Simon was jerked back to the surface, pulling Mickey with him and groaning against the bite of the rope line at his bare waist. Hundreds of pounds of man and river water ground the coarse hemp into his skin.

The boulder loomed high, cascading muddy water churning at its base as the current flung Ben toward it. The line between Mickey and Ben had paid out its full length and snapped stiff, halting Ben with a jerk just as his boot soles slapped against the granite surface. He dangled there, just before the crushing face of the boulder, bobbing in the surging water, his eyes focusing on the rugged details of the granite edge waiting for him just inches away.

"Jesus," Ben sputtered, his face drenched and water pouring down thick strands of hair along his forehead.

The three men hung by their ropes catching their breath, like three minnows rigged for fishing and cast by a giant pole from the shore. After a moment's rest, Simon and Mickey managed to work their way back along Simon's safety line to the bow of the *Turtle*. They looped Ben's line around the tow post on the bow and slowly pulled Ben back upstream to the barge. When all three were together, they stood several minutes in the relative lee of the current behind the bow of the barge, bracing their hands on their thighs and coughing up water, then wiping their faces with water soaked shirts, and refilling their lungs with fresh air.

Ben held himself up against the hull and looked between the other two with a half smile. "Thanks...So, who is going after the block and tackle on shore?"

Simon took in a few more deep breaths as he examined the ropes tied to Ben and Mickey. He eased the hemp noose away from the whelps and bleeding scratches around his waist and tucked his shirt tail between his skin and the rope. "I guess that'll be me, since I'm the only one still tied to a tree."

Mickey could only nod in agreement, still bent over nodding his head and taking in deep breaths through the water running down his face and dripping from his nose and lips. His head bandage was gone and a thin trickle of blood traced a small red line from his hair line down to his left ear.

Ben watched Simon care for his waist.

"Thanks, Simon."

Simon was too winded for anymore words, and waved away the comment as he turned and began pulling himself hand over hand along his safety line toward the bank.

Once the tackle was rigged and pressure brought to bear pulling the bow of the *Turtle* toward shore, the barge righted, shot out of the crevice like an escaping trout and quickly snapped to the end of its own retaining line. Getting the barges back in the canal had been decided the night before. They would have to float six miles down the river and make their way into the canal basin through the exit lock. With the only power available being the fearsome push of the river water, they tethered, played out, secured and tethered again, fifty yards at a time – the length of their longest heavy lines. Like a timid convalescent moving cautiously through his house from one hand hold to another, they first tied an upstream line to a tree or massive boulder as a safety against the push of the current, and then paid out the second line foot by foot as far downstream as it would reach. They re-tied to the next location and then slowly released the next fifty yards below that.

Shoulders and arms ached from the repeated strain on the line. Blisters whelped across raw palms and were almost immediately split open by the rasp of stiff hemp fibers. The river pushed and pulled and tugged at the barges, trying to snatch them away from the safety lines and send them crashing down into the rocks. Tie, release, tie. Tie, release, tie. Six miles.

Fifty yards each evolution. 212 evolutions. Mickey counted each one. 212 evolutions. Simon had long ago trained himself to go numb with repetitive harsh labor. 212 evolutions. Ben cursed the river at the end of each evolution. 212 curses. Sometime after 128 curses, the sun settled over the western ridge above the canal. Somewhere around 180 curses, they tied off with double knots and lay on the deck in dreamless, motionless sleep for a few hours. They rose in the gray predawn to continue the evolutions, not stopping even as they passed Lapidum; it was only a passing image under the rising sun.

Like the eerie quiet in the moments after a tornado, the barges emerged at the mouth of the river and glided almost serenely into the western side of the Susquehanna flats, where the river current faded against the incoming bay tide, and the men were able to pole the barges slowly through the lock into the canal basin. Soaked, mud splattered, scratched and bruised, Ben, Simon and Mickey at last tied up the barges near one of the new warehouses.

Dropping the poles from bloody palms without thought of stowing them away, they let them clack onto the deck where each man stood. They stumbled along the narrow board off the barge and collapsed onto the grass beyond the warehouse and below the lockhouse, letting the sun bake the cold river water, raw hands, and trembling muscles that had become their only awareness.

Will and Alice Boyd had watched their slow progress into the basin. Alice led the way from the lockhouse carrying a large basket of food to the spot where the three men rested. Will followed close behind with a wooden pail of fresh cool water dangling by its rope from one hand, and a modest-sized crockery jug nestled into the crook of his other arm. Alice pretended not to see the jug as she placed the basket in their midst.

"You boys eat on this and catch your breath a while. Sonja has gone up to Doc Harper's to speak with LuAnn. Said for you to wait on her and you can all ride back up together with Dan Bartlett on Number 26."

Pulaski's Canal

William set the jug in the grass beside Ben, and then placed his hand on his shoulder.

"This river seems to hold a grudge against your family, Ben. Glad to hear that Aaron is all right."

"Sometimes I could really believe that, Will. She – the Bitch as Mickey calls her - got a good hold of me again earlier today."

"She can be evil for sure, Ben. I've seen her devastation more than I wanted to."

William recognized the contemptuous name; knew it until that moment only as a nameless feeling standing on the bank when the Susquehanna was running angry. It was part of a recurring dream, staring down into the shallows and seeing his own pale bloated face looking back from among the crabs. He mumbled to himself the common name Ben had used and stood a moment looking at the barges; scarred, injured, floating high and empty.

"Not sure which looks worse, those boats or you boys."

He turned to go back toward the lockhouse, speaking again over his shoulder as he walked away. "Send that jug back to me when it's empty."

Mickey reached over and pulled the jug into his lap, then holding it up to his ear as he shook it to gauge the fullness of its content. He yanked out the cork and took a large swallow quickly followed by a second, before handing the jug to Simon. Looking back at William he added, "Ah-h-h, a true saint to the down-trodden." Soon the jug, the pail, and the basket received full attention until each was empty.

Not far away, returning from Adams Street, Sonja took a stroll to a place she had blocked from memory. She walked up the slope beyond the canal basin, above the warehouses to the large oak tree. It stood alone, once overlooking the lane that ran by their house and now covered by those warehouses. She turned to watch the sailboats working their way back and forth from

Perryville to Havre de Grace. Lost in her thoughts, she did not hear the approach of Martha Johnson. Sonja was startled from her thoughts at the voice behind her.

"May I tell you something, Mrs. Pulaski?"

Sonja quickly wiped a small tear from her eye as she turned.

"Hello, Mrs. Johnson. I did not see you there. I hope you don't mind my being here. This is the first time since…"

Martha hesitated to intrude into Sonja's silence, but then continued.

"My man, Josiah, wanted to build me a bench on the very spot. He knows how I love to look out over the bay from here."

"It always was a lovely view."

"On the day your Ben came home, I saw him out here. He appeared to put something in the ground near the tree, but I never thought anymore about it until Josiah went to build that bench for me."

Sonja looked into Martha's face, but only nodded, not knowing what else to do.

"Josiah dug holes for the legs, so the wind wouldn't blow the bench down? He brought up a small canvas bag from that same spot and we looked into it."

Sonja was curious, and waited for the gentle old woman to continue. Once neighbors, this was the first time they had spoken since the flood.

"Please don't think us awful, but I thought you should know that it was a little white christening gown."

Tears flooded into Sonja's eyes and she tried to smile through them.

"I told Josiah to put it back and move the bench out away from that spot. He dug the hole deeper and then put the bag back in the ground."

Sonja hesitated and then asked the question.

"Can you show me the spot?"

Martha took Sonja by the hand and led her the few steps back to the little hollow at the base of the oak. Sonja gripped Martha's hand tightly as she looked down at the small patch of delicate pink thrift growing in the hollow between two large root knuckles.

Martha looked into her face.

"Didn't seem right not to have flowers there."

Tears raced down Sonja's face and she began to sob. Martha wrung her hands, drying them on her apron in a nervous tic even though they were not wet, looking in the direction Ben had gone that day.

"He came back a few days before Josiah started to work on the bench, but not since. I can see here from the kitchen."

She paused, unsure if she should go on.

"But I never saw you come until today. When you didn't go near the tree, I figured maybe you didn't know."

Sonja could only shake her head no and wipe her eyes. Martha pointed a delicate wrinkled finger.

"I put the flowers there, 'cause I understood this was the place he said goodbye to that little angel. I've buried too many of my own, and I know you've got to have a place for her. You've got to have a place to leave your grief."

Sonja took in a deep ragged breath and looked up to watch a heron glide down over the shallows at the edge of the basin. A tear on her cheek slipped down her face in timing with the sweep of the heron.

"Her name was Alisha."

"Well," the old woman said, "this'll be her spot as long as I live here."

Sonja put her arms around the portly old woman and hugged her tightly. Martha slipped her hand under Sonja's elbow and guided her toward the little farmhouse. "Come child, I have some fresh coffee in the kitchen."

Sonja looked again at the modest patch of thrift. "Sometimes I forget he feels the loss too, though my own regrets often overwhelm me."

Together the two women walked up from the tree, past the little barn like the one Josiah had built for Ben, and past the tethered cow munching on browning grass, and into the house.

Later, Sonja made her way down the slope and along the mean little cart path that had once been the beginning of her lane, and wound her way around the warehouse to the front lawn of the lockhouse. She waved at Alice sitting on the porch mending one of William's large socks and then crossed the swing bridge to the towpath side. She found *Number 26* near the head of the line waiting for entrance to the canal and joined Ben at the bow. She tried desperately to keep her anger at Ben, but she could not put out of her mind the secret Martha Johnson has shared with her as she sat on the cargo hatch. Ben sat next to her without speaking. She released a heavy sigh, and then slipped her arm through his.

Ben looked down in surprise at his wife sitting so close to him. He noticed dried mud already caught in the yellow fabric of her dress.

"I'm awfully messy, you'll get your dress dirty," he said, but she did not move.

Dan's mule tender Thomas lead the team farther up the towpath and *Number 26* faithfully followed the towline into the canal. Sonja watched Thomas's back. *You seem older and thinner, Thomas. Are you not well these days?*

Along the way to Lapidum Ben and Sonja talked of Aaron and Isaac, the farm, the repairs to the barges, and the new mules they still needed. It was nothing unusual for a man and his wife living on the canal to discuss. It was nothing unusual at all, and Ben felt happier than he had since coming home. *Perhaps it is a start.*

"Ben," she said and he turned his face toward hers. "Ben, the boys must stay off the barges. They will not be boys much longer. They must go to school. Do you understand me?"

13

Ben and William Boyd shared cups of coffee in the early morning sunlight on the lockhouse porch, watching through squinted eyes as clustered seagulls dove for breakfast among a shad school near the middle of the river where the last of the morning mist lingered. The Susquehanna lay dozing, its undulating surface like the shallow breathing of a great animal, offering no color of its own, only the reflection of a perfect sky decorated with bright overlapping sun rings where seagulls pierced the mirror. Water droplets from the captured fish repeated the sun behind them in miniature, sparkling yellow flashes falling back to the river as the seagulls swooped away. Will agreed that prices for new mules would be far better among the farms just outside of Havre de Grace than dealing with the canal company. There was only so much Will could do even as the supervisor. It would not help his family for him to jeopardize his position. He needed to turn a profit from the barges even more than Ben, and needed it far more desperately than he would admit.

After registering his co-ownership in the *Ugly Boat* and the *Turtle* at the courthouse, Ben rented a horse from the livery stable in town and visited several farms by the time he had agreed to purchase his fourth mule. His precious seaman's pay was all but gone with having to buy mules twice during his first year as a canaller. He returned his horse in the early evening, and then continued up St. John Street to the Harford Hotel. The small restaurant off the front lobby was still open, and he stepped in only because the lights were bright and the sound of clinking glasses and conversation helped dilute the disappointments snaking through in his thoughts. He stopped a few steps into the room and decided he would rather go next door to the tavern. He needed a whiskey more than bright lights.

He saw few faces in the tavern that he recognized, but the bartender was quick to serve him in a good glass on a well-cleaned bar top. He propped his foot on the large wooden rail set out ankle high at the front of the bar, and leaned over his drink. He took the whiskey in a single gulp and motioned for the bartender to pour another. Buying small glasses of whiskey in a tavern was an extravagance, he knew, but he would allow himself this treat. It burned his throat and the fumes of it irritated his lungs. When the shot glass was refilled he asked for water, and traded sips between the two glasses until they were both empty again.

Another man stepped to the bar next to him. Another black wool coat in a sea of black wool. It was the only proper color for public. He could imagine his mother's voice saying the words. The man ordered a whiskey and then bumped into Ben as he threw it back. Ben inched away giving the drinker room, as the man slapped the counter top and ordered another. Again the head tilted back and again the man bumped into Ben's shoulder. From the corner of his eye, Ben could tell the man was looking directly at him, but he did not want the bother of a conversation with an unsteady drunk. Another flick of the wrist from the man next to him and the bartender refilled whiskey and water for both men.

Shit. The sot is buying me a drink. I don't want to fool with this.

The intrusive drinker slid one of the whiskey glasses in front of Ben, and picked the other up and tossed it down his throat as he had with the previous two. And as he had with the previous two he bumped soundly into Ben, although he had to take almost a full step to make up the space between them. Ben's remaining patience evaporated, yielding to his smoldering temper. He slammed his hands against the hard surface of the bar and spun around to face the drunk. The collection of men at the bar fell instantly silent. Some, more wary than others, quickly eyed Ben and the stranger, then looked for a clear path to the door.

Ben clenched his hands, bringing his right hand up between them. "Look you..."

But before he could raise a finger to point in the man's face, the drunk plopped his hands heavily on Pulaski's shoulders, and began laughing into his face.

"Goddamnit!" Ben sputtered.

The man ignored the threat of instant bodily harm and enveloped Ben in a bear hug and began jumping up and down with him.

"Pulaski! Pulaski! Pulaski!"

The man yelled into his ear, spraying water and whiskey on the side of his face. Ben shoved back to break the grip of this drunk who knew him by name and looked into a big round face, red from the whiskey and mirth, and framed in a thick shaggy beard. The man palmed meaty hands against Ben's cheeks, pressing his mouth into a pucker, and said again

"Pulaski! Pulaski! Pulaski!"

Ben stared into the face of a madman, and then at last roared his recognition of the stranger.

"Renowitz!!"

The old shipmates traded bear hugs and severe back thumpings and called out each other's names, to the enjoyment of the others. Relief and laughs rippled down the bar as loud conversations refilled the air, patrons returned to their drinks, and the bartender raced along the line refilling shot glasses.

Ben held his friend out at arm's length and looked into his beard-covered face.

"What are you doing here?"

"Things got too damned quiet in Philadelphia. I've leased a barge from the Chesapeake and Delaware and I'm gonna be taking her to Wrightsville for their black gold. Philadelphia's sucking up more coal than anyone can bring to'em. Bargemen are selling coal up there at half the price of railroad-delivered, and making twice the profit!"

Others drifted in and out of the tavern as the two friends tried to catch up with their lives and loves and sorrows, until finally there was only Ben and Anthony and the bartender.

The bartender began putting out the lamps, yawning as he moved toward the last one.

"Time t'go home, gen'lmen."

They each bought a jug and walked precariously down to the docks to sit on unattended crates, and watch the moon settle over the horizon to go fetch the sun. They were still talking and making plans when the sky over Perry Point began showing an edge of coming blue. Two hours later they burst into the front room of the Pulaski cabin, laughing and trying to hold each other up after too much liquor and too little sleep.

To her surprise and mixed anxiety, Sonja was scooped up into only a slightly more gentle bear hug than Ben had received, as Ben introduced his best friends in the world to each other.

Coffee and breakfast was an ordeal of reaching arms and spilled coffee cups passed overhead as the kitchen and front room swelled to accommodate Ben and Anthony, and Simon, and Mickey, and Aaron, and Isaac, and a stray dog Sonja had not seen before, but that Isaac kept feeding. Sonja returned with her own coffee, munching a biscuit, standing behind Ben, resting her elbow on his shoulder, then quickly removing it and straightening her back when he looked up.

Ben and Anthony talked until they finally fell asleep on the braided rug in the front room, while the others went about their more productive chores. Sonja watched the stray dog nestle down against Anthony and doze off with them, and then pointed her finger down at the sleeping visitor.

168

Pulaski's Canal

"We'll have no more of your adventures, Anthony Renowitz. I'll be damned if I will let you destroy my life again. Why the Hell did you come back?"

She kicked him with the toe of her shoe, and he raised his head to look bleary-eyed in her direction, frowning through his whiskey sleep.

"Not another adventure, Anthony. Do you hear me?"

He mumbled thick tongued.

"No,..not."

She kicked his side again, this time harder. And he raised his head again, looking at her in sleepy confusion.

"I mean it, Anthony. You swear to God you are not going to take him off somewhere again? I won't stand for it. I won't."

Anthony waved his hand and covered his eyes against the daylight and the pounding at his temples.

"No... Promise... not going anywhere but here... barges... just barges."

He laid his head back down on the rug and resumed snoring.

She kicked him again and then turned away.

It was late in the morning when Ben and Anthony emerged from the front room of the cabin to the fresh air of the porch, to wash up at the outside pump. Neither man could tolerate the idea of food at the moment and eagerly sought the cooling water pouring over their aching heads. Hearing the familiar chatter between Ben and Anthony from his room in the barn Simon came out shaking his head in amazement.

"Renowitz! What th'hell are you doing here?" The two ex-shipmates exchanged hugs and backslaps. "I figured you'd need help watching over this helpless pilgrim, Simon."

Anthony looked back at Ben and laughed. Ben wagged a crooked finger at Anthony. "I don't recall you helping last night. What I recall is helping you keep on your feet during the walk home."

Simon's smile faded and his eyes narrowed on Anthony. "How'd you know I'd be here Renowitz?"

Anthony gave Simon a quick appraisal noting the sudden change in demeanor. "Didn't. Just something to say to keep you two on your toes. What're you suspicious about, Simon?"

"Not 'spicious, jus' curious."

"Now I know you're suspicious. He's talkin' low, Ben. Always did that when he was hiding his thoughts. He's better educated than both of us put together!"

"Yeah, but you got the papers, Anthony..." Ben looked away and Anthony quickly changed the subject. "Got my own barge, Simon. Brought it all the way down from Philadelphia, well, had it brought. Pulled by steam tug that was on its way here anyway to pick up coal barges from your Canal Company."

Simon watched Ben, but spoke to Anthony, "I can't believe it's any better than the *Brzydka Łódź* "

"Actually, it's a piece of shit, but it was free and the owner will let my repairs to it count as rent for now. *Brzydka Łódź* ? Is that a name or a disease?"

"It's Polish, Renowitz. Don't you know your own language?"

"Simon, I'm as Polish as you are... what was it? Madingo?"

"Mandinka."

"My grandfather was from Poland. My Father grew up in Philadelphia. I'm from Philadelphia. My only language is United States American. And I have no idea what *Brzydka Łódź* means."

"Means '*Ugly Boat*'" Ben responded, "And it lives up to that name wonderfully. C'mon Simon, let's show this United States Philadelphia American to the *Ugly Boat*."

They stepped down between the two oaks and Ben gave a short wave of his arm towards the barges sitting in the canal. Anthony stared hard at the cabins and shook his head.

"Whoever built the things did a bad job on your cabin."

He pointed at the *Turtle*.

"That rook looks like a kid built it. There's a lot of tar to be seen even from up here."

Simon put his fists to his hips and leaned toward Anthony. "It was smashed all to hell in a flash flood, and was a hard job to repair, but it doesn't leak! Like to see you do better..."

Anthony raised an eyebrow to Simon. "So what are you doing down here, Simon?"

There was a small pause before his answer. "Just helping Ben." Simon offered a well-practiced vacant smile. Ben sighed to himself, knowing that Simon would be the one to discuss his own affairs in his own time. *What could he say?* He thought. *I killed a man?* The trio walked down the gentle sloping front yard to Isaac's two-plank wharf and onto the *Ugly Boat*.

Ben was proud to show the odd shaped hull that held placements for mast, sprit and outboards. "We keep the mast and sailing rigging here at the farm when we go upstream to Wrightsville. Then we pick it all up on our way back down to the basin. We pole it through the outlet lock, then rig the mast in the shallows just outside. From there, it's a sail boat," Ben explained.

"We had so much trouble getting up the Patapsco to Baltimore that first time. Had it rigged and loaded wrong for the weather and current. We had to run down bay to Annapolis instead. That turned out real good for us, though. Met some merchants who want what we carry and have cargo we can fill our holds with for the return trip."

Simon added, "We can't go empty. If we don't settle this hull a little lower in the water it won't sail worth a damned!"

Ben nodded in agreement. "We'd have to take on rocks for ballast if we didn't have cargo. Most barges get towed to Baltimore or Philadelphia full of coal, then come back up empty. We take cargo under our own power in both directions. That saves the tow fee and adds the profit of the return cargo."

Anthony smiled at the efficiency of Ben's trips. "What kind of cargo do you bring up from Annapolis?"

Simon answered, "Whatever they have that we think will sell in Havre de Grace, or on up in Wrightsville."

Ben nodded to Simon and added, "Sometimes it's household things, sometimes smoked meats, sometimes its cotton bales ~ anything but rocks. One trip we picked up a load of English dishes. I could not have afforded to buy a cargo of that, but the merchant fellow trusted me and we took it on consignment. I intended to take it all to another fellow I met in Wrightsville, but I mentioned my load in Havre de Grace and sold almost half of it right there in the Canal Basin. Then sold a set to almost every lockhouse between Havre de Grace and Wrightsville. Barely had a third of the cargo when we hit Wrightsville, and sold every bit of it to the first store I went."

Simon grinned broadly, raising his eyebrows, and tilted his head at Ben. "Now tell Anthony who DIDN'T get a new set of dishes."

Ben frowned back at Simon. "I already said I sold it all in Wrightsville."

Simon continued his grin, egging Ben on. "Yeah, and you sold a set to Bartlett at lock 9, just about two hundred yards from here. But you didn't..."

"Simon, don't you bring that up again..."

"You forgot to set aside a set of dishes for the wife of the barge captain..."

"Hell, Simon, I didn't mean to ... "

Simon chuckled and looked at Anthony. "Almost everyone around these parts got a set of the English dishes Ben brought up from Annapolis, except ..."

"Except Sonja," finished Ben, and resisted the urge to look back towards the house to see if Sonja was listening.

Anthony laughed. "I'll bet that caused you trouble."

"Came to sleep with us in the bunk room. Said he got tired of hearing about it up in the house."

Anthony and Simon laughed together at Ben's expense as he slowly shook his head and rolled his eyes.

"I'll never hear the end of that."

Ben thumbed in the direction of the house.

"And don't you dare bring it up to her again."

"Now, what we do on every trip up," Simon informed Anthony, "is let Sonja have first pick of anything she wants that we're carrying, even if it's just smoked fish or baled cotton."

Anthony slipped his hands into his pockets and

walked around the deck past the cargo holds. He stopped on the small patch of deck near the blunted bow where the resting mule usually mangered under a canvas sun cover. The running grain in the oak planking was crossed and pitted from scores of mule shoe scrapes.

"Not much of a bow, Ben, but plenty of cargo space in the holds and a decent size cabin. Not as big a cabin as on my barge, but fair size."

"We lost a few feet up there when I decided to turn this thing into a sailing scow as well as a barge. We take about half-ton less of coal than a regular barge, but pushing the *Turtle* ahead of us more than makes up for it."

Anthony swept his felt hat from his head in mock return salute.

"Now, what about mules?"

"You'll probably need'em, Anthony," Simon responded.

"Hurts like hell to pull these things yourself."

Anthony grinned.

"Where would be the best place to pick up a couple good mules."

Ben rubbed his chin whiskers and looked to Simon for his thoughts on the subject.

"Well, I just bought what was available on the farms west of Havre de Grace. Had to replace the ones I lost in the flood. The Canal Company barn has the biggest selection, but you'd get a much better price up the hill on into Webster or farther north. They've got a few farms there that keep more than they need..."

"Or over in Darlington," Simon continued.

"Yeah," Ben said, "there's a bunch of Friends in Darlington that raise'm to work hard, but treat'em well. They tend to be more even-tempered than the ones you'd get from the Company."

"Well then" Anthony said "show me the way to Darlington."

Pulaski's Canal

Ben clapped a hand on Anthony's shoulder. "We can do better than that, old friend. We leave for Wrightsville this morning with a load of cotton, and will go within a mile or two of Darlington."

Simon wagged a warning finger at Anthony. "And don't let'em sell you any double tree rigs either. We walk'em two in line, sometimes three, but you need to keep them in line. Side by side and they get ornery with each other and don't half pull."

With that they set to the remaining preparations for the trip up the canal to Wrightsville. Ben and Simon took turns looking up the towpath for sight of Mickey, but he did not return. Ben was sure he had met up with some old friends at one of the taverns in town. Mickey could take care of himself, but he had a real problem staying away from whiskey. They would have to pick him up on the way back.

Simon brought four mules around from the barn down the front slope and then up the plank walkway onto the barge. Ben and Isaac poled the barge across the canal to the towpath, where Simon and Isaac lead two of the mules down the plankway set onto the bank. The remaining two mules were left tethered under the canvas awning, munching on hay and flicking their tails with a frisky jerk, obviously enjoying themselves while watching the other two set to work. The two harnessed mules effortlessly pulled the barge up the wider canal below Lock 9, where the *Turtle* had spent the last two days tied out of the way on the western side of the canal. John Bartlett opened the mid lock gate and Ben guided the barge into the far end of the full-length lock. Simon and Isaac pulled the bow rope for *Turtle* and bumped it easily into the lock behind *Ugly Boat*, and John closed the upper gate behind it. Ben tied the *Turtle*'s towrope to the sternpost of *Ugly Boat* while the lock filled with water leveling both boats with the upstream canal.

Anthony watched closely as the practiced crew led the tandem barges out of the opened lock and into the upstream flow of the canal. He turned to look back at Ben standing loosely against the tiller bar, lighting his pipe, and casually tossing his hand in a friendly wave to Anthony. Ben followed his wave with a puff of gray smoke and a smile Anthony had known for years. He also knew that sooner or later he would have to explain to Ben what he was really doing, but not yet. There was still much to do. Somehow it seemed right to protect Ben by keeping the truth from him a while longer.

Will Boyd laid the reins gently against the neck of his horse. His weekly ride the length of the canal to The Line was complete, but he decided to steer the horse in a lazy loop around the far edge of the canal basin. The basin was as much his responsibility to manage as the canal itself. It had been an easy ride this afternoon and the horse was in no way winded. The gelding could wander a few more minutes before his feed and rub down. He continued around to the north end of the basin, past the warehouse farthest from the lockhouse.

There is still room for two, maybe three more buildings. River ice only yards away for the fetching during the winter. An icehouse tucked in there at the end would fetch a nice income in the warm days of summer, so close to the rail, shipping and canal business.

He pulled the horse to the edge of the basin, looking at the thick mud below the water's surface, and then at the steep rise up the hill behind. Half of the ice house could be set back within an earthen pit, helping to protect huge straw covered blocks of river ice well into June, or July, or maybe even August. Prices would triple then.

He sat there leaning on the pummel of his saddle picturing the building that could be there, letting his horse nibble at the wild grasses growing at the water's edge. The horse nosed into a clump of tall grass, scaring up a dozing muskrat who charged from the weeds to escape the horse. The quick dash of the muskrat startled the horse causing him to jerk back in reflex, twisting to face the dark form skittering over the

176

grass away from the basin, raising on its hind legs and kicking at it with his front hooves.

Even as William realized the horse was going to throw him, he was already in the air arcing toward the muddy basin water. His thoughts filled with curses for the horse that was about to ruin his new suit and quite likely the new hat as well. He knew the water was shallow and the mud was soft, and was angry over the bother he would now have to endure to clean his clothes and boots and hat. Even as he splashed into the water there was no fear. His dream had showed him in the river.

There was nothing to fear from two feet of water in the Canal basin. His fast racing thoughts were still thinking that, when his head struck the stump. Even then it was only an injury to add to the bother of the mud. But his head stayed perched against the rugged top of the stump left behind by the ice gorge of '39, and his body continued down passed the top of the stump, bending his neck farther and farther until it snapped.

His body was already numb to his mind when it fell flat, splashing into the shallow water, driving away the herons wading nearby and pulling his head off the stump into the water. He watched air rush from his nose and mouth, no longer able to command the muscles of his chest or throat. The water splashed back and forth across the surface six inches above his face. Unable to close his eyes, he could see the sky through the silting water and the heron that flew over as his body settled motionless into the mud. In the long moments while he was drowning, he remembered that the basin was always busy with crabs.

<hr/>

Sonja looked at the black bunting tied neatly on the swing bridge center post as well as the on the front door to the lockhouse. The wind had risen and little whitecaps formed on the waves out in the bay, and the black bunting streamed out in the breeze. No one was on the front porch, nor was anyone out in the yard around the house.

"They must have already left for the church. I hope we're not late!"

As they rounded the corner at the rear of the house they could see several wagons and surreys, and several men standing together smoking cigars. Sonja was relieved that they had not yet left, and wished she had tried the front door before coming around. She decided to go in through the winter kitchen with Margaret Bartlett close in tow.

Ben followed the ladies inside to pay his respects, while the rest of their group stayed outside. The kitchen was located behind the superintendent's office, so a quick turn to the left brought them through the dining room and into the living room of the house. Alice Boyd sat in the center of a large sofa against the north wall, surrounded by other ladies of the town giving solace to her by their presence. The wigs and coiffeurs nodded and bobbed to hushed small talk around her, but Alice stared blankly straight ahead. The dark under her eyes was more than the days without sleep since William's death. Her eyes held the torment of grief raging silently in her soul, discernable to anyone who had suffered such a loss, and incomprehensible to anyone who had not. Sonja stepped bravely into her line of sight to gain her attention and spoke quietly to Alice. There was a murmured exchange and their gloved hands met and lingered while the voices and their eyes seemed to carry on two separate pieces of the same chorus.

Ben glanced around the room seeing faces he knew, to whom he nodded. Standing aside a large high-backed chair at the east window, a smiling face nodded a second time to Ben. Herbert Binterfield stood next to his seated wife proffering a smile completely out of place for the moment and the history between the two men. As Ben fully noticed Binterfield, Herbert tapped Lydia's shoulder and pointed with his coffee cup toward Ben. Ben turned his attention toward Lydia who appeared to be staring intently out of the window across the river, not responding to the gestures of her husband. Sonja joined

Ben and the two withdrew to the edge of the room. John and Margaret made their condolences to Alice and joined the Pulaski's near the doorway to the kitchen. John leaned close to Ben keeping his attention on Binterfield and whispered out of the side of his mouth.

"What's that weasel up to?"

Ben arched his eyebrows and shrugged his shoulders.

"Don't know. Must'a run over a kitten or a puppy on the way here, or something."

Sonja gave the two men a reproachful look, but before she could say anything, most of the people within the room began to move toward the front door, and out the other side of the living room through the superintendent's office. They had all but missed the casket in the corner of the room, until the men raised it to take it out outside. It had been kept closed, draped with flowers. William had lain for most of the day in the water after he was thrown from his horse.

Ben shook his head slowly at the casket.

The crabs would not have left a body in any condition for a viewing.

Sonja shuddered at the picture forming in her mind. She had known Alice since before the flood of '39, but she knew that the ladies near her now were the ones best able to support Alice now. The casket was loaded into the hearse that had been brought around to the front of the lockhouse. The hearse was followed by the surreys. Alice was helped into the first. The Binterfield's were seated into the second. Herbert Binterfield caught Sonja's attention and motioned her to join them. She pretended not to see him. His smile faded into a scowl and he turned his attention to the driver, poking him in the back with his cane with a rebuke for falling behind.

Sonja stayed with her family and the crew of the *Ugly Boat*. The Pulaski's and the Bartletts began their walk toward the church, arriving long after the casket had been taken inside and all the wagons unloaded of their passengers. William Boyd had made many friends, who became part of a small throng accompanying the Pulaski's into the simple Methodist church attended by the Boyd's, and where William had become an elder. As Ben side-stepped along a rear pew with his wife and friends, he saw Binterfield turn almost completely around in his second row seat to look directly at Ben. Once again offering an unsettling cold-eye smile.

John Bartlett gently elbowed Ben's side.

"What in the world is up with him, Ben?"

"Can't be anything good for anybody but him."

Sonja "shushed" the men and was accompanied by a small scowl from Margaret. An hour later the service ended, and church emptied from the front back out into the street for the last part of the journey to the cemetery. Binterfield bestowed another animated nod and gesture upon the Pulaski's as he passed. Ben's curiosity was rising, as he and Sonja traded looks and small shrugs.

"Ashes to ashes, dust to dust; the Lord giveth and the Lord taketh away."

The minister informed the mourners, and followed that with a benediction for both the lost and the living. Alice could barely stand. The husbands of the ladies who had stayed at her side stepped in to assist her to the waiting carriage. Ben recognized the height and bulk of Wallace Harper, making Alice appear almost childlike beside him. LuAnn came by Sonja to trade a few words and quick hugs and was off with her husband. Sonja turned to Ben with tears in her eyes.

"That LuAnn is a saint. She has invited Alice to stay with her tonight. Alice will really need that..." She did not finish her sentence, but abruptly started another. "We should have a headstone for Alisha."

Ben put his arm around her, not knowing anything else to do.

Margaret appeared next to Sonja and began to walk with her out of the cemetery, leaving Ben standing where he was. A hand slipped onto his shoulders; a light touch, like a woman. He turned and faced Binterfield, grinning like a medicine oil salesman.

"Benjamin, we need to talk and come to terms like gentlemen."

Ben scowled.

"I don't think we have anything to talk about, Binterfield."

The smile remained.

"But Ben, we have so much more to talk about now."

Binterfield grasped Ben's wrist and pulled his hand into a handshake of his own making,

"Why, Ben, we're partner's now! I own half of the *Ugly Boat*!"

15

It was the only way he could contain his anger. Ben wrapped himself in silence on their way back from Will Boyd's funeral and kept his thoughts to himself the rest of the afternoon. He shared few words with anyone through dinner.

Isaac and Aaron shared a bed to allow Anthony a place to sleep for the night. Mickey and Simon had withdrawn to their room in the barn. Sonja placed the last dish to dry on the cloth-covered shelf above the washbowl, and Ben entered the latest figures in his business ledger. Sonja had printed the various categories and he could easily recognize them as he recorded the receipts and expenses of the trip. Sonja pumped a small cup full of fresh water into her cup and sat down beside Ben at the kitchen table.

"Ben..."

He finished his last entry and looked up into her face.

"Ben, it's time the boys went back to school. They've missed three years now. I kept them up as best I could with the books that Wallace and LuAnn loaned us."

Ben sighed.

"I know. I don't want them to have the trouble I've had. But,.. it's been so great to have them around me again. I feel like I just got back yesterday."

"It's time, Ben. We're really settled again here. They need to go back to school, so they can be settled too. And they need to learn more than you or I can teach them."

Ben nodded without speaking. He did not believe Sonja would feel settled if she knew that Binterfield was already trying to take the *Ugly Boat.*

"Well, we have what we need for a good business. I've got Mickey and Simon to help me with the barges and the mules. Since our first trip to Annapolis with both barges, I've been able to pay them real wages."

"There's talk about having a school here in Lapidum, Ben. Maybe even a post office. The canal took part of old man Walker's front yard, but it's brought so much here. Margaret is still sending her daughter, Susan, to Havre de Grace for school. It's only a four-mile walk to the basin, then a half mile more to the school. Margaret would really like it if Susan had some strong young men to accompany her to and from school. She worries about so many new faces coming and going on the canal. They would be doing something good for themselves and for another."

Ben lost himself in thought as his eyes fixed on the bright yellow light blinking through the cracks in the iron stove in the kitchen. He stared into the slices of firelight.

"I so enjoyed those days on my father's schooner, and I knew he was happy to have me along. I would not want to have missed those times with him. I also know the agony a grown man suffers when others have to read things to him. There is a lot of good honest work where a man doesn't need to read to do well and to take care of his family, but those days are fading. I don't want our boys to have to face that."

He hammered his ledger with his finger tips.

"These things are everywhere. And they can hide lies as well as hold figures. The men who hold the ledgers will keep us all slaves as long as they can keep us from reading what they have written there. And I don't want my sons...our sons, to be at the mercy of those bastards in figuring them out."

He reached his hand to hers, but she withdrew it to take up her cup. Ben exhaled heavily.

"You're right. It's time."

Sonja patted his forearm.

"We'll tell them in the morning then?"

Ben and Sonja stood, Sonja putting her cup in the bowl, Ben returning his ledger to the shelf in the front room.

"One more trip to Annapolis. They love that most of all."

Ben stood in front of Sonja and placed his hands gently on her shoulders to pull her closer. A long curl of her golden hair had slipped out of its bun and dropped to her shoulder. The color and shine had come back to her hair since that first day back. Ben delicately guided the curls behind her ear, feeling the smoothness of her cheek with the side of his finger. She looked into his eyes, but would not linger and looked away, scanning the kitchen for one last chore to end the day. As she took a cloth to clean the counter she spoke to him over her shoulder.

"One more trip, if the weather is right. Then they stay home and go to school. It's almost too late if they delay any longer."

"Alright, Sonja."

Sonja turned to him and smiled a small and fleeting smile, then looked down and stepped around him to go to the bedroom. There was still a small space between them, but it might as well be a mile when they were alone. It was always there, and the more Ben pushed into that space, the stronger it pushed him away, and they did not speak of it.

Ben went to the front room and retrieved his pipe, filled it with tobacco, took a small kindling light from the stove, and stepped onto the porch to light it. Sonja had always disapproved of the smell of burned tobacco on her curtains, but he had long ago accepted her oddity on that. He watched the moon rise into the treetops on the eastern shore of the Susquehanna. The near shore was covered in silver lace as the moonlight came through the thinning trees and the drifting swells on the river gently rose and fell like great sleeping fish. The far side was draped in blackness, an owl hooted to its neighbor and a disgruntled crow flapped into the air from its roost. Ben listened as Anthony's snore reached the iron furnace roar he had known aboard their old ship. He heard Isaac's muffled voice from the back room.

"I did not fart!"

He could not make out the muffled words spoken by Aaron, but recognized his voice from within the cabin. Ben finished his pipe and walked slowly to the wood pile next to the barn. The full moon had cleared the tree tops and the jumbled crevices running down the bark in the old oak trees were silver and black in the moonlight. The evening breeze rolled up the river and over the canal, bringing with it the scent of fish and the musty smell of the canal at slow water. He picked up the axe leaning against the barn and twirled its head in the moonlight, the sharp beveled cutting edge flashing as it spun.

"God damn that Binterfield."

He slammed the axe head into the sawed log sitting on the chopping block, sending the split pieces flipping through the air and landing heavily onto the damp leaves covering the ground ten feet away. He needed both hands to pick up the next piece from the woodpile and set it on the block. He grunted when he brought down a wide swing of the axe onto the log and sent its pieces out to join the others. The scar along his back pulled back against his skin as he swung the ax, and he cursed the scar and the man who had given it to him, and sent more pieces of split wood to join the others among the leaves.

"You gonna do that all night?"

Ben looked up through the sweat dripping from his forehead, his eyes stinging from the salt.

"Just chopping some wood, Simon."

"UnHuh. That next piece named 'god-damned Binterfield', too?"

"Just go on back to sleep, Simon."

"Can't. Not with some night demon chopping wood

about three feet from my head on the other side of that wall."

Ben twisted his shoulders to loosen the muscles, then rubbed a hand over his scar, the toughened tissue a long wrinkle under his shirt.

"She know about that, Ben? How it happened?"

"Not yet."

"What does she know?"

"Only what she already knew before I came back. That seems to be enough."

Ben slammed the axe down into the next piece of wood, then looked over to the corner of the barn, but Simon was gone. He let the handle slide down, resting the axe head on the ground and leaned the handle gently against the chopping block, then went inside the cabin.

He washed off in the kitchen and lay down on top of the blanket next to Sonja. Pulling the old quilt over him he stared at the darkened ceiling until his eyelids finally drew the day to an end and he slept.

At dawn Ben met Aaron and Isaac on the front porch. They were both excited and ready for the sail down the Chesapeake Bay to Annapolis. The mast, boom and spar were retrieved from their rack near the edge of the canal, and the canvas brought around from the barn. The extra bales of feed hay were tossed from the deck of the barges and the canvas awnings that served as a roof for the off-duty mules were struck and tossed onto the ground near the hay.

"Stack that hay and cover it with the canvas. No sense letting it go bad in the rain while we're gone."

The barges were too full of coal to pole across to the other side of the canal, so Mickey had taken the single team of three down to the crossover bridge near the lock, and had them waiting on the tow path.

Simon no longer joined Ben on his trips to Annapolis. Getting closer to Southern Maryland would be an unhealthy thing for Simon to do. Still, Ben relied on his friend and was happy to have his help for as long as Simon wished to stay, even though he knew there were parts of his friend's life he could not share and Simon had to have his own life. He had known Simon for over ten years, but there were many moments when he realized he knew him so little.

"Pa!" Aaron called a second time. "I said we're ready."

Looking about him, Ben realized he had been lost in his thoughts while Mickey and the boys had finished preparations, and he still stood on the planks next to the ugly boat. Ben shook his head at himself and smiled to Mickey, throwing his hand toward the southern canal as he stepped back to the tiller handle. Mickey kissed the air in front of the mule team, moving them to take up the slack on the towrope and starting them on their short jaunt to the canal basin. Simon walked along beside Mickey talking easily to the Irishman as the barge began to draw away from the planks. Simon would return the team to the Pulaski's barn, and avoid the boarding fee the company would charge to keep them in the company's basin barn. In three days, the Ugly Boat would return to Havre de Grace, and Simon would be waiting for them with the mules.

Ben stood at the stern with his hands on his hips watching the little crew. Three days to Wrightsville and back, and then three days to Annapolis and back.

If I time my trips right, I will be at home Wednesday evenings and then all day Sundays. Many men were gone much more than that. Already been gone too much. Missed too much.

Now his boys would be going to school and he would only catch glimpses of them as he went back and forth between Annapolis and Wrightsville.

"Can't be helped."

"What, Pa?" Isaac asked.

"Nothin', Son. Just talking to myself."

He looked at Isaac's half smiling face, and then at Aaron hopping lightly from the bow of the *Ugly Boat* to the stern of the *Turtle*.

I will tell them tomorrow.

"Hey!" Anthony yelled running down the slope. "Wait for me!"

Anthony scooted across the front yard with the brim of his hat in his teeth, and a steaming cup of coffee in each hand. He made the distance from the edge of the dock planking to the deck of the barge with a stretched step, holding the cups of coffee high before him as priceless trophies. Handing one to Ben and diving quickly into his, he surveyed the boats squinting through the steam rising at the rim of his tin cup.

"Beautiful day, Benjamin! Can't wait to settle the mules to their rig and start these trips in my own boat!"

"Don't blame you a bit, Anthony."

Ben pushed the tiller slightly bringing the barges to the center of the canal. The water was as smooth as glass this morning. The blue of the sky and the white of the clouds were painted perfectly on the surface. Even the seagulls had their double in the canal water surface. Ben looked back at his farm, and the smoke drifting up out of the chimney. Knew Sonja was there. Could imagine in the kitchen, and wished it was the kitchen at the end of Pearl Lane, where she always seemed to be happy. He looked back at the double lines slowly drifting outward behind the barge in a gentle wake, and then at the growing distance between the stern of the barge and the little wharf Isaac had built along the canal at the edge of their property. He looked back at Anthony, grinned broadly and said,

"So, ya can't wait to get your mules in a rig can you?"

"No! I have been looking forward to this for days! I still need to hire a crewman, but that shouldn't be difficult with all the men I've seen around this canal and the docks in town."

Ben nodded and continued to grin.

"Might have a little trouble getting the mules into

their rig though this morning, Anthony."

Anthony frowned, trying to remember what he may have overlooked.

"No. I am sure I have it all. I brought good stout trees with me. My cabin is full of all the supplies I could think of. No, Ben I'm sure I'm ready to pull the barge to Wrightsville, as soon as I have found a hand. Surely there cannot be a man within a hundred miles that doesn't know how to put a mule or a horse into its rig."

Ben pinched his face into a studied frown.

"Yeah, I guess that's for sure... except you've gotta have the mules with you."

Anthony peeked at Ben's face with his eyebrows raised, innocent and totally unaware of the point.

"We're going to sail this morning, Anthony, just as soon as we can pole through the outlet lock from the basin and out into the Susquehanna Flats."

Anthony's face was still a study in childlike wonderment, trying to connect Ben's comments with his mules.

"Anthony, your mules are still in the barn at my farm. We never intended to take them down to the basin this morning, because you never said you intended to use them today."

Anthony looked up toward the *Turtle*, where the canvas awning and bales of hay had been the day before, then back down the canal toward the Pulaski farm, up ahead along the thin ribbon of manmade towpath that ran into the river, arrow straight for the lockhouse gate three miles south, and then again into Ben's face.

"I thought..."

"No, ya didn't. Ya figured, but ya didn't think. You've still got a few things to do and learn before you're ready to hook up those mules you bought and drag that mildewed hulk to Wrightsville."

Ben still grinned at his old friend, but knew he would be too eager to start something new.

A scowl began to settle onto Anthony's face, replacing his cheery smile.

"So, you just let me hop aboard until I was too far to hop back off, to tell me all this. Isn't that so, Ben Pulaski?"

Ben's grin skewed lopsided.

"Yeah, I reckon."

Anthony finished his coffee and tossed the remaining liquid and grounds over the side.

"Guess I need to get off at the outlet lock."

Ben slapped his hand on Anthony's back.

"Simon will be taking our mule team back to the farm while we go on to Annapolis. I was thinking that you'd get a lot of help by asking Simon. I don't think he'd mind showing you a few things about the canal, maybe have your mules pull you up to Deer Creek and turn around at the flint mill and then back to the farm. It would give you a chance to get the feel of that ol' tub of yours in this canal. I can't speak for Simon, you and I never did, but I'm certain he'd help you."

As the mule team pulled the barges into the outlet lock in front of the Lockhouse at the canal basin, Anthony stepped off the barge onto the granite wall of the lock and onto the grass along the edge of the towpath. Simon held the mule team just beyond the lock near the end of the towpath, overlooking the river mouth and the Bay beyond. He slipped the braided loop of the towrope out of the harness hitch and watched it snake back to the *Turtle* where Isaac was coiling it down at the snubbed bow. The swing bridge was now parallel to the lock, allowing Ben, Mickey and Aaron to raise the mast and begin the process of securing it with taught lines in four directions, bracing it to become the center of sail power for both barges. Lines were looped and hitched tightly, tied at stern bow, starboard and port. The wooden loops of the main sail ran up the mast a few feet to make way for the boom attachment.

All hands pushed to move both barges out of the

lock into the northern edges of the Flats. This was a delicate time for the pair of boats. The *Ugly Boat* had to sprout sails and go from ugly duckling to swan before the wind caught her unready. The *Turtle* would go out first as it had traveled on the canal, but would have to be brought behind the *Ugly Boat* to take its lesser station to the stern when Ben's barge would become a sailing scow.

Each time through the evolution was a little easier for the crew. Each time there were fewer surprises and more preparations to make way. The jib sail ran along the line from the bowsprit to a block high on the mast. The mainsail rose along the mast and spread itself in a gentle curving triangle between its ends at the top of the mast and the tip of the boom swinging just over the tiller. There were a hundred things that could go wrong and dozens of steps yet to be taken, but slowly the outboards went down into the water on each side and were chained to the deck braces to keep them from swinging up and away from the water once in motion. The bow of the *Turtle* drifted slowly beyond the stern of the *Ugly Boat* searching for the reach of the towrope that earlier had been tied to the mule team. Now it was tied to the sternpost of the *Ugly Boat*.

The wind was mild and from the west today, slowly pushing the *Ugly Boat* out toward the channel, filling both sails. Ben swung the boom out, spilling the wind from the mainsail and releasing the pressure until everything was ready for the full push of the wind. The *Ugly Boat* began to take up the slack in the towrope to the *Turtle* until a subtle bump ran through the scow signaling Ben to let the wind take them. A nod from Ben to Mickey and then to Aaron were the only orders necessary as the boom was brought inward and the flapping tail of the jib brought tautly against the cleat at the starboard bow. The canvas stored in the Pulaski barn since its last trip to Annapolis shed its wrinkles as the wind smoothed its billowing surface. The mast leaned toward Perry Point across the Flats and Isaac ran the bright red wind pennant to the very tip of the mast where it gave a single loud snap, like a whip over a buggy team. The hull leaned into the water and the starboard outboard keel did its work to push back against the wind. In the manner of all sailing ships, the *Ugly Boat* made use of the opposing forces of wind and keel as she swam forward toward the center of the channel.

The wind pushed harder against the mainsail and the shoulder of the *Ugly Boat's* blunt bow took her first wave as they left the protection of the little point and anchored boats outside the Canal Basin. The wind was fresh and clean and the aroma of fish and tar blew across the decks chasing away the smell of damp coal and wet mules. The *Turtle* took its first wave and bucked only slightly against the towrope but settled into her rightful place astern. Men and boys shared the same excited grin, watching the Lockhouse and the groups of men near it dwindle in the distance. They sailed beyond the Susquehanna Flats toward Turkey Point, where the twin sister of the Concord Point Light house stood along their first bearing toward Annapolis.

Ben looked back toward Havre de Grace. Somewhere back there he knew Binterfield was doing everything he could to cause him trouble, but for now, for these next three days with his sons he would try to forget about Binterfield's connivances.

Simon and Anthony watched the sailing barge slip away from the shore, as did a few of the canal workers and warehouse laborers catching their breath from their work and watching this thing Ben Pulaski called the *Ugly Boat*. She was never ugly at this moment.

Across the canal bridge Simon could see the quick stepping Sheriff, his belly bobbing in his brisk walk, looking out upon the bay while one of his deputies pointed excitedly toward the *Ugly Boat*. Neither man wished to draw the attention of the Sheriff. After a quick stop at Anthony's barge, Simon and Anthony lead Ben's mule team up the towpath past the company barn for their return to the Pulaski farm.

"Wilhelmina, huh?"

"Yeah ."

"Why'd you name it that."

"I didn't. It was already named. Sign already on the bow and stern."

Simon pointed a crooked finger at Anthony. "You know Anthony, we could use this very team to pull your barge up to Deer Creek. There's still a lot you need to know about barges."

Anthony touched the side of his nose. "Not yet, but there are things you need to know about my barge, and I need to tell you."

Simon looked straight ahead. "I've been waiting for you to tell me what you're really up to."

He looked over his shoulder into Anthony's eyes. "It sure as hell isn't hauling coal down from Columbia."

16

Simon stared repeatedly at the bushy faced Philadelphian, as he and Anthony made the slow paced walk along the towpath back to Lapidum. He had known the man for over a decade, and had served beside him as a sailor on the *Philadelphia Star*. Simon was still in shock over his discovery of this other side of his old friend, this secretive side. Anthony was as always on the outside, always excited about some scheme or another. He had been the originator of many guileful and practical jokes.

Almost as if they had shared the same thought, Anthony turned his face to Simon.

"You remember Old Hoagg, the Bo'son on the *Star*?"

"Like a nightmare, when I do. Hateful man at the best of times."

"Remember the time we mixed dried pig shit into his snuff?"

"Wasn't any 'we' to that, Anthony. You did that all on your own. And he wound up blaming Ben for it."

"Ah, he blamed Ben for everything."

"Wonder if he ever died back in China."

"God Almighty, I hope so, Simon. The way he cut Ben, I would have taken his head off if I'd been there."

Simon pressed his lips together, withholding the urge to remark on Anthony's bravado.

"I wasn't there either, Anthony. The only thing Ben ever told me was that he gutted the man, and he was barely alive when Ben left him in that alley. But, Jackson was there. He told me on our way back. Said Ben wouldn't let them at that little boy. Said he knew Holmes was already dead for sure when Ben cut Hoagg the last time."

"One thing is for sure, Simon, neither of them were on the Star when she sailed – and the captain made Ben Bo'son..."

Simon only nodded, seeing again in his memory the little Chinese girls that came to get him, taking him to the house where Ben lay bleeding. Almost like he had been painted in blood. Anthony did things without thinking sometimes, and dangerous though it was, Hoagg was a frequent target for Anthony's tomfoolery. More than once Hoagg guessed wrongly that the culprit was Ben. It was always easy for a man like Hoagg to hate anyone, but he seemed to hate Ben most of all.

Something had already gone between those two before we ever sailed.

The ribbon of mule path slipped back next to the shore above the basin and Anthony shared his secret with Simon.

"I said, 'Did you hear me, Simon?' "

"Yeah, I heard you. I just don't believe all this. Not from you."

"Why not me? And why not you? You can help your people."

"Anthony, keeping a secret from Ben is the same as lying to him."

"Well, sometimes he's too law abiding. Sometimes doing what's right is more important than the law."

"You didn't come here just to work the canal, or just happen to visit Ben. You came here to do this, and you came here to lie about it!"

They stopped and faced each other on the tow path.

"Simon, you listen to me and stop being so high and mighty. I am one point on a line that runs hundreds of miles, and I have friends in places well outside of Havre de Grace and Philadelphia."

"Yeah, so..."

"So don't talk to me of lying. I have friends who know about a black man that killed the son of a respected land owner in St. Mary's County. A black man that grew up down there as a slave and came back to buy his wife."

"Ben knows about that."

"Bullshit, Simon! What does he really know?"

"He knows I killed a man down there."

Anthony held his mouth closed in silence for a moment.

"What did he say?"

"He asked me if the man deserved it."

Anthony peered into Simon's eyes and paused another moment.

"I believe our friend is tougher at heart than we think."

"You don't know that? We were just talking about him in a knife fight with two men, and he left them both lying in their own blood when he came out of that alley."

"Yes, I know that, Simon. But he has all that locked away now. Even I can see that. Some men can give all they can give, and there's just no more."

Simon had nothing more to say and they resumed their walk at the sound of a southbound mule team emerging from the tree lined towpath ahead. They walked in silence for several minutes.

"Simon, my barge is perfect for this. It looks like shit from the outside, needs paint, some of the deck boards are even rotting, but the hull is sound. When we rebuilt the cabin we saved all the wallboards we took out, mold, mildew and all, and then put them back. We used bilge boards from wrecks to finish out the cargo holds before and after the cabin. It looks like it's been hauling coal for thirty years, well, it has, actually. But, the places we worked, they look it too. They'll never be found."

Simon shook his head slowly and looked out over the river as they stepped into the shadows of the tree line. They said very little until the other mule team had passed.

"Come on, Simon. You've got to admit it. You stood in that cabin and I even told you there was an extra compartment behind one of the walls, and you couldn't find it!"

Simon shook his head, half smiling at Anthony's renewed excitement.

"No, I couldn't find it. I looked and looked for a separate door in the wall that might be an entrance."

"See? See? No one will realize it and so no one will suspect it even exists! There is no secret door in the wall. The whole wall is the secret door! The whole thing just swings up from over the bench on one side, and all the way from the floor on the other! "

Anthony checked himself in his exuberance, and quickly looked around, but the coal-filled barge was far into the basin and beyond hearing. The water in the basin and on the river were both smooth surfaced, with only the occasional ripple caused by a southerly breeze running down to Havre de Grace to help the Ugly boat on its way to Annapolis. Anthony repeated, almost a whisper.

"It will not be found, Simon. It will not even be suspected, especially with Ben along."

Simon clenched his fists, rippling the muscles along his arms below his rolled up sleeves.

"You can't do this without telling Ben."

"I will tell him, I will tell him. Just give me time to find the right moment. You know he will want to do the right thing. I just need the right moment to help him see it."

Even then these two men, these two friends who were becoming committed to an action of jeopardy, had difficulty overcoming that last wall between them to even speak the words.

Anthony stopped and turned to face Simon, keeping his hands in his pockets, which was unusual for the energetic little bear. Simon stopped as well, looked into his eyes and waited for Anthony to speak.

"You know that my grandfather owned and captained a slave ship. He made a fortune when he was young, and set himself inside a living hell when he grew old. He died last year and left our family a lot of money. Money that he made catching your cousins and grandparents and hauling them back to this country in conditions that would not have been allowed for cattle. We always knew that. It was accepted. It was business. Well now it's NOT business, and it's NOT <u>God's</u> <u>Will</u>."

Anthony was breathing hard expelling his anger. Simon's friendship had become both the embodiment of Anthony's shame and his commitment to act. It was more important for him to show the hidden compartments in his barge to Simon than to Ben or anyone else. Simon represented all the victims of his grandfather's greed, and it made the whole issue of the *peculiar institution* all very personal. It was no longer just business, and Anthony Renowitz was going to do what he could to stop it. Telling Simon was telling every black face his grandfather had brought over in the terror of the ship's hold. He pulled a hand from his pocket and pointed north.

"I can't do much, Simon. But, by GOD, I will do what I can, as long as I can, to bring as many people to Pennsylvania as I can haul up this canal. I'll never help set free as many as my grandfather brought into slavery, but I will do what I can. And I need your help."

Simon looked at the sincerity flooding Anthony's eyes and the trembling hand still held out over the water pointing toward Pennsylvania.

Please God, let it be true...not just for Anthony, but for enough white people that it will be over someday.

Even as he thought it, he felt foolish for believing it for the moment. He knew that such a prize would not be seen in his lifetime. He also believed that Anthony was committed to just what he promised, at least for now. If one man could do a thing, then two could do more.

"I will help you." Simon took in a deep breath."'Course if we're caught, they'll hang me and just put you in jail for a while."

Anthony brought down his hand and shook his bushy head. "Nah, these are changing times, Simon. No...they'll hang us both!"

Two miles south of the Pulaski farm the canal opened wide and formed the northern end of the canal basin. The ground above the water on the western side was a cliff face of granite running a hundred yards, affording no access to the basin from the land side. Anthony picked a spot not well seen from most directions and decided that would be a secure spot to anchor until the time came for his first trip up the canal. Near evening Isaac and Simon worked with Anthony to fix tie loops in the granite face for the Wilhelmina, and poled Isaac's old flat bottom duck boat back into the canal to the Pulaski farm.

When Ben returned, Sonja met him in the front room with her carpet bag packed.

"I need to go to York Furnace. I will be leaving in the morning. Dan Bartlett will take me."

Ben was confused.

"Why?"

"My father is sick."

"Well, I'm mighty sorry to hear that Sonja, but I thought you weren't welcome there."

"My father is sick and I am going. That's all you need to know. I have sent the boys to stay with LuAnn Harper while I am gone."

"Well, you didn't have to do that, I could have..."

"Ben, I can't be worrying about their safety around you, or that trouble-maker Anthony Renowitz. I know he's up to something. I feel it, and I won't have it again, and my father is sick and I am going to take care of him." She folded her arms and stared into his eyes without blinking.

"How long will you be gone?"

"I don't know."

She would not say any more.

He stared at her.

I guess this is it. This is her reason to leave, and I guess she now has a better place to go.

"Well, I just..." He started. And the silence fell between them again. He opened and closed his mouth, but could put nothing in it to say to her. Then he turned around and walked out the door and back down to the barge.

Ben spent the rest of the day at the barge. He was more ready than before to work with Anthony and agreed to travel along the canal together for a few weeks as partners. Ben listened intently to Simon as they sat on the front porch and Simon told Ben of his decision.

"You know he needs help, Ben. He's always been full of good ideas and excitement, but then he always forgets something important and winds up with shit on his face."

Ben smiled and nodded.

Shit. Is everybody going to leave?

"Ben, You got Mickey, when he's sober, and he's sober most of the time these days. And you got the boys."

Sonja sent them away!

Ben drew on his pipe and blew a thin cloud of blue smoke out into the yard.

"I know Anthony needs help, and I know you are an excellent teacher, Simon."

Simon looked down at his feet, then out toward the canal.

"Ben, you've made great progress with your writing. You're closer to it than you think. You just blocked it out of your mind for so long."

Ben exhaled a cloud of smoke and stared after it.

I will get by.

"It isn't easy for a grown man with a family and his own business to make himself a schoolboy again. My Father thought I had learned some things in school, but I hardly ever went. If I couldn't tag along on his schooner, I'd go on any other boat that'd take me. That's all I ever wanted then. Most of the crew didn't read or write either, and it didn't seem to bother them."

"I know this is what I need to do, Ben."

Ben only nodded, and smoke curled up above his head.

"Well, Mickey cooks a good stew, and there's no need in firing up the stove in both barges, just to feed four men. Why don't we plan on you and Anthony eating meals on the *Ugly Boat*? Then we could do a little reading after that, if we're not too tired?"

I am not going to beg you!

Simon smiled at his friend.

"That would be just fine, Ben. I'll tell Anthony. You KNOW he hates to cook, always has."

"You make sure that dreamer pays you, Simon. He makes great plans, but sometimes forgets the important parts."

"That's already decided and I'm satisfied with the arrangement, Ben."

"You two conspirators talking about me?" Anthony spoke as he stepped up on the porch. "Caught you, didn't I?"

Ben shook his head and pointed at Anthony with his pipe stem. "You couldn't sneak up on a dead man, Anthony Renowitz. I heard you clomping around on that barge clear around the point and heard that pole banging against the duck boat since you set off to come here. The granite face your floating hog trough is tied to makes any sound easy to hear!"

Anthony and Simon exchanged looks in the fading light of the evening. Without taking his eyes from Simon he spoke to Ben. "I will surely have to remember that valuable piece of information."

Ben stretched in his chair and then stood up to stretch again. "Gentlemen, Wrightsville calls us. We need to be on our way at daybreak, so I'm heading for the bed. Word has come from John Calvert that Sonja's father has come down with some flux or other and she's going to York Furnace with Dan Bartlett. Has anyone seen Mickey this evening?"

Simon chuckled, "He's had a second home since they opened that new tavern between here and the lockhouse."

Ben frowned about that. "Lapidum's growing too much, if you ask me. I was glad to see the dry goods store, and even the second one cause Willis's prices came down a bit after that. And we needed a good blacksmith, like MacMallery. But now they're laying rock foundations all along the hill up behind. One of these days it'll be too noisy to sleep at night. And if that Mickey is not on the *Ugly Boat* in the morning, his second home is going to become his first!"

Ben tapped his pipe against the porch post and flipped his pipe ashes out onto the moist grass of the front yard. "Must be going on seven o'clock now," he said to himself, and went into the cabin for the night.

Anthony broke the lingering silence first. "I imagine that if you and Ben could hear things from around the point, people straight across the canal basin would be able to hear noises even better."

"That may not be an especially good spot to load the last of the cargo, Anthony."

"No, I think not, Simon. I also think that seven o'clock is too early for me to go to bed. I think I should do my duty for our friend Mickey, and go see that he is reminded of his morning obligation."

Simon knew that Anthony liked to share the evening with a few glasses of beer as well as Mickey. Anthony lowered his voice slightly.

"Is the tavern a place that you can go with us, Simon?"

Simon shook his head, then realized that Anthony could no longer see him. There was no lamp lit in the front room to spray the usual faint yellow glimmer on the porch.

"There are very few such places for me, Anthony. It is not like China here. There are no Ale Houses where sailors of color are tolerated. There is a place in Havre de Grace that I sometimes go, but a lone black man walking along the streets of town in the dark faces too many risks. I will just turn in for the night. See you in the morning."

Simon slapped Anthony on the shoulder and stepped off the porch into the starlit night.

Anthony stood there alone on the porch for a moment, watching Simon's silhouette disappear around the corner of the cabin. The crescent edge of a bright moon began to peer at him through the trees, looking out from the ridge above Port Deposit. Anthony stepped off the porch into the brightening moonlight, patted his abdomen and felt in his vest pocket for the few coins he would need to buy a couple mugs of apple ale, and found the pathway up to Lapidum. He wouldn't stay long. He would have a few drinks and remind Mickey to be on board the *Ugly Boat* well before daybreak. He would not stay long. He would have a very busy day himself. He would actually begin to do what he swore he would do; what he had planned for many months to do. But planning a thing and doing a thing, especially when that thing was against the law, were two entirely different kettles of fish. Sleep was going to be a tremendous challenge this night, even as much as he really needed it, he knew it would be long in coming.

A few drinks of apple ale would be just the thing to help me sleep.

Sonja stepped from Dan Bartlett's barge onto the lock wall at York Furnace amidst a beautiful bright autumn day. The hardwood trees on the hillside above the lockhouse were a painter's pallet of reds and yellows and golden browns. John Calvert flashed a welcome grin,

"Emma will be real glad to see ya, Sonja!" And turned to call back at the house.

Emma flew down to the lock to greet Sonja and walk her back up to the front porch where she had set out the last of the lemonade. Women visitors to the York Furnace Lockhouse were rare, and rarer still, one that fully understood life on the canal. The two women fell immediately into conversation to fill the unknown with the known about places and family and friends.

"Sonja, John and I visited Burl's farm only two days ago and found him much weaker and experiencing periods of confusion. He was confined to his bed, unshaven, weak in his bed and unable to recognize me."

Sonja slowly shook her head at the news.

Emma set her glass down on the table with a hard thump.

"The room was so dark, and I don't think the chamber pot had been emptied in a while. The room was closed up, and I know lots of folk still close their windows against the night, but I think it's healthy to let in fresh air."

Emma flew on in her conversation, hungry to speak with another woman. "Why that Esther told me that she had sent word to you to come to help her father, but you didn't care to come and only Esther was willing to take care of him. I knew that was a damned lie."

Emma stopped herself and quickly looked back across the front yard to John, touching the lips of her suppressed grin with her fingertips at her own unaccustomed curse. "That's why I had Dan and ol'Thomas stop by your place on his way back to Havre de Grace. So you would know Burl was sick. And you didn't know, did you? Your so-called sister hadn't sent for you, had she?"

"No, she had not. I can't imagine why she would say such a thing, Emma. And she is definitely not my sister. She is the daughter of my father's second wife, and certainly not of my father's blood nor of mine, so we need not use the word 'sister' when speaking of that one, but that's not important now."

Sonja patted Emma's hand. Emma took another sip of lemonade and spoke again.

"I had offered to help Esther care for Burl, he is such a dear friend of ours, but Esther accused me of interfering with his care and then finally of attempting to steal money from Burl's room! Of all things! I couldn't believe all the half lies and accusations coming out of that woman's mouth. When I said I would have to leave, she actually bolted the door behind me!"

"Well, I was able to pick up a few things from Dr. Harper that might help Papa with fever, and Dr. Harper said he was coming by on his monthly trip to Wrightsville soon and would look in on Papa."

Sonja stood pressing out the front of her dress with the palms of her hands.

"Well, I must go see to Papa."

As Emma stood Sonja embraced her. "Emma. Thank you so much for trying to help with Papa. Honestly, I don't know what Esther is thinking, but I will explain to her how mistaken she is about our friends."

Emma called to the Lock, where her husband was still in conversation with Dan Bartlett. Thomas stood alone across the canal, in the shade of the trees on the far side of the towpath, his hair far more white than she remembered, and his frail frame almost lost in the old cast off brown coat he always wore.

"John, come help Sonja with her bag up to Burl's farm."

John nodded and raised a crooked finger over his head in acknowledgement and completed opening the upstream lock releasing Number 26 to the pull of the towline. John and Dan traded waves over turning shoulders, then John brought Sonja's bag up from the lock. Sonja hugged Emma again and stepped down off the porch to John for the walk across the browning grass and up the pathway to her father's farm.

After an easy walk up the path with John, Sonja mounted the steps to the front porch of her father's house, noticing that all the curtains were drawn, and tapped on the door. She heard quick footsteps on the wooden floors within and one of the window curtains whipped open but immediately flew shut. Moments passed with no sound coming from within the house and no movement of the door in front of Sonja's face. John mumbled, but only shrugged his shoulders when Sonja turned back toward him.

The clack of an iron bolt followed by the sound of it sliding within its own carriage announced the opening of the door. Esther stepped into the partially opened door and faced the visitors. Sonja smiled and began to step forward, but hesitated as Esther remained in the opening. Esther looked at both faces almost without recognition, but then quickly produced a beaming smile that did not reach to her eyes.

"Why, Sonja, what a pleasant surprise! I do wish I had known you were coming, sister, so I could have made things ready for you."

Before Sonja could respond, Esther turned to John, her faint smile fading.

"Tell Emma that there are still things missing in here."

Pulaski's Canal

She stepped back from the entryway and walked back within the house. Over her shoulder she said, "I will put us on some tea, Sonja, just set your bag anywhere."

John hesitated on the porch, his face reddened and his lips compressed looking at Esther's back as she walked away. Sonja thanked John for his kindness, picked up her bag and went inside the house as John spun on his heels and made his way back down the curving path to the lockhouse without once looking back. The front room was darkened and difficult to see after the brilliance of the autumn sun and Sonja blinked several times to help her eyes adjust to the dim light. As details of the room showed themselves, Esther stepped back from the kitchen.

The woman delicately pressed a loose strand of auburn hair back into its place among the others pulled back into a bun at the back of her neck. The deep Kelly green of the woven net around her hair bun matched perfectly the color of her dress, narrow tapered at the waist. A narrow white collar joined at her neck with an ivory brooch decorated with a green flower. The paleness of her skin stood out from the deep color of her dress. Sonja absently stroked her own tanned forearm under faded blue calico sleeves.

She is so out of place here, surely being here is not of her choosing. Maybe she has truly stayed only to care for Papa.

"Tea will be ready shortly, sister. The fire was already burning well and I had already drawn water for Father and me. You're just in time."

"I think I will step upstairs quickly and see him first, Esther."

Sonja did not care to be called sister by the daughter of her father's second wife, but wished that the feeling would fly away.

"No. I mean, he is sleeping now, and I would hate to disturb the angel when he finally gets a chance to sleep deeply. He is so disturbed, you know, his fever confuses him and he forgets what time of day it is. I have to get up day and night to attend to him, with barely a moment to myself."

"I will only look in."

Sonja spoke over her shoulder as she walked to the stairs and went up to her father's room. He was not in the room she expected, the room Abigail and he had shared, but in the room Sonja and Ben had used on previous visits. She opened the door slowly and indeed the old man was sleeping deeply. Gone was the ruddy complexion and full cheeks she had always seen, and in its place laid a gaunt old man of almost alabaster pallor. The reek of stale linen and human waste was almost overpowering. Sonja stifled the tightening in her stomach. Tears filled her eyes and slipped out to run down her cheeks.

A warm breath floated delicately on the nape of her neck, Esther's voice whispered into her ear.

"I said he was sleeping."

Esther reached in front of Sonja to pull the door closed. As Sonja stepped back from her, Esther slipped into the space she vacated, standing full in front of the door.

"Let me show you to your room, Sonja."

Esther escorted Sonja to the other small bedroom across the hall. Sonja could see through the doorway to the main bedroom and could see that Esther now occupied that room. The little bedroom for Sonja was sparsely furnished, long since last dusted and the old mattress uncovered. Esther brought sheets and blanket so that Sonja could make her bed.

"Don't forget your bag in the parlor," Esther said and was gone back downstairs.

In the quiet of the room, Sonja made the bed and retrieved her bag from the front room, and then found places around the room to hang the few dresses she had packed. She then sat in the ladder back chair near the chest of drawers, squeezing her hands together, reluctant to even go back downstairs. She felt like an intruder in her own father's house, just as Esther had made her feel in the first days after the flood. The knot returned to her stomach and the grief she had felt in those early days engulfed her again, and still Esther put herself between Sonja and her father. She resented Esther's intrusion into a time when she so desperately needed her father, an intrusion that finally drove her back to Havre de Grace and destitution.

The sound of something falling to the floor across the hall broke into her thoughts and she ran to her father's room. Burl was half out of bed, still reaching for the water that was no longer on the table where he rested his hand, staring at the table, trying to comprehend what had happened, or remember what he was doing. Stepping around the bed Sonja could see the fallen pewter mug in the midst of a small pool of water on the dark wood floor boards. She helped her father back into bed and under stain spotted covers, and then found the water pitcher near the bowl on the dresser and refilled the mug.

He sipped only droplets of water.

"Thank you, Esther."

And he slipped back into the heavy sleep from which he had only temporarily risen, unaware of Sonja's voice and her words to him telling him she was there.

"See? He knows it's me that cares for him, *Sister*."

Esther stood at the doorway, her perfectly manicured hands draped upon her hips.

"We must clean this room, Esther."

"I clean it almost constantly, but you are most welcome to make it better. But, do try not to disturb him any more than necessary with your scrubbing."

She turned and went back down the stairs.

The pungent air was almost more than Sonja could tolerate, and her first act was to open the window. The air was quite cool, so she added another blanket from her own bed to cover her father. She found the wooden bucket and made several trips to the kitchen for hot water and cloths, and then outside to wash out the chamber pot. She located more fresh bed linen and with reluctant assistance from Esther, changed her father's bed clothes and night shirt. The clothing held an odor that spoke of too long since it had last been changed. At least Esther was quick to care for the water mug, and brought up fresh water from the well in it. Sonja watched her.

She does not want to be here. That is the resentment she holds. I must find a way to ease that, to thank her for being here, and find a way to let her know she can go now!

The kitchen was only slightly better in appearance than Burl's bedroom. After the bedroom was cleaned, Sonja found herself in the kitchen, hoping for an opportunity for a friendly conversation with Esther, but received brief comments from Esther spoken over her shoulder as she left the room. From the front room Esther's voice drifted back into the kitchen.

"There's stew on the stove if you're hungry."

The outside of the pot showed drips and dribbles, heated and reheated dry and layer upon layer, but the contents looked wholesome and even appealing though it was starting to dry out on top. Sonja moved the pot from the cluttered sideboard onto the stove, poked the wood coals and added more firewood, then stirred in a small amount of water into the too thick stew. Only one clean bowl remained in the cabinet above the sideboard, with almost every other dish Abigail and her father owned food-stained and stacked on the sideboard.

Sonja brought in more fresh water from the well behind the house and filled a second iron pot for hot water, and sat at the small table by the window looking out at the falling leaves until the water was hot. She washed the dishes, and then the other dirty pots and pans, and then the soiled counter tops, and then swept the floor.

The sun outside began to sink low into the western sky behind the farm. Sonja remained alone in the kitchen, not yet wishing to attempt another conversation with Esther, eating and toying with her small portion of reheated stew. Esther trimmed the wick of the whale oil lamp in the front room where she had spent the afternoon reading a new novel recently arrived from her favorite bookstore in Philadelphia, and finished the bowl of stew she had brought out from the kitchen without speaking to Sonja.

Upstairs Burl turned onto his side in his bed, could see the partially opened window in the room and the near darkness beyond it. He smiled into the fresh air bathing his face, wondering whether it was a coming or a waning day, then wondered where he was for only a brief moment before drifting back into deep sleep.

18

Evening was beginning to draw near and the three barges were well short of Ben's usual progress. Even with Simon helping Anthony on the *Wilhelmina,* the day had been plagued with thoughtless mistakes and rotten luck. Ben could almost think that Simon was hardly paying attention to let so many small things result in so many stops along the canal. On the other hand, not only had Mickey been stone cold sober this morning, he was up before Ben and had the mules across on the towpath when Ben stepped down to the canal at dawn to gauge the weather in the sky. It was only fifteen miles from the Outlet Lock at Havre de Grace to the Maryland-Pennsylvania line and the group had been on its clumsy way since daybreak.

Even with a lame mule they should have made the line shortly after lunch!

Ben's frustration was growing by the minute. The sun was already dropping close to the tree line on his left, far from its rise on the Cecil County side of the river. Seagulls dived and squawked their insults from above the roaring spray of nearby river water slapping against standing boulders, laughing at the bungling humans as the gulls snatched small fish trying to hide under the downstream surface behind the rocks. Several barges had come upon them from the south, and had to pass their towlines over the three barges to keep their own pace to Wrightsville.

They had wasted hours at Darlington, for some fool reason Ben still did not fully understand. Anthony off loaded several crates at his first delivery to the farmer who had sold him the mules. Anthony must have bought the mules on trade for this delivery. He had never seen so many slaves ordered to help unload a single barge. It seemed an entire family and their cousins had been brought out to help unload the *Wilhelmina*. He had no idea that Friends had any slaves, but it was obvious by watching them move back and forth from the barn to the barge, that they were field hands well accustomed to detailed instruction. They kept looking at Ben and Mickey and then quickly back to their feet. Ben could not believe the Friends in Darlington could treat people so badly that their spirit would be pulled away, or pushed deep inside.

It has been a curious day.

Then he had to spend a good half-hour listening to the farmer talk about his other mules for sale. Ben had been quite clear that he had no need for new mules, but the farmer was insistent that he look at his little herd up at the barn, and that Mickey should come too. There had been fresh apple juice in a new crock waiting in the barn for them when they looked at the mules, and the man was extremely friendly, but it was impossible to tell him "no" until he had said his full piece. Then, to Ben's growing surprise, when Ben was finally able to say clearly that he had no need, the farmer simply nodded and took him back to the barges without another word said.

Damned curious day. Damned SLOW day!

They were still miles away from the line. The line. That ridiculous invisible wall so much preached about in the newspapers of both Havre de Grace and Wrightsville. It was nothing but trouble for the bargemen. Since the first year canal traffic extended down into Maryland from Pennsylvania, men had begun to show up at Pennsylvania lock number nineteen and stare intently into the barges passing under the line bridge just south of the lock. The men were strangers, but looked and acted so much alike. They all had the hunger for bounty, and eyes that spoke of fury if an opportunity arose. They were all well armed, heavy drinkers, and as quick to fight each other as an unfriendly barge captain. Some carried warrants, but most just bullied their way onto one barge or another looking for runaway slaves. Many spoke the thick American tongue of the Deep South, oblivious to the music of their own accent that conflicted with the meanness of their trade, but there were also plenty of men from Harford County who would make their money catching slaves. That was the slave owner's problems, and Ben wanted none of it. His only concern was keeping his friend Simon out of their sight, and keeping the worst of them off his barges.

The slavers took great advantage of the bridge, since it was on Maryland soil south of the Mason-Dixon Line, and their function was legal. Still, that did not keep them from lock nineteen only a few yards north, nor did the fact that the lock stood on Pennsylvania soil prevent them from bullying their way onto northbound barges. On occasion, the Harford County Sheriff would come up to the line and tell them to behave, or the York County Sheriff would visit the lock to remind them to stay at the bridge. The lockkeeper was known to go armed although it was contrary to his nature to do so, it allowed him to retain the respect he deserved. Ben had no fear of these slavers; he just did not like them. And he did not like to be around them as the day settled and the whiskey came out.

Just one more complication of this damned clumsy day.

Maryland locks number four, three and two raised them higher along the canal and were finally behind them. North of Lock Two the Wilhelmina slipped her towline and the mule just trotted on ahead knowing it was not her time to stop and enjoying the freedom of the pull against her shoulders, and Ben slapped his straw hat down on the deck at yet another delay. The canal current was mild there, and even though the full length of the barge wedged it's ends against both sides of the canal, it was not very difficult to pull the bow back into the current and stake tie lines into the towpath for all three barges while Simon and Mickey went after the wandering mule. Ben was surprised to see how low the *Wilhelmina* remained in the water. Even after the amount of cargo had been delivered in Darlington.

"Anthony!" he yelled to the barge behind him.

Anthony came up from the cabin and cupped his hand over his ear to let Ben know he was listening. There was a slight breeze, but Anthony would hear him clearly.

"You're sitting low!"

Anthony only shook his head and started to return to the cabin.

If you'd stay out of your cabin, you'd not have so many mistakes!

"Are you taking on any water, Anthony?" he yelled again.

Anthony stopped with one foot on the top step going down into the cabin and yelled back.

"Dry as a bone, Ben."

And he disappeared like a rabbit down a hole.

"You're sitting too low in the water to be half empty!!" he yelled to no one. He sat there near his tiller, hearing the breeze rustle drying leaves in the trees overhead and the water rushing along the Susquehanna. He opened the wooden locker attached to the deck near the tiller and pulled out the canvas bag that held his tobacco and pipe. He shook his head absently as he filled his pipe and then began searching for his flint kit.

Damned expensive habit, Ben. Pipe, tobacco, then start a small fire in the tender just to light a flim, so you can light your pipe.

Ben settled down on the barge deck to keep out of the slight breeze and brought a small flame from his tender, and then managed to transfer it to his pipe. The tobacco slowly roiled into a bright red surface, made brighter by a few additional puffs as Ben re-rolled his flint kit and tobacco pouch. Ben leaned against the locker and stared absently back at the *Wilhelmina*.

A head peeked over top of the Wilhelmina's cabin at

him and instantly disappeared.

What the Hell is Anthony up to?

Ben stood to see more of the Wilhelmina's deck. The small head reappeared and then shot down out of sight with a noisy thump from inside the cabin, followed by a short cry of pain.

What the Hell...

"Damn!"

Ben leapt the distance from the stern of the *Ugly Boat* to the towpath. He dug his heels into the soft dirt and swung his arms stiffly as he walked quickly toward the gangplank of the other barge. He heard a whimper from within the barge, followed by several shushes that sounded like a small steam escape.

"Goddamn it, Renowitz!"

There were a series of thumps within the cabin and a metal plate was knocked to the floor inside.

Ben's heavy heels clomped up the gangplank. As he neared the cabin doorway Anthony dashed up to meet him. Anthony placed his hand against Ben's chest and tried to speak, but Ben pushed him aside and staccatoed down the wooden steps into the dimness of the cabin.

"Anthony Renowitz!!" He bellowed again. "Are you out of your Goddamned mind? Do you want to get us thrown in jail?"

As the dimness of the cabin lifted and light began to fill the corners of the room, Ben Pulaski found himself standing in the middle of more than a dozen black faces. A boy's young face showed itself just above the waist of the woman holding his shoulders from behind. The bloody rag that had been wiping his injured nose dropped to the cabin floor. Ben slowly turned the full circle looking at the pitiful people standing around him. His own heavy breathing matched that of the people facing him.

"Good God Almighty!" he said as another voice spoke "Lord he'p us," at the same time.

Anthony charged down the steps, catching the fierce attention of Ben and all the secret passengers.

"Did all you people...What the Hell is...Anthony, did you..."

Ben's own mind gave him answers even before he could speak the questions.

"Goddamn it, Anthony! Take these people back!"

"We ain't goin' back," came a voice from someone in the corner.

There were murmurs from around the cabin. Somewhere in this press of people was a young woman or girl and she began to sob quietly.

"I was going to tell you, Ben, but I thought it would be better after we were across into Pennsylvania, and these folks were crossing the bridge into Columbia."

"Anthony! You insane Bastard! What are you doing to me? We can't take slaves across into Pennsylvania! You can't just break the law because you're from Philadelphia! Goddamn it, Anthony! These are slaves. They are PROPERTY. They belong to someone. If we take them into Wrightsville, we will be STEALING. Don't you understand that? The law can put us in jail, confiscate my cargo, and burn my barge. Goddamn it, Anthony, how could you risk my family and my business like that? Goddamn it to Hell!!!"

"Quit that cussin'." Said another voice from the little mob. The same voice that had spoken before.

"You do whatcha gotta do, but don't keep takin the name of th'lord in vain."

"Sorry, ma'am."

Ben spoke without seeing the woman, but looking in the general direction of her voice.

"You calls me ma'am, but you says I'm property."

Ben turned in the direction of the voice.

"One is my personal way, the other is the law."

He turned back toward Anthony. A shadow crossed the opening to the cabin and another body managed to come down the steps into the crowded cabin. It was Simon. Ben and Simon locked onto each other's eyes, each searching for the words, any words, that could be said at the moment for it all to make sense, and still do the right thing. There was only the sound of the breathing, and the muted sobbing of the little woman, punctuated by the occasional sniff of the little boy who had to have a breath of fresh air and a quick peek outside.

Ben looked from Anthony to Simon. Rage, entrapment, betrayal, anguish, frustration and fear all fighting for dominance in the man's mind and on his face. His fists opened and closed, and the muscles of his face flexed and relaxed under his beard. He opened his mouth and then closed it again. His lips compressed into a thin line of determined anger, but his trembling chin only confused the set of his face as the storm exploded within his mind. Simon slowly stepped past Ben, neither men taking their eyes away from the confrontation, neither shrinking back, neither advancing.

In the pressing dimness, Simon reached slowly past the shoulders of a tall lean black man in a tattered shirt, and gently pulled forward a slight framed girl with tears streaming down her face and a full round pregnant belly.

"These people are not 'They', Ben."

Simon brought the young woman in front of Ben.

"Saying 'They' is like saying 'herd', Ben. She is not part of a 'herd'. She is not just one of 'they'!"

Simon gripped the girl's wrist and raised her trembling hand to Ben.

"This is Melissa. She is fourteen years old. Her man laid a scent for the dogs so she and his baby could get away. Melissa is a fine seamstress and can play the flute. Her Momma and her Daddy and her brothers and her sisters love her. She wants to learn to read and write, like another one of my friends."

Simon extended her arm further toward Ben.

"Take her hand, Ben. Meet Melissa."

Ben's entire body tensed with physical rage at the trap that had closed around him. He was unable to escape; unable to will himself to turn on this rabble and walk up those stairs to the outside where there was sky and wind and river and the world he knew. He looked at the skinny girl with the big belly and the tear-filled eyes that screamed a silent fear, and extended a trembling hand beyond the firm support of Simon's grip.

"Goddammit, Simon!"

Ben stormed up the stairs of the cabin and stopped at the top.

Simon and Anthony looked at each other with pensive stares. The little girls hand slid from Simon's grip and sagged back to her sides.

Murmurs began to drift among the slaves.

"What he gonna do?"

Anthony whispered in the half darkness.

"Wait. This is not finished."

A long minute passed among the heavy breathing of all the people in the cramped quarters of the simple cabin. Ben slammed his fist on the edge of the hatch and slowy stepped back down into the cabin. He pointed a finger at Simon's face.

"You knew this. You helped Anthony bring us to this. You call me your friend?"

"I am your friend, but I am your black friend. I will never be white."

"Simon, color has nothing to do with right and wrong."

"Shit, Benjamin, listen to yourself. This isn't right or wrong. This is being alive or being dead. This is being a mule or being a human."

"We cannot do this Simon."

"What can't we do? What can't YOU do? I saw you gut a man in China who had abused a little boy of color."

"That was China. That was a fair fight."

"You left him for dead, his blood pouring into a stone gutter."

"It was a fair fight."

Simon grabbed the little girl's hand again and raised it up to Ben.

"Doing THIS is a fair fight. This is the fairest fight in my life; in your life. One little girl who just wants to get to the dirt on the other side of a little wooden bridge and into lock nineteen."

Ben looked into the little girl's eyes and could not be firm against her silent plea to have her chance to bring her baby into a land where it would not be chained, or collared, or whipped or sold; a land that was only two miles away. Slowly Ben raised his hand and took the little brown one in his. He easily and gently wrapped his hand around hers, and then she unfolded her hand and took his in a firm handshake.

She smiled slightly and shook his hand slowly.

"Name's Melissa."

"Ben." He barely whispered.

"Hey, Massa Ben."

"Just Ben."

"Hey, Ben."

"Hello Melissa."

Simon then pulled up the forearm of the little boy with the bloody nose who had peeked at Ben along the cabin roof.

"This is Toby."

And Ben shook his hand. There was John, and Mary, and Tom, and Jedediah, and Jobe, and then six others. Simon introduced each one to Ben, and Ben shook each hand. When they had all been introduced, Simon added,

"These folks aren't 'they', Ben. Each one is a person that ought to have as much chance in life as anyone else. No less and no more. All we're trying to do is get them into Pennsylvania. After that is up to them, but they need help getting over that line."

Ben said nothing.

"What do you think, Ben?"

Anthony spoke from the upper step where he had seated himself while Simon introduced his passengers to Ben. His usual exuberance was returning to replace the worried face that had appeared when Ben entered the cabin.

Ben placed his hand on Toby's head and slowly ran his fingers across the thick hair. Ben still said nothing, only shook his head and stepped toward the cabin stairs. He paused with his hand on the rail and looked down, did not look at the people in the cabin, did not look at his friends who were working so hard to have him break the law. Taking a deep breath and sighing it out, he climbed the steps back onto the deck of the *Wilhelmina*, and then down the plank onto the towpath.

Anthony and Simon could only stare after the man they thought they knew, as anxious murmurs grew among the people hidden within the cabin. The old woman was the first to speak.

"What's he gonna do?"

Simon had no answer for her. He did not want to think that Ben had reached his limit, but there was always a portion of each of them the other could never really know. Anthony turned back toward the old woman and merely shrugged his shoulders. Simon spoke at the unanswered question.

"Just wait here a while longer. We may have to make other plans, but we are going to cross that line. You folks just wait here."

The runaways traded looks among each other, only to have the growing worries reflected back. Jedediah spoke in a coarse whisper.

"We're too close not to try. If we can't go in these boats with these white men, then we make a run fer it through the woods. It's only a few miles. We already walked hundreds."

"Give'em a while longer, Jedediah." The old woman turned to face him, placing a gnarled hand on her hip. "Those woods are full of liquored up slave catchers. Which one of us you suppose would be alright fer them to shoot while we're tryin' t'run?"

Jedediah had no answer. None of them did. The air in the little cabin became thick with the scent of brassy sweat from the nightmare fear of capture that clung in their chests.

Ben walked up the plank onto the *Ugly Boat* and wandered to the bow. He picked up his pipe where he had dropped it and placed the stem in his mouth while he stared into the slow moving current of the canal water. Small leaves and twigs floated by the bow of the boat and then slipped along its outer side going south. The current began in Wrightsville where the water filled the upper basin and flowed gently downhill and southward all the way to Havre de Grace, stopping at the locks and freshening with stream and creek flow along the way. He wondered if the twig he watched would eventually find its way past the two old oaks in front of his home on its way to the Havre de Grace Basin.

Sonja was right. It's always some goddamned scheme with Anthony.

He shook his head and looked back up to Anthony's barge.

How could I help these runaways, by breaking the law? It'll stop someday. Good people will change the laws. That's how it's supposed to work. Why should all this be up to me?

"Goddamn it, Anthony!" He growled under his breath at the water, as another twig moved past him going south. "I'm not needed here for this shit," he told the twig, "as if I'm needed anywhere else – BY anyone else!"

Ben could tell Anthony to go ahead, or tell him to wait until he had gone ahead. Either way he could separate his barge from the insanity of Anthony's intention. There was no width to the canal for several miles in either direction to turn the barge around, and the *Ugly Boat* was scow-built, with no tiller possible at the bow. He'd have to go north as far as York Furnace before he could turn around, and that wouldn't help because he still had to pass lock number 19 to get back here, still had to pass the slavers.

Ben clenched his fists and gritted his teeth trying to force the dilemma away. The clay pipe cracked in his hand, crushing the bowl and freeing the unlit chopped tobacco. He tossed the pieces of his pipe at the next piece of canal debris to float by, wishing he could go with it. Brushing the tobacco from the palm of his hand he recalled the small hand of the little girl in the cabin.

What was her name? Melissa. Alisha would be three now, still far from the fourteen years Melissa had. She had a man? Her man laid a scent so she could get away. Probably only a boy himself. Laid a scent for the dogs.

Ben shook his head at the thought of a young boy being attacked by dogs. A heron glided to a near silent landing in the shallows near the bank just yards away from where Ben stood in the fading light. Mosquitoes found him and fell hungrily on his forearms and face, and he let them drink their fill.

I should have been with Sonja when the flood came. If I had come back after a year, I would have been there. I would have been able to save Alisha.

He patted his pocket. Felt the little leather pouch. His life was not in there. It was gone. What he had now was something else. Something different. Something less, but it was still more than Melissa had, or her man-boy had, if he was even alive. Would never see his child. Maybe a daughter? He wondered if Melissa's man would have tried to help Alisha, knew he would, knew what he was by his selfless act. He felt shame wash over him.

"I should have been there." Ben growled at the heron, sending it squawking and flapping back into the graying sky.

A man should be able to take care of his family.

He watched another leaf flow along in the current, and tried to imagine what it would have been like diving into the icy waters to bring Alisha back. He could almost imagine reaching out and catching her hand before she went deep, before it was too late to put the air back into her little lungs. He tried to imagine the feel of her little hand in his as he brought her to safety. Tears slipped begrudgingly from the corners of his eyes and moved slowly down his cheeks to fall onto the deck. He squeezed his eyes tightly, reaching with his mind to catch that little hand, to feel that little hand in his. There. Just on the edge of reality he could feel something small and gentle slip into his hand; just the breath of a touch. He could feel the hand in his and he would save her this time. He gently squeezed his left hand to hold onto the hand of a never known memory; reached deeply within his mind to pull her back to the surface; pulled her close to him so he could see her. A single great sob erupted from his throat as he tried to pull the imaginary into the reality, even knowing he could not, and his palm felt the memory of a little girl's hand, small and trembling in fear, and he knew it was Melissa's hand.

It was then that Ben Pulaski crossed into some new place. He opened his eyes and everything looked the same as it had before he closed them, but it was not the same place. There was no *legal issue*, there was no *slavery question*, there was no law to dispute. There were thirteen people leaving a hideous existence, and a little girl named Melissa, who liked to sew and could play the flute. Her man had given himself as a sacrifice to pass her along to Ben.

"Well, shit!"

He looked up at the same gray sky, across to the same river filled overhead with seagulls, and listened to the same breeze rustle the leaves in the trees on the high side of the canal, but it wasn't the same world anymore. It had just gotten more confusing and more dangerous. He had no idea how he could bring all this to Sonja, or even if he should.

Hell, all that's assuming I don't get jailed or shot

trying to cross into Pennsylvania helping runaway slaves!

Footsteps clomped onto the deck as Simon and Anthony stepped from the plank onto the *Ugly Boat*. Mickey came up from the cabin wiping fresh brandy from his lips. Ben spoke quietly over his shoulder.

"I think someone needs to keep a tight hold onto Toby, if we're going to get past the Line to Lock 19."

Simon and Anthony traded smiles.

"Come on over here and let's figure out how the hell we're going to get past those men at the Line."

19

Sonja slept poorly in the farmhouse. Night noises are common to all houses, but different in each, like the breathing of a child that awakens the mother when it is different. Late at night, long after leaving Esther wrapped in her own silence, long after taking a damp towel to dust her room against the sneezing she experienced, Sonja awoke from her fragile sleep to the sounds of footsteps going down the stairs. Quickly enough the footsteps returned and Esther's voice floated and cooed from Burl's room. Sonja could not hear the words, only the tone of voice or rather the tones of voices, because it sounded like more than one person and neither voice had the familiar tone of her father's. At the thought Sonja arose, put on her robe over her simple shift and crossed the hall. Esther looked up from her seat by the bed, the pewter mug in her hand, quickly glancing at the mug and then back to Sonja.

"What it is, sister?"

"I heard your voice and thought perhaps Papa was awake."

Burl's eyes were closed, a few droplets of water tracing their way down the side of his unshaven cheeks to his neck.

"He needs to take his medicine."

"Well, I pray it helps him, Esther. What is it?"

Esther looked into Sonja's eyes, her own unblinking. "I don't really know what it is. The doctor prescribed it and delivered it to us when he came by."

"I'm so glad to know he's been seen by a doctor."

Burl turned his head toward the sound of her voice and shifted one of his legs below the blankets.

Esther watched Burl's movements, placing the mug to his lips again, "Drink, sweetie. You must take your medicine." Then turning back to Sonja, a frown barely visible across her arching eyebrows, forcing a whisper to carry clearly to Sonja. "There, you're waking him. He must take his medicine and then sleep. That is the best thing for him. Why don't you go back to bed and we can talk about this in the morning."

Having little else to contribute, Sonja withdrew red-faced into the hall and closed the door behind her, noticing the window had been closed.

Maybe it was too cool for him.

When the sun finally peeked through the front window of Sonja's room, she was already out of it and sitting next to her father. She had brought a clean glass of fresh water to sit on the table near him. He took a few hesitant sips of the offered water, and then after his first swallow hungrily raised his head for more. Opening his sleep weighted eyes only briefly, he had stared at her for seconds, the puzzle of wondering who it was tending him was obvious on his face. Sonja leaned close to her father's face and patted his shoulder.

"Papa. It's me, Papa. It's Sonja, Papa"

Burl looked at her, his eyes shifting left then right to each of hers, looking at the details of her face, taking in the sound of her voice, and worked his jaw as if to answer, but his heavy eyelids slid down again and he drifted back into the heavy sleep that had its arms so fully around him. His breathing was slow but steady, and his chin settled lower over his neck.

"Where is his mug?"

Sonja turned to see Esther standing at the door. Her hands on her hips where they tended to be unless she was engaging them, wearing a dress so dark it almost looked black except for the dark green highlights shown by the morning light, the contrasting white of her cuffs and collar almost too brilliant to take in. Her eyes rapidly surveyed the glass on the bedside table, the straightened bed linen, and the opened window.

"Where is his pewter mug?"

"It's in the kitchen, Esther. It had become quite stale, so I left it down there to be washed and brought him up a fresh glass."

"That's his favorite mug. He drinks everything from it. You should not have taken it away from him."

She spun around to face back into the hallway, the edges of her dress billowing and flowing barely over and not touching the floor, and descended the stairs. Sonja took in a deep breath and sighed it back out, then followed her down the stairs and into the kitchen. As Sonja entered Esther was going through the cupboards, speaking softly to herself yet loud enough so Sonja would hear. "Everything is in the wrong place. No telling where it is..."

Esther stopped with a small gasp, reaching into the cabinet in front of her she slowly withdrew a battered well worn tin cup, much of the original green coating long since worn away from the edges and the handle. Its numerous dents were thrown into small shadows in its sides as the sunlight streamed in from the front room through the opened kitchen door. She turned toward Sonja holding the cup gently forward with the fingertips of both hands.

"This was my mother's. My father gave it to her before I was born. We don't hide it away. It always goes here."

She ceremoniously set the cup at the back of the counter, in the corner nearest the stove. She looked at it as she tilted her head once to each side, adjusted its position, and then stepped back as she viewed it again among its surroundings. "There. It belongs there, just like that."

"Esther, Papa's pewter mug is still next to the dishpan. I have yet to wash it out."

Sonja picked up a clean white wash cloth and stepped toward the dish pan, but Esther stepped ahead of her and retrieved the mug.

"I'll take care of this."

And she took it to the water pump. When she finished rinsing it off she started toward the kitchen door.

"Esther, lets wash that old thing out."

"It is clean as it is, sister."

"It's stale and soured, Esther. I smelled it. Now, please give it to me and let me wash it."

"It won't help our dear father take his medicine if it tastes like soap!"

"Esther, we will rinse it. Why do you refuse to wash it?"

Esther ran her fingertips along the top edge of the mug, looking at the kitchen door ahead of her.

"Sometimes he doesn't drink it right away and it settles, so I must add more water to make sure he gets his medicine. That's what you smell, the medicine, and I have so very little of it, I dare not waste it."

Without looking back she left the kitchen. Sonja stared after her, the kitchen door swinging closed as Esther's fingertips yanked it behind her, the kitchen silent except for the thump of the door finding its frame. Sonja extended one hand to the counter, leaned against it and settled her other hand onto her hip.

That is one strange woman.

Sonja spent the morning and early afternoon tending Burl as much as she could and trying to avoid spending much time with Esther. She was left alone in the kitchen, in her room, or on the front porch. Each time Sonja went to Burl's room Esther materialized to assist and give guidance and instructions. Sonja fixed lunch, thinking neither would have it otherwise, and served venison broth to her father. She spent time in the front room afterward, looking at the books and bric-abrac Burl and Abigail had brought together to fill nearly every inch of shelf and table space in the room. The little carved wooden horse and the little wooden bear she remembered from her own childhood home in North Carolina. Holding them, looking at the details given them by the carver, she was lost for precious short moments in the memories they held, and then returned them to their places. Esther came behind her and readjusted each piece Sonja touched, and pulled the curtains closed against the afternoon light.

Sonja escaped Esther's hovering to the privacy of her room upstairs, sitting in the ladder back chair, looking out the window to the trees that separated the farm from the canal down the hill, rubbing her hands, full of worry for her father and wishing Ben were there. Downstairs, beyond the front door Esther kept locked to the outside, heavy footsteps sounded on the porch boards. The front door vibrated as hard knuckles rapped on old wood. Sonja flew downstairs to find Esther peeking between drawn curtains, and mumbling to herself in whispers.

"I do not know this man."

"Well, open the door, Esther. See who it is."

"No, not yet. It is a man. A big man. You can't take such chances. They could..."

"They could <u>leave</u> if we don't answer the door!"

Sonja spoke as she reached the inside latch and threw open the door. The doorframe filled with the bulk of the man who still had his huge fist, raised knuckles first, in front of him to knock again. He lowered his hand and tilted his head up slightly to see below the brim of his hat and squinted into the dim front room. Sonja filled her face with her smile and stepped into the doorway taking the man's hands in both of her own to draw the man inside.

"Hello, Miss Sonja"

His bass voice marched in and echoed around the front room.

"Esther, this is Wallace Harper, a close friend of the family. My Friend."

Esther eyed him without response, but her eyebrows arched perceptively higher as Sonja continued.

"DOCTOR Harper, this is Esther Wilson. She is the daughter of my father's second wife."

I'll be damned if I will introduce her as my SISTER, half or otherwise!

Esther pursed her rose colored lips and looked from Wallace to Sonja, and then allowed a diminutive smile to form on her lips.

"Doctor? Harper ?"

To which Wallace nodded his head as she tilted her head slightly taking in the information.

"Well...how wonderful!"

She nearly beamed, stepping forward to slip her arm under his and taking his hat from his hand. Handing his hat to Sonja as they passed, Esther guided Wallace toward the stairs.

"Please, you must come see Father. He is so ill. Sister and I are at wits end to know what to do for him. And I fear the prescription fostered upon us by that simpleton poor doctor from Wrightsville is simply doing no good whatsoever."

Moments later Wallace was escorted back down the stairs, Esther looped again on his arm chatting amiably. Sonja followed from the stairs into the front room.

"Most baffling," Wallace said turning to face both women. "It is not a condition I can remember ever seeing before."

Hanging on his every word with feminine smiles and animated emerald eyes, Esther walked Wallace to the front room as Sonja slipped into the kitchen to put on water for tea. Seconds later Sonja returned to the front room to find Esther letting an almost confused Wallace Harper out of the door way and handing him his hat.

"It was so sweet of you to stop by to see Burl, Wallace. You are indeed a good friend of Sonja's. Please do come back when Father is well and we women are truly prepared to entertain visitors."

Stunned at the rapid departure, Sonja stood at the doorway to the kitchen as Wallace gave his goodbyes, speaking around the edge of the door as it closed behind him, and telling Sonja he would stop by again on his return trip. Even as the door closed Sonja spoke out.

"Wait. Wallace. Wallace." But the door was latched. Esther turned to face Sonja, her hands flying again to her hips.

"Really, Sonja. You should think of taking care of our father rather than chasing after this man friend of yours."

Sonja froze in her steps, her mind a confusing jumble of thoughts, until the clomping of Wallace's boots on the porch steps returned her attention to the door. She flew by Esther, unlatched the door and slipped onto the porch.

"Wallace, is there not anything you can do for Papa?"

Harper stopped and turned back to face Sonja, rubbing his right ear lobe between his finger and thumb, frowning at the steps.

"All very odd, Sonja. Doesn't really look like a pox, what little of him I could actually examine, but the symptoms Miss Wilson describes certainly sounds like it. Could be a different species of it I suppose. Sorry you were out of his medication, couldn't prepare a replacement when I don't know what he had been prescribed. I will stop by again on my return trip, when I am not, uh, intruding."

"No Wallace, you certainly..."

"Say nothing of it, Sonja."

He raised up the palm of his hand to her.

"Only came up when Emma told me of her concerns, and if he is under the care of another doctor I can't..."

Sonja moved quickly down the steps and placed her handkerchief into his hands.

"Look carefully at the stain folded at the center. It is the medicine that Esther insisted he must have – and without any such reservations she described today. Maybe if you can see what the medicine is it will help you decide what illness he has."

He took the handkerchief, patting her hand, and then turned to walk down the path. Sonja slowly mounted the steps back to the porch, took in a deep breath and blew it out onto the door and thumbed the latch, but the door did not move. She pushed again, but the door would not open. It was latched from the inside. Wearily Sonja called out Esther's name.

Esther's voice sang out from inside the house, "Coming, Dear."

Mickey tossed in his bunk on board the *Ugly Boat*, Ben's slow footsteps on the deck overhead echoed through the oak bulkhead. He decided to forget his attempts to sleep and light a fire in the stove. Dawn could not be far away, and he relished the thought of a good strong cup of coffee. Smoke puffed through the stovepipe above the cabin and drifted across the deck toward Ben. A single spark leapt from the narrow smokestack chasing the smoke away in the fading darkness. Ben looked from sleepless swollen eyes out to the light gray strip of sky daring to show itself just above the tree tops across the river. He took a final sip of brandy and water from the last of numerous cups poured throughout the night, and tossed the meager remains into the canal. He watched another twig drift by the boat, outlined by the ripples of the fading starlight reflected off the surface. It moved faster than the others he had watched the evening before, and the water swirled gently around it.

Someone was coming south through Lock 19 a mile or so ahead, the water released by the opening locks momentarily adding to the current of the canal. The lockhouse had been stirred to business for the day. It was time to move the boats. Mickey slid back the cabin hatch, silhouetted in the yellow lamp glow from below. He poked his head above the rim of the hatch to look for Ben. Seeing him at the stern of the boat, he called out in a soft early morning voice that carried easily across the dew painted cargo hatches.

"Would ya care for a cup of coffee, Ben?"

Ben answered hoarsely that he would.

"and put a little brandy in the coffee, Mickey."

Mickey tsked and shook his head slightly, went to the stove to pour the boiling coffee, and then pulled down the brandy keg.

"Might as well fortify me own cup as well"

After a quick sip through the steam of fresh strong coffee, Ben set the cup on the cabin roof and stepped down the plank to the towpath to meet Simon bringing the first mule team. In the gaining light Ben could see the fullness beneath Simon's eyes, marking his friend's sleepless night as well.

"Remember, Simon, I need you to stay here with the *Turtle*, and one of the mule teams."

Simon only compressed his mouth and nodded in resignation. He had agreed to Ben's plan, but still did not like much of it.

The *Turtle* was untied from the *Ugly Boat* and pulled back up the canal. Then the Wilhelmina was manhandled by ropes to sit in front of the *Ugly Boat*. The two barges drifted together as the stern line was tightened until the two hulls kissed between the drive wedges built into the blunt bow of the *Ugly Boat*. They could be controlled by a single rudder at the rear and pulled by a single mule team at the front. The switch would allow Ben to steer both barges, and try to keep the attention of the slavers on the *Ugly Boat* while both went through the lock. They did not want to risk waiting at the Line for two cycles of the lock gates. The lock could hold two barges at a time, if end to end. A third barge in the procession would only delay everything. They had to get through the lock as quickly as they could, but it would not be fast. Simon would bring the Turtle up through the lock later.

The darkness of the sky was melting away to lighter shades of gray and beginning to show hints of clouds drifting in from the east. Ben took that as a good sign. He knew game was slower to move and less confident on overcast days. He always thought it was due to the fact that they could not see as well without the bright sunshine; part night and part day. They seemed to doze more on days like that. He could always get closer to a deer on thick cloudy days. Maybe the slave chasers would be that way. The thought of those men with guns at the Line tightened his stomach. Simon joined Anthony on the stern of his barge. The four of them looked around to see that the boats were joined properly, and then at each other. There was little else to say. The ideas, the arguments, and suggestions had all been discussed for hours until all the options had been swept away and only the plan remained. Ben pointed at Anthony

"You keep those kids quiet."

"There's some coffee left," Mickey offered, but no one answered. "Guess I'll put the fire out."

Simon extended his hand to Ben. "I'll come in the early afternoon."

"If you see us in trouble, or don't see us at all, go on through to York Furnace. Don't you stop. Don't you act like you even know us. Tell'em your boat belongs to Herbert Binterfield in Havre de Grace, and get th'hell on outta there. Then go tell Burl Jundt I'm in a shitload of trouble."

"I know what to do."

Silence settled among them, holding them, letting them linger a while longer before the next step. Only Simon had faced the law from the outside before, but he had been able to run through the woods; to be where they were not looking. This would be straight to the Slavers.

Mickey broke through the silence.

"When me father wanted t'beat me, I learned not t'run from him, cause he always caught me in the end, and the beating would be all the worse."

The three looked at Mickey.

"'Least, 'til the day I knocked him out with a fine oak slat from me bed."

Pulaski's Canal

They matched his smile and still smiled after him as Mickey went down the plank to take up the mules. Anthony retreated to his cabin to ensure all was ready. Simon padded down the plank and went up to the *Turtle*. Ben pulled the plank in from the towpath, stowed it against the cabin wall, then yelled for Anthony to come out and do the same. Anthony still had much to learn – and remember - about canal barges. Ben only hoped that would be the worst of their worries when the evening finally came.

"They gotta keep that little boy out of sight... and quiet! You tell'em again, Anthony!"

Anthony waved a thick hand over his head as he ducked again down the cabin steps.

Ben took in a deep breath and then turned his attention toward Mickey and the mule team waiting on the towpath beyond the bow of Anthony's barge. It was light enough to see Mickey's face, although the sun would not show above the tree line for a couple hours yet. Looking up at the sky Ben saw more clouds gathering.

This day may not have a sun to see.

Mickey pulled the mule harness to get the pair walking forward and take the slack out of the line. He looked back at Ben while pointing up the canal.

Yes. It is time to go.

Ben waved to Mickey, pushing the air in front of him in the same direction as Mickey.

Pull us on Mickey. Pull us north to Pennsylvania Lock 19.

A breeze ran off the river and through the tops of the trees, scurrying over the canal and above the forest on the hillsides above. Ben settled against the tiller, pushing the rudder over to guide the stern of the double barge to the center of the canal. The tops of the trees waved in the breeze. He felt like waving back, like he was leaving something behind here. He had taken risks before, but they had been in the heat of the moment, or the scream of an emergency.

All of this is too damned slow.

Ben looked along the lines of the *Ugly Boat* and the length of Anthony's barge before it. He scanned the edges of Anthony's cabin looking for the outline of Toby's head peeking out into danger, for the sound of voices that ought not to be heard, that would call the attention of the men at the Line. The clouds overhead continued to bump into each other like a heard of cattle driven into a pen barely big enough for their number, until the sky was filled with them. The grayness of the earliest hour of morning did not fade to blue and was not joined by the bright yellow of the sun. Without the sun to track the progress of the day it would be difficult to mark its passage until it finally darkened in the evening. Ben's hands absently felt at the pockets of his shirt and his pants, until he felt the leather pouch again. The letter. Her letter. He focused his attention on Mickey's back; watched the steady rhythm of his limping gait next to the lead mule; watched his occasional slight head movement toward the mule. Ben noticed Mickey's head rock slightly back and forth over his shoulders.

Mickey is singing to the mules.

Ben heard the soft gurgle of water run around the stern of the boat. The mules would pull the barges no more than three miles an hour, but the south bound current fed by the spill from a full lock would more than equal that in the opposite direction. The little current dashing around the stern of his odd barge-scow could be running at seven or even eight miles an hour. Ben looked down at the canal water and watched it run past the barges. Seven knots on the Bay would be satisfactory travel, he thought. Looking at the slow passage of the trees lining the towpath, Ben wished the barges were actually moving seven knots, wished they were actually out on the Bay.

No. They must be here. He must do this thing. It must be done by someone, and he is here.

Pulaski's Canal

The water gurgled again around the stern and he wished he had gone into the bushes before they started this last section of canal leading to the lock.

Ben watched the long gentle curve to the left begin to straighten, opening the canal to his view for two hundred yards or more before it would curve slightly back to the right. The small maple growing alone among house sized granite boulders formed a rude cliff near the canal. Around the next turn they would come to the lock. Ben opened the locker near the tiller and pulled out the conch shell with the hole bored in the tapered end. Holding the tiller in place with his hip, he took in a deep breath and brought the hole to pursed lips, and blew the sound of the conch horn along the canal and among the trees. An unseen deer dashed through dry leaves, his hooves sounding like a drummer slapping sticks into the forest floor, running from the sound of the horn. Ben blew again, the sound echoing off the nearby granite and reverberating along the canal. Ben watched among the trees in the lowland, to see if he could spot the deer, but it was already gone. He returned the conch shell to its place in the box.

They know we are coming. It is the way we always come, all of us.

The horn tells the locktender to be ready. To come without blowing the horn would have been unusual, and generated a mild scolding or comments or unwanted questions. Ben shook his head and gave a small smile to himself at the contradiction of blowing his own horn to avoid undue attention. Anthony had come on deck and was standing just forward of the cabin corner, looking along the canal as the lower outflow walls of the lock came into view. He looked back over his shoulder and traded nods with Ben. With his straw hat jammed down over his bushy head and his leather straps over his shoulders he looked like every other Quaker in this area. Anthony turned back toward Ben and then pointed out into the woods. Between the trees near the edge of the river a horse stepped among the scrub bushes carrying a rider pulled deep into his cloak. There was no trail there.

Travelers took the readily available towpath, they did not force their horse to walk among the scrubs and briars at the waters edge.

Ben knew the look of a man on sentry. He was probably near the end of his shift. It drove a chill along Ben's spine that they were actually patrolling this area. Those men were like the bear that converged on the narrow river rushes when the shad ran up to spawn. They came for the feeding frenzy to pack their bellies after the long winter. These men knew this was a narrowing of the path for runaways. The river forced the escaping slaves to look for passage by boat or bridge, and the men would converge there to hunt their quarry. The barges and the rider all moved beyond the stand of trees and gained a clear view of each other over a rock cluttered clearing. The rider raised his hand toward the barges and Anthony returned the wave, but Ben did not.

Lock number19 was up ahead, across the state line into Pennsylvania. The wooden arch bridge crossed from the towpath side high over the barge cabins and back down onto the other bank. The air smelled of fresh coffee, fried bacon, damp straw and mule droppings. The mule barn and tack shop was to the right of the bridge, on the towpath side of the canal. The land had risen enough to hold the building, and the river was still ten to twenty yards behind that. The lock tender's house and general store stood on the left of the canal, and the bridge crossed the canal along the middle of what everyone thought was the actual line between Maryland and Pennsylvania, although no one was really sure. The canal company never surveyed the actual line, it was just generally agreed to by the folks who lived there that that was the spot. Two men stood close together at the arch of the bridge looking down at the oncoming barges. Anthony waved to the men as they neared the bridge as he had to the rider in the woods, but no wave was returned. The men separated and began to walk down the arch to the towpath. A third man rose from a rough wooden stool placed in front of the open barn door and stepped down toward Mickey and the oncoming barges.

All three carried rifles. Two carried their rifles across the crook of their arms, the man from the stool carried his by the barrel as he had picked it up from leaning against the barn.

Slowly and purposefully the men converged on the towpath as Mickey approached the bridge with the mule team and stopped before the men standing in the path. The hundred feet of towline between the barges and the mule tree slackened, sagged, and then set in the water as the barges continued to drift several yards closer toward the bridge. Ben could hear voices in quiet conversation, but could not hear what was being said. From the stern of the *Ugly Boat* he was almost eighty yards from the bridge. He craned his neck toward the path to watch the four men talk near the stone abutment to the bridge. Mickey was rocking back on his heels and tilting his chin up as he spoke and one of the men laughed.

Good, Mickey, charm them. Tell your tales, make them laugh.

Anthony stepped onto the deck and toward the bow, only once glancing over his shoulders back toward Ben. He placed a shoe on the path side rail and leaned over to rest his elbows across his raised knee as the bow of the lead barge neared the men on the towpath. Ben could see Anthony's left hand raise and twist and turn as he joined the conversation with the men. Anthony could not talk without moving his hands. Sometimes it seemed as if he had to form each word in his hands and then toss them to the listener. One of the three men stepped back to look back at Anthony and gave a short hand gesture, not quite a wave, and a nod. The forward motion of the barge had stopped and the hull was angling toward the bank as the gentle current from the weirs around the lock allowed the upstream water to overflow from the upper holding pond and find its way south. Ben whistled at the group and flicked his finger toward the lock gate.

Nothing unusual in that. We've got business to attend to. Get out of the way. We need to get through the gate.

The lock tender was standing near the lower gate, waiting on them.

Ben could just see another barge sitting high and empty in the holding pond above the lock. His full barge would have the right of way. The tender would have to wait until the *Ugly Boat* had passed before he could allow the other barge to come through. Impatient at the delay, the tender flicked the cord to the bell near the lock. Get on up here, the bell said to them. Mickey waved back at Ben and then clapped one of the men on his shoulder and pointed to the lock. The man shook his head, but was smiling, his belly jumping a little. He liked Mickey's joke, and nodded his head toward the lock, letting him go on. The two other men stepped across to the abutment, allowing Mickey to move forward with the mules.

Ben sighed.

Maybe all that worry was over nothing. Maybe I have just worked myself into a lather over nothing.

The towline came up out of the water as the mules drew it tight and began to pull the bow straight again. Ben angled the tiller to put the barges back into the center of the canal, and laughed to himself over nothing at all.

Maybe the men did not cross into Pennsylvania. That must be it. They watched from the bridge, but did not go back to the lock.

But the men turned with Mickey as he went under the bridge and began to walk with him.

No. It will not be easy for us. These men go where they please.

The distance to the lock finally slipped behind them as Mickey led the team along the path beyond the open lock gates and to the subbing post near the opposite end of the lock cavity. Anthony's barge entered the cavity first and moved deeper into the little granite canyon, the *Ugly Boat* slipping in as the stern, and Mickey pulling loose rope around the snubbing post until the bow of

Anthony's barge kissed the inside of the upper lock. Ben pushed the tiller all the way over to bring the rudder flush against the stern so the lower gates could close behind him. The muffled stillness in the well formed by the granite walls and huge wood beamed lock gates was only momentary, as the locktender leaned against the iron rod at the top of the upper gates opening the sluices at the bottom, to let five thousand gallons of water rush in from up canal to fill the chamber. At first the water sounded like a raging flood until the level rose above the tops of the sluices. Water quickly rose within the chamber bringing the barges up toward the tops of the granite lock walls, bringing the barges up to the waiting men. Ben snatched up his cup of cold coffee laced with brandy still sitting on top of the cabin.

The men had separated along the lock walls, with one near each gate and one near the center. The man that had been sitting on the stool in front of the barn had brought his rifle up and rested it in the crook of his arm. A pistol was tucked inside a wide harness belt. He looked down into the lock cavity watching the boat rise before him. He must have watched that same feat a hundred times since he had come to the Line from South Carolina, but still found it amazing. He watched the straw hat rise from below and looked into the tillerman's face as his head rose above the capstones of the granite wall. The bargeman was drinking from a battered tin cup and talking into it at the same time.

"...the Goddamned Hell a man can't get his work done without somebody stopping things or slowing things down!"

The boatman leaned forward slightly and pointed his cup toward the other's face.

"What the Hell is so all fired important that you had to stop my barges before we got to the lockhouse?!"

He waved his cup in the general direction of the locktender's house, sending a spray of coffee over the rim of the cup into an arc that traced his movement across the wall caps, the dust of the tow path and across the boots of the slave chaser, the sound of the liquid falling on stiff leather reaching the owner's ears. Ben continue his tirade even as the two men came eye level to eye level, and the sound of liquid on dry leather continued. Next, there was the sound of raindrops falling onto a puddle that became the sound of a small trickle of water pouring steadily into a bowl, and then the sound of water being poured onto hard leather.

The slaver breathed heavily from lack of sleep, from the want of breakfast and a good cup of coffee he could smell coming from the lockhouse. He was not in the mood to hear whatever complaints this water floating farmer had to say to him, and certainly not in the mood to let a farmer cuss him in front of other men. His rising anger found its way through the grog of night watch and he opened his mouth to give the boatman a blast of his own oaths, and maybe the butt of his rifle as well, when a piece of his mind that had been napping, but also listening to the water pour on his boots, told him to look down.

To his horror, the sound of water pouring was actually the sound of this cussing farmer rising up with the barge deck riding the climbing water from the deep well of the lock cavity pissing on the wall and his boots! Frozen for a moment while the realization that this damned farmer was actually pissing on him while the man continued to cuss him, holding his tin cup in his other hand and spraying its contents as well, the slaver nearly shrieked.

He jumped back from the yellow stream still arching out of the farmer's open fly and still continued to receive droplets of spray on his boots and lower pant legs as the spray dashed itself into the muddy puddle forming in and around the foot prints where he had stood.

"What the hell??!!...You Goddamned son of a bitch!" he yelled, lifting and shaking first one boot then the other, flicking droplets and urine soaked mud. He looked back at the farmer and then down at his pants surveying the damage, and cussing into his knees as he grabbed the seams of his trousers and shook them violently trying to rid himself of the contamination. He looked up again at the boatman, unable to find the right cussword to fit the situation and none would do, so he worked his jaws in silent rage and then stomped his feet into the dust of the towpath. He managed to find his voice and let loose a stream of profanities, not even forming a cussing sentence, just emitting a series of obscenities, his mind reaching into the darkened vault of the vilest words he had ever uttered or heard, and flung them out at the farmer still standing there waving his cup with one hand and holding his prick with the other, and still trying to direct his urine toward the slaver's boots. Spittle emerged from the corners of the slaver's mouth as he raged at the farmer, and began to step toward him menacingly.

Ignoring the continued stream of urine, the slaver moved toward Ben, bringing his rifle around, not butt first, but barrel first. Still cursing over his rifle, the slaver brought the barrel up toward Ben's face, quickly stepping forward again and brought the tip of the barrel within inches in front of Ben. Ben hooked the edge of his tin cup over the end of the barrel and pulled it aside, and then grabbed the barrel with his other hand and quickly pulled the rifle from the man's grip. The slaver was able to grab back at the weapon with his extended hand that had been under the barrel, and seized the stock before Ben could toss it away. The slaver reached far forward with his other hand to regain possession of his rifle. He was going to shoot this pissing farmer and nail his body to a nearby tree as soon as he got his rifle back!

Ben and the slaver both saw it at the same time, almost as if both were bystanders watching two other men quarrel over a rifle. Ben was standing firmly on the deck of the barge as it rose with the water, bringing him slightly higher than the level of the towpath. The slaver, standing on urine soaked mud, leaning far over his center of gravity, his toes holding his entire weight, his heels off the ground, and his arms far out in front of his body. Even without looking down the slaver realized he was beginning to slip within the pool of urine. Nor did

Ben need to look down to see where the man was going. And then it happened as if they had both already seen it happen.

Ben leaned back further, gripping the barrel of the rifle, holding its deadly end pointing beside but away from him, pulling the man farther off balance. The slaver loosened the grip on his rifle as his mind yelled for him to find something to hold on to. Obeying the orders to seek support, the slaver's hands flailed out in all directions bringing his arms out in deformed arches and looking like a plucked chicken trying to fly. The worn boot soles below his toes began to slip backwards, the wet powdered clay performing as grease to enhance his movement. His rifle slipped to Ben, the man's shoulders, arms and hands shot forward and his feet were sent flying behind him. In an instant he was spread eagled in the air above the ground, above the puddle of muddy urine, and he just managed to look down at his descent and scream.

"Son of a Bi-...!!"

And his chest and face slapped hard into the puddle, sending mud in a sunburst array onto dry dusty ground around him.

Ben glanced at the rifle. The stock was ancient, the wood near the lock was burned down some telling him that it had begun life long ago as a flintlock, but it had been converted for cap and ball. It was not an especially good rifle like an Armstrong or a Hawkens, but it would fire in the rain or a wet snow.

But it will not fire with a barrel full of water lying in the bottom of the canal.

He let the rifle fall from his hands into the narrow space between the side of the barge and the lock wall. It clattered briefly between the wood and the rock and then splashed easily into the now deep water, sending out a farewell gloop as the water rushed into the barrel and it sank down to the mud lying over the teak wood bottom.

21

The slaver lying in the urine-soaked mud continued to curse loudly and struggled to regain his feet. He pushed himself up on his hands and knees, flicking mud drops from side to side shaking his head, not wanting to touch his own face, and reaching for his pistol as he forced one foot in front of himself and came to rest on his other knee. Ben watched in surprise as the man began pulling the pistol from his belt and saw the murder in the man's eyes. Drawn to the noise, the other two men and Mickey were running toward Ben and the man kneeling in the mud.

"God damn you!" The man before Ben growled, spittle joining the mud on his chin. The pistol barrel cleared the man's belt and the hammer was being thumbed back as the man threw his shoulder aside to allow his arm the room it needed to complete the motion. Ben could see from the corner of his eye that others were rushing back toward him from the direction of Anthony's barge.

They will not come in time. This man will kill me and then they will look in Anthony's boat and they will kill him as well.

He did not know these men, but he did know men that killed, and knew that killing was a thirst that a single death did not always slake, once it started. And it would start with him, but he would not be there to see it finished.

Almost by their own control, and without his conscious order for them to move, his shoulder and arms raised his hand that had clenched to the tiller grip, lifting the heavy wooden bar free of its spindle as if it had been designed and greased to come off so quickly. His shoulders began to rotate and his arm dragged his clinging hand and the oak tiller bar around his body in a wide arc toward the man in the mud before him. The man's eyes stayed on Ben's face as his hand and arm brought the pistol up so he could kill this farmer who had pissed on him. Aligned with his side, the pistol began its rise showing the 50-caliber opening at the end of its stubby barrel.

Ben watched the opening become more round and darker as it came closer to his face and took its position along the line of sight from the man's eyes to his. The man's eyes blinked as he realized something was coming his way and he first shifted his eyes, then his face to better see the dark object flying in from his unprotected side. The man's left arm rose to block the tiller bar while his right continued to follow its instructions to kill the farmer, and his eyes tried to feed his brain images of both sides at once, only showing him Ben's face in the middle. The gun's cap and powder exploded at the same moment the wooden bar flew above his left arm and smashed into his head. For an instant both men were enveloped in the gray cloud of gunpowder gases, and an instant later the cloud moved away as the kneeling man fell to the ground and Ben fell to the deck behind.

Ben watched the gray clouds spin over him as he fell back onto the deck and began to slip away from consciousness. There was no sound in the world outside his body, only his own breathing and the ringing in his ears after the gun went off so near his head. A sharp pain spread along the left side of his skull and he could feel warm liquid pour down the side of his face and over onto his shoulder as his head silently landed on the deck. A seagull flew overhead, come to see what the humans were up to. A darkness ran in from the edges of his vision to grab the seagull in the center of his view, and then there was nothing to see but the darkness.

He heard his breath leave his chest and he waited for it to return, but the darkness ran deep into his mind and it all became nothing.

Ben stumbled along in the darkness, hearing the sound of his own footsteps echo off the rock walls of the unlit cave. He could not remember entering the cave, nor where the cave was, but he set that aside in his mind while he worked to find his way out. He stopped walking for a moment to listen for that other sound.

Wait. Wait. Yes, that was it!

It was a voice farther down or up the cave – he wasn't sure which direction was correct, but he traveled in the direction of the voice.

"Who are you?"

He yelled again, and the voice answered, but he could not understand what the voice had said. He yelled again. This time he heard several voices. They were yelling and whispering and echoing in the darkness. Something touched him on his arm and he reached out into the blackness beside him but found nothing to grasp. The voices grew louder. They were coming. The voices grew louder yet, and the left side of his head began to throb, the pain growing more severe as the voices neared. He heard a young girl scream, a long wailing scream, and the pain in his own head became worse. Something grabbed his arm and spun him about, dizziness and nausea sweeping over him with a vengeance. That voice again. Louder and closer, and light beginning to show in that direction. His heart thumped within his chest fighting the dizziness to see and face this thing in the fading darkness.

The voice boomed within his ears matching the iron hammer throbbing of his skull.

"Ben!" Simon called his name again.

Ben rolled over onto his back among sweat drenched covers of his cabin bunk. He tried to look at Simon, but only one eye could send him the image, his other eye still in a brown haze of semi-darkness.

"C-can't see..."

The words halted in his chest, unable to struggle their way out through the dry throat and the cracked lips. Simon slipped one arm under Ben's pillow and gently lifted his head toward the cup of water he brought to Ben's lips. The first minute spill of water over the metal rim slipped onto Ben's lips and down into his mouth. Ben swallowed first at nothing, but the water that soaked into his lips and under his tongue was joined by slightly more that found its way down a dry plaster throat. The liquid made its way past his tongue and announced to his body that water had arrived. The desperate need for water brought Ben fully awake and he reached with his hand to tip more of the water into his mouth, hungrily working his jaw to draw in more of the nectar.

Simon moved the cup back away from Ben's lips, while Ben tried to track the cup's movement with his head, to stay in contact with that wonderful little flow of water.

"Easy does it, Ben."

"More," Ben pleaded.

"You drink too fast and it'll just come right back up, if it doesn't drown you."

Simon lowered Ben's pillow back down and Ben settled into it, not trying to raise up himself.

"Can't see much out of my left eye. Is it there?"

His hand automatically reaching up to his face, feeling a coarse stiff covering at his cheek just under his eye.

"Ben, you took bad powder burns to your face and that left eye. It's suffered a lot, but you must have been squinting or already had your eye closed when the gun went off, else you'd be full blind in that eye. As it is, Miss Mauzy thinks it'll be alright, except maybe your cheek is going to stay pocked after that scabbing comes off."

"Mauzy?..."

Ben delicately placed his fingertips along the

surface of the series of scabs spread across his cheek to just below his eye.

"How did it form so quickly?..."

Simon turned his head away from Ben, staring intently through the wooden bulkhead toward the bow as another scream penetrated the oak boards surrounding them.

"Melissa's having a hard time of it, Miss Mauzy said she thinks..."

"Who the Hell is Mauzy?"

Simon did not turn away from his sightless vigil toward the forward barge.

"You met her the same time you met Melissa, the other night before we crossed the line."

No more screams came. Simon let his shoulders settle a littlet and turned back to Ben.

"She's the old woman. Came up from North Carolina. Say's now that she's in free Pennsylvania, everyone has to call her "Miz Mauzy".

"We made it across to Pennsylvania? Did they find anyone in Anthony's cabin?"

Simon shook his head.

"Never even looked. They were trying to decide whether to hang you from a tree for near killing their friend when me and Toby got there..."

"You and Toby? Why was Toby... what were you...?"

Ben struggled to rise up on his elbows to continue with his questions. Maybe all this would be straighter in his head if his head were straighter. Simon blocked Ben's shoulders from rising off the bunk and firmly kept him down amongst the loose covers.

"You need to stay down, Ben. You're not ready to be up. We weren't sure if you were even going to live, so don't mess it all up now by breaking your stitches and bleeding to death. Mauzy said if you got up and then died, that she'd bring you back from the dead just so she could slap you!"

Chuckling under his breath Simon added, "And I believe she could do just that."

Ben let his aching head settle back into his pillow. "What in th'Hell happened?...How long was I unconscious?...What happened?"

Simon patted Ben's chest. "You just lay still and I'll tell you everything, but you got to lay still."

Ben relaxed fully and Simon rested an elbow on the bunk frame near the upper edge of the mattress, and recounted the events of the past three days.

Hearing the cursing and yelling, Mickey and the two other slave chasers raced back toward the stern of the *Ugly Boat*, and were only yards away when the slaver fired his pistol at Ben from less than two arms length away. The gray gunpowder cloud was still drifting over the deck of the barge when the trio came to the sides of their fallen companions. Mickey hopped onto the deck of the barge and the slavers knelt next to the man laying face down in the mud. Each little group flashed quick looks at the other to ensure nothing else would happen and then began to provide aid. Both men were unconscious. A wide puddle of blood had spread across the deck from Ben's head and the left side of his face was covered in black powder and still smoking.

Mickey quickly ran his hand across the powder and then pulled off his shirt to staunch the flow of blood and see if Ben was alive. Ben's hair was soaked in blood, his neck and upper left shoulder was covered in it. Dabbing first at the neck and then at the side of Ben's head, Mickey was able to soak up enough blood to see the actual wound. There was a flash of sickly pure white instantly covered again in bright red blood. Mickey blotted the area again and determined the size of the opening. In the middle of the small field of white was a shallow groove which filled with blood first, surrounded by a grotesque smile of split scalp and tissue slipped away from the exposed skull itself. Anthony had leaped across from the stern of the *Wilhelmina* and joined Mickey at Ben's side.

Mickey looked up at Anthony as he came near.

"Doesn't look like it tore into his brain. But I've seen men die from less damage. He's bleeding awfully bad."

Anthony had brought a bag with him from his cabin. It had been prepared by the Philadelphia Anti-Slavery Society so he could tend to brutalized runaway slaves, and it was full of clean linen strips and a variety of salves. He pulled the first bundle of strips from the bag and with Mickey's help began to wrap the strips around Ben's head. Seeing that the gunfire had apparently ended, the lock tender had come up to the lock wall, and had been joined by the other bargeman and several other people on that side of the canal. Three men from the barn and tack shop were standing in the dusty clearing near the fallen slaver.

One of the slavers stood and turned toward Anthony and Mickey.

"Is he dead?"

"Not yet," was all Anthony could say.

"Well, Charles here almost got his brains bashed in. His skull's caved in some under his scalp, but his heart is still beatin. What the Hell happened 'tween these two?"

The slaver picked up his dropped rifle and brazenly stepped past the men kneeling on the deck and barged down into the cabin. The other men remained near their comrade and looked over at the cabin as the other slaver came back up and shook his head. He had found nothing they were looking for. Nothing to explain why Charles had tried to kill the boatman. The slaver stepped away from the cabin and gripped the lower edge of one of the cargo hatch covers. Keeping his eyes on the barge men he strained to lift the hatch and quickly looked down into the hold. He looked over at his partner next to Charles.

"Looks like bales of cotton."

The man kneeling in the dust next to Charles nodded toward the forward barge. The slaver dropped the hatch cover and spoke to Mickey and Anthony.

"What's in the other barge?"

Anthony answered over his shoulder.

"Same thing. Good Georgia Cotton. Pennsylvania folk buy a lot of it."

The man next to Charles patted the downed man's face, allowing his head to roll to the side. He spoke toward Anthony.

"This boy dies, and I'll gut that other from prick to heart."

The other slaver stepped past the bargemen, keeping the killing end of his rifle barrel in their direction and glancing down at Ben's pale battered face.

"You'll need to do it quick-like, Andrew, if you want to do it before he's gone anyway. This ol'boy ain't long for the world. Charles killed him for sure."

Andrew slapped Charles face again.

"Shit." He looked down again and slapped Charles face harder. Charles emitted a faint groan and turned his head away from the slap.

"Charles, you Goddamned swamper. Sheriff said if we killed a white man we'd answer to him. And we here on Pennsylvania dirt. I told you we ought t'check the barges still down at the bridge, you stupid swamper!"

Charles moaned again.

The tissue on the side of his head swelled noticeably, deforming the shape of his head. Andrew slapped his face again harder and Charles moaned again.

If he was awake he'd kill me for slapping him.

Andrew looked over at the barge, saw that his partner was still looking at the fallen boatman, smiled a small smile to himself and then slapped Charles face again, as hard as he could. The slap split Charles lower lip and blood began to drip down across his chin. Charles growled at the pain and rolled over on to his side. The dizziness and nausea following the head injury caused him dry heaves. He then rolled over onto his stomach and back into the dwindling area of caking mud. Andrew stood and stepped away from Charles.

Pulaski's Canal

The locktender yelled across the lock, some of his bravery returning as he sensed a waning in the confidence and bravado of the slave chasers.

"Is either of'em dead?"

He did not like them there, did not like the way they strutted across the line into Pennsylvania, like their kind of trash belonged there. He did not care one way or another about slavery – he had none, but if he had a large farm and the money, he probably would need them. Fact was, it was the law down south, and it ought to stay down south. Pennsylvania had its own law, and that law said no slaves up here. It also said if people got to shooting at each other or otherwise trying to kill each other – or even worse, harm good Pennsylvania folk – then the Sheriff came and took them off to jail and judge.

"Maybe I ought to send for the sheriff!" he yelled out, fingering the bell rope waiting to see the kind of response his statement would get.

Andrew had returned to look down at Charles, and used his boot to roll him over onto his back. Squatting down, the other man reached over and brushed the mud and dirt from Charles face, and then stood up. Both men faced the bargemen deciding what to do next. Each man still held his rifle, and each barrel drifted almost of its own accord in the direction of the barge. Mickey and Anthony rose and turned to face the men from the deck. The men up from the barn stepped back down the path, but still watched intently. The locktender released the bell cord, and began to move back away from the lock. The small knot of people that had surrounded him to watch the excitement moved back with him. A faint whisper of wind drifted through the treetops above and the water gurgled over the tops of the lower gate tops. Mickey watched the slavers closely, the movement of their jackets as they breathed, the tight grips they had around their rifles, the lean of their stance, trying to guess what they might do next.

Keeping his head still he quickly scanned the deck area close by, looking for anything he might be able to use as a weapon. Nothing. The tiller bar was on the ground next to the downed slaver. Anthony began to raise his hand and open his mouth to speak among them. Something had to take the coil out of this spring that had caught them all. He stopped his hand movement when he realized it resulted in a similar rise of Andrew's rifle.

Andrew's movement was echoed and magnified in the other man, who moved one foot a half step back and brought the butt of his rifle into the crook of his arm. Andrew peered from one angle then another trying to see if either of the boatmen had a pistol, and the movement caused Anthony to turn slightly away. Anthony reacted to Andrew fearing he might shoot. Andrew raised his rifle higher, fearing the boatman was trying to hide his pistol while preparing to draw it out. The faint wind dropped down out of the trees and ran across the dust of the towpath between the groups, creating a small dervish – a dust devil, the miniature cousin of a tornado, no higher than a man's knee. It spun three times and then fell to the ground, its miniscule wind exhausted, laid down between the two groups of men.

A conch shell horn erupted from down canal. The slavers' rifle barrels instantly came up pointing at the heads of Anthony and Mickey, but down as quickly and the slavers looked back down canal in the direction of the horn. It sounded again, and the barge's mule team came into view from the bend in the canal a hundred yards away. The conch shell sounded a third time, echoing off the granite boulders in the hill side above the locktender's house and the dry goods store. Anthony turned to look at the oncoming barge as well. Sitting atop the lead mule was a little brown boy, who could not stand to be boxed up inside Anthony's cabin. Toby. The barge came full into view and letting the gray light from the overcast sky place its meager illumination on the black man at the tiller. Simon. The steady forward movement of the barge slowly bringing the normal activity back to the lock.

One by one the people at the edge of the towpath and behind the locktender began to awake and look around themselves, trying to find the threads of reality that slipped through their fingers to watch those men step closer to mutual destruction and death.

The rifle barrels were back down pointing toward the ground. Charles rolled onto his side and begin to spit mud, dust and dried blood from his mouth. The locktender found his voice again.

"Do I need to send for the sheriff? Is that barge man dead?"

Anthony placed his fingers against the side of Ben's neck and felt his pulse.

"He's alive!" he yelled back over his shoulder.

The Sheriff won't help Ben. That would only make things all the worse, and it could take two days by the time someone from here found the Sheriff in York, and then brought him back here.

Anthony spoke to Mickey.

"Help me carry Ben down into the cabin, then let's get out of here. Do you know if there is a doctor in York furnace?"

Mickey slowly shook his head while he looked down at Ben's pale face.

"I know, and there ain't one. Closest one is Wrightsville."

"Then we have to take him there."

Anthony looked over at the slavers.

"We have to take this man to Wrightsville."

The slavers nodded and backed away still facing the barge. Then Anthony and Mickey carried Ben down to his bunk, and as they returned to the deck the lock tender reasserted his authority over the lock by yanking on the bell cord several times. Anthony took the tiller as Mickey limped to the mule team, unwrapped the towrope from around the snubbing post and began to pull the line along the towpath. The locktender leaned against the beam extending from the lock gate and began the ponderous swing into the upper holding pond to open the lock up canal. The mules seemed to sense Mickey's urgency and had stepped out handsomely, taking up all the slack in the line by the time the gate was open far enough to let the barges out.

As soon as the stern of the *Ugly Boat* cleared the opening, the waiting barge was already running its bow across its faint wake. Ten minutes later the barge was on its way down canal while Simon, Toby, and the locktender watched the *Turtle* rise in the lock to the level of the upper holding pond. Toby was completely lost over what to do, but the mule knew to stop at the snubbing post, and Simon had pulled the barge into the lock hand over hand, letting the wet towrope pile onto the deck.

Simon shook his head and gave a big toothy grin and chuckle to the locktender.

"Boy ain't learned nuthin'!"

The locktender smiled at Simon, and did not even consider the little black boy standing near him. He knew Simon worked for Ben, though he did not know either well. He kept his own counsel, and talked freely to only a few of the bargemen. Ben was simply not one of them. Simon would never be. He asked Simon no questions, but handed him the clipboard. There was no need to carry a lie on the clip board, so Simon placed a third vertical mark next to Ben's signature. The locktender accepted it with a silent nod and opened the lock gate.

With no one on board to check on Ben, less than thirty minutes away from Lock number19, Anthony signaled Mickey he wanted to pull against the towpath. The barge secured, he went down into the cabin to find Ben on his side, but fresh blood was beginning to pool around his head. He found the society assistance bag and pulled out another bundle of bandages. He was uneasy about removing the previous bandages, thinking some of the area may have begun to clot, so he simply added another layer. This layer was tighter and created a firmly seated cap around his head. Another loop of bandages went over the fresh salve on Ben's left cheek. Anthony knew that if Ben were going to live, his scalp would have to be stitched. He also knew that he was unable to do such a chore.

There was a thump against the hull of the *Ugly Boat*, and the heavy first thud of bare feet jumping onto the deck. Before Anthony could reach the steps to the cabin, the hatch was blocked of the gray light slipping down from the sky, and then large black calloused feet stepped down bringing Simon to the cabin floor. Anthony released his breath.

"Ben was shot in the head!"

Simon asked a short series of questions forcing Anthony to refine his description until Simon had a better idea of the damage to his friend. Simon turned and went back up the stairs speaking as he went.

"At least we got Mauzy with us. That's pure good luck for Ben."

Simon returned to the cabin of the *Ugly Boat* carrying a small body wrapped in a wool blanket. Mickey held on to Mauzy letting her step sideways down the same steps, fighting age and arthritis in her hips, they worked their way down into the cabin. They moved past Anthony, Mauzy's bent frame almost shifting him aside as she went straight to examine Ben.

"Need some light in here," she said from Ben's side without turning. "There's a heap of blood here, some still fresh. He's bleeding awful."

Simon pulled a whale oil lamp from one of the cabinets near the bunk and set it on the table while he pulled out and unwrapped the flint kit and loose wick to light it. As soon as he had a small flame, he transferred it to the wick of the oil lamp and covered the flame with its glass chimney. He set it in a gimbal on the wall near the bunk. Mauzy turned to Mickey.

"You got more cloth?"

Anthony held up the bag from the Society and handed it to Mickey. She glanced into the bag seeing the generous amount of bandages within and raised her eyebrows.

"Good for you, young'un. Your friend here need a lot of patchin, do he?"

"Supposed to be for you," He mumbled. "They sent it down from Philadelphia. It's got an assortment of salves."

Turning back to watch her own hands, she continued to unwrap Ben's bandages as she spoke to Mickey.

"Open'em all up child, and put'em on the table over there. I'll need ta smell'em to see if any of'em will do this boy any good."

She uncovered Ben's scalp and looked down at the four-inch gash showing shiny white skull centered in the spread of bright red blood.

"Well now," she said to the wound, "ain't you pretty. Clean cut with a nice big scratch on his head bone. Head cuts bleed awful, like all the blood's gonna come out, but some ain't all that bad in the long run."

She placed a blood-soaked bandage back against the wound as fresh blood poured into the gash and ran down Ben's neck. Mauzy turned to face Mickey keeping one hand holding the bandage on the wound and pointing a gnarled blood covered finger from her other at Anthony's bag.

"You got any stitching twine in that there bag?"

"Y-yes. I think there is some silk thread for stitches."

"Silk thread for stitchin' skin. Now ain't that somethin'," Mauzy said to herself, as she continued to look at Anthony's face and as he continued to stare at her. After a silent pause she said, "Well young'un, you gonna just stand there wasting this good whale oil and that boy's blood, or you gonna get me that silk thread?"

Mickey jerked into motion searching the bottom of the bag for the thread. She reached up to the underside of her old smock collar and pulled a shiny steel needle into the lamp light.

"Here," she said handing the needle to Mickey. "Thread that needle and then wipe it off with somethin' clean. I ain't been able to thread a needle in years, but I can still sew up a storm. Calico or people skin, don't make no difference to me. I do'em either one, but it's easier to see stitchin' on white folk."

She pulled a second needle from her collar.

"You boys lucky I carry two needles, and ain't lost either of them. This feller's head going to take a lot of work."

She handed the needle to Mickey in trade for the one he had threaded.

The wrapped body Simon had placed in one of the bunks on the opposite side of the cabin began to moan. Anthony spun around to look in that direction.

"I gots to look after both of'em , so I brung the girl with me. You make that there patch on your trousers, young man?"

"Yes ma'am." Mickey said.

"Then you're gonna help me stitch. I got to get this head done and look after Missy there."

Mickey slowly shook his head.

"I don't know if I can do that."

"Course you can. You did them trousers. You use the same stitch on this head."

She turned to Simon.

"You get a fire going in that little stove and boil some fresh river water. Don't you get it from this filthy canal. Been too many people spittin an pissin in it – you go on out to the river and put your bucket where the water's runnin fastest."

Mauzy pointed her needle at the ripped skin nearest Mickey.

"You start there. Work toward me."

Melissa rolled onto her back in the narrow bunk. Her breathing grew deeper and harsher, each exhale rasping out of her little chest while she fought the growing strength of the next contraction. When her breathing quickened and deepened until it could do no more of either, she sucked in a lungful of air, raised her knees until they bumped the slats of the bed above her, and screamed. The sound pierced the ears and mind of everyone in the cabin. She screamed with a pain that nothing in her fourteen years had prepared her to endure, no pain had ever been this bad. She was terrified that the pain exploding between her legs would split her body open like an overripe tomato, and at the same moment another part of her mind prayed that someone would stick a knife into her just to release the pressure.

"Fight it, Child!" Mauzy commanded from beside Ben's bunk. "Turn over on your side. You got to git that youngun in you to slip around so it'll come out right!" She added to herself, "Child's too damned young to be havin a baby of her own."

She emphasized her thought by yanking on the first stitch she had just run between the two lips at the edges of Ben's wound, pulling the skin there together in a small pucker.

"I was only a year older than that child when I slid my first onto a pile of rags in Charleston. They took it as soon as the cord was tied off, didn't even know if I'd had a girl or a boy, then stood me up on the block for sale, with stains of afterbirth still on my legs."

Mauzy placed another stitch into the skin of the white man who had tried to help them on their way, and looped the shiny silk into a knot keeping the skin tight and her line straight.

"I think it was a boy. If he' still alive he's probably picking cotton or cutting sugar cane somewhere down in South Carolina, no thought or image of a momma anywhere in his mind."

Melissa screamed again as Simon came back down the cabin steps. The sound of his big bare feet thumping down the wooden steps told Mauzy that he was there and she did not take her eyes from the seam she was sewing along the side of Ben's head.

"You get one of them clean rags from that other boy's bag and wipe Melissa's head, Simon. Try to keep her still if ya can, and get her to roll onto her side. It'll help her baby."

Simon nodded to Mauzy's back and dipped a handful of linen strips into the bucket of cold river water. He squeezed much of the loose water out and knelt down beside Melissa to place the rag on her forehead. Mauzy took a quick look at Simon over her shoulder then shook her head.

Won't help anyway. That baby ain't comin out alive. Probably kill Melissa too.

She looked into Mickey's eyes.

"You doin fine, young man. You got doctor stitches there. You got healin hands."

"I have the devil's hands. And they'll make mischief as soon as I'm done here."

"You talk a lot of horse shit, young man. You got healin hands there. Takin to that like you was born for it."

Melissa screamed again. Mauzy made several more stitches then tied off and stepped back.

" You finish it. I got to tend to this child."

Mickey did not look up from his work. His stitches as secure and neat as Mauzy's.

Anthony had a fire going in the small iron stove in the corner of the cabin. In the fading gray daylight managing to find its way through the small windows near the roof of the cabin, the yellow and red of firelight from a poorly covered pothole in the top of the stove flickered around the room. Melissa screamed again, a long wailing shriek. Mickey dabbed at the blood oozing from Ben's wound so he could see where to put his next stitch. Blood and stitches in a ghastly wound. Melissa screamed again, and Mauzy tried to help the baby turn inside of her. The firelight flittered about the room throwing shadows of Mauzy, Simon, Mickey and Anthony, first on one wall then on another. Anthony took in the scene. Mickey paused to straighten his shoulders and relieve the strain out of his back, took in a deep breath, then bent down to sew another stitch into Ben's flesh.

Pulaski's Canal

This must be what hell is going be like.

And Melissa screamed again.

It rained during the night. The water washing dust off the leaves and softening the soil along the river bank on the towpath. In the rare hours after midnight thunder rolled along the Susquehanna River, throwing lightning out into its path to light its way. Two miles south of the three barges staked together along the towpath, Charles Lamoor Worthingood sat up from his pallet in the barn at the Line. His head pounded with each heartbeat, and he felt the stab of a dozen nails run deep into his brain. He walked out the small back door of the barn to stand under the eve, staying out of the rain while he relieved himself in the darkness, adding his own stream to the rush of raindrops falling from the night clouds.

The wind shifted, slightly tossing misted rain into his face, and his right arm fell limp by his side. He had to struggle to put himself back within his wool britches and button his flap with only his left hand, and tried to figure out what was happening. He had laid wrong on his arm before and woke to find it numb, before the pine needle stabs ran along its length as it reawakened. He turned to reenter the barn, but leaned with his right shoulder against the wall, his right leg joining his arm in numbness, forcing his shoulder and his chin against the rough cut vertical boards of the wall. The pain in his head worsened.

Lightning in the sky tossed splashes of white light around the barn and he could see the green of the moss and the gray wood grains in front of his eye, and watched unable to close his eyelid as his face began to slide slowly along the rough surface. Unable to keep his stand or bring his left leg to support himself, he endured splinter after splinter being harvested into his chin, jaw, and cheek. He tried to curse at his fall but his lips and tongue no longer responded to his command. Lightning continued within his head and the feeling of razor cuts whirled within his brain.

He managed to bring his left hand against the barn and push himself around and get his face off the wall, but continued his slip toward the ground, his legs folding beneath him like old leather chaps. The pain on his face stopped and he felt nothing on his back as it slipped along the vertical surface of the rough hewn board, tearing his shirt and gouging his skin. The pain in his head grew worse and felt like it could explode out through his very eyes. He sat in the mud and straw under the eve of the barn, slumped against the wall and the wind shifted again bringing the raindrops onto the top of his head and down his face. He looked out from inside his head feeling nothing except the stabbing pain and saw the world tilt around him as his head leaned down to his shoulder, let down by sleeping neck muscles.

The blow to his head earlier that day broke a tiny artery no bigger than a pin head just inside his skull bone. The whiskey he drank throughout the afternoon kept his blood thin and the little artery did not clot. The blood seeped by drops into the space between the skull and the brain with nowhere else to go. The pool of blood was now almost as big as a child's fist, spreading out, pushing against the sponge-like brain and one by one turning off the controls to his body. His body ceased to be a slave of his mind, responding to his every thought or instruction, and became a slumping vessel responding only to gravity. At last the pain stopped and his head fell forward over his folded knees. He noticed he had missed a button of his fly. Lightning flashed again but he could not raise his head or move any part of his body.

The old hound that slept on the locktender's porch made his nightly rounds along the outer edge of the barn, sniffing the ground as he came. Seeing Charles he trotted toward him under the eve and nudged up against his elbow with his loose jowled snout looking for a tidbit for chewing or a rub behind his long ears. The man's arm fell limp to the ground and the dog sniffed at the body and backed away into the rain. The lightning came again but Charles could not see the flash.

Goddamned farmer.

Pulaski's Canal

The rain poured down upon the form against the barn wall and the vapor that rises from a living body caught in cool rain, thinned and faded away.

The rain stopped and daybreak finally came to the canal, stopping briefly to look in on the people in the barge tied to the towpath, and then moved on keeping ahead of the sun. The clouds stayed where they were, content to rest in the sky above Pennsylvania and Maryland, recovering from the thunder and lightning hurled back and forth over the humans during the night. Mauzy wrapped an unmoving light skinned infant girl in a blanket scrap and laid it on the top of one of the cargo hatches for Simon to collect when he returned from his digging. The rain had swollen the river and added some height to the canal, and the canal water current whispered as it ran along the sides and ends of the barges. Ben slept a deep sleep, his newly stitched wound wrapped in clean bandages, while Melissa laid on her side with an old striped pillow padded between her knees and quietly sobbed her remaining tears into the blanket at her face. Anthony snored in the bunk below Ben, and Mauzy sat next to Mickey on the stubby bench at the little corner table smoking her pipe. All of her joints ached and her usual sparse ankles were swollen from the night of work. Mickey wiped the blood from his hands with a wet rag.

"You did mighty good, young'un. I tell you, you got healin hands."

Mickey shrugged his shoulders and leaned forward resting his elbows on his knees, and hanging his head.

Mauzy looked down at her wrinkled hands.

"Most places got lots of men with strong killin hands. Killin is easy, and there's a whole world of hurt and meanness out there. There are rivers of blood flowing from here to Jordan – so much blood it must make God cry. He must cry to see the meanness we set upon each other down here."

"Then why doesn't he stop the bloodshed?"

267

"He don't work for me, chile. I work for him. He ain't stopped slavery, but he led me to get out of it. I did that with his help to hold my mind together long enough to git gone. You ain't stopped the killin in this world, but tonight you kept one fella from being dead. That's the best thing you're ever gonna to get to do. Don't you waste that."

At the Line, one of the men who worked at the mule barn for the S&T Canal Company, led Andrew out the small door at the back of the barn. Andrew stood a few moments looking at what the man had found, looking down at the ashen skinned form staring with sightless eyes down at its own knees.

"Shit." was his only comment, and he kicked the hip of the stiff body.

As the sky brightened by an unseen sun rising above the clouds, an odd trio of an ancient black woman, a large straight black man, and a wild bushy bearded white man, stood over a small grave on the hillside above the canal. Mickey had stayed with Ben, but had poled the *Turtle* across the rain swollen canal to put the three on the upper side.

South of the Line, a handful of men slid a folded hard body into a shallow grave on a tree studded flood plain between the canal towpath and the river. The body would spend eternity laying on its side because the men at the barn could not straighten it out from its folded pose.

On the hillside the old woman reminded God that he had taken too many babies, but that she hoped he would still take this one unto his bosom until it was time for her momma to come get her. She asked God to look after them all, the living and the dead, and that she would appreciate it if he could find it in his heart not to test them too much that day, as they had all had a hell of a night of it as it was.

The men in the stand of trees said nothing and covered Charles with the dirt from his hole, and kept his one other good shirt, his rifle and his pistol. Andrew won the draw of cards over the grave and got the pistol, and then reminded Geoffrey that Charles' rifle was still down in the lock water.

Only one other barge moved up the canal from Havre de Grace that day, and at midmorning it passed the three barges tied together north of Lock number 19. A man with a limp seemed to be the only one about, but he helped pass the towrope over the three barges so the traveler could keep on his way. He was lucky to get so far. The towpath wall just south of Maryland Lock number 2 had given way and most of the canal down that way was too low in water for anything to move. The word had spread up the canal about the break and barges tied up as soon as they heard. No sense going on then. It would only create a jam at Maryland Lock number 1, and the up canal holding pond was too small to handle more than a couple barges.

Ben, Anthony, Melissa and Mauzy slept through most of the day and into the night. Simon and Mickey spent the day doing catch-up work on the barges, and teasing with young Toby. During quiet moments they would glance up to the narrow landing near the maple tree on the hillside above the canal. Andrew spent the rest of the morning watching Geoffrey trying to fish Charles' rifle out of the lock without getting wet, and then went up to the dry goods store, bought a jug of Apple Whiskey and drunk himself to sleep by early evening.

Geoffrey finally had to jump into the lock to find Charles' rifle in the mud and bring it up to the barn. When he finally got all the mud off of it he could see that the hammer had been snapped off when it hit the rock wall on its way into the water the day before.

"Well Damn!" he said to himself and tossed the useless rifle into one of the empty mule stalls. He spent the evening drinking the rest of Andrew's Apple Whiskey trying to decide if Andrew had cheated him or not. Finally, after dark, as he was slipping off to sleep on Charles' pallet, he decided he had been.

Goddamned farmer.

The water in the canal began to rise at noon of the second day after the shooting. The three barges tied along the towpath were briefly visited and passed by two company barges, eager to resume their trip to Wrightsville once the lower canal wall was repaired. Ben had slept the greater part of those two days, while Mauzy visited him often, bathing his new scar in boiled water and changing his bandages. Anthony, Simon and Mickey held a worried conference on the bow of the *Turtle* and decided it was time to move the small convoy on to Wrightsville. They passed through York Furnace just before sunset, not yet wanting to stop at Burl's farm until Ben had been seen by the doctor in Wrightsville; not knowing that Sonja stood at the window of her room looking at the trees standing between the farmhouse and the canal, thinking of Ben. Mauzy told them that Ben was of good stock and would likely be up and about by the time they reached the Wrightsville doctor.

Anthony recalled the wide pool of blood spreading across the deck under Ben's head and resisted Mauzy's optimism, anxious that Ben be treated by a physician. He held his guilt close to his heart knowing that Ben had taken such a ridiculous risk only because Anthony was trying to smuggle slaves across the Line into Pennsylvania. The moment when Anthony told Ben that most of the slaves had decided to go on through the woods by themselves had strained Ben even more. None of that had gone well. Ben was merely to engage the attention of the slave chasers to his own barge by appearing drunk and belligerent, while Anthony was to be the accepting Quaker guiding them through a cursory look in his cabin. The attention was to be focused on Ben's barge and cabin. That part, at least, went as planned.

"They weren't even there?" Ben rasped at Anthony from his bunk.

"No, Ben. Most of them decided to take their chances in the woods. They knew you had to make your decision whether to help. I knew you would, knew you wouldn't turn your back on them. Simon knew it too. But, see, they didn't."

"All this for nothing," Ben said and turned on to his side away from Anthony .

"All that for something," Anthony countered, speaking at Ben's back.

"Mauzy, Melissa and Toby crossed with us. Mauzy was too old and joint-stiff to try to walk through the woods anymore, and probably saved your life!"

In pairs and threes the slaves had found their way across the Line and made their way back to the barges inside Pennsylvania. Those that said anything said they came to check on Mauzy and to hear news about the others. None had heard from Jedediah, but all nervously assumed that the big man had just gone on without them to slow him down. Jedediah was bound for New York State and was not going to stop in Pennsylvania.

Those people had walked a thousand miles and more, daily placing their lives in the hands of strangers. Maybe they had developed a sense of recognizing those white people who were obviously committed to helping them escape, and did not feel Ben had made that commitment.

Looking at the deep stains still enmeshed in the woven cloth of Ben's bunk, Anthony knew Ben had made that commitment. He also knew Ben could have been killed, and that it would have been a guilt Anthony could never escape.

Ben was sitting on the locker near the stern of

the barge sipping Mauzy's broth as Anthony steered the *Ugly Boat* into the holding basin at Wrightsville. The washout at the southern end of the canal had prevented and delayed much of the usual traffic into the basin, leaving the docks open without the usual several hours wait. Anthony and Mickey were off to find the doctor as soon as the barges were tied to the heavy wooden posts supporting the dock. With Mauzy to guard him from becoming too active, Ben waited until Simon arrived in the *Turtle* and allowed his friend to arrange help to hoist out the cotton bales from the three barges. The bales were stacked neatly on the cobblestone roadway when Simon brought the weaver down to look at the cargo.

Mickey and Anthony had Doctor Redding in tow only steps behind the weaver. Dr. Redding stepped briskly in well shined boots onto the barge deck and over toward Ben, naturally drawn to the bundle of bandages wrapping Ben's head. The weaver eagerly pulled white strands from the bale ends checking the quality of the cotton, nodding and smiling to himself over his decision to have this boater bring him less costly cotton. His cotton mill would make a tidy profit from these bales. Yes, he would do this again if the bargeman would bring more.

In his stylish vested suit and beaver skin top hat, Dr. Redding introduced himself and confirmed that Ben was indeed the man to be seen.

"Your friends described a most harrowing hunting accident, Sir. I am amazed to find you sitting up and sipping..."

He bent down to sniff over the cup and nodded approvingly.

"Broth by your own hands. Perhaps the wound is not nearly grievous as your friends supposed. May I examine the wound?"

Ben nodded slightly, still barely whispering his "yes."

On removing the bandage, Dr. Redding stepped back giving Ben and then Anthony and Simon a stern look.

"I am not in the custom of double checking the work of one of my colleagues."

Anthony and Simon traded looks not understanding the doctor's response.

"It is quite obvious, that Doctor Thompson has already seen this man. I recognize his tight stitches with the silk thread."

Mauzy had approached the men at the stern locker to watch the doctor work.

"That there's the handiwork of Mr. O'Grady, young sir..."

Dr. Redding turned to see the old woman now standing beside him. Her palms were planted on her hips and she nodded her chin toward Ben.

"...though the silk thread come from that bushy feller," pointing her chin toward Anthony.

She introduced herself to him as "Miz Mauzy". Dr. Redding began to ask Mauzy a series of quiet questions about her method of stitching, allowing a small smile to emerge beneath his mustache as she spoke. When she was through, she asked if there was something else she should have done, and he shook his head slightly but keeping his smile.

"No, Miss Mauzy, I think you performed an excellent service."

Dr. Redding looked at the men around him.

"Are, um, do any of you gentlemen, that is to say, does Miss Mauzy <u>belong</u> to any of you?"

Before anyone else could speak Mauzy cackled ,

"You mean, is any of-em my man?" and then cackled even louder.

"No, ma'am. What I meant was..."

"I know what you meant, young sir. Don't none of'em own me. I own myself, always have. Just needed to git someplace where folks'd see that."

"Well," Dr. Redding continued "that was real good handiwork - showed great skill. And I know you are not from this county. If you weren't passing on, that is if you were planning to stay...you see I have several free black families, and frequent... visitors on their way farther north, that come to me. Your assistance would be extremely useful. They pay me in chickens and such, but with that and the meager pay I could provide you for just a couple hours a day, you would live well here."

Mauzy patted the doctor's arm, then gave his arm a tight squeeze with her twisted fingers.

"Thank ye kindly, Doctor Reddin. If I'd heard that ten maybe twenty years ago, I woulda made a stay of it. But now I just got enough gittin' left in me to go on to New York. Up near the Canada line, I hear there's places with lots of free black folk. I been hopin ta go there for quite a while."

"Our loss. Still, you said most of the stitching had been performed by Mr. O'Grady?"

Mickey returned the nod to the doctor. "It was indeed, doctor."

"Have you had such training?"

"Just last night."

"Um... I could still use an able assistant. Please come see me if that interests you. Good day, all." and offered Mauzy his hand. She placed hers in his, and he bent over and gently kissed the back of her hand. She laughed and looked away in embarrassment. "Good day to you Miss Mauzy."

He turned to Ben. "Sir, you are obviously in good hands. Your wound is clean, your stitching excellent, and does not have the angry look of putrification." He then turned to Anthony. "For coming to see a patient that has already received proper medical care, there is no charge. For meeting Miss Mauzy, I would almost pay you. However, for leaving my office full of paying patients and trotting down here for no actual emergency, that will be half a dollar."

And he held his hand out to Anthony and kept it out until Anthony dug deep into his trouser pockets, withdrew his coin purse, fetched out two silver quarters, and laid them in the doctor's hand. Dr. Redding then tipped his hat to all in turn, slipped the coins into the pocket of his pressed wool trousers, and stepped across the deck to the dock ramp.

Anthony watched after him as the doctor stepped down the plank way and then called out in curiosity.

"How much would it have been if Ben here still had an open hole in his head?"

The doctor spoke over his shoulder as he walked up the dock toward town.

"Half a dollar!"

Seeing the doctor leave, the weaver stepped over toward the side of the barge holding samples of the cotton in the fingertips of each hand.

"Wonderful!" he exclaimed. "We must all do this again soon!"

Ben gruffed loudly under Mauzy's arm as she rewrapped the bandages around his head, "Not likely!"

Mickey and Anthony laughed among themselves as the man could only stare dumbly at Ben's response.

Simon wondered if the weaver had any idea of the toil that had gone into that flimsy white tuft in his fingers, but at the same moment knew that he did not. And even though Simon did know, he would still help Ben bring another load of it from Annapolis. That was the lure of cotton, everyone that touched it after the slave, received gold from it.

Simon looked over at Mauzy. He saw too the way that Mauzy looked at the cotton, and could see hate in her face. That plant put gold in your hands or scars on your back. It put the hate in Mauzy's lined face and the childish happiness in the round faced weaver. It was all too complicated to think on any more right then. Simon walked over to the dock plank to get the *Turtle* ready to receive the load of coal she would carry back down the canal. Anthony followed Mickey's lead to begin the same for the *Ugly Boat* and the *Wilhelmina*.

Ben watched the men take to their work and felt guilt that he could not yet help. They would not be ready to return until the following morning. And then they would have to pass through the Line again to go home.

Dr. Frederick Redding returned to his office in Wrightsville, apologizing to each waiting patient in his outer lobby as he passed through. He hurriedly removed his frock coat and slipped back into his office smock, not very stylish if his fellows back in Baltimore got a good look at him he thought, but kept his clothes from drips and splatters. Being a bachelor he always looked for opportunities to avoid domestic chores like cleaning clothes. As he reached for his door to go back to his patients, there was a quick rap on the other side and it opened of his own accord. The doorway filled with the bulk of his old friend and school chum visiting in town.

"Ah Wally, how was your visit with Doctor Thompson?"

Without allowing time for an answer Redding continued.

"Had an emergency right after you left, well, at least I thought it was an emergency when the fellow came to collect me. Canaller shot in the head."

Wallace Harper ignored the first question. Even in medical school Redding had always been a chatter box, allowing his mouth to dump his thoughts as they came to him, while his school mates helped him make sense of them. It was only a small chink in the armor of a man the entire class and most of the professors thought of fondly, like an adopted relation.

"Well, Red, that certainly sounds like an emergency to me. Local man?"

"No, not one of mine, and most of the cracked heads and broken ribs from down there do usually find their way to my doorstep. No, these were from the southern end, went down to their barge here at the canal basin. Didn't get their names, though."

Wallace peaked his forehead with lines above raised eyebrows at the mention of Canallers from the Havre de Grace end of the canal.

"I have several friends and acquaintances among the Canallers from Havre de Grace, Red. Describe them to me."

Redding stopped, bringing his forefinger to his chin.

"Well, let's see. One was a big burly fellow, not as tall as you but broader. Shoulders like a miner. Big bushy beard, but his speech was well-mannered and very Philadelphian. There was an African man, quiet, also well spoken – unusually so. The victim was average size, actually he was sitting down and essentially all I looked at were his pupils and his new stitches. And, oh yes, the most marvelous elderly African woman having such skill with silk stitching, I at first thought Thompson had already been there. Tried to hire her on the spot. Goodly portion of my practice is African, you know."

Harper smiled at the collection of people Red described in the barges.

"Now I do believe I would surely recognize such a party if they were among my friends, Red, but I do not know them. I do not even know 'of' them. Maybe they were from across the river after all?"

"Well, could be, but I don't think so. Anyway, the man was stitched and bandaged as well as I could have done. The African woman had no interest in coming to work for me, and I had to get back to my patients – which I must do now."

Patting Harper on his arm, Redding slipped out into the hall toward his lobby, but stopped after two steps.

"Oh by the way, how did your visit go with Thompson? Was he able to tell you anything about your nasty little rag?"

"Yes. Thompson is quite the chemist, trained in

New York, not Baltimore, but really knowledgeable about chemicals. There appeared to be an awful concoction of debilitating nastiness within the handkerchief Mrs. Pulaski gave me. Not really very much in the handkerchief, just enough for old Thompson to identify it. He admitted he was guessing about some of it, but it seemed to pass the tests he had in mind for it. If this actually came from the dregs of Mr. Jundt's drinking cup, and not some cup accidentally brought in from the barn for cleaning, I fear her father is being poisoned."

"Good God, Wallace! You must get back down there and raise hell about this before the man takes in too much!"

"And I am about to do just that, Red, but there is still one last piece of information I need from you. What is it you actually prescribed for the man."

"Which man? The canaller... or the gentleman in York Furnace?"

"Your patient in York Furnace."

"Me? He's not my patient, Wally. I don't think I've ever even been to York Furnace. Been by it, on my way to Havre de Grace, but don't recall stopping there, ever, except maybe to dine on the way ~ and I don't believe I will eat there again!"

"Well, it's not the town doing anything, Red, it's what that young woman at Mr. Jundt's farm may be doing."

"You mean this Mrs. Pulaski?"

"Oh no, not her! Mrs. Pulaski is timid as a church mouse and has never a cross word for anyone, most certainly not for her father. No, I refer to the other young woman staying at the farm. She claims Mr. Jundt as her father, and even calls Mrs. Pulaski 'sister', although I must admit Sonja looks as though she has been slapped each time the other woman calls her that. I think she was introduced as the daughter of Mr. Jundt's second wife, yes, that's it. Step sister, I suppose. Esther. That's her name. The other woman at the farm. Esther."

"Wally, I've seen no one in York Furnace. Maybe she referred to Thompson, or maybe Wolcox over in York..."

"No. I asked her where the doctor had come from, and if he was from York, even gave Wolcox's name as a reminder, but she said no, it was a doctor from out of town, came down the canal from Wrightsville."

"If that's the case, Wally, then it must have been Thompson..."

"No, Red. He has not been there in years, he said. No, I am afraid something sinister has come to York Furnace. I will leave you to your patients now, Red."

"You're off to York Furnace, then?"

"Yes, as soon as I pack my bags and my horse is saddled."

"Do let me know how all this comes to an end, won't you Wally?"

Harper nodded his answer as the two shook hands and each turned to his task.

At Burl's farmhouse in York Furnace, Sonja placed the fresh cup of water on the table near her father. The medicine was not helping. Each day he slept more and spoke less. His pallor was deathly pale. He awoke late morning in a rare moment of clarity and smiled at Sonja, calling her daughter as was his custom. He even managed to take a few spoonfuls of broth; the spoon nearly lost to the bedclothes as trembling pale hands reached out to pull it to parched lips, but then quickly returned his slumbering state. The window was open again. The sick room smell was much milder since she had been there to clean each day. Esther was near her little and said almost nothing, except what was absolutely necessary. Another day crept by, sliding from sunlight to gray light of the evening. Sonja was accompanied only by her near comatose father, her cleaning chores, and her worries.

Without bothering to return down stairs for supper, knowing it would again be in strained silence, Sonja went to her room as it filled with the darkness of the night and of her heart and fell into a fitful sleep.

Long after the evening sounds of the forest around the farmhouse had faded into fragile silence, Sonja awoke to the sound of soft singing. Thinking perhaps it was a dream, she sat up silently on her bed, listening to the sounds of the house and the farm, and then it came again. It sounded like a little girl singing a nursery rhyme.

Another waking dream to haunt me. It is a sound I will never hear in my own house.

The voice began to talk in the darkness, from outside in the hallway. It was the sound of a question.

What are you asking?

Another voice answered the question. It was a woman's voice.

Sonja stepped down from her bed and went to the door of her room, leaning her head against the cool wood, trying to remain silent and hear over the thunderous pounding of her own heart. She could not hear the words, only the sound of words finding their way through the wooden door. Her heart slammed within her chest and the blood pounded within her ears as she quietly opened the door to the hallway, not wanting to see but unable not to look.

Nothing was there. The voices arose from her father's room. Again the question of a little girl. The answer from a woman. Sonja tiptoed across the hall and carefully opened the door to her father's room. Esther sat up from the edge of the bed and stood facing Sonja before the window. Her body was silhouetted within a near transparent cotton shift by the moonlight flooding in through the window, the narrow space between her legs traced by silver light.

" Oh, Sonja, it's you."

" I thought I heard voices in here."

" I-I must have fallen asleep when I came to give Father his medicine."

Sonja looked around the room, but only her sleeping Father and Esther were in it.

"I thought all of Father's medicine had been given?"

"Silly me, I found a second vial in my dresser from that nice Doctor from Wrightsville."

Sonja could not see Esther smiling in the darkness with the moon behind her, but could sense it. Esther reached down to the bedside table and picked up the small tin cup and then walked slowly around the bed to the door. Sonja kept her place in the doorway urging herself to confront this woman, but Esther slid herself between Sonja and the doorframe, brushing Sonja's arm with her breasts, her nipples hard and erect, whispering warm breath against her ear.

"Good night, sister."

Sonja turned her head to face Esther, noses almost touching, saw her smile in the moonlight as she hesitated in the doorway, and then Esther was gone down the hallway. Esther closed the door to her room and latched it from inside.

Something repulsive slipped through the back of Sonja's mind and sent chills down her spine and raised the hairs on her arms. She looked down at her still sleeping father, faintly breathing and unaware of almost everything, and she cried into her hands. She cried until her palms were dripping and her ankles ached from long standing barefoot on the cold hardwood floor.

When she stopped crying, she retrieved blankets, coverlet and pillows from her room, and brought them to lay in the square patch of moonlight on the floor next to her father's bed, kissed her father on his forehead, and laid down on her pallet. She did not sleep, could not sleep, dared not sleep.

The locktender at the Line had watched the progression of barges through his lock the day of the shooting; had seen the pool of Pulaski's blood on the deck of his square ended barge; had seen the black that worked for Pulaski yet tillering another barge and almost acting as if he didn't know his own boss. That bushy headed fellow with Pulaski was new, too. It didn't really surprise him all that much that one of the slavers had shot someone, it was bound to happen with all those guns, but glad it wasn't one of his people.

Wouldn't have thought a guy like Pulaski would be in all that. Didn't know him well, but wasn't what I would expect from that one. Too many strange things at once though. And I don't like the slavers worth a damn.

He had sent for the York County Sheriff after all.

Three days after the shooting, two days after they had buried that Worthingood man, the Sheriff had finally arrived. The locktender had sent the Jenkins boy, old enough to be on the road by himself. The Jenkins boy helped out around the lock some days, when his father had had enough and sent him off the farm for part of the day for his own safety. The boy went running off to get a horse from his father's barn as soon as the locktender had asked him to fetch the sheriff. Lost in his excitement to ride to Lancaster, he did not stop to pack food, rain slicker, or sleeping roll. His imagination was full of adventure and his common sense left behind.

Not a whole lot of sense that one.

The Sheriff had been out hunting and was another

day coming home while the Jenkins boy waited, fed by the Sheriff's wife and sleeping in the man's barn that night.

The rain was heavy when the boy and the Sheriff finally arrived. The Sheriff was tucked down inside his rain slicker with only his eyes and his great mustache showing between collar and hat brim. The rain soaked Jenkins boy, his clothes pasted to his skin looking like a wet cat, sitting proud in his father's saddle peering under the soggy hanging edges of his father's cast off felt hat, guided him straight to the scene of the crime. The clearing along the towpath next to the lock where the shooting had taken place was then nothing more than a wide gray mud puddle. A small vapor cloud slipped out from under the Sheriff's hat as he grunted and immediately turned his horse toward the barn behind the lockhouse and the comfort of a roof over dry ground.

After bedding his horse he made his way to the general store, where the open area around the iron stove served as local tavern for those with coin to buy the liquors sold there. The Sheriff spent the afternoon and evening sitting near the stove, listening to accounts from the local folk, and sipping whiskey-laced coffee while his clothes dried.

The rain stopped the following morning, the fourth day after the shooting, and the Sheriff walked down from the lockhouse, his long double barrel shotgun hanging easily across his forearm and the butt snugged under his armpit. It was well after eight o'clock in the morning, but the sun was still trapped behind steel gray clouds, and rainwater continued to slip off leaves and roof edges to tap on the ground in dollops of twos and threes. Hangers on who had been eager to stay close to the Sheriff to hear the comments of others telling their version of the story, lingered back farther and farther as the Sheriff neared the bridge and mule barn at the line. He was alone when he crossed the invisible line separating Pennsylvania from Maryland and approached the small gathering of slavers come together to watch this man. His badge of office, rarely on display out of his coat pocket, since everyone mostly knew who and what he was, was this morning shined and prominently pinned on his chest.

Andrew stepped forward from the small group. Since Charles' death he had assumed a leadership role among the disparate band of slave chasers formed at the northern edge of slave country.

"You got no powers here, Sheriff," he said for the benefit of his new followers. "You just crossed into Maryland."

"I know that, mister. Don't need official powers to ask another man questions, though. Unless you got some reason you don't want me to hear the answers."

Andrew shrugged his shoulders, facing the sheriff squarely, showing his own rifle hanging from his arm much the same as the Sheriff's. "Ask away, Sheriff."

These men don't need my introduction. They know damned well who and what I am, and they sure as hell ain't hiding in the bushes from me. Go easy old boy, they don't give a hoot about that little piece of tin pinned to your chest.

He nodded to Andrew and then to the other five.

"Need to hear your version of what happened here the other day."

"What d'you mean, 'our version' ? Wha'd those farmers up there tell you?"

"Each man sees things a little different. Each time he tells it he forgets one thing and remembers another. It's always that way, 'specially with a knifing or a shooting."

The other men mostly remained silent while Andrew recounted the events, occasionally punctuated by supporting remarks from Geoffrey. Andrew told the Sheriff about the incident, what he and Geoffrey had seen of it, and Charles' death during the night, and of the burial among the trees next to the river south of the barn.

"Don't really make much sense."

The Sheriff nodded and then looked into the face of each of the other men, hearing no additional words, and not reading any expression that would lead him to believe any more would be forthcoming. The Sheriff looked from the men up toward the lockhouse and then back again.

"I haven't heard anything from anyone to make me think anyone was involved but the two that got hurt. Seems providence has taken care of them both. I'll tell you something else, though, not from what I've heard but what I see for myself. You get a bunch of men together, all carrying guns, and all with strong feelings about one thing or another, and sooner or later something like this is going to happen. What you fellahs do is legal in Maryland. Hell it ain't really illegal in Pennsylvania – I mean going after a man's property that's run off. "

He looked down at his feet and used the toe of one boot to knock a dried ball of mud from the other heel, then slowly looked across the faces of the men standing around the room.

"But I'll tell you this: I ain't having no more shooting around here. You ain't the law. I am. If a law needs enforcing, I'll take care of that, or I'll deputize a dozen men and then get it done. You can carry a gun to protect yourself, but you don't use it to hurt or even scare Pennsylvania folks. You boys keep down here below the line, and put your guns away unless there's a righteous reason to have them out."

The sheriff had spoken stronger than he had planned, the attitude of those men had provoked his sense of authority. Andrew had enough sense to let the man go on without challenging him.

Let this farmer with a star on his chest have his say and then be on his way out of here. Their business was to catch runaway slaves. Trouble with the law was more trouble than it was worth.

Andrew leaned to the side and spit into the weeds next to the barn, and then nodded to the Sheriff. That's all the satisfaction he was going to give this farmer. He nodded back at Andrew, and then cast his glance across the faces of the quiet men. The Sheriff grunted to himself and turned to walk back up to the lockhouse.

Ten steps north along the towpath he crossed the centerline of the bridge going over the canal to his left, and he was back in York county, back in his county. Only the slight built locktender had advanced far enough toward the barn to greet the Sheriff as he stepped back into Pennsylvania. The Sheriff answered the unspoken question on his face.

"They pretty much say the same things I'm hearing up here. Two men got into it. One man armed and one not. One man shot but the other dead. Hell, for all we know the one shot may be dead, too. The Pole, say you know him? Have you heard about him?"

The locktender shook his head.

"Haven't heard anything down from Wrightsville. A dozen or more barges have come down since the shooting, but none of'em knew anything about it. One, the barge this morning, said he thought he saw Pulaski's barge in the basin up there, waiting to take on coal, but didn't see Pulaski. Saw his black, though."

"Slave?"

"Freed or slave, don't know. They're Marylanders, so it could be either. The black seems to like working with Pulaski, always in a good mood. Course you can never tell with them."

The Sheriff grunted.

"Well, maybe that was part of all this. Maybe those slavers were bothering his black."

"No, he wasn't even along, not then."

"Thought you said he worked for the Pole."

"Yeah, but the black came on later in a separate barge, a third one. Put his mark down under Pulaski's name though. Pulaski be the one pays the toll at the end of the month."

Pulaski's Canal

"How many barges this Pulaski run?"

"Usually just the two. The other day he was tied up with another, one I hadn't seen before. In all the excitement, no one ever really talked about that other barge. Then the black came later with the usual other barge – Simon – that's his name. Pulaski's black. His name is Simon."

The Sheriff was thinking about the new barge and wondering how it connected with the slavers and shooting, if it did at all, and then the locktender mentioned the name of the black. Simon.

"Now, something comes to mind about a man named Simon. Black man. Yeah, a black man named Simon. Got a bunch of postings up from Annapolis last month, or the month before. Now, what was it? Damn. It's right on the edge of my memory, but I can't for the life of me remember what it was. Hell, might have even been a for sale leaflet. I once got a packet that was supposed to go to the Sheriff down in York, South Carolina. Came in off a ship into Baltimore, forgot to put it off in Norfolk and sent it off from there. Got sent in the wrong direction and came to me."

The Sheriff shook his head.

"Going off in too many directions here, too. Believe I'll just spend the day here, just watching things. Might give me more to think about that I'm not thinking now. Listen to what folks have to say when they're not all bunched together in a crowd."

The morning passed, marked by a free lunch with the locktender and his wife. Ugly woman, he thought, but an excellent cook. Rabbit never tasted so good, though he generally liked it well enough almost any way it was cooked. The sun finally peaked between begrudging clouds in the mid afternoon, but shedding no sun on the Sheriff. He spent the afternoon on the front porch of the locktender's house whittling and sipping applejack sent up for free from the general store, and listening to the same story told by a dozen and half people with each telling slightly different and pulling the truth ever closer to the center. Well before sunset, the smell of roasted chickens, boiling buttered potatoes, and baking apple pie was far more alluring than either the locktender or the Sheriff could resist, both hovering not far from the door until it was ready to be eaten. Supper was served early that afternoon on brightly colored unchipped crockery plates not used in years, and heaped high with wonderful food by the locktender's wife, eager to serve this man who bragged on her cooking, included her in his conversation and looked into her eyes when he spoke to her.

Supper was long and lasted until sundown, with two helpings of everything, and cigars brought to the table by the wife to keep them there and keep the conversation going in a room that went for months with little more sound than the chomping of food and monosyllable grunts in answer to her few questions. The Jenkins boy watched the lock and then paced the hardboards of the porch until she invited him in to join the meal that scented the air all the way down to the mule barns causing the slavers to salivate and remember home cooked meals while they ate their hard tack crackers and dried beef from the general store.

The Sheriff put up both hands in mock surrender as the woman offered him another piece of apple pie sweetened with both molasses as well as her precious sugar.

"No more, Madam. My tongue is willing, but my belly has nowhere to put it. The chefs of Philadelphia are put to shame by your skill. I have never eaten so well."

The glow on her face was far greater than that from the candle flame on the table. Looking to his left, the Sheriff gently slapped the back of the Jenkins boy as he shoveled the food into his mouth.

"Take time to breathe, boy!"

And they all laughed, while he grinned through the potatoes and nodded his head, bobbing at the waist.

"I'll need your help to watch for this Pulaski fellow."

The boy looked at the sheriff, his cheeks now puffed out with chicken, looking like a squirrel with jowls full of acorn, and managed a guttural "Huh?" around the food.

"I think we need to talk to that man, or his friends, or whoever is getting his barge ready to take on coal in Wrightsville. That means they plan on coming back down, so we'll wait for them at this lock while they're still in Pennsylvania, by God."

The boy's eyebrows went high and other sounds fought their way around the biscuit now meeting its end within the boy's cavernous mouth. He gulped mint tea from his mug, shaking his head and reaching for another biscuit.

"Already gone by."

The laughing ceased and a frown began to spread across the face of the Sheriff.

"Already gone by?"

Spooning potatoes onto his plate the boy nodded.

"Yeah, they done came and went whilst you was eatin'. Got'em to sign the clip board, all proper and everything."

The sheriff looked at the boy in dead silence. The sounds of the room died away to nothing more than the sound of the boy's chomping, and then it too stopped as he looked up at the adults staring him down.

"What?"

"I wanted to speak to them, boy."

Sinking into his seat under the scrutiny the boy swallowed and spoke at the same time.

"I didn't know. Didn't see the fellah that got shot. Simon guided the two barges in, with Mickey at the mules. And then the bushy fellah came after that with his own barge with the little black boy on his mules. I let'em through just before I come to the porch and got supper here."

The Sheriff looked from the boy to the locktender and back again.

"Damnation!"

The smell of the locktender's supper had driven nearly everyone in to dinner early, and even the slave chasers were sitting around their makeshift table in the mule barn eating whatever food they had or could bring down from the general store, and did not see the barges pass. Did not see the wary looks or the guns carried in plain view and ready to use if need be. Did not see the four additional travelers standing loosely on the barge decks with guns already in hand, offered free transport to Havre de Grace for any man with a gun and no love of slave chasers.

The sheriff stepped out onto the porch looking down the canal, now empty of barge traffic and fading into the charcoal gray dimness of nightfall.

"Damnation!"

Sonja awakened on her pallet, her shoulder and her hip sore from the hard floorboards beneath the quilts. Esther was standing in the doorway, holding a bowl in front of her, its contents sending steam up toward her face. Sonja rose to her feet.

"Wh-what's this?"

"I have been so worried about Father. I know you are exhausted from your vigil, but honestly, Sonja, I don't think he's eating as much as he should. I have brought him a bowl of the wonderful broth you prepared."

"He has been fed, Esther."

Sonja looked out of the window to see the moon high over the forest behind the farm.

"What time is it?"

"Not late, but very early, Sister."

Sonja turned back to Esther.

"Esther, it must be after midnight."

Noticing a large object in her gown pocket and stretching the fabric down, Sonja pointed at it.

"Is that more of Father's medicine? It seems such an awfully large vial if it is."

"I heard a sound outside. I thought someone was out there, so I took down Father's pistol to keep with me." Esther abruptly smiled and whirled in her spot to return back down the hallway. "Never mind sister," echoed in the hall after her. "We can feed father in the morning."

Morning finally came to find Sonja half sleeping with her pallet against the inside of the closed bedroom door, listening to Esther sing nursery rhymes to herself in that child's voice as she dressed within her own room. Sonja heard the latch freed on Esther's door and shoed footsteps patting down the hallway to stop outside Burl's room. There was a faint tap on the door from Esther.

"Sonja, sweetie, I must run on an errand, but will be back long before lunch and I will have a visitor for us. Do please straighten yourself up a bit," and she was gone down the stairs. Moments later the barn opened allowing Burl's mare to trot out pulling the light framed surrey Burl and Abigail had purchased in York. The mare trotted around the farm house, beyond sight around the turn of the pathway, and down toward the canal at the edge of the property. Instead of going along the canal road to the lockhouse, Esther turned the surrey back up the hill at the next trail and headed up the steep incline and the forest road beyond, flicking the whip on the rump of the heavily breathing mare to keep the pace.

Sonja was left to wonder where Esther had gone and who this visitor would be, but also grateful for the respite of not having her in the house for a few precious hours. Soon the iron stove in the kitchen was ablaze, coffee steaming in the pot, and grits laced with ham grease bubbling in the pan. When she brought it to his room, Burl was already awake and bid good morning to his daughter as she came in the room.

"When did you get here, Daughter?"

Sonja smiled, glad he at least recognized her, but sad that he was unaware of her presence through the previous two nights, feeding him morning and evening. She set the tray on the table and began to offer him slim spoonfuls of grits and coffee. She blew on the spoons to cool the content even as he raised still slightly trembling lips to the spoons eager for her feeding. As the last of the coffee slipped down after the last of the grits, he focused his weak eyes clearly on her.

"Thank you, daughter. I've been mighty sick here

lately. Esther helped me. But, I am happy to see you here."

The twenty words were more than all the words she had heard him speak since her arrival. Sonja leaned over him and kissed his forehead. He smiled, tired from even the activity of taking nourishment and from saying a few scant words, and settled back into his pillow, and then back to sleep. Sonja picked up her quilts and blanket from the floor and took them back to her room to spread them over her bed. The sun was almost summer bright as it beamed in through the window, creating a warm rectangle across the quilts. Spreading out the cloth Sonja could feel the warmth quickly seeping into the material, and the warmth seeping into the back of her hand. She stepped around the bed and sat on its edge on the sunbeam, her eyes closed and chin raised to put her face full in the sunlight and bathed in the warmth finding its way deep inside her. Slowly without plan or awareness she settled deeper onto the mattress and folded herself within the rectangle of light spread across the bed, and sank into an overpowering opiate sleep.

"You still love me, don't you Burl? I've come back to take care of you. And you'll want me to stay here after you're gone, won't you?"

Burl stared up at the ceiling still confused, but answered that he would. The voice was not the little girl, nor was it Esther. It was the voice of Abigail, Esther's mother, and a voice she knew well enough to imitate. Esther sat upright on the edge of the bed, holding a small sheaf of unfolded papers in her hand. A slender dark haired man in a vested suit stood near her.

"If you love me, Burl, sign these papers so I can always stay here. You need to change this will, Burl, so I'll have a place to live."

Esther was speaking but the voice was Abigail's. Calvin Turner shifted his feet uncomfortably as he stood by the doorway within the room.

"Esther, are you sure he wants to do this?"

Esther turned her head to look at the man over her shoulder.

"Why, of course, silly man. He told me he wanted to do this, since I was the only one in the family that came to care for him, he wanted to make sure I was included in his will. Then you and I can do that other legal thing later on. Don't you worry a bit, honey."

"But, Esther, he doesn't sound very clear headed this morning, maybe we should wait..."

"No. We should NOT wait. He's confused because my sister won't let him have the medicine prescribed by the doctor. I'm sure that Emma Calvert told you the doctor came by from Havre de Grace. I'm sure Emma has told everybody everything, and some of it even true."

She turned her face back toward Burl, but still speaking to Turner.

"You must ask her someday, what she did with father's gold medal given him for fighting the British in '13. Ask her to tell you the story about THAT."

Esther retrieved the pen from the bedside table and dipped it again into the uncapped small inkwell next to it.

"Burl, dear, raise your sweet little hand and take the pen. You love me, don't you?"

"What is going on in here?" Sonja asked from the doorway. Her eyes were swollen and she was unsteady on her feet, trying to climb up from the well of sleep she had fallen into, trying to focus her eyes on her father and Esther and the visitor.

Esther flashed her eyes upon Sonja, and then at Turner.

"See? See her? See this, this is what I have to tolerate, what Burl must endure. Were it not for me he would have passed long ago. She had abandoned him and now lies about the house in stupor, unable to care for herself, let alone her father."

Confused at the situation and Esther's outburst, Sonja rubbed her eyes trying to force them to behave, to focus on these people. She shook her head trying to clear the syrup fog covering her brain, keeping her from thinking clearly.

"She is drunk again, Calvin. Can't you see that? Push her away. Push her back into the hallway and shut the door."

Calvin reached for the door. Esther flipped her hand in dismissal toward Sonja.

"Go back to sleep, Sonja. Sleep the day away. I will take care of Father, like I always have. Close the door, Calvin."

Sonja screamed at Esther. "He is NOT your father!"

"He is my father and I am his only daughter! I am the only one who has cared for him. Close the door, Calvin! You abandoned him, Sonja, and, if he wants to take care of me as I took care of him, it's his right! You can't stop it!"

Esther turned back toward Turner.

"He asked you to come here so he could change his will in front of a witness he could trust. And I'm sure you'll have all the access to the canal you need as long as I stay here. Now close the door!"

Turner hesitated. Sonja stepped into the doorway, her hands at her sides clenched into fists. Turner looked between the two women. Esther placed her hand on Burl's chest and spoke into his ear, her voice almost singing.

"Father, isn't this what you want?"

Burl mumbled after her. "...what I want"

"See! It is what he wants."

Sonja pulled at Turner's sleeve.

"He is confused. She is poisoning him!"

"He does seem a bit weak, and possibly a little confused, but I do not see him as often as Miss Esther ..."

He turned back to Esther, his hands out toward her.

"Perhaps we should try this again in a week or two."

"No!" screamed Esther. "He wants this done NOW!!"

Turner shook his head slightly and folded his arms across his chest.

"Burl, tell me what you want. Do you want to do this now or wait a week?"

"...wait a week," mumbled Burl.

"He didn't mean that. He still wants to change it now, don't you Burl honey".

"...Burl honey," he mumbled.

Turner exhaled deeply, making his decision.

" Esther, I want access to the canal in a bad way, but I'm not prepared to get a confused man to change his will. I don't like what's going on here. You come get me when he's better, or ...whatever."

Turner walked out of the room. Esther sprang from the bed and followed Turner down the stairs yelling and trying to convince him to go through with the change in the will. Sonja stepped to her father's side and closed the inkwell, looking at her father, but listening to Esther's tirade continue on the front porch and out into the front yard. Sonja looked down at her father and squeezed his hand. Burl looked up with a faint smile and winked slowly with his left eye, his voice a ragged whisper.

"Daughter, that woman is crazy."

Sonja smiled down at her father, took up the green tin cup of medicine left there by Esther, and hid it in her room.

Wallace will get this when he comes back.

She went to her room to look out the window and watch Turner walk away from the house, catching a glimpse of the canal in the distance.

Ben, I wish you were here.

Fatigue swept through her body. She had been awake for three days, and still groggy from the short broken nap, but dared not allow herself to fall asleep again with only Esther around. Sonja returned to her father's room pulling a rocking chair from Esther's room – Burl's rocker - next to her father's bed. She drew her feet up into the rocker with her hands around her knees and listened to the sounds of Esther's unfettered anger as she thrashed around within the rooms below her and shivered.

Esther spent the rest of the day and into the night walking around the house rearranging furniture, slamming doors and cabinets. In the evening, she began to yell at the cabinets and the furniture and the air downstairs.

"Where is it?!!"

As darkness settled around the house, Esther came up the stairs and into Burl's room.

"Where is it? What did you do with it?!!"

"Where is what?" demanded Sonja.

"My mother's cup! The green tin cup! It was my MOTHERS! Where is it??!!"

Sonja realized that Esther was looking for the tin cup she had hidden in her room, but said nothing. It is hidden behind the chamber pot in its cabinet, and she smiled to herself.

Esther will not look there. Esther hates chamber pots and only begrudgingly empties her own, and rarely Burl's.

"Somebody STOLE that cup!" Esther screamed and stamped her foot.

"It must have been those damned Calverts!"

Esther stormed out of the room.

Sonja curled up tighter within the rocking chair and pulled her quilt over her shoulders, and rocked slowly through the night listening as Esther's rampage through the house continued. Slowly the blackness of night drifted into the gray of early morning. Esther's voice ground on in yells and curses.

Finally sunrise, and precious golden beams slipped though Sonja's window, the open doorway across the hall, and settled gently onto the surfaces in Burl's room. Sonja's eyes were swollen from lack of sleep and felt like they were covered in sand. She had sequestered a sewing needle under her quilt, and stuck it into the tenderness of her thigh whenever sleep tried to pull her from the chair.

Esther came to the doorway smiling and wearing an ill-fitting dress that Sonja recognized as Abigail's. Her hair was bundled on top of her head as her mother used to wear it and a large ivory brooch at her neck. Her face was sickly pale, dark circles hung under her eyes, her lips thickly painted clown-like and the red smudged on her chin.

"Don't you stir, sister dear. I just have some broth and medicine for our father."

The sweetness of her voice was a grotesque contrast to her rants during the night.

"I'll feed him."

"Oh, pooh, Sonja. Just look at you. You are a mess. Go lay down."

Esther stepped toward the bedside.

"How can you look after Father, if you don't look after yourself?"

The innocence of her child-like voice was unnerving to Sonja.

Sonja rose from the rocker and stepped between Esther and Burl.

"Just leave it!"

Their eyes met, and for an instant fire raged in Esther's eyes, but she handed Sonja the tray and left the room. As she went downstairs she spoke into the air of the stairwell.

"Be sure to give Father his medicine."

Sonja snatched up the medicine and poured it out the window. Burl awoke and looked up to his daughter.

"That broth smells good."

Sonja smiled and smelled of the broth herself. She

sat down and placed the bowl on the table next to Burl's bed. It did smell good. She dipped the spoon into the bowl taking in the aroma of the soup. It smelled of slow simmered chicken and stewed vegetables. She lifted the spoon to her father's lips. It smelled of...she dropped the spoon on the floor and stood quickly. It smelled of that medicine! Sonja slapped the bowl off the table sending it crashing against the wall and into pieces.

"Damn her!" She growled through clenched teeth.

Esther yelled from downstairs, "What was that?"

Sonja chirped in her best southern belle drawl.

"Oh, clumsy me, Esther. I have made a real mess."

Esther trundled up the stairs and stood frozen in the doorway. She screamed and fell to her knees picking up the pieces.

"That was my MOTHER's dish!"

"Here, Esther, let me help you..."

"Leave it alone!"

"No, I insist, Esther. I am SO sorry."

Esther grabbed for the porcelain pieces held in Sonja's hand, but before Sonja could release the broken porcelain it cut across the palm of Esther's hand.

"Oh dear, Oh dear! Esther, you have cut your poor self."

Esther stared into Sonja's face, her eyes turning to ice.

"Esther, I am so sorry. We must cleanse the wound or it will become infected. Here, let me go with you to the kitchen to wash that hand off."

Sonja escorted Esther downstairs to the kitchen. She washed Esther's hand with a clean wet cloth and then bound the wound.

"I will fix us some tea, Esther," Sonja whispered as she also began to prepare a fresh bowl of broth for her Father. Sonja smelled carefully of the broth from the pot and determined that it was free of the *medicine*.

"You just sit here and rest, you poor dear, and I will feed Father."

Sonja returned to her father's room to feed him the broth.

Burl eagerly accepted the nourishment, his chin angling forward for each spoonful.

"Good soup," he said weakly, "good soup."

While Sonja fed Burl, she heard Esther walk slowly up the stairs to her own room. Esther unlocked her room door and then locked it behind and gently lay down on her bed muttering to herself. "Momma's good dish. Momma's good dish.", and fell asleep.

Sonja was happy to be free of Esther for a while and double happy to feed her father a second bowl of broth when he asked for more. Moving as if in a trance, she closed and latched the bedroom door, drug the rocking chair behind the door and then propped it against the door latch to secure the room from the inside. She could go no longer without uninterrupted sleep. Eyes already half closed, Sonja kissed her father's head, telling him she must have a nap, and then curled up at the foot of her father's bed and allowed herself to sink into sleep.

Faces swirled around her mind's eye as she sank deeper and deeper into the desperately needed sleep. Darkness drew around her consciousness in a slowly moving curtain, until there was only black silence in her mind. A reluctant corner of her mind fought weakly to remain awake, to warn herself, to watch for Esther, but soon it began to slip away as well.

Surely we are safe with the door barred.

"Yes, surely," she mumbled to herself.

Sleep wrapped around her like a warm embrace and she slid gently into that place people go when they give themselves over entirely to the luxury of a deep sleep.

The barges were drawn down the canal toward Havre de Grace, floating on a surface almost as smooth as glass. The mules walked lazily, even with the barges full of coal and low in the water, they were moving down stream. Thousands of gallons of fresh rainwater rushed into the canal system from dozens of feeder streams. The rush of water added to the movement southward toward the canal basin and the Chesapeake Bay. It pushed against the stern of the barges trying to elbow them out of its downhill way, ignoring the tremendous weight, lifting and pushing the barges along and making an easy walk for the mules.

Ben stood a watch at the tiller, easy enough to sit there steering the barges to the deeper center when the rain made it deeper everywhere, keeping the barges high over the muddy canal bottom. The slow routine of minding the barge, watching the mules, signing the clipboard at each lock as the lock number began to climb again after the Line, all that forced the reality of the work that must be done now to the forefront, and what had happened four days ago to the back of his mind. There had been moments in the quiet darkness before they left their tie-up to cross the Line northward when he had pictured the celebration they would all have in Pennsylvania, as he bid the slaves farewell and accepted their gratitude for helping them to freedom. But they could not trust him, had no reason to trust him. His plan to distract the slave chasers with cunning and guile, but without true criminality, had crumbled immediately resulting in an avalanche of regretful actions. In his mind, the distraction was to be so easy; barely more than a prank, and he almost got himself killed.

Ben shifted in his seat on the stern locker, not really moving against the stiffness of the oak slat top, but against his own nagging recriminations. He was terrified of breaking the law, but his true danger had been with the slavers. He puffed on his pipe and raised a hand up to his head to rub the bandage over the newest spot of itching that was spreading around his stitches. The four passengers lounging around the cargo hatches, finding whatever was acceptable as a place to sit at the moment, chatted among themselves and looked at the river rushing by on the other side of the towpath. Their pistols and rifles long ago uncocked and secured. Mickey had found them and had gained their support to cross the line in force. Good men, needing to travel south, but already harboring the distaste for the slave chasers and bore sufficient ill will toward them to risk a shooting as price for the passage.

Ben watched the men and shook his head. Another plan not met in reality, he thought. Only the kid at the lockhouse; no one else in sight in the full afternoon well before supper, no one to challenge them. No Sheriff, no canal men, not even slave chasers appeared as they passed the barn. It had all been easy and silent. During the chuckling and quiet conversation that follows unfulfilled danger, Mickey had been good naturedly accused of having more brandy in him than facts when he recruited their passengers. Ben spit over the stern of the barge. The contradiction of the two trips though the Line gnawed at him, and he immediately scorned himself for the regret that he felt over the absence of action.

The barges had slipped though the Lock, seen only by the pimply youngster proud to posses the clipboard. The men on the barge smelled the aroma of an excellent meal up at the lockhouse, but had no idea that the aroma had driven men to an unusually early supper and kept the locktender and the county sheriff only yards away from them as the water level rushed down in the lock to match the next section of the canal.

Pulaski's Canal

The barges continued their invisible slide down through the Line and past the mule barn, without a single slave chaser to see them pass. The bargemen did not see the slavers gathered around their meager fare responding to the aromas of food prepared by an oft-ignored woman and served to a boisterous sheriff who paid her only slight but well chosen attention. Did not see the slaver with the broken jaw trying to sip beef broth painfully through toothgap and broken teeth, or the other with freshly broken arm slung in one of Charles remaining shirts and with his face battered almost unrecognizable. Did not see in the stand of trees near the grave of Charles Worthingood, where a heavy form swayed from the branch of a nearby tree. Did not see the body of Jedediah, tongue protruding and neck stretched grotesquely long by the hemp rope around it as if he were looking up at the stout limb that held him there.

The slavers caught Jedediah in the woods outside Wrightsville the day after Charles died, and had given up on taking him back to his master when the seven of them could not subdue him to accept the shackles. One slaver had screamed through his broken jaw. Another man, his arm twisted horribly at the point of its fracture, used the rifle butt as a club in his other hand to batter Jedediah unconscious while the others held his arms.

Not wishing to confront the big slave again, the battered and bloody men gave their reward over to hatred and decided his fate while he was still unconscious. Andrew tossed a length of hemp rope over the nearest stout tree limb and looped the free end around the pommel of his saddle. One of the other men tied a simple but deadly slip knot at the other end and looped it around the big man's neck. Andrew spurred his horse and quickly pulled the big man into the air. He guided the horse around another tree as the body rose and tied the end of the rope there, watching as Jedediah's neck stretched beyond the limit of his neck bones by his own weight. He grunted in disappointment that there was none of the kicking feet he wanted to see, to indicate the big black even knew he was being hung.

They left him there, swinging slowly below the limb as a monument to Charles' grave, and in plain view of anyone trying to walk around the lock by taking the pathway along the river. Andrew decided there was still room on the limb for the farmer off that barge if they could find him.

Mickey came up from the cabin, with several cups dangling by their loops from his fingers, and holding a pot of fresh boiled coffee in the other. After providing coffee to each of the four passengers, Mickey made his way back to the stern locker. He poured the last two cups, set the near empty pot on the deck and handed one of the cups to Ben.

"Almost a shame nothing happened. Aye, Ben?"

"It would have been a blood bath, I'm afraid, Mickey."

"No matter the side of the fence yer stand on, it drives a man hot to make his stand. It's like yer Alamo a couple years ago, Ben."

He nodded toward the passengers sipping his coffee.

"Them Pennsylvania boys, or the Slavers, each feel they ought t'stand firm against the other. Either one would be on the walls of their own Alamo and stand against a thousand times their own number – cause they think they're right."

Ben swallowed some of his coffee.

"That was no Alamo at the Line the other day, Mickey. That was one dumb bargeman pissing on another man's boots, and almost getting killed for it...for nothing."

Mickey chuckled into his coffee tin.

"Twas mighty funny, Benjamin. You've got to admit."

"But he may well have died because I hit him."

"Aye, but ya had no choice. Had ya not hit him he'd a blown your head off, and we'd be bringing a headless corpse back to your sweet Sonja."

"And that poor fellow could be lying in a grave, hundreds of miles from his own home and family."

"Poor fellow me ass, Benjamin. Ya don't shoot a man in the head fer gettin' piss on your boots. He had a belly full of hate for almost anybody, you could see that in all those fellows. You just got his attention at the wrong time. Besides, ya told me yerself you were in the Army some ten years ago. Wounded when ya met yer Sonja. Had to shoot some men back then, didn't ya?"

Ben lowered his cup and turned to look Mickey full in his face.

"I don't do that anymore, Mickey."

Mickey met his glance and did not blink.

"Might be what ya wish for my friend, but some people get t'be like animals, and they won't stop comin at you until you put'em down forever."

Blue Jays screeched in the trees on the high side of the canal and both men turned to watch them call at each other and jump among the branches. Mickey turned back toward Ben.

"So, does this mean your little foray into helping the blacks up the canal is over?"

Ben looked into Mickey's face. The Irishman's permanent smile was boldly on display, but his eyes were intent, searching.

That's the real question here, isn't it?

He blinked his eyes, and swallowed.

"No. I don't believe it is."

Mickey nodded and reached for the coffee pot as he stood. His empty cup clinked against the pot as he picked them both up by the same hand. He looked again at the blue jays and then down at Ben, placing a hand on his shoulder.

"Then you got to be ready to do whatever it takes to get those people up there."

"I know...and I am...until good men make better

laws that end it."

"I don't know about that, Ben. The same men that burned your sweet little town almost thirty years ago, been keeping their heel on the backs of the Irish for a couple hundred years – and they have all sorts of good laws for themselves, laws that even forbid slavery."

Mickey poured the contents of the pot overboard into the canal and then pointed the pot at Ben.

"'Course they don't need slaves, when they got the Irish on their knees killin each other over their table scraps."

"They'll fix it here, Mickey, I'm sure they will."

He placed his hand on Ben's shoulder.

"You are 'they'."

Ben just stared at him, and Mickey only sighed and shook his head like a patient father.

"You're a darlin' man, Benjamin Pulaski. I only wish I could visit the kind world ya keep in yer head, 'cause I've never been to such a place."

Ben rubbed the long knotted scar on his side.

It has a Hell of its own, too, that would send you screaming into the night.

"Mickey, I just can't see it coming down to some kind of an 'Alamo' between Americans. It'll get fixed, but I'll help out until then."

Mickey kept his smile, and limped back down into the cabin to wash the pot and cups.

The gentle outward turn of the canal straightened again, and the shape of the tree line told Ben the next lock was near. He stood and raised the locker lid, taking out the conch shell horn from its nest of rags where he kept it in the corner. Three slow howls from the conch echoed down the canal. The locktender half dozing in his chair on the porch, tilted back against the front wall of the house, raised his head and lowered chair legs and his boots onto the floorboards of the porch. As he walked to the swing bridge he pulled his watch from his vest pocket. It was nearly supper and a barge was coming. He would charge ten cents for a barge man to join him and his wife for supper. Maybe the mule rider would join them, too.

"Set out extra plates, Sally. We'll make a little money this evening."

Ben was weak and suffering another bout of dizziness again by the time the barges had made their way to the small holding pond above the lock. There was just enough room for three barges, and a passage way for any other barge determined to make its way south that evening. Havre de Grace was only three or four hours further south, if there had been enough light, but it was decided by all to take the offer of supper and then bunk in the cabin. The locktender and his wife couldn't have been happier with the barge's arrival. Eight men and a boy for supper, ten cents each for the men and a nickel for the boy.

All that and the S&T Canal Company would not see a penny of it.

After supper the travelers bedded down, and while Sally washed dishes in the kitchen, the locktender counted the money he had collected into his leather pouch. Sally would have new shoes by the end of this month, he thought, just in time for her birthday, maybe even enough for a couple yards of that new light green cotton weave come in at the General Store. He had seen her fingering it when she thought he wasn't looking. He smiled to himself in the growing darkness and looked down toward the boots he could no longer see. He could go a while longer with these old brogans.

She sure would look nice in something made out of that green cotton.

Before the next morning sun had peaked above the rim of the trees on the eastern side of the Susquehanna River, the three barges had cleared the lock and were moving south toward Havre de Grace. It was late morning when the barges slowed into lock 9, slipped down to the last level and poled their way across toward the Pulaski place and then tied up at Isaac's wharf. No sooner had they halted than Anthony was untying the *Wilhelmina* for the last leg of the journey to the Canal Basin. Mickey and the armed passengers went along, the travelers eager to make their destination or make their next connection by boat or steamer.

Simon and Ben walked slowly to the house, Toby's chatter almost nonstop with recollections, thoughts, observations, and questions. Toby kept them from noticing the dead quiet of the place.

Looking back at the youngster, Ben asked the question.

"What do you plan for young Toby, Simon?"

"I'm going to see what I can find for him. Didn't think you would mind if I looked after him till he was settled."

"Thought he would have gone on with the others into Pennsylvania, or on to New York."

"His folks didn't make the journey. He came on with his Uncle Jedediah, and no one's seen him since the crossing. Others said maybe he just went on, but neither Toby nor I believe he'd leave the boy behind. Especially not once they made it to free land."

"You do what you think is right, Simon. He can stay in the house with the boys."

"No I don't think so. For now I think he'll feel better staying with...other colored folk."

Ben smiled at his friend.

"Yeah, like you and Mickey?"

"Like me and me, for now. When this boy gets worried and wants something solid to hold onto, he's going to need mahogany, not oak. With what he has been through, we can't ask him to pretend it didn't have anything to do with his color, because you and I both know it had EVERYTHING to do with it."

Ben nodded, seeing the logic of what Simon made quite clear.

"As you see fit."

They parted at the porch. Simon took Toby to find him sleeping arrangements in the barn.

That's quickly turning into a boarding house. We have more people sleeping in that thing than animals.

The area where Mickey and Simon slept had been turned into a bunkhouse, and Sonja's old stove sat in the center of the bunkhouse to keep it warm on winter days. There would be plenty of room for Toby, especially since Anthony slept on board the Wilhelmina.

The house was empty. The boys were still in town at the Harper's, and Sonja had not yet come back from caring for her father. He regretted not stopping to see her on his way down from Wrightsville, but with his head bandaged and the story he would have to tell her, he would have provided no comfort to her or her father. Better to wait until she comes home. Burl will bring her back down when he is up and about again, or he will fetch her himself on his next trip.

Ben walked though the empty house, exhausted from his experiences, feeling his reserve drain into the floorboards now that he was home. Without thinking he found himself sitting on their bed, laying back to allow his head to sink into the down pillow.

Need to take my boots off.

Even as his feet seemed to find their own way onto the end of the bed, making a vain attempt to prop his boot heels over the edge of the bed rail to keep them off the quilt covering.

Sonja'll kill me if I get dirt on this quilt.

He thought another half thought about something, but it made no sense, and a dream already in the making rushed forward to pull the thought down and mixed it with a rush of unconnected scenes from different times and different places. For a moment he was a young boy standing next to his father on their schooner, with the deck tilted steeply away from a fresh autumn breeze on the Chesapeake Bay rushing down from Baltimore.

To...somewhere...Wrightsville maybe? No not there...not then...

He slipped deeper into his dream world and then down past it, below sights and sounds and thoughts, deeper into the quilt as his own body heat soaked into the fabric and kept himself warm from below. He let himself go like a child slipping off to sleep in a sunbeam, and true sleep wrapped her warm arms around him and pulled him to her bosom.

"Ben! Ben!"

The voice was coming from far away, cruelly pulling him up from his unfinished sleep. He opened one eye looking for any reason to send the voice away so he could go back to sleep.

"Massah Ben, get up, Massah Ben."

Toby yelled into his ears, making his breath felt on Ben's face. He opened his other eye, turning to look at Toby, looking earnestly back into his face.

"Ben!"

Simon shouted from above. Ben turned his head to look up at Simon who was holding out a weathered paper in his hand.

"Ben, this warrant was nailed to one of the big trees in front. It's a foreclosure notice! It says you must pay the balance of everything owed on the *Ugly Boat* to Binterfield's bank by the fifteenth of the month or you forfeit the barge!"

He stared wild-eyed down into Ben's face.

"Ben, today is the fifteenth! You've got to get to the bank today, and it's already four o'clock!! You got to pay Binterfield or do something to stop him!!"

Ben snuggled back into his pillow, still lost in sleep's confusion.

"No... not time yet...got a couple days before that."

"No, Ben! It's today! Today is the fifteenth! Now get up!!"

Ben opened his eyes and slowly sat up on the edge

of the bed, shaking his head and trying to force himself up out of a deep sleep. Everything had become so confused and tangled with the slaves and the slave catchers and his head wound.

"Ben, God damn it, it's the fifteenth day of the month! You've got to get your ass to Binterfield's!"

The meaning of the facts were like cold water, hitting Ben in the face. Ben stared wild eyed at Simon.

"Shit!"

He jumped up, grabbed his hat and began pulling together as much cash, coins and canal script he could find. He knew it would be more than enough to pay off that snake Binterfield. Simon and Toby brought the Pulaski's one horse around from the barn.

"Shit!"

Ben yelled at no one as he spilled the contents of his pouch trying to shove it into his pants pockets as he walked to the door. Invaluable seconds were lost to recollect the money, recount it, and put it back into the pouch.

Simon looked back into the front room at the clock on the mantle.

"Hurry up, Ben! It's 4:30!"

Ben made it out onto the porch and toward the barn, wiping sleep from his eyes with his shirt sleeve.

"Ben! Here! Here's the horse!"

He turned back, stepped up into the stirrup and threw his other leg over the saddle as he rose, and then almost immediately began to dismount.

Still have to cross to the other side of the canal, have to pole the barges sideways across the canal to get over there. Hell, that'll take 10 minutes!

Then he shook his head, still trying to clear it of the heavy sleep trying to claw back into his brain.

No, ride back up to the lock and cross the swing bridge. That's faster.

Simon and Toby traded unasked questions as they

watched Ben's motions.

Ben was back up into the saddle pulling the reins around to face the horse toward the lock and slapped its haunch with his hat sending it charging up toward the lock.

Seconds later the horse slid its rear hooves in an arch as Ben held its head toward the entrance to the swing bridge and it bumped his rear hip into the bridge railing. His front hoof slipped on the wood, but regained its direction and the horse shot onto the tow path and turned again, reaching a full gallop as it sped past the Pulaski place in a dead run toward Havre de Grace, with Ben shouting "Shit!" with each swat he gave the horse's haunch with his crumpled hat.

Toby pulled himself close to Simon, curling a handful of Simon's woolen pant seam in his hand, watching Ben gallop down the towpath. Simon placed his hand among the thick stiff curls on Toby's head.

"This is not good."

Simon and Toby watched the horse and rider round the canal bend in a flurry of thrown mud.

"This is not good."

"Open the door! Open this door, you Bitch!!"

Sonja awoke to the thunder of fists against the wooden door. The rocking chair jumped and jerked as Esther pounded and flung herself against it from the hall. Burl raised his head from the pillow and looked over at his daughter.

"Sonja, that woman really wants in here."

Sonja stood up from the bed trying desperately again to wipe the sleep from her eyes and the fog from her mind. It was near dark. The gray light of late evening lingered outside the window, casting heavy shadows in the room. The rocker jumped again as if it were alive.

"Open this door, Sonja! How dare you lock me out of my father's room! What are you doing in there?! What are you telling him?!"

Esther pounded on the door again.

"Open this damned door, or so help me, I will shoot it down!"

Sonja struggled from the depth of sleep to answer Esther.

"What's wrong, Esther? W-what has happened? W-wait a minute! I will open the door!"

As Sonja slid the rocking chair back out from under the doorknob, Esther kicked the door open.

"This is my house!" she screamed. "How dare you lock me out of this room?! You have to get out of this house, you meddling Bitch!!"

Esther stood trembling in the doorway, her hair

313

fallen about her shoulders in disarray. She shook a clenched fist in front of Sonja's face. Burl's pistol was hanging from her other hand. Cocking and releasing the lock again and again, she stepped into the room, frantically looking around the room and settling her attention on Sonja. Esther pointed the cocked pistol absently toward Sonja.

"You get out of HERE! "

Burl tried to rise from the bed.

"Put that damned gun down, Esther! What has got into you?"

"I'm just trying to protect you, Father." Esther cried. "Everything was just fine until SHE came here. We don't NEED her!"

Burl reached a weakened hand for the gun.

"You got to calm down, girl! Give me that thing."

Esther whirled around pointing the gun at him.

Sonja caught her breath and her heart stopped.

"Esther..."

Esther kept the gun pointed at Burl. Sonja fought her voice to keep it steady.

"Esther. Please be careful with that. Why don't you just point it down for now, all right? Point it down, Esther. Everything will be all right. We can work this out. Just point the gun down at the floor."

Slowly Esther turned the gun toward Sonja, her lip trembling and tears slipping down along her cheeks.

"You're all against me. You hate me! You just want to get rid of me."

Her breath came in short contracted sobs.

"Esther, please put the gun down..."

Slowly the gun barrel drifted down toward the floor.

"Why don't you give Father his gun, Esther. It will be all right."

"No!" spit Esther. "I need this to protect me. You just try to take it from me and I'll..."

Sonja spoke very softly. "Esther. I don't want it, Esther. "Why don't you just put it in your pocket for now? No one is going to hurt you. No one wants to do anything to you."

Esther stared blankly at Sonja and Burl. Her fading sobs and sniffs added small sounds to the ticking of the old clock in the room. No one moved. The gun floated in the air at the end of Esther's arm, neither up nor down, then at last drifted downward. The ticking of the clock seemed to become louder.

Esther's eyes flew up to focus again upon Sonja's. The moment seemed to freeze into hours as nothing moved in the eerie silence except the brass pendulum below the clock face. The ticking filled the room. An ember snapped within the potbelly stove in the kitchen below. An old floorboard creaked in the empty upstairs hall.

Esther cocked and then uncocked the gun, cocked and uncocked to the rhythm of the clock. The wind stole in under the bedroom windowsill to deftly nudge aside the hem of the curtain. The walls held their breath. A curl arose from the corner of Esther's mouth, and a frown began to descend along her brow. Her eyelids drifted closer together and her head tilted slightly as she came to her decision.

"Esther..." Sonja tried to talk, but the name could not escape from her throat except as a ragged trembling whisper.

The gun barrel began to rise.

"Esther, *sister*, you need to put the gun down, *sister*."

Esther's smile was frozen on her face, glazed in place. The gun came up in line with her eyes and pointed directly into Sonja's face.

"I'm not your sister, you bitch."

She brought up her other hand and cocked the hammer all the way back, then held the handle with both hands.

Knock! Knock! Knock!

"Hello in the house! "

The words drifted up from the front porch.

Louder the second time.

"Hello in the house!"

Knock! Knock! Knock!

Trancelike, Esther turned her head, listening in the direction of the voice downstairs while the gun hovered in front of Sonja, it's single dark eye at the end of the large barrel drifting back and forth across her face.

"Hello in the house!"

A different voice boomed from the porch this time, through the front room and up the stairs, echoing off the walls. Esther's eyes widened and she gasped, then whirled around and flew down the stairs. Sonja exhaled in a gush of trapped air from her tightened lungs and turned to her father.

"It's Wallace!"

Esther flew to the front window and peeked between the heavy curtains. The porch was filled with men: Wallace Harper, John Calvert, and Dan Bartlett, accompanied by a very unhappy looking man behind a thick mustache and under a drooping wide-brimmed hat.

"Why are you here?" she demanded.

Wallace stepped forward to the window.

"Where's Sonja?"

"Go away! Father is sick!"

She pulled the gun up near her face so they could see it.

"You shouldn't be here!"

Wallace took in a deep breath when he saw the gun.

"I should be here indeed... Miss Esther. Surely you recall my visit a few days ago. I am Doctor Wallace Harper. You so kindly asked me to stop by to...to look in on your father... and of course to have the pleasure of seeing you again. "

She looked into his face, and smiled brightly, reaching up with her empty hand and delicately patting the loose strands of her hair.

"Yes...yes I did. How kind of you to return to my aid, Doctor."

Esther moved to the door and removed the bar. Allowing the door to swing partially open she leaned into the doorway, her wrinkled and smudged dress blocking the entrance to any of the men, and keeping the pistol held behind the door. Her feminine tilt of the head and slightly arched eyebrow unable to divert attention from the frayed unkempt hair and ponderous dark bags below her eyes. She presented the men with a gaudy smile and her silky voice drifted among the men.

"I am so sorry to be rude, gentlemen, but as you can see we are not properly attired for visitors, and poor father is finally sleeping after a very disruptive night. Perhaps tomorrow would be a better day to come for the others. But dear Doctor Harper, please be so patient as to allow me to complete my preparation for your visit. I have yet a simple chore to complete upstairs and we shall meet in the parlor."

She stepped back smiling and began closing the door. Harper reached a meaty hand up and gently opened the door against her shoulder.

"I do apologize, Miss Esther, for being forward, I am so concerned for your well being..."

Esther hesitated, her smile fading into a frown and then returning.

"Yes, of course. It would be a great service for you to examine dear Father. I fear my sister is fostering questionable medicines upon him in his weakened state, and is refusing to allow me to check on him. Perhaps, as her...physician, you can convince her to go home."

She then stepped back, adjusting her hair with her empty hand, pulling the pistol behind the folds of her dress.

Sonja ran down the stairs and to Harper.

Surely he has her gun!

She took his hand into hers.

"Thank God you are here, Doctor."

Esther looked to Dan Bartlett with a diminutive smile and knowing eyes.

"Isn't it wonderful to have a personal physician so...attentive?"

Bartlett had not seen the gun, said nothing and looked away.

"I need to see Mr. Jundt right away, Sonja. I have an idea what's wrong with him."

Sonja placed her hand on his arm.

"I have something in my room I need you to look at."

Esther snickered and curled her lip.

"I'll just bet you do, you tramp."

Sonja did not hear her and Bartlett did not respond to the remark obviously not meant for his ears. He stepped toward Esther.

"We've been real worried about Burl...and what's been going on up here."

Esther looked at the fourth man, who only returned her stare and nodded without removing his hat. Esther looked among the men's faces, looking for a receptive face, but found none. The fingers of her empty hand running, tapping across her thumb, beating a near silent tattoo. Her eyes flickered from person to person within the room. She watched Harper walk toward the stairs. Sonja moved toward the stairs with Harper, looking back in cold silence at Esther.

"Stop!" Esther yelled, pulling the pistol from the folds of her skirt and pointing it at Sonja. "She has been trying to poison Father! Don't believe her lies! She's trying to kill him and have everything! Everything! We've got to stop her!"

The fourth man was slightly larger than even Harper, and he shocked everyone in the room with such swift fluid movements, more like a young dancer as he moved forward to sweep the pistol up and out of Esther's hand, grabbing her around her slim waist with the other and took her off her feet in a sweeping turn as smoothly as a waltz. With practiced dexterity he uncocked the pistol and twisted his head to avoid the fingernails Esther sent toward his face. He dropped the pistol onto the nearby sofa and grabbed one wrist, then letting her drop to her feet he spun her around, grabbing her other wrist and brought them both behind her back.

"Help me! Help me!" Esther screamed to the other men in the room. "Oh, help me! Please! I know this man. He has accosted me before, please do not let him put his filthy hands on me again! Help me! Help me!"

But the others did not rush to her assistance. Bartlett and Calvert stepped nervously farther away from the woman as Harper turned back toward her.

"This gentleman..." He said gesturing to the fourth man, "is Mister Matthew Nayers, Sheriff of York County. I hardly think he has ever accosted you."

Esther twisted against the sheriff's grip, looking wildly into the faces of the other men.

"No! No! You are wrong. He did. He Did! And, and Calvert held me down! Down you see? They were in it together! They held me down."

She thrust her chin at Dan Bartlett

"And him, he did it! I will swear in a court of law they held me down and he did it!!"

Dan sputtered at the lie. "I never did anything of the sort to you!"

Esther continued to fight against the sheriff's grip. Twisting and turning her arms and her shoulders, kicking at him with her feet and trying to bend around to bite him.

"Help me! They raped me! They raped me. They were all in it! I remember every detail now, doctor. Save me. I'll tell the judge you saved me!"

She kicked and twisted and danced to loosen the hold on her wrists, but the sheriff did not release her. Her hair was beginning to cover her face, wet strands of it stuck to her lower lips as she spit and bit at him, growling and grunting as she struggled.

"Save me! Save me! Rape!"

The scream of rape froze the canallers for a moment, but the sheriff held on, and the doctor braced himself against her accusations. Sonja was mesmerized by Esther's demonstration, and her mouth opened in amazement to the nonsense that exploded from Esther.

Esther turned tearfully to John Calvert.

"John. I only told this to your sweet Emma, but when I stayed with Ben and Sonja, that man raped me! He told me he'd kill me if I ever said anything. I tried to tell Ben and Sonja, but they protected him. I can't stand the thought of him touching me again. You've got to stop him! Help me get loose!"

She saw the gun lying on the sofa near her.

"Grab the gun, John, Honey. Grab the gun and shoot him! Shoot him! Shoot them! Shoot Sonja first!!"

Esther collapsed against the sheriff, folding into his arms and slipping to the floor. He released her wrists to grab her waist and keep her head from falling to the floor. She continued her dip toward the floor and the sheriff matched her movement, bending one knee to allow himself to settle to the floor and still support her head. As he continued downward, Esther rolled to her side pushing the floor with her hands and bringing her feet beneath her body. Before the sheriff could detect the movement, she kicked to bring herself to her feet again, moving away from the sheriff and out of his grip in a single swift motion, and grabbed the pistol from the sofa.

Sonja and Harper rushed Esther to keep her from cocking the pistol.

Pulaski's Canal

"Kill you. Kill you!" Esther raged through clenched teeth. "Bitch! Bastard! Kill you! Kill you!"

Saliva drooled from her mouth as she spit out the contemptuous words.

"Rape! Rape! They're trying to rape me! RAPE!"

Sonja rushed forward and grabbed for the gun with her left hand, pushing the barrel up toward the ceiling when the room thundered to the explosion, and the smoke of the gunpowder billowed out from the gun. She yelled, "I've had it with you, Esther!!"

At the same moment Sonja brought a round house punch learned as the only sister of seven brothers, and threw the full weight of her body behind it, driving it hard into Esther's cheek . Esther's head snapped to the side, her eyes rolled toward the ceiling and she slid down limp into Harpers arms. Harper pulled the gun from Esther's hand and tossed it across the room to the sheriff. Esther was lifted to her feet again, her arms swinging loosely. Harper smiled in astonishment at Sonja.

Sheriff Nayers chuckled and said, "Just the thing for that young lady." Then he tipped the brim of his hat toward Sonja. "And nicely delivered by the other young lady. Well done, Ma'am."

Still, Harper kept her tight within his bear hug.

Then Esther's body stiffened, she shook her head and focused her attention on Sonja as her eyes cleared. She kicked out toward anyone close enough to try to reach with her feet. One of her shoes flipped across the room shattering a glass trinket next to an oil lamp.

"Bastard. Bitch. Shit! Kill! Bastard! Rape!"

The sheriff shook his head at the spectacle as Harper took her up the stairs, and still Esther continued a string of curses and accusations.

"I'll tell everyone you tried to RAPE me! I'll ruin you!"

Harper ignored her screams and held on to her arms as Bartlett held tightly to her ankles, and Sonja followed them upstairs.

"You BASTARD, I'll ruin you! I can do it! I've ruined men in Philadelphia. I'll tell everyone in the county that you raped me!"

The sheriff slid Burl's pistol into his belt.

"At the rate you're going, honey, you'll already have accused everybody in the county. You're a sick woman and need watching real close."

Esther emitted a primal scream and kicked wildly with both feet as she was forced upstairs to her room. Her hands and feet and waist were tied to the bed and then Sonja covered her with a blanket against the room chill. Sonja looked down at Esther as she thrashed under the blanket. Esther's head and wild eyes were swiveling frenetically between her restraints and the people in the room, her back arching and her limbs yanking frantically.

Sonja smiled, "Don't worry, Esther. We will help you get well. I will bring you some nice broth. And some of that good medicine you brought for father..."

Esther screamed, "NO-o-o-o-o!!" And she began another series of breathless curses to the ceiling and jerked madly at her bindings.

As Sonja slowly closed the door to Esther's screams and stepped into the upstairs hall another voice spoke from behind her.

"That's a crazy woman, daughter."

Burl was standing in the doorway, his legs trembling from weakness.

"I tried to help, daughter..." he said softly, his hands clutching the door frame for support, "but this is as far as I could get."

Sonja and Wallace helped Burl to his bed.

"Mr. Jundt, I am Dr. Wallace Harper, friend of your daughter and her husband. I was here a few days ago, but you were not aware of me. With your permission, I would like to re-examine you, to see what this fever is all about."

Burl nodded in assent. Wallace turned to Sonja.

"Perhaps you could bring us some tea or coffee while I am in consultation with your father."

Sonja soon returned and set the wooden tray on the bedside table in front of her father and Wallace. There were two cups of steaming tea, coarse sugar, cream, and a green tin cup.

"Do not drink from the green cup, Wallace. It contains the <u>medicine</u> brought into this house by Esther."

Dr. Harper, carefully raised the cup so he could smell of the contents. The cup had set in Sonja's room, which had allowed the heavier contents of the liquid to settle to the bottom. Slowly Wallace poured the liquid into the chamber pot until only the settled residue was left in the cup. Again he sniffed the concoction. He slowly shook his head and set the cup on the table.

"As I have come to suspect, Mr. Jundt's condition has not been a natural fever at all. I was troubled by his darkened gums and confusion, but since they can be seen in the final stages of some other dire conditions, I did not wish to concern you further. I believe that sometimes nature must take its course, and it is only detrimental to the patient and his family to interfere. Too many patients in the past were ushered into their graves prematurely by ignorant physicians who felt compelled to at least DO SOMETHING, even if it was ultimately wrong. Look at the travesty of bleeding that was so rampant in the last century and even practiced in some locations to this day. Why, when I was in medical school..."

"Doctor, your opinion of the *medicine*, please," urged the sheriff standing at the doorway.

"Yes, of course. This residue in the bottom of the cup contains three elements. One is fulminate of mercury, once used in small quantities with clay to treat syphilis. One is powdered lead, probably from one of your own molded bullets," he said to Burl.

"And the third is arsenic. Quite a nasty concoction, even though it was being given to you in small amounts, the intent was to slowly poison you while your neighbors saw you suffer from what they were to believe to be a terminal fever."

Wallace noticed Burls' drooping eyelids and gently patted his shoulder. "You just rest for now, Mr. Jundt. The good news is that your recovery has obviously already begun, which tells me your doses were blessedly small."

Burl leaned back on the pillows, and Wallace patted his hand. "We will look in on you again shortly."

Burl's eyes closed, exhausted from his earlier attempt to walk out of the room. Sonja straightened the quilt over his chest and kissed his forehead. She and Dr. Harper walked into the hall and to the next room. Sonja opened the door and pointed into the room at the chiffonier that served as a clothes closet in the main bedroom.

"I suspect the poison is in there."

Esther had settled into exhausted silence, but awoke with fresh curses when they entered her room.

"Stay out of here! This is my room! You have no right! Untie me, you Bitch! Bastard! Kill you! Kill you!"

Esther's keys were on the dresser. Sonja tried the keys one at a time, until she unlocked the wooden cabinet in the corner of the room. In a cedar box kept in the back of a lower shelf, Sonja found small bottles of perfume and two other marked arsenic and mercury. Burl's will was folded into the box as well. There was also the nutmeg file and a lead bullet partially filed away. The nutmeg file was colored gray where Esther had filed on the bullet, and some loose lead grains in the bottom of the box.

"Stay out of that! That's MINE!"

324

Wallace adjusted his glasses to see the objects more clearly. He picked up the small bottle of mercury and then the ampoule of arsenic.

"The arsenic vial is mostly full. That's good. It tells us your father had not received much of it, yet"

"I don't know what you're talking about!" Esther yelled from her bed. "I had that to deal with all the rats this damned place has!"

Sonja picked up a thin head scarf lying across the back of the chair near Esther's bed. "The only rat this house ever had was the female one that came from Philadelphia!" With that, Sonja wrapped the scarf around Esther's mouth and tied a large knot between her lips.

"Now, shut up! YOU bitch!"

Harper looked into Sonja's face with raised eyebrows.

"That's the very treatment for the moment, I think," he said looking over the rims of his glasses at Sonja's handiwork. Sonja smiled, placed her hands on her hips and blinked her eyelids coquettishly at Harper. Esther raged in half formed profanities under the scarf, and kicked a vicious drumbeat against the footboard that echoed throughout the house as they left the room, slowly closing the door behind them.

Sonja and Harper visited Burl again before going down to the kitchen.

"Tomorrow we will move you back into your own room, Papa."

Burl settled back into his pillow with a smile and closed his eyes. Sonja found John Calvert and the sheriff in the kitchen drinking coffee. The sheriff nodded to Sonja.

"Miss Jundt, looks like everything is under control here for the time being. I must tell you though, I don't rightly know what to do with that woman up your stairs. Ain't no doubt she was doing devilish things to your father, but I can't take her to jail. Got no place for a woman there. Never arrested one. Believe I need to hear what old Judge Cameron over in York has to say about this."

Sonja ignored the sheriff's mistake with her last name.

Harper peered over the rim of his glasses.

"That woman is insane, Sheriff. She needs to be confined for her own good – and everyone else's, but I'm not so sure a jail would be the place for her."

"I don't know where to put her, Doctor. York County doesn't have an asylum for such people, though I've heard of one in Philadelphia, but I don't have the authority or the means to send her there. No, this will have to be sorted out by the judge."

Harper wagged a finger slowly in the air.

"Just don't lose sight, Sheriff, of the fact that there is real evidence that Esther Wilson was attempting to poison Mr. Jundt. Had it not been for Mrs. Pulaski you would be investigating a murder. If not for that, then a travesty would have been committed with no one the wiser and Sonja Pulaski left to mourn her father."

The sheriff had blinked at the first mention of the name Pulaski, and blinked again understanding that Doctor Harper was referring to the woman sitting across the table. Ignoring the doctor's further comments, the sheriff focused his sight directly at Sonja, who sensed his attention and met his eyes with hers.

"You have a question, Sheriff?"

"Your name's Pulaski?"

"Yes."

"Just my time to hear that name again, I suppose. Didn't think there were so many by that name in these parts."

Sonja straightened in her chair. "There are none other, that I am aware of, Sheriff, except for my husband's mother in Baltimore, and us, of course."

The sheriff smiled and shook his head.

"No, this other Pulaski must certainly be another. He runs a barge, I am told, and was involved in a shooting down at the Line. I was just returning from there when the good doctor came to the Lockhouse during my breakfast. Mrs. Calvert cooks a most excellent venison loin, I might add. No, no, this fellow killed a man and was shot in the head for it."

Sonja grew pale and began to tremble.

"Was the man's name Benjamin Pulaski?"

"Why yes..."

Sonja's hand flew to her mouth.

"Dear God," she whispered as tears began to well up in her eyes. "Dear God!"

The sheriff exchanged looks among Harper and Calvert, realization spreading among them. Sonja looked about the room for some object to focus her eyes upon, to force herself to keep thinking, to hold on to the world around her. The sleepless nights, the terrible fear of Esther, the fear for her father.

"Is...is he alive, Sheriff?"

"Far as I know, Miss, that is, Mrs. Pulaski. I was told his barge slipped through the gates of Lock number nineteen even as I supper'd last night."

Harper rolled his eyes and slapped the table top.

"Balls of Fire! He was the one seen by Red. Had to have been him!"

The eyes within the kitchen turned to Doctor Harper.

"Red, Dr. Reddington in York Furnace, told me he had just this morning examined a bargeman, a canaller, with a gunshot wound at the head. Across his skull, not in it, mind you. Had received stitches for it and was expected to recover."

"Expected to?" Sonja echoed the statement as a question. "What can I do?" She said to them all. "Surely that is Ben! And I have Papa here...and that devil upstairs. What else will fall upon me?"

She began to sob into her hands, the men at the table looking from one to the other, silently searching their thoughts anew for the things that must be done. Doctor Harper was the first.

"I will stay with your father, Sonja. He is stable and will recover. You must go to your Ben."

The sheriff pointed to the ceiling, meaning the upstairs. "She needs to be out of this house and confined somewhere. Calvert, you have that upstairs room at the lockhouse you let for travelers, why not rent it to the county for a few days, with board by Mrs. Calvert? I'm certain you two would be able to keep her out of mischief and out of this house."

John Calvert nodded to the sheriff. "Why, yes, yes. We can certainly do that. I'd expect you to put a manacle at least on the woman's wrist or ankle, though."

The sheriff nodded to Calvert and Harper went to Sonja, placing his hands on her shoulders.

"You must go to Havre de Grace."

He turned to look at the sheriff.

"That only leaves you to escort the lady to Havre de Grace," but before the sheriff could respond, Dan Bartlett spoke up.

"Won't be necessary, Dr. Harper. Number 26 sits down there in the holding pond. Mrs. Pulaski will ride with me all the way back to her place. It will be far better on her than bumping on the back of some horse."

In a whirlwind of packing and confused emotions and making her way to the canal, Sonja left Dr. Harper watching over her father, saw the Sheriff and John Calvert escort Esther to the lockhouse, and managed to find herself aboard Bartlett's barge as it settled within the lock just moments later, listening to the water gush into the downstream canal. Down canal at the far end of a hundred foot of hemp line, Old Thomas tapped the haunch of the front mule with a thin switch and the barge slid out of the lock. She paid no attention to how tight the old coat looked on him. Sonja looked back at the tree line separating the lockhouse from her father's farm, knowing he was safe with Doctor Harper.

I owe you again, Wallace Harper!

Sonja turned her attention to the thin strip of water ahead of them, wishing the mule to walk faster, trying to remind herself of Harper's reassurances about Ben's condition.

I could not take care of my baby, but I could take care of my father! And maybe now I can take care of my husband.

She looked up at the breaking clouds, saw small patches of blue beyond the angry gray pillows.

Do not take my Ben from me again! I tried to hold on to Alisha! I tried! You let Ben come back to me. Do not take him again!

She stood at the bow of the barge. Tears dropped to the deck and she looked at the river beyond the towpath, and then looked to the farthest view of the southward canal where it gently turned into the trees.

"Oh, Ben."

Evening was fast approaching when Dan Bartlett pulled the tiller over and nudged barge Number 26 against Isaac's wharf. Sonja looked at the house up the slight rise between the two oak trees and saw her sons coming toward her. She turned to thank Dan with a pat on his gnarled hands and he beamed through his blush at her attention. Boy's boots clomped across the wooden planking of the little dock and Sonja gathered her sons into her arms, plying their foreheads and cheeks with kisses.

"Did your father bring you down from the Harper's?"

Aaron frowned at his mother.

"No. We walked down on our own. We're not little babies."

Both boys began talking together creating a chatter that Sonja could not understand.

"How is your father?" she demanded.

They had only heard stories from Mickey. Had not yet seen their father. Anthony mounted the porch and was soon joined by Simon and Mickey.

There on the porch Sonja heard the story of Ben's actions; of Anthony's barge, the runaway slaves, the fight with the slavers, the healer Mauzy, the trip to Wrightsville and finally Ben's ride into town to pay Binterfield. In the silence that fell into the moments after the last story had been told and retold, Sonja closed her eyes.

Pulaski's Canal

Thank you that Ben is alright, but please don't take our home! No more, please, No more!

⊱⋅ ☙❦❧ ⋅⊰

As Ben had ridden to Binterfield's bank, he pushed the horse hard past the lockhouse and up into town, then on to Oyster Street and the Tidewater Bank and Trust Company. He tied the reins to the ringed iron post at the edge of the wooden sidewalk and left the horse breathing heavily as he reached for the door handles – and stopped.

What the Hell?

The doors were locked. Ben leaned his face against the glass and covered the glare around his head with his hands, peering into the gloom of the bank. In the back of the room an oil lamp hung on the wall burning brightly over Herbert's desk. Ben knocked on the door, but Herbert did not raise his head. Ben knocked harder, and looked at the teller booths. Both were empty. He turned and looked at the new post mounted clock in front of the tavern across the street.

Five minutes until five.

Ben pounded on the door frame, and peered in to the bank again. Binterfield had not moved from his desk. He was calmly writing notes and signing papers, but he did not look up. Ben beat on the door again.

"I know you hear me, you bastard! Open the damned door, Binterfield!!"

Ben spun around on the sidewalk, looking for something, anything to help him. There was a piece of brick nestled against the edge of the wooden sidewalk near the clock. He dashed across the street, his head pounding under the bandages, black splotches arising and drifting along the edge of his vision. He returned to the bank, stumbling his foot against the edge of the boards as he stepped up.

He pounded on the door frame with the brick, gouging the painted wood and chipping the shining black paint.

"Open the door, Binterfield!!"

He stood back, and then hurled the brick through the door window, shattering the glass into a rain of shards onto the floor inside. Binterfield stood up from behind his desk.

"You'll pay for that, Pulaski!"

"I'll break more if you don't open this door!"

"Alright, alright. I'm coming."

Binterfield ambled leisurely toward the front door, slipping his hands into his pockets, and then stopped at the edge of the broken glass several feet short of the door.

Ben yelled again.

"Binterfield!!"

The banker nodded smiling toward Ben and held one finger up in the air, tilting his head, still smiling. The clock across the street began to chime.

Bong! Bong!

"Damn it, man! Open the door. I have all the money. You've won, damn it!"

Bong!

"Not quite, Pulaski."

Bong!

"Binterfield!!"

Bong!

Binterfield withdrew his pocket watch and released the catch to the cover, allowing it to flip open in his palm. "Now I have, Pulaski." And he snapped the watch closed.

The thunder roared in Ben's ear. His head throbbed and his temple pounded against the bandages as if his very head was about to explode. He stepped back. He grabbed the handle of his seaman's knife, his knuckles white over the grip slipping the blade out of the scabbard, and he raised his foot to kick in the door.

"That's it, Pulaski! You're done here!"

Hands grabbed Ben's arms, pulling him over his heels and out into the street. Briscoe let go of Ben's arm, holding a cocked pistol in his other hand. Another hand grabbed Ben's knife from the other side. The constable held the knife out away from Ben's reach, and placed his other hand on the handle of his own pistol stuck into his belt.

"Stop, Pulaski. Unless you want to go to jail."

Ben looked at their faces.

"No! I have his damned money! I have it right here!"

He slapped his trouser pocket.

"All of it. I came to pay the bastard off...buy the whole damned barge!"

Briscoe sucked air between his teeth, dislodging a piece of meat and spit it on the ground.

"You missed your deadline, Pulaski. He don't want your damned money. He has your ugly barge."

"It's still five o'clock! I can pay him. Let me go."

"No, it ain't, Pulaski. It's AFTER five o'clock. Inch is as good as a mile"

Ben knocked the gun from Briscoe's hand and punched the man hard in the face. Briscoe's knees buckled and he plopped down sitting on the dirty street with his legs spread out in front of him, staring at the multicolored lights flashing in front of his eyes.

The constable tossed down the knife and yanked Ben around by his arm, and at the same moment drew the pistol from his belt, cocking it as he put it in Ben's face.

"This is over with, Pulaski. Go Home."

Ben glared at the constable and then looked back at the bank. He could see Binterfield smiling and retreating back into the shadows returning to his desk.

"Go home, Pulaski."

Briscoe shook his head and rubbed his jaw, and smeared the blood running down from his nose. He spoke from his sitting position in the street.

"Lock his ass up!"

"Shut up, Briscoe. You think I don't know what you two did. None of this had to happen, except that snake in the bank wanted it this way."

Ben held his hands open toward the constable.

"Then let me go in there and finish this up."

"Yeah, you'll go finish it up. I let you go and there's a dead banker in this town and I'm out of a job. Nope. It's done, Pulaski."

Ben stood there with his palms still up in front of him. A carriage trotted by going around the men in the street.

"Go Home, Pulaski. Go home or go to jail."

"Put him in Jail!" Briscoe's words bubbled through the clotting blood on his face.

The constable kicked Briscoe's hip.

"Shut it, Briscoe, or I'll put you in there with him."

Ben stood there staring at nothing.

"Go home, Pulaski. I'm going to take this man around to Doc Harper. You can pick up your knife in a couple days."

The constable helped Briscoe to his feet, while the man held both of his hands around his nose and spit out a tooth. His voice echoed within his cupped hands.

"Broke my nose, bastard."

The constable watched Ben to ensure he would not attack, then he turned Briscoe toward Adams Street and they walked away.

Ben stood in the street alone. The pounding within his head wound was unmerciful. Everything he looked at appeared behind frosted glass. Dizziness and nausea pulled at him. He stumbled to the sidewalk in front of the tavern and sat on its edge, his feet in the gutter with fish heads and oyster shells, and put his head in his hands resting his elbows on his knees.

"C'mon, matey. You need some help. We'll take you to that doctor, too."

The seaman and his shipmate had been drinking in the tavern and had heard the whole conversation from the tavern door as they finished their beer and watched the drama. Their voices were loud enough so that the others in the tavern could hear them.

"That's what your friends are for..."

"...Pulaski..." the other said.

"Right as rain, you are. That's what your friends are for, Pulaski."

They supported him on each side, Ben's eyes unfocused and his hands moving out of time with the motions of his body, and the three of them walked in the direction of the constable. Around the corner, past the second building, well before Adams Street and blocks away from Doctor Harper, was a narrow lane between the backs of two stores. The sailors walked the confused man back into the shadows of the alley and began searching through his pockets. Ben passed out while they robbed him, and they let him slide down into the mud.

They didn't even bother to go to another location to count out and divide up the money.

"Jesus! Look at this. Must be almost three hundred dollars!"

They each took half in cash and coin. The canal script they threw down at the unconscious form, where a urine stain began to spread on his trousers. They laughed at the man's continued misfortune.

"Just ain't his day, is it, Freddie?"

"I just hope he had a lot of good luck before today."

They laughed at the joke and walked away, stuffing the money into their pockets.

29

Sonja waited into the night for word of Ben. She sent off Mickey to go down the towpath into Havre de Grace to look for him. Then, when Mickey did not return she sent Aaron. Aaron finally returned near midnight. He had found Ben in one of the taverns, drinking with Mickey. Aaron said he told his father to come home, Mother was worried.

Ben had only put his hands on Aaron's shoulders, filled his face with the vapors of exhaled alcohol and sent his son home.

"She'll have the better night for me staying here," He had told his son.

"Better night, be damned," Sonja muttered through clenched teeth.

The curious statement had only added to her concern and perplexity over Ben's. It had not been too long ago that she had sent Aaron into town to find Ben singing songs with a bushy headed fellow in that same tavern, but although Aaron had brought Ben home, at least she knew he was alright – in his own way. This time she had feared he lay dead or dying of a gunshot wound as she had imagined during her trip home. His message gnawed at her. She was terrified for him only to hear he is drinking in Havre de Grace. She was furious. She was not able to sleep. She busied herself through the night with one chore after another. Staying awake. Staying busy.

In the small hours before dawn, when even the night noises in the forest had stilled, and the only sound was the river sluicing among the rocks beyond the towpath, she sat on the porch waiting. The struggle in York Furnace still keen in her mind, made the more maddening by the trapped stillness of her vigil. Under the starlight and waist deep in the mist slipping over the towpath, a figure moved northward; a man who coughed once and nearly stumbled. A moment later, a boot heel hard on the swing bridge down at the lock, and then later another muffled cough just beyond their little barn. She heard the wooden latch spun open and stood to the edge of the porch.

"Who is that? Ben, is that you?"

A form stepped away from the barn and stood in the starlight.

"No, Ma'am, t'is just..." and he retched, falling to his knees.

She stood there furious.

"God damn all of you! You rule the world, fill your bellies with whisky, and come home vomiting children - for us to clean you and help you to bed!"

"No Ma'am..." and he retched again.

"Mickey?"

The man stayed on his knees and dropped to his hands, moaning and crying. She stepped down into the yard and saw him near the barn, and he moaned again.

"My humble apologies, Ma'am. Please forgive my state...your husband is well enough..."

"Well enough for what? To keep drinking the night away?"

"...until he is ready to come home, Ma'am."

She stepped near the man, the base human aroma spoiling the night air near him, and then a fresh wind puffed it away. The starlight faded as clouds scudded across the sky.

"And when will he be ready to come home this time? 'Til this place is swept away, too? 'Til we have lost another child? 'Til I am destitute? A banker's whore?"

"Forgive me, Ma'am. I am in an awful state."

Mickey was still on his hands and knees, trembling to remain above the ground, and whimpered, "I am ashamed of what I am."

The rain came quickly, dashing across the yard, encircling the barn and the woman and the man on the ground. Mickey said something else, but she did not hear him. She stood there for a long moment, letting her hair wash down over her shawl and into her eyes. Then she stepped next to him, pulled the shawl from her shoulders and placed it over him. She placed her hand on his back.

"If I can't forgive you Mickey, I can't forgive anyone. – I was far lower than you, the night you pulled me from the river."

"Maybe it's ourselves that's the hardest ta forgive..."

His back shuddered and he cried in the rain, his falling tears lost in the mud. " 'Twasn't you I saved, Sonja. It was me. It was my sweet wife that I had failed..."

He sat back, looking up at her and took her hand, while the rain cleaned his face."

"She came to me the other night in a dream. 'What have ya done with yerself, Micheal?' she asked me."

Sonja nodded, "What have either of us done with ourselves?"

He let go of her hand. "I must be leaving you, Madam."

"You go sleep it off, Mickey."

He stood and wiped the mud from his hands.

"No, ma'am, I must never let myself sleep this moment away. I have to be off and doing something with myself." He stumbled to the barn and leaned against the corner, turning back to her. "I can no longer help yer beautiful man, for I am far weaker and more in need of salvation than that one."

The rain poured down heavy upon them both.

"Oh, Mickey..."

"I must go from this place that I have come to love. I have been offered salvation in Wrightsville, working with a Doctor there, if he will have me. The slave woman said I have healing hands." He looked down on his open hands, the rain running in rivulets from his fingertips. Then he went into the barn and closed the door.

She stood there a long moment, letting the rain wash away her tears, then walked slowly back onto the front porch, and then into the cabin to dry off and change clothes.

Dawn arrived and the cabin was perfectly cleaned. Every dish she owned had been taken down and washed. She had built a fire in the iron stove and boiled the water, and washed dish and surface in the cabin, except the room where the boys slept. Isaac's room was empty.

Anthony had been welcomed by Ben to sleep in that room, but Anthony was raised a gentlemen and would not sleep there without Ben in the house. She did not know that Anthony had also found Ben in a tavern, had also told him Sonja was worried, had been told to join them drinking or go away, had been told he was the cause of their ruin once more. Anthony found his way back in the rain alone, and went to the bunk room in the barn.

Sonja heated the iron on the stove and took down the curtains in the front room to iron the wrinkles from them. She emptied the big water pot and pumped it full again from the well and then heated that. While the water heated again she walked down to the little wharf, 'Isaac's Wharf' they called it now. She stared up the towpath on the other side of the canal as far as the light would let her see, and still nothing. A duck quacked and splashed away from the wharf in complaint of her disturbance by being there.

"Oh, shut up!" she snapped at the duck.

She stood there a while longer, slowly rubbing her long dry hands with her apron. There was enough light now to see all the way to the bend in the towpath. She could see as much as she could ever see, and he was not coming yet. She turned and walked slowly back up the gentle slope between the huge oaks and back into the house. She would wash her hair with the warm water.

The sun rose above the tree line over Port Deposit across the river, and flooded the front room and part of the kitchen with a golden glow. She sat in her rocking chair in front of the stove, felt the warmth of the sun's arrival on her back. Toweling her hair, she would stop for moments to listen to the morning sounds outside for a step on the porch that would tell her that Ben was home. Twice she had considered getting one of the mules from the barn and riding it into town to find him, but she would not embarrass him by having his wife nag him home in front of the other men in the taverns. That time was past anyway. No tavern had been open for several hours now. She stood and walked to the front room, rubbing plaits of her hair between layers of the towel. Sonja stood facing sunlight with her chin up and eyes closed, feeling the warmth on her face. She spoke to the sun.

"Benjamin Pulaski, you ass, get home and explain yourself!"

She stepped out onto the porch and pulled a chair to its edge and sat in it, letting her hair fall down in front of her to dry in the sunlight. It's once brassy hue now finally a healthy golden yellow again. A tear dropped onto her lap inside the flaxen cocoon formed by her cascading hair, and she began to doze there, head down in the sunshine, exhausted and unable to remain awake another moment.

"Good morning."

He spoke from the water pump near the porch. A wisp of air pushed the vapor of stale alcohol and tobacco and urine between the strands of her hair like smelling salts. Sonja jerked upright in her chair and fingered her hair back over her head.

"Benjamin Pulaski, what the hell have you been doing this whole night?"

Ben pumped the cold morning water up from the

well, rinsing one hand at a time and then dipped his head under the flow. He looked down at himself, his nose crinkled at his own smell, and reached for the lye soap near an oil lamp on the edge of the porch.

"You look awful," but there was no hatefulness in her voice, only concern.

"We lost it, Sonja." His voice was almost a tremble. "I took too much time on the trip, doing things I should have left to others. I was stupid and did not honor my own obligations."

He pulled his clothes off, piling them nearby. Standing naked in the yard with his back to the house, Sonja could see the long red scar that ran along the left side of his back just above his hip. She could also see other scars latticing across his back, ones he had always refused to discuss. She shook her head at the sight and tears filled her eyes.

"Ben we had not been...I mean I had not seen,..your back, was it..."

"None of that matters, Sonja."

"We both have scars, Ben. Ugly scars, and not only on the outside, where others can see them. Maybe we should talk about them, maybe..."

Ben ignored her comment. He pulled the oil lamp from the edge of the porch, opened the cap to the glass oil reservoir and poured the oil onto his clothes, then slipped off the chimney glass and touched the exposed flame to the oil soaked cloth. His clothes erupted into flames.

Sonja stood up on the porch, her hand knotted around the corner post, "Ben! What are you doing!!"

Naked, Ben moved back to the pump, soaped himself down and then doused himself with sprays of water, rinsing away the foul odors drifting off his body. Sonja dashed into the bedroom and retrieved a blanket, then stood at the edge of the porch, handing it down to Ben. Water still trickled from his bandaged head, draining through his hair and down his neck in thin pink rivulets of diluted blood.

Sonja looked at the flames lifting off his piled clothes and the sight of the bloody bandage loosely wrapped around his head.

"Good God, Benjamin, what happened to you??"

Ben stood barefoot in the yard wrapped in the blanket, staring up at her through red swollen eyes.

"I happened. I had the best of plans, and then let them slip into shit while doing something else."

"Ben, what is it?"

"I knew Binterfield had papers for me, was avoiding the sheriff until I had the profit from the last trip to Annapolis. And then... and then, I lost my way! I got involved trying to do Anthony's goddamned work. I got shot and let everything else just go to hell."

"That's what happened to your head? You were shot?"

Ben took a deep breath and shook his head slowly.

"Binterfield called in the loan on the barge, but I got involved with helping slaves cross into Pennsylvania –"

"Slaves!?"

"- and didn't learn of the new deadline until yesterday afternoon. Yesterday was the deadline for paying off the note. I missed it."

Sonja brought her fingertips to her lips, staring into his eyes.

"The bastard was still in there. He stood there looking at me knock on the door, with his damned pocket watch in his hands. I couldn't get in and he just stood there and smiled while the street clock chimed. I was there just in time, but he wouldn't take it. I could see him through the glass, but he wouldn't open the door. I even took the money out of the purse and showed it to him. Banged on the door to make sure he saw it. Yelled at him to open the damned door. Threw a brick through it!"

Tears flooded Sonja's eyes.

Pulaski's Canal

"The bastard just looked at me from that damned desk and grinned. Had a constable and Briscoe waiting for me. He got me. He's got the boat. Without the boat we don't have enough money coming in to pay the rent to stay on this farm. All the money I had left was stolen from me, except for some canal script. Hell, even the goddamned horse is gone. I've lost it all, Sonja. I've failed you again. I wanted you to have one more night in this house before you knew the truth. I wanted it to be yours one more night."

He gave her a cold menacing smile.

"And then I am going to go kill that son of a bitch, Binterfield."

"Ben, none if this makes any sense! Everything is gone? We've lost everything again??"

Ben brought his hands up to his nose, turned from her and stepped back to the pump.

"I still smell. I may never be clean — inside or out. Maybe I should have stayed in China. Maybe that was where I was supposed to be all along."

Dropping the blanket on the ground, he began to pump water over his head and spit curses at Binterfield through the cold water. Sonja turned in silence and slowly walked back into the house. She was still standing in the front room, staring into the empty fireplace, as Ben walked by, unable to look into her face again, and went into their room.

After dressing, Ben went to the kitchen, reached up to the shelf above the window and pulled down a half-full jug of whiskey. He turned and walked unsteadily back onto the front porch and took a long drink from the jug. The whiskey burned as it slipped down into his stomach. He went back into the front room and pulled the old pistols down from their place on the wall and looked at them for a long moment.

"I should have had these old pistols converted to cap and ball, but the flints will do the job this day."

He stepped back onto the porch and laid them on

the little table next to his chair on the porch. With the second drink, the cloud that had enveloped his head for most of the night began to return. He sat there with one hand holding the jug on his knee, and the fingertips of the other drifting along the surfaces of the pistols, staring at the canal and the river and the tree line over Port Deposit.

Ben's chin was already settled onto his chest, and the near empty jug dangling above the floorboards from his fingertips when Sonja stood at the doorway looking out at him.

"I don't know who I hate more at this moment, you, or Herbert Binterfield- or myself."

She walked back inside through the front room and into the kitchen. She stared out of the back window at their little field nestled against the hillside, placed her hands on the counter as her eyes filled with tears and she lowered her head.

"No more! No more!" She spat out the words, teardrops and spittle falling onto the countertop. "No more! I've had enough! No more! No more! No more!"

Boots clomped on the porch, but Ben only barely heard the noise. The number of drinks went uncounted and the jug was empty, when Isaac stepped onto the front porch. He did not notice the whiskey jug held in his father's far hand.

"Where's my boots?"

Ben shook his head only slightly.

Isaac placed his hands on his hips.

"I left'em by the stove so they'd dry out from yesterday, and now they're gone."

Ben only stared out across the river.

Isaac looked inside the house then back out at his father.

"Where's Ma?"

Ben shrugged and pointed his thumb back over his shoulder into the house.

Isaac looked at his father for a moment, and then shrugged his own shoulders and went back inside.

Ben heard a pot or a pan go down onto the stove. He still had nothing else to say to her. Hoof beats shot along the towpath, but Ben did not look up to see who or what it was. Moments later, a rustle in the grass and then more boot heels on the floorboards forced Ben to focus his blurring eyes on the figure sitting in the chair next to him.

"Oh, my achin' head," Anthony whined.

Ben offered the near empty jug to Anthony who only waved it away.

"No more of that, for me. Sonja laid into you, did she?"

"You know the whole story, Anthony," Ben spoke into the neck of the empty jug, then threw it out into the yard.

"Well, she was certainly angry. Damned near ran me down."

Ben looked at Anthony with a wobbling head. "W-what?"

"Ran me down, I said. Came heading for the swing bridge like a banshee, riding one of the mules bareback. Never seen a mule run at full gallop before. Didn't know they had it in them."

Ben sat forward and tried to make sense of Anthony's words. He stared at the empty little table next to his chair.

"Ben, there is something I need to speak to you about. It concerns Mickey..."

"Later Anthony..." Ben stared across the canal at the towpath and then looked back down at the empty table.

"Mickey's gone, Ben. He's left us," Anthony said, but Ben was no longer listening.

30

A mile south of the Pulaski farm, Sarah the mule was running her heart out toward Havre de Grace. Sonja was straddling her, her knees and feet tightly wrapped around Sarah's belly, the only thing holding Sonja on and keeping Isaac's warm boots from slipping off her feet. She held Sarah's short mane in a death grip by her left hand, while her other hand tightly held her freshly ironed front room curtain, wadded into a bundle around something hard. A smudge of black powder was spread across the back of her right hand, and the mate to the smudge on the side of her nose.

Sarah ran as fast as she could, faster than she had ever run. Something was different and she did not understand. She only knew that she must run for this woman, and she gave herself into it. Sonja's full skirt and petticoats gave her scant padding over the bony jostling back of the mule. Her knees strained against the fabric at the front and the wind slapped the ends of it against the sides of the mule as she rode the mule hard into town. Her golden hair sailed away in its own directions behind her in the breeze. The ride along the towpath and across the swing bridge was no more than a blur. She heard voices of men calling in surprise or anger as she pushed the charging mule past them at a break-neck pace. The mule made the turn onto Oyster Street and Sonja almost lost her seat, but leaned forward against Sarah and wrapped her free arm around her neck, the bundle bouncing under Sarah's white-gray chin.

Sonja brought the mule to a halt in front of the bank , looked up at the sign atop the building and shook her head at the word 'Trust'. She opened the bundle and took out the two heavy iron and walnut flintlock pistols, and let the curtain drop into the dust. She started to slip one into her apron pocket, but realized it would not stay there, so instead slipped the barrel down inside the waist of her skirt. She slid the barrel of the second pistol into the waist on her other side. They were so large and took up so much room at her waist that it almost made it difficult for her to breathe. The butts of the pistols tapped against each other as she walked. She ran her hand gently along the surface of Sarah's back as she stared at the bank. She took in a ragged deep breath, blew it out, then drew in another and spoke to the mule.

"Go home, girl."

She gave Sarah's rump a hard slap to send the mule trotting back the way she had come, but the mule only stepped away a short distance. Sonja turned to face the front of the building. She stepped up onto the wooden walk, Isaac's boot heels making a comforting sound as she did. The sun was behind her and she could see easily into the small bank. Boards covered the front door where a pane of glass had been broken out. Brown was at the teller window.

What did Ben say was his first name?

In the back office area, the sunbeams penetrated to show Binterfield at his desk busily hunched over some ledger or paper, his pen jiggling its dance as he wrote. She walked up to the door and slowly pushed down on the thumb latch. The clock on the wall above the teller window said eight fifteen. She thought it was much later in the day, or did it feel earlier?

Sonja gently pushed the door handle and the door swung full open, jingling the entrance bell above. The sound seemed so loud, and Brown looked out at her. She froze in her footsteps. Up to this very moment it had been a ride of anger, an act of force only upon those things around her she could normally control. Across that threshold would take her to another part of her life she could never undo. Where she stood at that moment was her present and her past. On the other side of the doorway was a dark future. A horse whinnied down the street. Ben would probably be here any minute. He would kill Binterfield, and the law would hang him. She did not have much time. She did not know if she had the strength and the anger to do what she came to do. Somewhere a little girl screamed for her mother, but it was far in the back of her mind. She took in a deep breath; set her shoulders back and her spine straight.

"God damn you, Herbert Binterfield! God damn you to hell!"

She tilted her chin down and stepped into the bank lobby.

Boot heels slammed onto the floorboards creating a series of clomps that matched the beat of her heart. One step, two, three, four, five. She was at the little gate to Binterfield's kingdom. She could see Brown coming around from his teller window, but her eyes were on Binterfield. Brown extended his hand out slightly, but she did not stop or even hesitate.

The clomp sounded again. Six! In the same movement, she kicked open the gate with Isaac's boot, stiff-armed Brown, who was caught off balance and almost fell, and pulled the first pistol from her waistband with her left hand.

Clomp. Seven! She threw her left arm in Binterfield's direction, knowing from her father how to use the weight of a gun to force its own hammer open, and cocked the pistol in the air as she brought the barrel down in the direction of Binterfield's head.

Clomp. Eight! Binterfield had looked up when the door opened. Had seen the woman at the doorway hesitate before entering, heard her speak, but not the words. The sun was behind her head keeping her face in shadows while filling her billowing waved hair with intense sunlight. The sun stayed behind her head as she had kicked open the gate and pushed Brown aside. He thought to yell at her audacity, to put her in her place, but her pace and her stance showed something ominous.

She pulled something from her waist. He could not see in the blinding light of the sun in his eyes. He tried to shield his eyes from the sun, but that covered the form of the woman as well.

Clomp. He heard the sound of her heavy boot heels on the polished wood floor.

Clomp. She was pointing something at him. He stood up to raise his head above the sunbeam stabbing though the window and could see her more plainly. It was Mrs. Pulaski. The beautiful radiant Sonja. Like an angel bringing the sunlight.

What was that in her hand?

She yelled his name.

"Binterfield, you Devil!"

Clomp. Nine! Binterfield's eyes went wide. He threw his forearm in front of him and tried to back away. Kicking over his chair and spilling the contents of his desktop onto the floor, he turned to make a dash to the back door. He took a step away, turning his back to Sonja.

Clomp. Ten!

Sonja could see the back door and knew he could easily outrun her. The pistol shifted only the slightest angle. The hammer struck, fell against the grate and the flint threw its spark into the flash pan. The fine powder flashed into a bright flame and smoke. And then the whole world exploded. The echo of the booming shot filled the office and reverberated off the walls. Her wrist and shoulder shuddered from the force of the recoil. Pain shot along her arm from the butt of the pistol to her shoulder. Her whole arm almost numb. Gray-black smoke filled the air and Sonja could no longer see the man.

Binterfield was slammed by the noise and concussion of the old sixty-caliber pistol. A bullet larger than the size of his thumb tore through the air near his head and shattered the oil lamp near the rear door. Whale oil and glass shards rained down upon him and his desk and the little iron stove nearby lit against the morning coolness. He covered his head with his hands, screamed in terror, and threw himself back toward his desk. Whale oil pooled on the floor and drifted in a little rivulet toward the front leg of the iron stove.

Even as she dropped the discharged pistol from her pain-filled left hand, Sonja reached across the waist of her skirt and pulled out the second pistol with her right hand.

Clomp. Eleven! Her next boot heel hit at the same moment as the butt of the first pistol found its way down to the safety of the floor. Sonja reached Binterfield as he was trying to slip back behind his desk, but he had taken the habitual front instead of the safer side. She was at him and on him in one sweeping motion. The forward motion of her determined walk carried her into him and his own terror bent him way from her. In a single motion she grabbed the front of his throat with her throbbing left hand, pushed her knee up against his abdomen, pushed him back down against the desk top, mounted his chest with her other knee, and as he opened his mouth to scream, shoved the barrel of the pistol into his mouth.

There was a satisfying <u>chink</u> as the end of the pistol broke off a piece of a front tooth. Little oil flames erupted and danced on the hot surface of the iron stove.

Like a desert turtle caught on his back in the noon sun, Binterfield lay pinned to the desktop by Sonja's perch on his chest, flailing his legs and arms in the air. The echo of the shot faded and the smoke drifted away from the desk. Sonja kept the pistol in his mouth. Squeezing the trigger. Preparing herself for what she had come to do, had to do. Looking Binterfield in his eyes along the barrel of the gun, she watched his eyes, listened to his labored breathing and heard him gurgle around the end of the barrel. She watched his eyes flow from the ceiling, the wall, to her face, to her finger on the trigger, to the uncocked hammer on the pistol. She brought her thumb up just enough to catch the upper edge of the hammer and drew it back through its two clicks. Binterfield gurgled again in renewed terror. Brown was pleading. She tuned out Brown's voice.

"Binterfield, you devil! You don't deserve to live. You made a game of taking advantage of me and my Ben. You ruined him with his barge. Not that you give a shit about owning a boat. It was because it was his."

Binterfield's eyes flickered back and forth from trigger to hammer.

"You cheated him and you ruined him, and then you grinned at him through those front windows, all just because you could. Now he's ruined in his own eyes, and when he quits blaming himself he'll come here. He'll come here wanting to do what I'm going to do."

Binterfield tried to shake his head no, but dared not move too much and cause the gun to go off.

"Ben will come here and kill you, you snake. Then the law will come and hang him for murder - and I will have lost my husband a second time, as well as my baby. You stole from me, you bastard! And now you've stole from my Ben. You stole our property for almost nothing when I was in grief over loosing Alisha. You stole my dignity when you had me as your housemaid, fondling me in the hallways when that nappy-headed bitch of a wife wasn't around. You stole my hope by convincing me that Ben was dead at sea, and I had no one and nothing but a shack in Wallace Harper's back yard. You don't deserve to live, but my Ben does!"

Binterfield gurgled and whimpered through the spittle and the tears.

"I won't let him kill you, you bastard! When he gets here it will be too late! I'm going to do it for him – Hell! For the both of us!"

"I'll take his payment!" he was able to say around the barrel of the pistol. "Have him come back. I'll take the payment."

"Payment be damned, Herbert Binterfield. Your payment is stuck into your lying mouth. And I'm going to pay you in FULL!"

She raised her shoulder over the pistol. The knuckle of her trigger finger began to turn white. The gun began to tremble. The hammer was ready to jump.

"No!!!" Screamed Binterfield. "I'll mark it all paid! I'll write off the note. Cancel it. Please God, don't kill me!"

"You'd never honor that. As soon as I let you go you'd get the sheriff. No. There is only one thing I can do to protect my man and the rest of my family. I couldn't save my baby, but I won't have my sons lose their father again."

"What about you?" Binterfield mumbled around the barrel. Sweat was pooling on his forehead and running down the sides of his face with the tears and the spittle.

Sonja smiled with ice in her eyes, and rasped into his ears.

"I'm just a poor weak woman." She took in a deep breath. "Every man on the jury will know how weak women are, and how we go crazy all the time. And here I am still in mourning for my baby. They'll probably never even take me to court..."

"And don't worry about that woman of yours." Sonja spoke through clenched teeth. "Some other man will have her bedded and wedded in no time."

"No! Please don't kill me. I will cancel your note. I swear I will! Brown! Brown!"

Sonja looked over her shoulder to Brown where he patted out the flames on the stove with Binterfield's hat.

Sonja shifted her hold on the gun to relieve the ache in her shoulder. Her movement on Binterfield's chest made him cry out in fear.

"Can he do that so he can't change his mind?"

Brown nodded emphatically yes to her question.

"I'm not robbing this bastard, but if I let him up I want it in writing that he won't call in the note on the *Ugly Boat* until my Ben has time to come pay him."

"All the time in the world, take all the time in the

world," Binterfield gurgled around the end of the barrel.

"On the off chance that Mrs. Pulaski might accept your kind offer, sir, I've taken the liberty of filling in the blanks for you."

Brown looked sheepishly at Mrs. Pulaski.

"May he be allowed to sign this, Ma'am?"

"Read it out loud to me."

She nodded in acceptance when Brown had finished reading the word on the paper.

"You know my Ben will hold the same malice toward you as Binterfield, if you are misreading any of that."

"You can trust me, Mrs. Pulaski. More than you may ever know." And then added, "I think your husband would trust me."

Sonja nodded again.

"Hold it so this shit can sign it where he is."

Brown held the ink pen and well next to Binterfield. With trembling awkward hands Binterfield took the pen and wrote against the form with a ledger held behind it by Brown. Black ink ran down his arm as he struggled to sign the papers.

"And this one too, sir," Brown added.

Binterfield shook his head and gurgled forcefully against the barrel of the gun.

"Sign the goddamned forms or tell the Devil why not," Sonja said leaning down against the gun.

Binterfield signed the second form and gave Brown a steely stare of hatred.

"You're fired!" he screamed through the spittle.

"Mrs. Pulaski, please just leave that gun right where it is for just a moment longer."

Brown then went to the unlocked bank vault speaking as he went. "He has fired me about every six months since I started working for him, but this time it is finished." He spoke to his previous employer over his shoulder. "I'm taking Mrs. Pulaski's account money, and my last two weeks wages, Mr. Binterfield."

He then counted out two stacks of bills onto the desk next to Binterfield's head. One was a small pile, the other rather large. The large pile of notes and the two signed forms he placed into a large envelope.

"These will be yours, Mrs. Pulaski, whenever you have completed with your business here this morning." He looked down at Binterfield blowing spittle into the air with his labored breathing and smiled. "Good bye, Mr. Binterfield, it has definitely NOT been a pleasure working for you. You are NOT a gentleman." With that Brown poured the remainder of the ink bottle over Binterfield's forehead, then turned his face back to Sonja. "Oh yes, I believe there are letters in his desk drawer that belong to you." He slid open the center desk drawer and then backed away.

Sonja kept the gun barrel firmly against the back of Binterfield's throat, and then began sliding the contents of the drawer around with her other hand so she could see it. Binterfield's eyes frantically shot to the that side as far as he could make them.

"No no no no no no. No. No. No!"

Spread around inside the desk were dozens of unopened letters. Some held her own handwriting, the ink long faded from the day she had mailed them to Ben. She tilted her head, and frowned at the man's face, then leaned closer to his ear, her voice an animal rasp.

"You son of a bitch! These were letters you said you took to the post office, said you would pay for the post. I thought you were so kind."

She gritted her teeth, rummaging the envelopes to see what else he had hidden.

There! One with my name on it! And another! And Another!

All had the company stamp and the hand written notation, 'Aboard the Philadelphia Star'.

Another one!

But this one more official, the letter addressed more formally, did not have the stain of letters long held in a ship's canvas mailbag, but still had the stamp of the shipping company.

Sonja looked across the room. Brown still stood there.

"Come here. Open this one."

Brown was quick to respond. The envelope was badly stained by spilled black ink, but dry, stained long before this day. He tore the envelope open and held the letter toward the light coming in the front window. He swallowed hard and peered at Sonja over it's top edge.

"Read it!" she yelled, her shoulder beginning to tremble.

"Much of it is ruined, madam, but I will read what I can. 'Dear Mrs Pulaski, it is our unfortunate duty to inform you that the ship on which your husband has served'..."

"Oh. THAT Letter. I might as well hear it from the shipping company to learn what else this weasel lied about."

Binterfield gurgled and yelled.

"NO-o-o-o!!"

Sonja looked at the letter in Brown's hand.

"Go on."

"... 'has been confiscated by the Chinese and will likely be much delayed in its return. We regret this incident but are told that your husband and his shipmates are well. The enclosed check for one hundred dollars is an advance of your husband's earnings to assist you in your time of worry'..."

"What???"

"I'm sorry madam, but the ink has covered the remainder of the paragraph, and it ends with the signature of a captain, something-or-other, and his company title, etcetera."

Sonja's eyes flashed wide, her eyebrows shot up, her

mouth worked silently a moment.

"Binterfield! You slimey God damned bastard. You told me he was DEAD!!"

"No no no no no no!"

"You made me a widow and tried to make me your whore! And now you think you can buy me with my own damned money!!"

Sonja smiled grimly down at Binterfield.

"You really believed you could buy your way out, didn't you? You thought a few dollars would settle the rage against you, the hatred, the death wishes!"

Binterfield's expression returned from anger to one of horror, as he understood her message.

"You still don't deserve to live, Binterfield. You will just go on ruining someone else's life, even if you are out of ours."

"NO! NO! NO! NO!"

Binterfield gagged as Sonja's shoulder went forward again to be over the recoil of the pistol, spittle ran down his face and sprayed up into the air. Once again he focused in terror on her trigger finger, as the knuckle grew white against the pressure of the trigger. The gun trembled. Binterfield let out an animal wail, and the trigger snapped, freeing the hammer.

All sound in his world stopped and he watched in slow motion as the hammer gracefully swung though its arch toward the grate, carrying the flint down to do its duty. The flint struck and the sparks sent out on either side of the pan, and he screamed to drown out the sound of his own exploding death and his mind slipped into the blackness of death.

The quiet in the bank was overpowering. The blood gushing in Binterfield's ears was a thunder. His body was numb from being over backwards across the desk. He felt the pressure release from his chest as Sonja stepped down, and felt the world spin around him in tighter and tighter circles as he was swept deeper into the blackness. There was a thud of something hard hitting the polished floor. He wondered only momentarily what that was and then his last thought was the recognition that the sound was his head hitting the floor boards.

Sonja stepped back from Binterfield as he slid to the floor, and stared at the pistol in her hand. Brown leaned over the edge of the desk and looked down at the prostrate form on the floor.

"Fainted dead away. It was providence that made that gun misfire, Mrs. Pulaski. You should take what God has given you," *and the bank,* he smiled to himself, "and leave quickly."

Brown had retrieved the other pistol from the floor and holding it between his fingers by the still warm barrel, handed it back to Sonja.

Sonja stood silent, looking at Binterfield lying in the floor, and then at the unfired pistol in her hand. The fine grained powder in the pan was clumped and damp from the man's spittle. She gave a brutish laughing snort, then let out a long slow ragged breath blown through trembling lips, and spoke to Brown.

"I meant to kill him. I was really ready to do it, but I'm glad the gun didn't fire. By God, not that Binterfield didn't deserve it, but I'm glad I wasn't the one. And with what you have done, I don't have to worry about what Ben will do."

She raised her right hand still holding the second pistol and wiped her nose with the back of her hand, adding another smudge of black powder to her nose and cheek.

Brown smiled at her.

"Mr. Pulaski is a <u>very</u> lucky man."

Brown extended his hand in the direction of the front door and escorted Sonja back out into the sunlight on the boardwalk.

"Is Will's note really secure, Mr. Brown?"

"Oh, yes. And I will be happy to come to your assistance and swear in any court of law that I witnessed Mr. Binterfield sign the extension papers deferring calling the note for four years. That boat as good as belongs to Mrs. Boyd and Mr. Pulaski now."

Sonja and Mr. Brown stood in silence on the boardwalk for a moment, until a few local merchants began to gather on the other side of the street looking toward the bank. She dashed back to the desk and clawed out all the letters in the center drawer. She stood for a moment deciding what to do with them, then twirled around and kicked open the front of the little stove. The desk area was bathed in red-orange light, flickering in the shadows. She took in a deep breath and looked back at Brown.

Brown shrugged his shoulders.

"They are yours madam. Do whatever you feel..."

"They belong to no one, Mr. Brown, only people that used to live around here."

She threw them all into the fire and kicked the stove closed, then walked briskly to the front of the bank.

Brown pulled her arm gently through the boarded front door onto the sidewalk.

"I do imagine that pistol shot was well heard outside the bank, Mrs. Pulaski. If you'll excuse me, I think I should seek the counsel of Mr. George Milton, esquire."

Brown tipped his hat to Sonja and stepped away.

Sonja looked down and saw her window curtain lying in the dust of the street. It must have lain there for hours. As she stared at the curtain, the large clock across from the bank gave out its half hour gong, and she turned back to look at it. It was eight thirty. She stooped to pick up the curtain and slowly, numbly, walked back down the street toward the canal basin, a few faces in the shadow of the tavern door watching her in barely contained curiosity as she went. A man stepped out from the doorway and stared as she walked away.

As Sonja neared the end of Oyster Street, she saw Ben walking toward her leading Sarah. Ben stopped to stare at his wife, concern painted on his face below the fresh bandages on his head. Her hair was dried and standing away from the sides of her face, searching the breeze in all directions. There was a dark smudge across her nose and cheek. In one hand she held a pistol and a large envelope, in the other another pistol and one of her front room curtains trailing in the dust.

"Sonja? Are you all right? What in the hell happened?"

"Nothing," she sniffed. "I just convinced Binterfield not to call in the note. And I closed our account with the bank."

Ben stepped up to her and removed the guns and envelope from her hands, but she would not let go of the curtain.

"Need to wash it again. It's one of our good ones."

"Sonja! What did you do?" He looked at the pistols. "Is Binterfield dead? Did you kill him?"

"No. But I wanted to. This is better."

Ben slipped the fired pistol into his belt and looked at the unfired pistol closely, blowing away the clumped primer.

"I've got more primer with me."

Sonja shook her head.

"No, Ben. It's over."

Ben handed the envelope back to Sonja.

"If Binterfield's still breathing it ain't over. The man needs killing." He put his hand on Sonja's shoulder. "He needs killing and then I'll be gone. You'll be rid of both of us."

Sonja dropped the envelope and clenched her fists by her side.

"Damn you, Benjamin Pulaski. I said it was over."

Ben pulled his hand from her shoulder and turned away from her, walking back up Oyster Street.

"Benjamin, turn around, you don't have to do that."

Ben walked farther, and Sonja called after him.

"Stop Ben! Turn around. We can go home."

Ben kept walking, half cocking the pistol. In the quiet steps between them, Sonja spoke again.

"Ben, do you still love me."

He slowed and spoke over his shoulder.

"Since the first time you ever smiled at me."

"Then, turn around. Turn around, Ben."

He stopped for a moment, sighed, and then pulled a small flask of primer powder from his pocket, and refilled the flash pan to the pistol. The edges of his vision were curtained by red and black tentacles twisting in toward the center.

"Turn around Ben. I don't want to lose you again. If you still love me, just turn around."

Ben took in a deep breath, and the roaring in his ears began to fade. The sounds of the seagulls overhead, and the wind coming up the bay, and the barges bumping together in the canal basin filtered into his brain.

"Turn around, Ben."

He spoke without turning, "It isn't over with Binterfield. He will come at us again, or he will send someone else. He will only stop if he is dead, and I am going to kill him."

"And then you will hang."

"So be it."

Sonja took a step in his direction. "No! Not 'so be it', but what we make of it."

He turned to look at her, "There is nothing left to make of it. There is nothing left of what we had, of what we were."

"But there is what we can make by who we are now, Ben."

"It can never be like it was. We will never get back there, Sonja. I accept that now."

She sighed. "No. Those people are gone. Gone with

Alisha. But we are here now, and our sons still need us. We need us."

He stood there a long moment, looked up the street toward the bank, then back at Sonja. He looked down at his feet, and let out a long breath. He uncocked the pistol and slowly slid it into his belt. Then walked back to stand in front of her.

"Are we enough? Is there enough of us left?"

She reached up and tucked a loosened end back under his bandage on his head. He looked over toward the warehouses. She turned his chin back toward her face.

"There is enough for a new start. I know that now."

He placed his hands on her shoulders, sliding them close to her neck, gently stroking the edges of her chin with his thumbs. She smiled at him.

They turned and walked without direction. Then stopped and looked back toward Oyster Street. Sonja ran back and picked up the envelope, then returned to Ben's side. He put his arm around her and they walked together.

"How is your father?"

"Wallace is with him. I will tell you more later."

Walking an old memory together, crossing a lane that no longer went anywhere, then up a gentle hill to an old oak tree spreading its massive branches into the breeze off the bay. There was a bench there now that had been added since Ben visited the tree a year ago. He was not sure if he should tell Sonja what he buried there. Now was not the time for all the details why, but he needed to tell one part of it.

"This is Alisha's tree."

Sonja reached down and took his hand, squeezing it tightly.

"I know."

She sat on the bench and looked down at the little pocket of pink thrift growing at the base of the oak, and pulled him down next to her, and placed her hands in her lap. She sat there staring out at the Bay. Ben opened the envelope and found the note deferring his debt to Binterfield for four years, and stared in amazement at Sonja, but she said nothing.

Sonja looked down at the warehouses at the bottom of the slope. Before the warehouses, there was a little lane down there that ran between a half dozen houses. Ben unfolded the second paper wrapped around a very large stack of money and read it.

"Sonja, this bank withdrawal... We did not have this much money in Binterfield's bank."

"Did today."

Sonja pulled her feet out of Isaac's boots and up onto the edge of the bench within the folds of her skirt, and wrapped her arms around her knees. She began to tremble slightly. Ben put his arm around her and drew her near to him. She leaned down, resting her head on her knees and began to cry. At first it was the quiet cry of old pains, but then they became great sobs of fresh grief, and her body was wracked by them within Ben's arms. She cried until the tears were gone and the sobs were dry, and her voice was hoarse. Then Ben pulled her toward him and wiped away the smudges on her face with his fingers.

"Let's go home."

They rose and left the tree together, walking down the gentle slope to the canal basin under a pale blue cloudless sky, Sarah walking obediently behind them.

Sonja looked up at Ben as they walked.

"Tell me about China."

"No. That doesn't matter anymore." He swept his hand out over the canal and the basin. "This is what matters now."

Ben and Sonja walked to the towpath, but were called after by Dan Bartlett.

"Seems like all I do is ferry Pulaskis these days. You folks want a ride?"

Pulaski's Canal

Ben tied Sarah with the off duty mules at the bow, then he joined Sonja and Dan sitting on the locker near the tiller. Dan whistled and Thomas flicked a switch across the rump of the lead mule. Ben watched the man with a spring in his step and bushy hair barely able to accept the old black hat Thomas always wore, above the ever present brown coat almost too small to hold his frame. Ben slapped Dan's back.

"Thomas is looking real good today, Dan."

Dan leaned over the boat rail and spit into the basin. "You got an opinion about him, Benjamin?"

"No. Just a question."

Dan looked straight ahead. "Well, have at it."

"How many Thomases have you walked up this towpath into Pennsylvania?"

Dan kept his stare forward, but showed a smile in his silhouette, then he spit into the basin again. "This'uns number thirty two."

Robert F. Lackey

Pulaski's Canal

Bibliography

Pulaski's Canal is an historical novel, and writers of novels take liberties with dates and incidents to blend them into the story. We are known to fold the actions of multiple historic incidents and people into a single character for continuity. Although no academic work is actually cited in this book, I would be neglecting due homage to my interesting sources of historical information, without sharing a bibliography with the reader. At least here, I can identify the original truths I 'massaged' in writing this story. I also offer my humble apologies to the historic researchers I so crudely burglarized.

Please visit my website www.rflackeybooks.com and select the page titled "Pulaski's World" to see a complete list of books I read while developing this series, plus historic photos, maps and displays of the period.

ROBERT F. LACKEY lived in Havre de Grace, Maryland, for 23 years. Moving there from North Carolina in 1993, he immediately fell in love with the little town sitting at the mouth of the Susquehanna River and head of the Chesapeake Bay. The area is rich in history and watershed culture reaching back to the beginning of the country. Among the many historic themes coexisting within the nearby sites and lanes, the Canal Era drew the author's attention first. Stepping outside technical writing, ***Pulaski's Canal*** was his first book-length work of fiction.

"I wandered the trails and historic marker sites along the old Susquehanna and Tidewater Canal route, and it was easy for me to picture families centering their lives around the canal, the way community centers spring up along the interstates today. Of course I was drawn to the simpler times, barges only moved at three miles an hour, but my research identified not only the hard demands and historical challenges of that simpler life, but the richness of the world the people lived in then. Having access to the original gateway Lockhouse, still maintained by the local historical society, was an absolute thrill and it gave me my first backdrop.

Once the core characters of the story tumbled out of my imagination and onto the computer screen in front of me, they almost took on their own life. They frequently went in directions I had not planned in the earlier part of the day, but evolved as the story evolved. Ben and Sonja, and their sons Isaac and Aaron, ARE the 19th century. Ben was born on the first second of January 1, 1800. The Pulaski experience encompasses the national experiences of that century, but from the eyes of a Maryland family on the canals. Much as today's national news is perceived from the living rooms and household budgets of American families.

Now they are dear friends, and I look forward to keeping their story going through the years after 1842. We will experience the changes that occurred in our country over the next two or three decades through them."

Please visit Robert's website and Facebook^(TM) page to learn about his current and future projects:
www. RFLackeybooks.com
https://www.facebook.com/RFLackey.author